Shroud
for a
Sinner

The Thirteenth in the
Murray of Letho series

Lexie Conyngham

Shroud for a Sinner

Lexie Conyngham

Copyright Alexandra Conyngham 2022

ISBN: 978-1-910926-80-2

Cover illustration by Helen Braid at
www.ellieillustrates.co.uk

DEDICATION

Many thanks to Elizabeth Fitzsimmons, Markus Rieder and Kelly Jo Sweeney, who won the prize of having a character named after each of them. Congratulations, and I hope you like the characters

ACKNOWLEDGMENTS

Thanks, as always, to valiant beta readers Jill, Kath and Nanisa, who, if nothing else, keep reminding me how to spell 'dilapidated'.

Dramatis personae:
At Letho House:
Charles Murray of Letho and his daughter Augusta
Alester Blair and his daughter Isobel
Deborah Scoggie, as was, and her husband Richard Wedderburn of Kineden
The staff, as mixed as ever: Henry Robbins, Mrs. Mack, Iffy, Jennet, Daniel and William, Elizabeth Fitzsimmons the governess, and at various points the housekeepers Mrs. Warner and Mrs. Gilmour
Daniel's family, his wife Artemisia, and his sons, Janny and Jackamo
Mr. Thalland, the factor, and two engineers, Mr. Edward Kelly and Mr. Jo Sweeney

At Collessie:
Mrs. Pillans, and Mrs. Skead her mother, but lately arrived.
Mr. Pillans, a late arrival
Sundry unpromising servants

At Dures:
Francis George and his sister, Lady Rocheid
Lord Rocheid, his brother-in-law, even later

In the vicinity:
The minister and his wife, Mr. and Mrs. Helliwell
Dr. Feilden, physician
Macduff, sheriff's man
Markus Rieder, a music tutor in search of his position
Ninian Jack, a clever old man
A busy innkeeper

In Edinburgh:
Mrs. Miller, manager
Susan Knox, shop girl
Sergeant Clyne of the Edinburgh police

Chapter One

'We seem to be lacking men this evening!' said Mrs. Pillans brightly, fiddling with her cutlery.

Since she was one of the women missing her man, it seemed to be her right to be cheerful about it.

'I look forward to meeting Mr. Pillans,' said Mrs. Helliwell, the minister's wife, warmly polite. 'We have heard so much about him already. And it is a delight to see people at Collessie once more.'

Charles Murray, laird of Letho, the estate adjacent to Collessie, was also eager to meet Mr. Pillans who had leased Collessie for the summer in the first instance. He was curious to meet a man who could possibly, in his right mind, have taken on such a wreck.

'He is already a week later than he said he would be!' said Mrs. Skead, Mrs. Pillans' mother. 'I think he has abandoned us to the damp cellars, the leaking roof, and the grass on the lawn that will need, I believe, something in the nature of a herd of elephants to reduce it to a manageable level.'

Murray glanced at Robbins, his butler, who was overseeing the service of the second course. Robbins was very fond of elephants, having met his fair share of them in the past. He would have liked nothing better than to have a herd of them across the woods at Collessie.

As to lacking men, in fact the party was well balanced, considering the dinner had been put together with little notice, in the way of the countryside. Mrs. Pillans and her mother, Mrs. Helliwell and her husband the minister, Mr. Murray, the host, and Mr. George, laird of Dures, the third estate that met to form the triangle of Letho parish. Mr. George, of course, was not lacking his husband this evening. Rather his sister, Lady Rocheid, had asked to be excused as she was also awaiting the arrival of her husband, who was expected at any minute from Edinburgh.

'I'm sorry to say that Collessie has very much missed having a laird in residence these several years,' said Mr. George. 'It would be a fine thing for someone to take up a permanent place there.'

'There is certainly work enough for a lifetime,' agreed Mrs. Skead, with mock dismay. 'I am quite daunted!'

To be fair, she did not look like a woman often daunted. Both she and her daughter were – not stout, exactly, but strong, healthy individuals, with attractive faces. Murray could not detect anything too unladylike about them – he had the impression they were both working hard to behave correctly – but they reminded him strongly of milkmaids – not the flowery, Staffordshire type that would fracture limbs at the very sight of a dog's wagging tail, but the real kind, who milked cows and churned butter and hauled mighty cheeses about the dairy without a moment's thought. He had not known them long, but he was inclined to like them both very much.

'Then you would not think of taking it on permanently?' asked Mrs. Helliwell, mischievously. 'We could do with some feminine energy in the parish! There is plenty to do.'

'As to that, Mrs. Helliwell, we are very happy to help while we are here, are we not, Mamma?' said Mrs. Pillans. 'We know what it's like in a large parish. Point us in the right direction, and we shall have broth made, or take bread in baskets, or whatever you desire.'

'Oh, do, please, Mrs. Helliwell!' her mother urged. 'Neither Annie nor I like to be idle.'

'Then I shall take you at your word!' said Mrs. Helliwell. 'Mr. Murray, you and I both know that the kitchen gardens at Collessie leave much to be desired. If you can provide, as you so often do, from your own gardens, then I'm sure Mrs. Pillans and Mrs. Skead will be able to transform the produce into nourishing food, and deliver it to our most deserving parishioners.'

'Of course,' said Murray dutifully, used to being organised by Mrs. Helliwell. 'Though it will be hothouse produce for now: for one thing it's early in the year, as you'll know.' Mrs. Helliwell nodded sharply: she was a keen gardener. 'And for another, I fear there might be some disruption to our gardens here again. I have engineers coming to work on the dreaded culvert again.'

'Again!' The minister, Mr. Helliwell, set down his knife and fork and looked appalled. His own manse had undergone so much rebuilding over the last few years that he had great sympathy for anyone in similar disruption. 'What now?'

'You must know, Mrs. Skead,' Murray said, 'that a number of years ago I made the mistake of employing a very difficult character to sort out a problem with severe damp in my servants' wing. The result, unfortunately, was a partial collapse of the building, and the necessity to rebuild with room for what was, to all intents and purposes, a stream running beneath the building. Now I find that the work requires extending back into the hill where the water is coming from, a tedious and muddy business.'

'How does that affect your kitchen gardens, though, Mr. Murray?' asked Mrs. Pillans.

'They are on the downstream side of the servants' wing,' Murray explained. 'I'm told there is no more need for work there, but the water coming down from the culverting, or whatever it is they intend to do, may not be quite what the gardeners would like.'

'I'd like to take a look at that, if I may, Murray,' said Mr. George with affable interest.

'By all means. The engineers are to arrive within the next few days, I believe.'

'Anyone local?'

Murray shook his head.

'Two Irishmen. They come highly recommended by friends in Wigtownshire. Edward Kelly and Jo Sweeney, I believe, are their names.'

'I hope you find them good, after the last time.'

'Oh, believe me, Mr. George,' said Murray, 'not as much as I do!'

'Shall we see Mr. Blair this summer, Mr. Murray?' asked Mrs. Helliwell. Her husband made some kind of face, and swiftly controlled it.

'Another arrival we are expecting soon!' said Murray.

'That is excellent news!' said Mr. George, and Mrs. Helliwell, whatever her husband thought, nodded agreement.

'It is, isn't it?' said Murray. But though he smiled sincerely, he could not help feeling a pulse of anxiety at the thought. Blair back at Letho. Would it work? Would he be all right?

Robbins left the dining room in the almost reliable hands of Daniel and William, the footmen, and returned to the servants' quarters. His mind, behind those odd, luminous eyes, was busy. They were low on the brandy that Mr. Helliwell particularly liked – there would be enough for today, as Mr. Helliwell was not a heavy drinker, but he would need to order more when he had the chance. The cottage where the Irish engineers were to stay, close to where they were to work, was not yet cleaned and prepared. They had candidates coming to be interviewed for the post of housekeeper, vacant for some time. Elephants … He missed elephants.

The passage along to the kitchen was quiet just now – in a few minutes no doubt maids would appear carrying more dishes towards the dining room. The kitchen itself, even from here, conveyed a comforting sense of bustling activity. For a moment Robbins felt an urge to go and sit quietly in his pantry, writing an order for that brandy, for he was not a man who sought company generally. But there was so much to do at present that he felt he would be failing in his duty if he went and hid. Instead he stepped briefly into the pantry, wrote a note to remind himself to order the brandy later, then carried on to the kitchen.

'Oh!' Mrs. Mack, the cook, spotted him immediately. 'Mr. Robbins, can you help take these dishes along? Yon one's too heavy for Iffy – she near dropped it the last time and I don't want to let her anywhere near it again. See the effort I put into arranging yon sparrowgrass? Ken if she so much as looks at it they'll go all agly.'

Iffy, a young woman of unpromising appearance, nodded at this. She had as much confidence in her abilities as anyone else.

'Is Jennet not helping?' asked Robbins, taking the dish regardless.

'Jennet's upstairs dusting out the rooms for Mr. Blair and Miss Blair. Tell me, Mr. Robbins – or tell me when you're back – where are we with getting a new housekeeper? It's all very fine when Mr. Murray's away or just here on his own with the Blairs, but the minute he starts entertaining,' she gave the word an emphasis she never used to do, 'we're in a stramash. How are we supposed to cope? I mean, I ken your wife comes in now and then …' If 'entertaining' was something of which Mrs. Mack now disapproved, Robbins' wife was a well-established bugbear. Robbins was trying to decide how to defend his wife without causing trouble – more trouble – in the kitchen, when the maid Jennet came in, carrying a copy of the *Edinburgh Courant*.

'I dinna ken if Mr. Murray still wants this, but Daniel's boys were making a tent of it in the library,' she said wearily.

'Were they, indeed?' said Robbins. 'Where are they now?'

'Och, they fled,' said Jennet. 'Again. They're too fast for me, Mr. Robbins.' Robbins propped the heavy dish he still had against the dresser, and took the paper from her, setting it down to attend to later. It might well need a bit of straightening out. Daniel's boys were in much need of discipline: they should never have been anywhere near the library. None of the children was older than seven. Robbins dreaded to think what they might be like if they survived to a greater age. Jennet in turn reached out for the dish, and took it off up the passage to give to the serving men in the dining room. Robbins sighed.

'We've two women coming to be interviewed as housekeeper,' he told Mrs. Mack. 'Both sound promising enough.'

'They're no from an agency, are they?' asked Mrs. Mack. Her tone seemed particularly acidic this evening.

'No, they're not. Both are here from recommendations that Mr. Blair received when he was down south.'

'English women?' Was that better or worse than being from an agency?

'One is, I believe, though she's lived in Scotland. The other is Scottish. What are their names again?' He scrabbled in his busy head, picturing their letters of application. 'Mrs. Gilmour and Mrs. Warner,' he decided. 'I was hoping they would be here and interviewed before the Blairs arrived, but I'm sure Miss Blair would be good enough to advise us if Mr. Murray asked her. She kens the household better than most.'

'She's been coming here since she was born,' Mrs. Mack agreed, her face softening very slightly.

'Aye, one of the family,' agreed Robbins. Jennet returned with a couple of empty dishes, and took them to the scullery.

'What next?' she asked as she emerged. She looked tired, and when an answer did not immediately come, she drifted back to the dresser and unfolded the newspaper. The front page of advertisements was folded back, and the news inside was revealed. She propped her elbows on the dresser and read.

'This is terrible,' she said after a moment. 'Yon girls disappearing in Edinburgh?'

'What girls is that?' asked Mrs. Mack. 'The wrong kind of girls, I daresay.'

'That's no what it says here,' said Jennet, who had learned to read late and was rather proud of her skills. 'It says they worked at a warehouse – the Oriental Warehouse, on South Bridge.'

'Oh, aye,' said Robbins, who was aware of the shop's existence. 'Cloth and such. It's a fine place, I believe.'

'And what kind of a girl works in a shop?' Mrs. Mack demanded.

'I cannot see that they would be any worse than any other girls,' said Robbins reasonably.

'I'd like fine to work in a shop!' said Iffy, breathless at the thought.

'Aye, but whatever shop girls are like,' said Mrs. Mack, 'I doubt they'd take a'body as daft as you.'

'Anyway, you'd need to be able to count,' Jennet put in, not unkindly.

'Oh, aye, I suppose,' said Iffy, deflated.

'But three girls, in the course of a couple of months?' said Jennet, eyes still on the paper. 'Where could they have gone?'

'Aye, well,' said Mrs. Mack, 'such things might happen in Edinburgh, of course. That's what you get for letting yourself be inveigled into going to the big town.'

'But it could happen in Letho!' said Iffy, her eyes wide again.

'Ach, dinna be daft, lass,' said Mrs. Mack firmly. 'Nothing of the sort could happen here.'

Chapter Two

'I suppose they could just have left,' said Robbins. 'Has nobody seen them?'

'Never seen since, it says here,' said Jennet.

'Like yon Ninian Jack's lass,' said Mrs. Mack darkly.

'Ninian Jack? The session clerk? Did I know he had a daughter?' asked Iffy. It was always hard to know what Iffy knew, even for Iffy.

'Aye, he had,' said Robbins. 'She went down south to a position in a lady's house, years ago. She wrote, I believe, for a bit – or did someone write for her?'

'Then she vanished, and was never seen again!' Mrs. Mack wanted the exciting bits of the story. 'Aye, poor Mr. Jack – she was a great favourite with him when she was wee, and then just to disappear ... he's always hoped she might appear one day. Mind, that was years ago. Aye,' she finished, wiping her hands with emphasis.

'I've news of more visitors,' said Robbins tentatively. There was likely not going to be a good time to tell Mrs. Mack.

'More!' Jennet and Mrs. Mack exclaimed at the same time. It was the cook, though, who went on, 'Who this time?'

'The Wedderburns. But not to stay over,' said Robbins, offering it as a comfort. 'Just for dinner, and probably supper. The master doesn't know when yet. They're to be staying somewhere nearby, I believe.'

'Dear grief,' said Mrs. Mack.

'I don't think he had the choice, Mrs. Mack.'

'Aye, well. We need more staff, and that's a fact.' Jennet nodded, dolefully. Mrs. Mack turned to her.

'Who's taking these ashets up this time? Iffy, you could maybe manage – no, on second thoughts you get on with washing the dirty plates. Jennet, have you the time?'

'I still need to make up the beds, Mrs. Mack,' said Jennet. 'But I suppose I could do that later …'

'Oh, give them to me, Mrs. Mack,' said Robbins. 'I'll take them.'

'Thank you, Mr. Robbins. Roll on the day we get this housekeeper. And maybe she'll find us another maid or two …'

In the dining room, William was trying to hide the fact that he had spilled some cream down the front of the sideboard, where it stood out dramatically against the polished burr walnut. Robbins set down his dishes, took a cloth from a drawer and discreetly wiped the cream away, giving William a look that sent him scurrying off with the cream jug to serve it to the remaining guests. Daniel, the other footman, suppressed a smug grin, but then he did not know that Robbins was planning to have some words with him later about his children. William's daughters were much better behaved.

Murray noted the cream incident, but left his servants to it. They all looked tired, he thought. He hoped that one of the housekeepers Alester Blair had had recommendations for might turn out to be suitable. Since the death of his old housekeeper he had been, he thought, unlucky with new servants – and one or two of the old ones needed watching. Nevertheless he would not want to lose any of them: the new housekeeper would have to be an understanding, tolerant sort of a woman. Probably with a good sense of humour. And she would have to get on with Robbins, and with Robbins' wife Mary. And be … well, normal, he thought, remembering one past servant.

Of course some housekeepers preferred to be in a household without a mistress, so that they could be in charge. And some preferred to have a mistress, for whatever reasons – support, direction, safety, even, in some households. He wondered what these candidates would be like.

Absently listening to his guests' conversation, he finished his pudding and laid his spoon on his bowl. Mr. George and Mr.

Helliwell were managing, as usual, to sit at the same table and pretend the other did not exist. Mrs. Helliwell could talk with anyone – and listen, too, always the sensible peacemaker. The newcomers, Mrs. Pillans and Mrs. Skead, seemed very happy to be here and to join in with village society. He wondered what Mr. Pillans was going to be like – a merchant, he had heard, in Edinburgh. There would be a good few people here from Edinburgh over the next month or so: the Blairs were already staying in their house there for a week or so before making the journey onwards to Fife. Lord Rocheid, Mr. George's brother-in-law, was there, too. It seemed unlikely that either party would seek out the other's company, though Blair would talk to anyone. One of the candidates for housekeeper had been in Edinburgh, too.

The Blairs were in Edinburgh. So close, and soon to be on their way.

His thoughts were interrupted by the dining room door opening softly, and a squeal of 'Papa!' His daughter Augusta, four years old, in a flurry of skirts, bounded across to fling herself on to his lap, leaving her governess shamefaced at the door.

'Come in, come in, Miss Fitzsimmons!' called Murray. 'Robbins, a chair?'

But already Robbins had the extra chair ready, and a dish of pudding for the governess, as well as a small one for little Augusta.

'Good evening, Augusta!' said Mrs. Helliwell.

'Good evening, Mrs. Helliwell,' said Augusta obediently, beaming through lips already well creamed. Mrs. Skead and Mrs. Pillans smiled on indulgently, not at all taken aback by the invasion.

'Our governess, Elizabeth Fitzsimmons,' Murray explained. It was an informal dinner, after all. 'Mrs. Pillans and Mrs. Skead, staying at Collessie.'

Miss Fitzsimmons bowed her head, a little shy. Augusta reached out a hand to her.

'Miss Fizz,' she said, 'have you enough pudding? I have lots!'

'Thank you, Augusta, I am very well provided for,' said Miss Fitzsimmons with a smile.

'Papa, when is Isobel coming? I want Miss Fizz to meet Isobel! Isobel is my friend,' she added firmly, not only to Miss Fitzsimmons but also to the Collessie ladies, who might not be expected to know.

'The Blairs should be here soon,' said Murray, using his napkin to remove some of the excess cream from his daughter's paws.

'Today?'

Murray shrugged.

'Probably not today. Maybe not even tomorrow. But soon.'

'Pff,' said Augusta. That was clearly not soon in her head. In some ways it was not soon enough for Murray, either.

'Have you had a good day, Augusta?' asked Mrs. Helliwell.

'Yes,' said Augusta firmly.

'Yes, thank you,' murmured Miss Fitzsimmons.

'Yes, thank you,' repeated Augusta with care. 'I rode my pony and I played with my dog, and I did some numbers. And things.'

'She is progressing very well with her numbers, sir,' added Miss Fitzsimmons, looking proudly at Augusta rather than meeting Murray's eye.

'Good girl,' said Murray. 'And now, I suppose, Mrs. Helliwell, would you like to lead the ladies into the drawing room, and we shall follow fairly soon?'

No sense in lingering, when Mr. George and Mr. Helliwell tried to avoid speaking to each other, and when Augusta was entertaining the ladies with an early attempt at some simplified Mozart on the fortepiano. Murray grinned when he saw her sitting so straight on the piano stool, balanced on two extra cushions, though he did hope that someone had managed to wipe her fingers properly first.

With Mr. Helliwell going to talk to the Collessie ladies, and Mrs. Helliwell chatting with Miss Fitzsimmons and Augusta, Murray had a chance to speak with Mr. George. Mr. George was perhaps ten years older than Murray, approaching fifty, and still a lively and vigorous man – as a few of the local girls could attest. He had always seemed to Murray to be a man at ease with himself and who he was. His sister, however, was a very different person.

'I am sorry Lady Rocheid could not join us this evening,' said Murray, perhaps not entirely truthfully. Mr. George gave a rueful smile.

'As I said, she's waiting at home to see if her wretched husband will arrive. He's three days late already, if you go by what he told her, though I've rarely known him turn up when he said he would. And the later the better, between you and me, if I had my choice in the matter.'

'Oh?' said Murray. There was barely a question he could ask that would not sound intrusive, so he stopped. Blair would probably ask, with a look of baffled innocence, and receive an answer that would tell him everything he wanted to know, and more besides. But Mr. George was used to being discreet, and even what he had already said was more than usual.

'Let me just say that I am delighted that my sister has found a husband to please her, and leave it at that. It's good to see someone take on Collessie again, is it not? I wonder how long they will last this time?'

Dinner had already been served and cleared down at the inn at the foot of the village. Supper was now in preparation. The supply of hot food there was a kind of ongoing process, designed to peak when the mail coach stopped but not fail when other independent travellers passed, or a lone villager, like the schoolmaster with no wife of his own to cook for him, would drop in for a bowl of broth or a couple of chops. The inn was no larger than it needed to be for a village of the size of Letho: no one changed coaches here, and few arrived to visit anyone without being able to go straight away to their house and stay there. One private parlour and a couple of tiny rooms were all that was offered besides the common dining room. In the dining room, above the doorway, hung an oversized clock, bought, apparently, when Collessie was last cleared, a little too large for the space but relentlessly warning the inn's customers of the imminent arrival or departure of the next coach. Relentlessly until now, anyway: the clock had stopped, suddenly, at half past three on Tuesday morning, and now refused to make so much as a random tock. The innkeeper had called in Ninian Jack.

'I mean, you could understand if someone had been doing anything with it at the time,' said the innkeeper anxiously. He had, with the potboy's help, lifted the mighty clock down and laid it, face down, on the dining table. 'But half past three in the morning – I tell you, I woke up myself because the ticking stopped. Just stopped, aye?' He cast a nervous glance at Mr. Jack.

It was not as if he could not afford a new clock, if he needed to. The inn was quite prosperous, by local standards. He would like the clock working as it was such a big, fine one, that was true. But also because he knew that if he were judged to have somehow mistreated the clock, he would never be able to look Ninian Jack in the eye again.

'I mean, I wind it every Saturday night, just like you tellt me to. Just the right number of turns, and I never overwind it, I promise you that! And it's dusted every day, just lightly – I watch the girl myself.'

Ninian Jack said nothing. He removed the brass backplate with reverence, and began a slow, steady scrutiny of the workings.

'Excuse me, innkeeper?' came a voice from the dining room's doorway. A woman stood there: she had been one of the passengers on the mail coach, and, surprisingly, had left it here. She was travelling alone, but she looked respectable: dressed in sober grey, she was perhaps in her fifth decade, with hair still fair and a complexion more used to indoors than out. The innkeeper had given her one of the tiny rooms, the one facing the yard, for the one facing the green was occupied already.

'Aye, mistress, how can I help you?'

'I need directions to somewhere. I have to go in the morning and I want to be prepared.'

'Oh, aye?' Half his attention was on Ninian Jack, still probing delicately into the clock's innards.

'Yes, I need to go to somewhere called Letho House? This is Letho village, is it not?'

'Aye, you're right,' said the innkeeper. 'You've no far to go – well, it depends on whether you want to go by the road and the drive, or over the fields.'

'The road and the drive, please – I have no wish to arrive looking like a farmhand.'

'Aye, right,' said the innkeeper, abashed. He glanced back at Ninian Jack for reassurance, but Jack had straightened from his task. He was staring at the woman, as intensely as if she were a piece of clockwork.

Chapter Three

When the woman left them, Ninian Jack nodded in the direction of where she had been, without looking at the innkeeper. The innkeeper knew he was supposed to respond, though.

'Aye, that's Mrs. Warner, she said. She's one of the women going to be interviewed for the housekeeper, mind?'

Ninian Jack grunted, and returned to the clock, but just as the innkeeper was about to look away that odd expression passed over his face again.

The innkeeper thought about that look later, after he and the potboy had carefully reattached the clock – now working – to the wall above the door. When he had finished the job, Ninian Jack had taken an ale, and left, as silently as he had come, and the woman had retired to her room, presumably to prepare herself for the next morning. The innkeeper wondered if she would be appointed as housekeeper up at Letho – he had been told to expect another candidate, too. He hoped they would find someone good, someone who realised that relations with the village were important. He hoped they would not be put off by Ninian Jack glaring at them. Aye, the old fellow was getting more peculiar every day as he aged. But there was still not a clock nor a fiddly bit of mechanics in the whole parish he could not persuade to work, or build from nothing.

Next morning, Murray waited about upstairs, watching the drive from the landing window, wanting to catch a glimpse of at least one of the women coming for interview. He would not be interviewing her – that was the job of Robbins and perhaps Mrs. Mack, for decency. He might not even meet the woman until an appointment was made, but he could not help being curious.

He saw her about half past nine, just when he thought he would have to give up. She was at first a blur of black bonnet and short spencer and a dark grey skirt, with a small reticule of some kind. As she approached, she became a strong-looking woman, well-used, you would have said, to a life of hard work, striding out confidently. Closer still and he could see she was pale with blonde hair, and blue eyes that were busy taking in the modest sandstone house with its low central door, the two flanking houses, in one of which Robbins lived with his family, the clean paintwork, the neat grass, the smooth gravel. Letho was looking its best on this spring morning.

She hesitated a moment, clearly recalling her directions. Her black-gloved fingers made a little tattoo on her reticule, as though it helped her to think. Then she veered off to Murray's right, between the main house and the factor's house, and disappeared from sight, heading for the servants' wing. Murray hoped she would not take one look at the damp conditions and turn on her heel. Mrs. Warner, then, this one was. And there was to be another in the afternoon – Mrs. Gilmour. Both had come from recommendations Blair had passed on, but he knew nothing further. He hoped one of them would be good: Letho had been without a proper housekeeper for too long.

Since he could not interfere with the interview, and since the bright morning was calling him to come and breathe the fresh air, Murray decided to take a walk down to the village and see who was about. Once the Blairs had arrived, he might have more commitments about the house, but for now his morning correspondence was attended to, his factor and butler had both called with little to report or request, and he felt surprisingly free. He hurried down the stairs before he could think of anything more urgent he should be doing, collected a number of dogs from around the hall fireplace, seized his hat, gloves and stick, and headed out.

Eschewing the drive, he headed across the lawns towards the shortcut he usually took to the village. Beyond the haha, sheep lifted their heads from grazing to check he was not intending to snatch their lambs, but he held the dogs well back and the ewes relaxed. Dandelions sparkled in the grass, and the hedgerows were glowing with gorse blossom. The last of the primroses lightened the ditches, sparrows and blackbirds hurled song into the air, and swallows darted back and forth high above, sign of good weather to come. As he passed along towards the little wood that stood near the kirk, he could smell may blossom, and the branches of Mrs. Helliwell's apple trees poked above the manse garden wall, dropping petals on to the path. The dogs, now released, tracked every glorious scent, and Murray, too, sniffed the air and grinned in delight.

He emerged into the village proper beside the kirk at the top of the triangular village green. The fine weather, some of the best of the year so far, had encouraged many of the villagers to venture outside: several women were spinning at their front doors, enjoying a gossip, while others had taken the chance to clean windows and generally spruce up. The goats that were pegged to graze on the green looked as if they had just been groomed. An open carriage, rather daring even though the day was fine, had pulled up outside Dr. Feilden's house, and Murray could see that he too was gossiping, with Lady Rocheid. Whether he was enjoying his chat or not, he was quick to hail Murray and bid him good morning.

'Good morning, my lady, Dr. Feilden,' said Murray, bowing and trying to catch hold of his three dogs at the same time. The spaniel in particular found wheels fascinating, and tried to get under them wherever possible.

'Good morning, Mr. Murray,' said Lady Rocheid graciously.

'I am glad to see you venturing out, Lady Rocheid,' said Murray. 'Mr. George last night suggested you were anxious for news about Lord Rocheid.'

Lady Rocheid's face crinkled.

'My brother does not take me seriously! It is too bad of him. And still there is no sign of my husband. I cannot fathom whether I should stay at Dures or go and see if he has met with some accident along the road. Yet if I should go, and find later that he had taken another path, been called away north, perhaps ...'

'Was he expecting to be called away north?' asked Dr. Feilden, and Lady Rocheid blushed.

'I don't believe so. But he leads such an eventful life, almost anything could happen!'

Her husband would have sent word, Murray thought, if he had the least chance. Lady Rocheid was clutching at straws, and yet from what Mr. George had said last night, his brother-in-law was not so very late arriving.

There had been no girlish bride so happy in the whole Kingdom of Fife as Miss George when she married her Lord Rocheid, yet she was twice the age of most other brides and, it was estimated, a good fifteen years older than her new husband. Miss George lacked the handsome vivacity and strength of character of her brother, and it had been no great surprise to anyone that she remained unmarried for so long, despite having a generous dowry to bestow. She must have given up hope when a chance visit to Edinburgh had seen her return, to everyone's astonishment, with the news that she was to be married, and if Rocheid was a minor title, it was a title all the same. To do Miss George credit, there had not been the least hint of 'I told you so' about her betrothal. She had simply been thrilled, and had shared her happiness with everyone she met. Murray had been away in England at the time of the marriage and so had not had much acquaintance with the fortunate peer: from Mr. George's strong hints of either dislike or disapproval Murray was curious, and disposed to feel very sorry for the new Lady Rocheid. He would have liked her happiness to persist, at least for a decade or two. But now here she was, clearly anxious about him, looking about her even as she tried to talk to Murray and Dr. Feilden, as if Lord Rocheid might suddenly appear from behind a wall and leap out to greet her. She, at least, was still very attached to him, whatever her brother's views.

Dr. Feilden, observing the spaniel, had embarked on an anecdote concerning a patient's dog when Lady Rocheid broke in.

'I should enquire of the innkeeper, of course,' she said. 'Perhaps word has been received there, or perhaps he has arrived fatigued and taken some rest there.'

'Do you think –' Murray began, but already Lady Rocheid had flung open the carriage door and caused her groom to rush to adjust the step. She seized Murray's hand to steady herself, stepped down, and made her way at some speed down towards the inn. Murray and Dr. Feilden, taken by surprise, watched her go, with her groom scurrying along behind.

'I wonder what the matter can be?' said the physician, his hand to his hat to make a farewell.

'I'm not sure that anything is the matter,' said Murray. 'Mr.

George was not too concerned.'

'Ah, but a lady has feelings,' said Dr. Feilden solemnly.

'That much is certainly true,' said Murray. 'Though I believe some men are endowed with them, too. I wonder if one of us should follow – in case there really is bad news? Her feelings then might be too much for her.'

'The coach is not due for an hour or so yet,' said Dr. Feilden. 'And while I am concerned for the lady, I'm afraid I have patients to visit.'

'Then I shall go and see she is all right, or at least safely settled to await it.'

'Mind,' said Dr. Feilden, 'I thought I did hear wheels not long ago – it can't have been the coach, but perhaps it was some private vehicle. Does he keep his own carriage, or is Lady Rocheid's the only one they have?'

'I have no idea,' said Murray. 'I shall go and see what I can find out.'

He strolled down the green, nodding to almost everyone he met and stopping for conversation with a couple, so that it took longer than it might have done to reach the inn. Once there, he found that Lady Rocheid had disappeared inside, along with her groom. In the stableyard, when he poked his head through the archway, there was no sign of an unfamiliar carriage. He wondered if Dr. Feilden had been imagining things, but he decided that he would go inside and make sure.

'Och, she's all right, sir,' said the innkeeper. 'She's taken herself off to the private parlour to sit for a wee bit. She's done it a couple of days this week already. She's quite safe here, you ken.'

'Oh, I know, indeed,' said Murray. Safe, yes, but not happy, clearly. 'How long does she tend to stay?'

'Only till the coach comes, sir. Then she comes out and sees who's arrived – ken, not many get off here anyway, not for long – and once that's done she's back into her carriage and away home to Dures. I mean, that's not her home, not now, but her old home, sir.'

'Well ... I suppose it's up to her.' He wondered if Mr. George knew how his sister was spending her time. Perhaps this was why he had a low opinion of his brother-in-law. Mr. George had many faults, but he was punctual and reliable, and often those who are find the opposite hard to bear in others. 'Did a vehicle come through not long ago? I saw no sign in the yard, but someone said they had heard one.'

'Oh, aye! Though that was nothing to do with Miss Ge – I mean, Lady Rocheid,' said the innkeeper.

'So who was that, then? Was it a carriage?'

'Aye, it was, sir. The two fellows are out at the front just now, getting themselves sorted. I have their luggage there.' He nodded at a couple of packs and a tantalising wooden box, tucked under a table.

'Where are they bound, then?' asked Murray.

'Och, they're off to Letho House, sir. A couple of Irishmen. They said they've a meeting with you.'

Murray felt a jump of excitement. The engineers had arrived.

Chapter Four

It took Murray a moment to leave the inn and go about to the front, where the long, low building edged the main road to Cupar. It gave him just enough time to remember the last engineer who had worked on the problem behind the servants' wing.

Mr. Elliot had arrived full of ambitious plans in the year '08, and in order to solve the issue of the terrible damp on the ground floor of the wing had elected to tunnel beneath the building, allowing the water, which flowed down from the higher ground behind the wing, to be channelled into a kind of canal in the kitchen gardens at the front of the wing, rather than being dammed against the wing's sandstone walls. It had been a splendid idea, and quite exciting. Less splendid had been the subsequent partial collapse of the servants' wing, leading to an expensive and lengthy rebuild and, more importantly, to injuries to several servants. However, the new wing, designed without any major input from Mr. Elliot, had been well-received and the burn now ran well under the building. Further back, though, on the higher ground where they had thought the spring rose, there seemed to be new problems. Murray had taken a solemn vow never to call in Mr. Elliot again. He hoped these two young Irishmen would be as good as their recommendation.

On the bench outside the inn sat a young man, perhaps five or ten years younger than Murray himself, with a scramble of dark curly hair and a look of solemn intensity as he carefully removed his boots and socks. Beside him lay a fresh pair of socks, exactly arranged, ready for the moment when he had finished flexing and stretching his long, pale toes. Standing and surveying him with a look of patient amusement was a taller man with ginger hair and freckles.

'Now Jo, make sure those feet of yours are well looked after, will you not? I'd hate to have to carry you up to the big house.'

The dark-haired man said nothing, carrying on with his important task, and the ginger man smiled to himself, then turned a little and caught sight of Murray.

'Good day to you, sir,' he said politely, with a nod of his head.

'Good day to you. Would you happen to be Mr. Kelly and Mr. Sweeney, by any chance?'

'We are that, sir. I'm Kelly and the man here arranging his toes is Mr. Joseph Sweeney. How may I be of service to you?'

'My name is Charles Murray of Letho,' said Murray. 'I believe you are on your way to see me.'

'We are that, sir!' Edward Kelly bowed again, lower this time, and Jo Sweeney picked himself up, bare-footed, and made his own bow, unabashed. 'I am sorry that you find us in this unready state. I hope you were not troubled by coming to look for us.'

'Not at all – I had not expected you today, but was passing the inn and found that you had arrived. I am here on foot myself. Are you able and willing to walk up to the house with me – once Mr. Sweeney is ready? Or would you rather I sent a gig when I return home?'

'Oh, now, we would not have you take the trouble to send a gig out for us when we're grand at the walking, would we, Jo? Jo's feet are very strong and healthy, for he takes such care of them. We'll be ready when you are, I should think, sir, if it suits you to be so good as to lead the way.'

'If I may?' Jo Sweeney gestured to the socks, and Murray nodded at once. He and Kelly waited while Sweeney packed up the socks he had just removed in a linen bag, then slid the fresh socks on to his feet and replaced his sturdy boots, lacing them with exactitude.

'I see your packs are in the inn,' said Murray. 'We can send the cart down for them later, unless there is anything you want to bring now.'

'Oh, my box,' said Mr. Kelly, and darted into the inn to fetch the smart box Murray had seen in there. He had a notion that whatever it contained, Blair would want to see it. Mr. Sweeney placed a black hat on his curls, and stood, testing his feet warily and finding them good. Once Mr. Kelly was out again, Murray gestured to the path around the inn and led them back to the village green and up the hill towards the shortcut to Letho House.

Mr. Kelly dutifully admired the simple, graceful shape of the main house and its two lesser houses as they reached the haha. Mr. Sweeney did not say much – Murray had the impression he was a little alarmed by the dogs and, when the dogs were safely on their leads, by the sheep. Nevertheless, Murray felt he had found out more about the pair than he would have in a formal interview in the library, say, for Mr. Kelly was very happy to fill the fresh air with talk. He and Jo Sweeney were from Dublin and had met at the university there. They had discovered a complementary aptitude for the engineering life, particularly enjoying working with water and water courses, and had decided to enhance their professional experience and build up their reputations in England and Scotland before returning home in, Edward Kelly thought, about five or seven years' time, when he himself hoped to marry his sweetheart, Martha by name, if she had the common decency to wait for him. Jo Sweeney did not, it appeared, have a sweetheart waiting for him in Dublin: perhaps he spread his affections more broadly, but Murray thought not – unless he attracted the kind of woman who wished to fathom the mystery of a man. Mr. Sweeney said barely two words on the whole walk.

'I believe my factor mentioned a cottage on the estate where you would be welcome to stay for the duration of your work,' said Murray. 'If you wish, the kitchens can provide you with your meals there, or you can join the kitchen table if you prefer the company.'

'As to that,' said Mr. Kelly, 'I love a bit of company. Jo here might prefer to sit on his own in the cottage, though. He'll want to think about the engineering.'

'And do you not think about the engineering?' asked Murray, half-smiling.

'I love the engineering,' said Mr. Kelly sincerely, 'and I enjoy every minute of my work. But when I stop in the evening for my supper, I don't need to see streams and bridges every time my eyes close. Jo, here – he thinks of nothing else. Do you, Jo?'

Jo's eyes were all over the buildings they were now passing, and Murray felt he was already looking for the problem and the stream they would have to manage.

'What's that?' he asked after a moment, realising they were waiting for an answer.

'We'd best see the water,' said Edward Kelly. 'Will it be your factor we'll be dealing with, sir?'

'Generally, yes,' said Murray, 'but he's out at the moment. I'll show you the place. Unless you would rather see your cottage first?'

But just as he expected, they both said no. Murray led them round the side of the house to the servants' wing, pointing out, when they were far enough along, the way the wing had been restructured to accommodate the water flowing down the hill behind it. There was much stooping, hands on knees, so that they could peer along the passageway under the wing, glimpsing the kitchen gardens beyond, and nodding as they examined the floor of the channel and the stonework of the wing above it.

'Maybe we could see inside some time, sir? I know it's not part of our own work, but it's an unusual way of dealing with the matter and I think we'd both like to take a look. The ground floor is split in two, then?'

'That's right. The further rooms, being very cool, are used for storage, while the kitchens are this end. There are stairs at both ends up to the first floor, where the men sleep, and then the women are above that again. It is not a large household,' he added, thinking to himself that it should, soon, be larger.

'Right, well,' said Kelly, straightening. 'Now for our own little challenge!'

'It's behind you,' said Murray, and they all turned around.

The rising ground behind them was topped with trees that continued on the far flank of the little hill. The near side, though, was muddy, between mossy rocks and spiky clumps of reeds. Though it faced west, it had a shadowy look to it as though it never saw the sun – the foot of it, indeed, was shaded by the servants' wing. The track between the hill and the building was thick with mud, rutted by years of carts and carriages being taken to the stables.

'We need to cassie the road, anyway,' said Murray. 'That's a task left over from my father's time, and we've simply never got round to it. But it's the spring that rises in the hill that's the problem.'

'What's the stonework?' asked Kelly, pointing. A rudimentary arch shape could just be seen, well mossed over.

'That was the factor's idea in my grandfather's time. He thought that with the spring cooling the stones around it, he could dig out a good icehouse, much handier for the servants than the conventional idea of having one by a lake. Of course the ice still has to be brought from the lake, but at least when the servants want to chill something they don't have to go so far. But unfortunately he could not seem to get the structure strong enough – I think, myself, that the spring kept everything moving, but you gentlemen will know more about that than I do.'

'So what's the solution you want, sir?' asked Kelly.

'Well ... I suppose I want the road dry, if possible, and I'd like the hill here not to be constantly washed down across it. The mud carries through under the servants' wing and makes it hard to keep the canal sweet, which is unpleasant for the servants and for the gardeners. Beyond that, I'd be interested to see what your ideas are.'

'Oh, he'll have ideas, all right,' said Kelly, nodding at Sweeney. Sweeney was already all over the hill with his eyes, barely moving but taking everything in. Kelly, by contrast, was stalking up and down the muddy road, considering different angles, moving in to touch the damp stonework, peering amongst brambles and ferns, poking the toe of his boot into the soft soil, even as he continued the conversation. 'We'll take a good look, and some measurements. We have all we need here,' he tapped his wooden case, which he held firmly under one arm, 'except a table to work on.'

'There's a good-sized one in your cottage,' Murray reassured him.

'That's grand. I'll do some drawings. Oh, is there a door here?'

His tapping knuckles had suddenly produced a hollow sound amongst the undergrowth.

'Yes, to the icehouse. I should imagine it's rotten.'

'I see – from what you said, sir, I thought the idea had been abandoned long ago.'

'Well, the icehouse was, yes: it isn't used. But behind there the hole must go back maybe twenty or thirty feet?'

23

'Now there's a thing,' said Kelly thoughtfully. 'Can we get the plants stripped back, and that door off?'

'You can, yes, I'm sure. As I say, it's probably rotten. A good kick would do it! But perhaps you'll want some help there, though, in case the stonework isn't sound? A few men with props, perhaps?'

'Oh, aye, that's a good idea.' Kelly, who had been prodding the weathered wood, backed off. 'And maybe then, as we're thinking of safety, some means of blocking up the hole again afterwards? Just in case,' he said cheerfully, 'someone should think of wandering in, and the whole thing collapse on their heads.'

Chapter Five

Robbins glanced out of the still room window when the movement outside caught his eye, and saw the master with two strangers, inspecting the stonework of the old icehouse. That must be the engineers, then. He hoped Jennet had had the chance to finish preparing their cottage – they were earlier than he had expected. Everything seemed to be happening at once.

'Aye, well, the last housekeeper seems to have labelled everything very nicely,' Mrs. Mack was saying. 'You shouldna have too much difficulty finding your way around. If you're appointed, ken.'

The woman, Mrs. Warner, gave a brief smile of acknowledgement.

'Can I ask why the last housekeeper left, Mrs. Mack?'

Mrs. Mack sniffed.

'Aye, you can ask. She –'

'She had business to see to elsewhere, Mrs. Warner,' said Robbins smoothly. 'Otherwise I'm sure she would still be here.' That was as ambiguous as anyone could want, he thought. 'Then with the master away for some months we have not been pressed to fill the position again. The last housekeeper was not here long, but before her Mrs. Chambers was here for many years, into her old age. Her niece Jennet is still here.'

'You'll ken as well as anybody,' said Mrs. Mack, 'that there's servants that come and go, but the most of us here has been here a long time, and many are local. Mr. Robbins here, and the men Daniel and William, and Jennet, of course. And – oh, not Mrs.

Robbins, of course. Not her.'

Robbins cast his cool gaze upon her. Rarely did Mrs. Mack pass up an opportunity to have a dig at his wife. Mary never minded, though: it was Robbins who noted them all.

Mrs. Warner nodded, apparently satisfied. Robbins put Mary and Mrs. Mack from his mind and focussed on her again.

He had been quite impressed so far. Her letters of recommendation had looked genuine and favourable, and the answers she had given to the questions he and Mrs. Mack had thought of had been sensible: what she would do if unexpected guests arrived and in what order; what would she do in case of fire; how would she address an earl; had she experience dealing with animals, and what kinds; what recipes would she use for preserving raspberries, for curing headaches, for cleaning oil off a curtain?

'And you've been working in Edinburgh till now?' Robbins knew the answer but he wanted to hear her speak more, see if he could draw her out.

'That's right, Mr. Robbins. A family in the New Town.'

A family Robbins had not heard of, but the New Town was growing all the time: there was no reason why he should know everyone there. And Mr. Blair had met them, apparently.

'A fine situation. Why did you leave?'

'I was – tiring of town life. I wanted something quieter. I was brought up in the countryside, in the West Riding.'

Much the answer she had given before. Not much more. She had all the right responses ready, but there was something – what? Withdrawn about her, maybe. But perhaps she was the kind of person who did not settle quickly with strangers. He himself was not, he would fully admit, an outgoing man. And a quiet, sensible woman would not be a bad appointment. He wondered, though, how he might discover whether or not there was more to her. Had she, for example, a sense of humour? That was often helpful in service, as long as it was an appropriate one. And it was almost essential when trying to deal with Daniel and William.

A bell rang in the passage outside, and Robbins went out to check.

'Library,' he said, almost to himself. 'Daniel!'

'Aye, Mr. Robbins.' Daniel's response trailed off behind him as he began to make his way up the passage to the main house, reluctant as a schoolboy dragged in from his play.

Murray was glad when Daniel finally appeared at the library door.

'A glass of wine for these gentlemen, Daniel – and can you ask Mr. Robbins, please, if their cottage is fully prepared?'

'Yes, sir.' Daniel's bows had not really improved over the years, not helped by his increasingly portly shape.

'We'll organise the removal of that door in the morning,' Murray went on to Kelly and Sweeney. Sweeney was eyeing up the books on the shelves with a happy expression on his dark face, as if he were greeting old friends. 'My factor should be free to supervise it then: I'll have a word with him when he returns. I'd better write him a note.' He went to his desk and found some paper.

'I'd like fine to see what the inside is like,' said Mr. Kelly.

'Dreadful, I should think,' said Murray. 'I can't see that foxes could have got in, but anything smaller than that is more than likely.'

'It's possible we can use part of that structure,' said Kelly, looking over at Sweeney, but something about Sweeney made him stop that line of speculation. Murray did not catch what it was.

'The blacksmith can rig up a gate that you can use to close over the entrance when you're not working there. Then, presumably, it can air at the same time, instead of being closed in.' Murray was glad that Kelly had mentioned such a thing: he was positive that Daniel's children would be into the icehouse like a shot. And annoying as they were, he did not want the roof to fall in on them. He finished writing the note to Thalland, the factor, explaining about removing the wooden gate, replacing it, and having men on hand to shore up any minor collapse – if it looked like becoming a major collapse, they would just have to run and leave it. He had no great interest in preserving a building that had never really functioned, anyway.

Daniel reappeared with the decanter and glasses, managing to look as if he had never seen such things in his life and had no idea what anyone might do with them. Mr. Kelly grinned and took the tray from him, leaving Daniel free to be summoned to Murray's desk.

'Take this to Mr. Thalland, please, as soon as may be. And

Daniel: we'll be opening the old icehouse behind the servants' wing tomorrow. For their safety, can you keep the children well away? There could easily be falling masonry.'

'Falling masonry? Like when the kitchen fell down?'

'That's right.'

All the colour had washed out of Daniel's face, but he managed to pull himself straight.

'Aye, sir, I'll keep them clear. And anybody else, too, sir.'

'That would be sensible, yes. Thank you, Daniel – the note?'

'Oh, aye. Sorry, sir.'

Daniel left with Thalland's instructions, and Murray went to pour the wine. He would talk to Robbins later about Daniel's reaction to the thought of falling masonry. He had thought that the staff were, for the most part, recovered from that dreadful day.

But the next morning Murray was distracted from the arrangements for the icehouse by a note arriving by express from the inn at Cupar. He called Robbins.

'The Blairs will arrive this afternoon – are we ready?'

'We should be, sir,' said Robbins. 'The small parlour at the back of the house has been arranged for Mr. Blair with all that Miss Blair suggested he might need. There is room for Smith to sleep nearby. Miss Blair will be in her usual room, sir.'

'Very good – could we go along now and see the parlour?'

The parlour had been Murray's mother's favourite room, looking out over the gardens.

'That seemed the best place for the bed, sir. We took out much of the original furniture, to leave as much floor space as possible. Miss Blair said that Mr. Blair would need that for using his crutches, but that he now has a wheeled chair, too, that he sometimes uses.'

'And they are here long enough that we can adjust as need be,' Murray nodded.

'There is room for a bed for Mr. Smith just here,' Robbins indicated space behind a screen for Mr. Blair's manservant, 'but Miss Blair will have her accustomed room.'

'Perfect. No doubt Miss Blair will tell us if there is anything else. I've been trying to think what else might need adjustment. The steps to the front door will be his only impediment, but they are shallow.'

'I've spoken to Mr. Thalland, sir: the gardeners can bring planks if they are needed. The dining room is on the ground floor, so that is convenient.'

'Along with the library: I cannot see Blair spending time here without wanting to be in the library. What about the drawing room?'

'I wondered, sir, if, while the Blairs are the only visitors, we might use the library after dinner, too?'

'I think that would please everyone, yes. There will be no piano, but I suppose I shall have to manage without!' Isobel was not the most musical woman in the world, he well knew. Isobel …

'A larger party might be accommodated in the entrance hall, sir, if the fire were lit and some more chairs brought in. And in that case we could bring the fortepiano down from the drawing room, if we were careful.'

Murray winced at the thought of Daniel helping to carry the fortepiano and the tuning it might require afterwards.

'Perhaps we can have guests that bring their own instruments. But yes, the entrance hall at this time of year might well be acceptable. Good work, Robbins. How did the interview with the women go yesterday?'

'In appearance they could almost be sisters, sir. Aside from that, they both seem very suitable. Mrs. Mack and I discussed them at some length yesterday evening. To go by meeting them and reading their recommendations, there is little to choose between them.'

'And in personality? Which of them did you like more?' It would be important that Robbins could get on with whoever they appointed.

'The first, Mrs. Warner, was a quieter, calmer person, we felt, sir.'

'That's good.'

'But then the second, Mrs. Gilmour, she seemed to have more energy. There was an excitement about her, we thought, as if she were really looking forward to working here. It's not a clear decision, sir.'

Murray frowned.

'Could we somehow give them a trial? A week each?'

'I don't know how they would feel about that, sir. You might be keeping a woman back a fortnight when she could be finding work elsewhere. Yet I don't know how else we might choose between them.'

'Perhaps Miss Blair might advise us. She has more experience, certainly in recent years, of good housekeeping.'

'That would be very helpful, sir, if she were willing to meet the two women.'

'I'll speak to her this afternoon. How did you leave it with the women?'

'They are both staying at the inn, sir, until we reach a decision.'

'We cannot leave it too long, then, or they'll be at additional expense. Yes, Daniel?'

Daniel had appeared at the parlour door.

'A note, sir, from Mr. Thalland.'

'Oh ...' Murray read it quickly: Thalland's hand-writing was elongated, like the man himself, but clear. 'Oh – well, that's not entirely bad news. The opening of the old icehouse is delayed until after dinner, because of a problem over at the Mains farm that has to be dealt with this morning. Daniel, will you go and tell Mr. Kelly and Mr. Sweeney in the cottage? No doubt they can do some surveying this morning.'

'Yes, sir,' said Daniel, and left.

'And Mr. Blair will be delighted if he can watch them take down that wooden gate,' Murray went on. 'Either from his wheeled chair or something we could carry out for him.'

'Yes, sir, that should be easy. Mr. Smith and I can arrange that and make sure Mr. Blair is comfortable.'

'Comfortable and entertained,' Murray said, nodding. 'That's the aim for the time they are here. And, Miss Blair insisted, not too much excitement.'

'As to that, sir, I'm sure we can guarantee it.'

Chapter Six

Traditionally, the Blairs' arrival at Letho would consist of
Alester Blair hurtling out of the carriage almost before the groom
had time to fold down the steps, followed at a more ladylike pace by
his daughter Isobel. Between him shaking out his wig, greeting the
dogs, patting his enormous pockets to check that nothing had fallen
out (though how he could possibly tell was a mystery), surveying
the front of the house as if checking the health of an old friend,
bowing to whatever servants were there to meet him and asking after
each of them by name, skipping up the steps towards Murray,
beaming, chubby and full of inquisitive energy, just getting Blair
into the house could be exhausting.

This time, however, it was different. Smith, the manservant,
was there with the groom at the steps, and first handed Isobel down
on to the gravel drive. Murray's heart filliped twice over. It was the
first he had seen her since he had left the Blairs in Sussex last
autumn, and he had been looking forward to this moment almost
with bated breath. She looked tired, and there were a few lines on
her brow that had not been there in the autumn.

'Charles!' she said at once, and hurried over to him, both
hands out to take his. He grasped them and grinned, not wanting to
let her go, but she was already turning back towards the carriage.

'How is he?' asked Murray quietly.

'He's – travel wearies him and enlivens him at the same
time. But he's doing very well, really.'

Smith and the groom were working at the carriage. A
wheeled chair was ready to receive its occupant. Isobel seemed to

run through some mental list of things to be done, then went to say hello to Robbins, Daniel and William, waiting for instructions by the door. Robbins allowed the men to bow to her, then sent them to deal with the luggage cart that had followed the carriage more slowly up the drive. Better that than standing there watching the carriage and waiting.

A flurry of movement at the carriage doorway, and the groom held the chair steady as Smith lifted a bundle clear and deposited it gently in the seat. Then the cushions were arranged, and the wig straightened, and a silk shawl thrown across the absence of leg, and in a moment Smith had turned the chair and begun a difficult progress across the thick gravel.

'Not the easiest surface,' Isobel explained almost apologetically, but Murray was looking at Blair.

The beaming smile was the same, but his old friend seemed to have shrunk. Of course he lacked one leg after what had happened in Sussex, but his face was thinner, older.

'Charles!' he cried, like his daughter reaching out both hands. 'Oh, Charles, you are a sight for sore eyes! My dear boy – I would embrace you if I were not in this chair! Charles!' He seized Murray's hands and shook and shook them, and Murray was shocked to see traces of tears in his wide eyes. 'Never have I taken so long to travel from Sussex to Fife – and never have I been so glad to be here! Mr. Robbins, come here so that I might see you. Oh, the house has not changed one jot! Mr. Robbins, tell me, how is your good wife?'

'She is very well, sir, and presents her compliments.'

'And the very same to her, Mr. Robbins. And your children? How many now?'

'Two, sir,' said Robbins, a little pink. He was a private man.

'Two! Wonderful. And have you found a housekeeper yet? I daresay not, or she would be here.'

'We are interviewing, sir.'

'I hope you find someone magnificent! Or at least, well, interesting.'

'And competent, Father,' Isobel suggested with a smile.

'Will you come in?' asked Murray, 'or are we to have our dinner sent out here?'

Already Blair had encouraged the smallest dog to jump on

32

to the base of his chair and Smith, with a hint of an eye-roll, pushed the contraption up and into the house, tilting it back carefully to negotiate the steps.

'Thank you so much, Charles,' said Isobel. They were in the hallway, Isobel at the foot of the stairs ready to go and settle in her own room. 'It's perfect for him – right in the middle of things, and easy for him to manage. He has longed so much to be back here, even more than in Edinburgh. Edinburgh seemed so busy, and he felt so much out of it, that he was more upset than he would have been if there had been nothing happening at all. Here, I know he can find peace, even when he is involved in everything. If that makes any sense!'

'If anything is the least bit wrong, only say. You know that.'

'I can't think of anything at all. You have thought of everything.'

'I think Robbins simply followed your instructions,' he smiled.

'No housekeeper yet, then?'

'He interviewed two good candidates yesterday. I think he would value your advice, if you were happy to give it.'

'Of course, I'll do that. It would be good for the place to have someone in charge. I know Robbins – and Mrs. Robbins – are invaluable, but still ...'

'I know, I know.' If you were here all the time, the thought popped into his head, then you could oversee things. Mistress of Letho. That would be ideal. When could he ask her? How? The circumstances would have to be just right, he thought. But what?

'Well ...' She gave him an odd look, and he wondered how long he had stood there without saying anything. 'Dinner at the usual hour?'

'Yes, indeed. Yes.'

'Then I shall see you then. I hope you still have a cook – I'm famished!'

'That's the Blairs safely arrived,' Robbins told Mrs. Mack. 'Mr. Smith will be along shortly, when he has Mr. Blair settled in.'

'And Mr. Blair – is he ...'

'It's just his leg, Mrs. Mack. There are plenty of people with only the one leg.'

'But is he all right in himself?'

Robbins thought about it. Mr. Blair had not entirely looked all right in himself, at least, not until he had smiled, and started to ask his usual questions. Then he had seemed to come alive.

'I think he's pleased to be here.'

'The master will be glad to see him, and see him safe here.'

Robbins nodded.

'He'll need to rest a few days, anyway. I daresay we'll not see so much of him as we would have had before.'

'Him and his pockets!' Mrs. Mack smiled, though she had always found Mr. Blair's habit of collecting random items on his travels a bit off-putting.

'He'll find it harder to gather up so much now. He'll be missed, wandering about the place and turning up when he's least expected.'

'I daresay he'll spend his days in the library by the fire, like a proper old gentleman, reading his books and getting his strength back. And Miss Blair will be painting and drawing, no doubt. It's fine to have them back,' said Mrs. Mack in satisfaction, for any cook likes an appreciative household to cater for, rather than one lone widower and his small daughter.

'Isobel!' shrieked Augusta, breaking free at once from Miss Fitzsimmons' hand and hurtling towards Miss Blair.

'Augusta! Are your hands clean?' Murray cried.

'In a minute, Pappa. I haven't seen Isobel for long time.' Her words were muffled in Isobel's skirts as she hugged her friend. Isobel, laughing, detached her and knelt down to even their heights.

'Dear Augusta! How are you?'

'I need to show you my new puppy and my new doll, Isobel. And my new governess. I don't have a nurse anymore! Come and see her.'

Poor Miss Fitzsimmons submitted to being shown off to Isobel in much the same way as the puppy would be later. They had chosen to sit in the entrance hall after dinner as the afternoon light was so pleasant there, and it meant there was more room to move about. Murray was seated by Blair, who had taken an armchair for a change.

34

'Your daughter and mine are firm friends as ever, Charles!' said Blair, watching them.

'Isobel has been wonderful to Augusta,' said Murray. 'Augusta has missed her very much.'

'The governess seems a pleasant young lady. Where has she come from?'

'From York, via Inverness: a very pleasant and intelligent young lady, and strict enough to keep Augusta under control. They share a keen interest in mathematics.'

Blair's watery eyes widened.

'Good heavens,' he remarked. 'Was she a governess in Inverness?' And the conversation continued along the lines of trying to find a point in Miss Fitzsimmons' life where she might have known someone that Blair knew, though since Murray did not himself know every moment of his governess' background it was a little frustrating. No doubt Blair would corner Miss Fitzsimmons later and subject her to a proper interrogation.

'But now, Charles, tell me about the icehouse and the Irish engineers!'

There was no point even in wondering how he knew. He told Blair about the problems with the spring – Blair had been there when the servants' wing had collapsed, and knew all the history – and how they planned to investigate the old icehouse.

'It was never used, was it?' Blair asked. 'I don't believe I have ever seen the doors open. May I – oh, please, Charles – may I come and watch when it is opened?'

'Of course you may!' said Murray at once – though he had no idea how, should he have wished it, he could stop him.

The weeds had been cleared from the face of the rotten planks, and a couple of self-seeded shrubs had been rigorously hacked back. The three men that Thalland had brought to help, armed with solid wooden posts and an iron crowbar, approached the door. Mr. Sweeney joined them, and exchanged views in a low voice, pointing up to certain stones in the lintel, perhaps indicating the ones he thought most likely to fall when the support of the door was removed. The wooden door frame did not extend all the way around the aperture: there were uprights only, which tapered off as the doorway rounded into its low arch. An arch, thought Murray: it should hold, if the stones had been properly laid. Unless there was some pressure behind them to push them outwards.

Mr. Thalland, thin and chinless, stood watching, but clearly trusted the men he had picked to do a sensible job.

'Have you ever looked in there?' Murray asked him, nodding at the doors.

'Once, long ago, in your father's time,' answered Thalland in his reedy voice. 'There's been no reason to go in since. The doors should have been better maintained, though – my omission.'

'There were other priorities,' said Murray. Rebuilding the servants' wing had taken up a good deal of the estate's finances. He still blamed himself for that.

'I think we're ready,' said Mr. Sweeney to his colleague.

'Right, then, ladies and gentlemen, we should clear away over here,' said Mr. Kelly, waving them backwards. 'Jo, get yourself clear!'

Mr. Kelly stood well back but Mr. Sweeney ignored him, staying close to the edge of the doorway, watching intently. Blair was equally focussed, though further away, beside Murray, sitting forward in his chair. The men with the posts inserted them as best they could under the least stable-looking stones. The man with the crowbar slipped it into the gap between the doors, and applied a little gentle pressure, then pushed harder. The wood was not, Murray thought, quite as rotten as they had expected. At last, with a heart-rending creak, something – perhaps an ancient lock – gave way, and the left hand door swung outwards a few inches before sticking on a stone. The man with the crowbar pulled it again, freeing it quite easily, and opened it wide, then returned to open the other side. At last they could see clearly, straight into the icehouse.

Chapter Seven

And inside, there was nothing.

Well, there was clearly enough to interest Mr. Kelly and Mr. Sweeney. At once they hurried to direct the men to set the props up more securely, then tentatively inspected the stonework left inside. It looked, to Murray's inexpert eye, fairly stable: it was effectively a short, dead end tunnel, six or seven feet high in the centre, and stone-lined, until it ended in a wall of rubble and earth and tree roots, perhaps the original constituents of the hill into which it burrowed. There must be larger rocks somewhere behind there, supporting the weight of the trees, and perhaps the workmen had reached one of those and stopped. The tunnel could not have been particularly appealing to the local wildlife, for the stone-flagged floor was pretty much clean: a few pieces of wet straw and moss had gathered or been gathered in one corner, as if some adventurous mice had tried it out and found it wanting. It was, indeed, very damp.

'Wheel me forward, please, Smith!' Blair called, and Smith obeyed, eyes on the roof-props. Blair was clearly itching to get up and into the tunnel, but even from the point where Smith stopped he could see the stonework quite clearly. Murray was content that the whole thing had not collapsed when the doors were opened. He turned to Thalland.

'How soon can we have a gate across that with a lock? It looks safe enough, but once work starts ...'

'The blacksmith is on his way, sir. He found an old piece of railing from Collessie he thinks will fit with a few adjustments, and I have a chain and padlock ready. I'll give one key to the engineers and keep the other myself, if that suits, sir.'

'That's perfect, thank you, Mr. Thalland. I'm not sure if the engineers will need any more help before they prepare their plans, but if they do will you be able to provide it?'

'Of course, sir. Though the more notice we have the better, of course.'

'Of course. Did you hear that, Mr. Kelly?'

The engineer was approaching, and nodded briskly.

'Aye, we'll give you all the notice we can, sir. The cleaner we can work together, the better for all of us.'

'What do you think now you've seen it, then, Mr. Kelly?' Thalland asked. 'Is it any use, or is it just going to be in the way?'

'It'd be a terrible shame to waste all that good stonework that's been there for years,' said Kelly thoughtfully. 'But I don't know yet. We'll give it some thought before we decide anything. Is there anyone about now who might remember exactly why it was abandoned the first time round?'

Thalland and Murray looked at each other. Blair would have remembered, but his links with Letho dated back only to Murray's father's time.

'Maybe Ninian Jack?' Thalland suggested. 'He'd have been a lad, I should think, but he's always been interested in that kind of thing. If it was happening and he could be here, I think he would have been.'

'Could we talk to him, do you think, sir?' asked Kelly. 'Or would there be anything written down?'

'Not much,' said Thalland definitely. 'I've taken a look: it's just the accounts. Unless Mr. Murray kept anything like a diary?' he asked Murray tentatively. Murray shook his head.

'Not that I've ever found,' he said.

Thalland nodded.

'You'd be better to talk to Jack.'

'He's a quiet man,' Murray added. 'But if it's anything to do with mechanical things, he's the best for miles around. I don't suppose there was anything mechanical in there?'

Kelly shook his head.

'There might have been something planned, but there's nothing there now but stones.'

'Still, Ninian Jack will be interested, I should think. I could ask him to come up here tomorrow and talk with you,' said Thalland.

'That would be grand, thank you,' said Kelly. 'The more information we have, the better. Now, those trees round the top of the hill – are you keen to keep those? I'm not saying we'd have to take them down but if you need them to stay there, I'll make a note of it. At this minute, they're likely the best thing holding the hill together, with all that water coming up out of it.'

The conversation continued along technical and arboricultural lines for several minutes, until Thalland and Kelly agreed to go up and take a closer look. Murray felt a touch on his elbow.

'So this is your plan for the summer, Charles?'

He turned in delight to find Isobel coming along from the stables.

'I need something to keep me busy! Have you been inspecting Augusta's pony?'

'Oh, yes – she wants me to make a drawing of the pony, but now she is being taken away by Miss Fizz for a bath. She has grown so much!'

'They do that, I find. Alarming.'

Isobel was inspecting the icehouse opening.

'I'm afraid it's not really picturesque enough for a painting,' she said, 'if that was what you had in mind. What is it?'

'It was to be an icehouse, about fifty years ago. It was never finished, and now it might become part of the great Letho water management system.'

'Oh, that one! I'll look forward to seeing that. And I see that my father is already taking an interest. Poor Smith! He has had to roll that chair into the most unexpected places.'

'You're happy with his interest here? I could find some means of delaying it if you think –'

'No! no, this is perfect. It's a delicate balance – is he bored? Or is he overdone? A tunnel – as long as it does not bring down a building again – would give him plenty to think about but no real excitement. To lose a leg is one thing,' she said, dropping her voice even lower, 'but the damage to his head and his heart, that is more lasting.'

'His head and his heart?'

Isobel's lips twisted quickly and smoothed again.

'You know he was hit on the head. He's – he is still as quick as he ever was, I believe, but if he thinks too hard, or for too long, it hurts. His heart – he knows he is vulnerable now, knows he is dependent, knows – though he is grateful, I know he is – that you had to make special arrangements for him even here, where he feels so much at home. That is what I mean when I say that his heart is damaged. But I believe – I have to believe – that he will heal.'

'It's a joy for us to make him comfortable, believe me. Not just for me – Robbins and Mary and all the others would do anything for him. You know that.'

Isobel drew a deep breath, tried a smile, and was in control of herself again. She rearranged her shawl.

'So what other entertainment are you to provide for us this summer? You have us here now for at least four months: a dilapidated icehouse is not going to last! Are the Georges at Dures? Is Collessie let? Are the Helliwells in good health? Come, tell me about all that is happening!'

Murray laughed.

'You only want to see people so that you can draw them. The Helliwells are in excellent health, so far as I can tell: he is as grumpy and she as pleasant as ever. Mr. George is in residence – you know Miss George is married?'

'What?'

'Yes, she married at New Year. I must have told you. I knew you did not read my letters.'

'I read them several times each – but only because my father asked me to. Surely I should have remembered such momentous news! But who is the fortunate husband?'

'His name is Lord Rocheid – from Haddingtonshire, I think, or perhaps Linlithgowshire. South of Edinburgh, anyway. I have barely met him.'

'Well! A title, too! Well done, Miss George! There is hope for all of us,' she added lightly. Murray looked at her sideways.

'You are not in despair of a husband, are you?'

'Not at all!'

She gave a shrug and a light laugh, and his heart sank.

'Did you go and form an attachment in Sussex?' He tried to make it sound accusatory, rather than anxious. 'For if you go to settle there, no doubt you will take your father with you, and I shall miss him, you know!'

'No, I formed no attachment in Sussex,' she said firmly, which made Murray sure there had been at least one offer. An offer that could be repeated, even by letter. He would have to pre-empt it.

'Well, thank goodness for that. The options did not look promising. Anyway,' he said quickly, 'you asked about Collessie, and I fear the options there are no better. At present it is inhabited by a woman and her widowed mother – they are every day awaiting the arrival of the woman's husband from Edinburgh. A Mr. Pillans – he has a warehouse of some kind, I believe, but both women are very charming. I don't believe there is any other family, and they are keen to help about the parish while they are here.'

'And are Lord and Lady Rocheid in residence at Dures?'

'She is – he is also expected from Edinburgh soon.'

'Edinburgh is decamping to Fife.'

'Oh, yes, including the two women being interviewed as housekeeper. The engineers at least are Irish, and have been working on the west coast.'

'They look more competent than the man you had here before.'

'Almost anyone would,' said Murray. Perhaps it had been a bad idea to try to solve the water problem: it was bringing back some very painful memories.

Without discussing it, they turned and began to stroll towards the front of the house. Murray offered her his arm, and she took it, using his support to negotiate some of the muddier parts of the path. The dogs followed, hoping for entertainment.

'And are you expecting any other visitors here at Letho?'

'I have none planned, with no housekeeper in post. Dinners, of course, and suppers, as the nights are lighter, but nothing more complicated. Mrs. Pillans and her mother have been here already. I believe that Deborah Scoggie is also intending to stay somewhere nearby, so she may visit.'

'Deborah Scoggie? I have not seen her for years! That would be delightful.'

'It would indeed.'

'You've always kept in touch with the family, haven't you?'

'I have. I feel a responsibility for her brothers, even though they are now grown.' Henry and Robert Scoggie had been his charges in Murray's brief career as a tutor. Henry was now Lord Scoggie, and Robert had distinguished himself in the army, rather more than his early years had promised.

'Of course you do,' said Isobel, giving his arm a quick squeeze, 'you feel a responsibility for everyone.'

'Do I?' Murray was taken aback.

'Anyway, it would be lovely to see Deborah. Mrs. Wedderburn now, is she not?'

'That's right. Her husband has friends near Cupar, so they will be staying there on their way home from Edinburgh.'

'Edinburgh again. The town will be empty this summer, and its entire inhabitants will be encamped in Fife.'

'I hope not, but you cannot blame them, can you?'

They had reached the front door, with its shallow sandstone steps, and stopped to gaze down the drive. The dogs at once took to the steps, sprawling in their accustomed place to enjoy the heat of the stone. The sky was wide and blue, the trees placed like sentinels, the sheep and their lambs beyond the haha peaceful in the sunshine. Even from here they could smell the chestnut blossom, the may in the hedges, the gorse further off, slow-baking and sweet. Perhaps, thought Murray, the moment had come. He drew breath.

'Oh, look – here's another arrival!' said Isobel, pointing down towards the gate. 'No doubt from Edinburgh.'

'No,' said Murray, recognising the grey horses pulling the smart dark blue carriage, 'no, that's Lady Rocheid. What is she here for?'

It would not take long to find out, for the carriage was speeding up the driveway in a way that scattered the dogs from the doorstep and caused Murray and Isobel to step back. The driver turned so that the side of the carriage faced the door. The top was still down, and Lady Rocheid clutched the edge of the door with one hand and her bonnet with the other.

'Mr. Murray!' she cried. 'Have you seen my husband?'

Chapter Eight

'Miss – Lady Rocheid!' cried Isobel, going at once to the carriage. 'Are you quite well?'

'I am perfectly well, Miss Blair,' said Lady Rocheid. 'Only that my husband has not yet arrived from Edinburgh!'

'When was he expected?' asked Isobel, in what Murray thought was intended to be her most calming voice.

'At any time! Any time! And he has not yet arrived! I have been looking out for him since last Saturday!'

'And it is now Thursday,' said Isobel. 'That is not so very long, I think. It would be easy to be delayed – perhaps he met a friend, or had to go out of town for a few days? His estate is, I think, somewhere south of Edinburgh?'

'Yes, yes, near Haddington,' said Lady Rocheid quickly, as if it were immaterial.

'So if he had been called away to his estate – in the opposite direction from here – perhaps urgently, so that he had to go before he could send word – or the letter miscarried, as they often do, you know – he could be here soon and perfectly well, and anxious that he has made you so concerned.'

'Soon and perfectly well! Oh, that would answer all of my prayers!' cried Lady Rocheid.

'And of course, he would not expect to find you at Letho – though if you were to step into the house I'm sure Mr. Murray's servants would quickly find you a restorative glass of wine, or cup of tea ...'

'No, no, you are quite right, Miss Blair. I should be at Dures, waiting for him, exactly where he would expect me to be. You are quite right.'

'Are you sure you will not stay? The drawing room is quite cool in this warm weather.'

'No, I must be there, ready. Good day to you, Miss Blair. Good day to you, Mr. Murray. Please to drive back to Dures, Mason,' she urged the coach driver, who sighed, and turned the coach slowly in the circle of gravel, and headed off once again.

'I hope she goes straight home,' said Murray. 'The horses could do with a rest.'

'Poor lady. What like of a husband has she married? Or is it a case of nervous excitement?'

'Mr. George does not care for him: that's all I can say.'

'To wait so long and so anxiously for marriage, and then not to have joy of it. Poor lady,' Isobel repeated thoughtfully. Murray promised himself that if he persuaded Isobel to marry him, he would keep her informed of his every movement, just in case.

Blair was quite exhausted by all the excitement of the icehouse, even though it had proved to be empty, and took his supper in his room. Isobel, too, tired by the journey, chose to retire early, and Murray was left contemplating his plans in the library. He had requested a whisky toddy, and Robbins appeared with the accoutrements on a tray.

'Any further thoughts on housekeepers, Robbins?'

'Not yet, sir. I sent notes to both of them asking them to remain, if they could, for two more days.'

'It's a small inn: I hope they get on well.'

Robbins smiled a little.

'That had not occurred to me, sir.'

'Any problems with the engineers?'

'No, sir. They dined with us but supped at the cottage, which they say – or rather Mr. Kelly says – is beyond satisfaction. Mr. Sweeney says little, but he seems happy enough.'

'Good. Mr. Thalland seems content with the arrangements, and he has sent for Ninian Jack to come up tomorrow and see what he can remember about the time it was built. Now, most importantly, anything else we can do for the Blairs?'

'Mr. Smith says no, sir, all is well. And Miss Blair has not mentioned anything.'

'Then we are settled. If the Wedderburns – Miss Scoggie – write to me to say when they can dine, I'll let you know at once. Otherwise it looks as if all is well. Miss Blair has requested a summer of peace and quiet with just a few things to keep Mr. Blair entertained. Do you think we can manage that?'

'It looks very much like it, sir. And that will be a good time to introduce a new housekeeper and make sure she is accustomed to the household, when all is running smoothly anyway.'

'Excellent. A time of peace and recuperation.'

'Let's hope so, sir.'

'If it's that lock you're on about, I can tell you straight away it's no work of mine.'

'Of course not,' said Mr. Thalland. 'You can see for yourself I picked it up cheaply at Cupar market. It's not intended as anything more than a deterrent.'

'Aye, for those that do not know their locks.' Ninian Jack pursed his lips ominously. Those who did not know their locks, it seemed, deserved all they got.

'No,' said Thalland, 'it's what's beyond the gate that we're interested in. Do you know the place?'

'The icehouse? Or that was what it was supposed to be. I wouldna say I knew it well.' He peered through the makeshift railings. 'I have not seen it from that day to this, to be honest with you.'

Mr. Sweeney peered, too. It was not clear from his expression what he thought of the icehouse that had never been an icehouse. Mr. Kelly, on the other hand, smiled at Ninian Jack.

'We're very grateful you were able to come up to the house today and give us the benefit of your advice.'

'My advice?' said Ninian Jack. 'Get a new lock.'

'And your memories, too, sir. Do you remember when this place was built?'

Ninian Jack gave him a long, steady look, while the smile on Mr. Kelly's face loosened a little.

'Are you Irish?' Jack asked at last.

'I am that,' said Kelly, 'and so is my colleague here. From

Dublin,' he added, clearly feeling his statement needed additional verification. Ninian Jack sometimes had that effect on people.

'And you're too young to have been here when this place was thought of. So are you,' he added to Mr. Thalland. Thalland shrugged.

'That's why we thought to ask you. That and the fact that you know about things like this.'

'About icehouses?' Ninian Jack looked dubious.

'About all kinds of clever devices.'

'I was just a lad,' said Jack. 'But I mind it well enough. They had plans for a kind of clockwork train that might run inside and get the ice, to stop mud being trodden in. That was what I was here for, the clockwork train. I'd have liked fine to work on that, but it wasna to be.'

'What happened? Why was the icehouse never finished, Mr. Jack?'

'Och, they thought the spring would cool it. But they didna think of the power of the water. It made the whole thing unstable. They couldna get the stones to stay put as they went on into the hill, so in the end they gave up. I think in the end they used all the stones they had brought in to build a wee pantry at the back of the manse kitchen, for they'd no use for them here and as you can see, they're grand worked stones.'

'So that was all it was? They gave up because it was hard to build it with the spring there?'

'That's plenty, I should say. Of course,' said Ninian Jack, eyeing the hill, 'the tree roots would be holding it together more now. But then they're a problem all on their own, are they no? So if you're thinking of trying again, I'd say forget it and go somewhere else.'

'That's not the plan, Mr. Jack,' said Thalland, reassuring. 'These gentlemen are going to try to find a way of controlling the spring a little more, so this road does not flood so much.'

'Controlling the spring? Aye, well: good luck to you.' Ninian Jack laughed, a rare enough sound. 'Aye, good luck to you! That I'd come to see. But you need a better lock on yon gate.'

'So that's as far as we've got,' said Murray at dinner.

'Property is just a constant worry,' said Mrs. Pillans, who

with her mother had again been invited for dinner, along with her violin. Isobel noted that they both wore particularly lovely silk gowns, perhaps a little too grand for the occasion. 'That's the reason my husband will not take a long lease anywhere – sorry, Mr. Murray! I know you want Collessie to have a good owner again, one who lives there. But I don't believe it will be us!'

'Oh, even someone staying long enough to care would be good,' said Murray.

'If we stay any longer we shall need a good housekeeper,' murmured Mrs. Skead.

'There are so many things that could be done with a house like that,' Blair put in. He was a little brighter this evening than he had been at dinner yesterday, so tired after his journey. He was energetically grating nutmeg over his creamed potatoes from a grater shaped like the Brighton Pavilion. Murray was not sure it was somewhere from which he himself would have kept a souvenir, not after last year. 'But the trees make it so dark.'

'Oh, I like that!' objected Mrs. Pillans. 'I love to hear them creak at night – I feel I am in the middle of *The Mysteries of Udolpho*!'

'I think I should prefer *Northanger Abbey*,' said Isobel, smiling.

'Or *The Bride of Lammermoor*,' suggested Mrs. Pillans. 'That is where we are from: it was so exciting to read a book set there! I love it when a book makes me really shiver.'

'Well, dear,' said her mother, 'we're not from exactly there.'

'Oh! Well, no,' agreed Mrs. Pillans, blushing prettily.

Isobel herself liked a book that would teach her something and make her laugh at the same time, but on the whole she would read anything, and the Lammermoor book was one she had snapped up in Edinburgh when it first appeared a couple of years ago. Mrs. Pillans, though possibly not someone who would have been in the same circle as her in Edinburgh, seemed likely to be a good companion for the summer, unless her husband, when he arrived, took up all her time.

The discussion of novels was not wide-ranging, but it took them to the point where Isobel, acting as hostess, rose and led the ladies out into the hallway.

'I hope you will not mind sitting here,' said Isobel, ringing for tea. 'It is quite cosy, as you see, and the evening is mild.'

'Oh, to make things easy for Mr. Blair! Of course,' said Mrs. Pillans, finding that her violin had been laid on the hall table. She went to it at once like a mother to her child, and brought it over to where the chairs had been arranged around the fireplace.

'It's delightful,' said Mrs. Skead. 'We should try it at Collessie, when Mr. Pillans comes. The drawing room ... well, you'll know it.'

'Oh, yes!' said Isobel, though she was momentarily distracted by the look of worry that passed across Mrs. Pillans' face. It could have nothing to do with the violin, for she sat still with the unopened case on her lap. Something her mother had said? The look faded only slowly as Daniel and William arrived, set up the tea things without incident, and retired. Isobel was curious. 'Your husband is in business, I believe?'

'That's right,' said Mrs. Pillans. 'He should be here any day, perhaps even with my new music tutor I'm to engage,' she added proudly. 'In fact, I had a letter from my husband this morning saying he himself would likely be here before I received it. I hope he has not met with some misfortune along the road.'

That was the cause of the worried look, then.

'What line of business is he in? I'm sure any businessman might be detained at any moment by some crisis!'

'Oh, he has a – a shop.' Mrs. Pillans glanced at Isobel sideways, presumably waiting to see if she would pick up her skirts and bar such a lowly individual from the house. But Isobel was her father's daughter.

'Oh?' A shop that allowed him to take a house – even Collessie – for the summer must be quite a concern. 'A shop in Edinburgh?'

'That's right, yes. I believe you are from Edinburgh, Miss Blair – perhaps you know the place? It's the Oriental Warehouse, on South Bridge.'

Chapter Nine

Isobel had been in the Oriental Warehouse on South Bridge several times over the years: the rich Indian fabrics that Mr. Pillans sold appealed very much to her father's taste, and there were also more subtle lawns and cambrics that Isobel liked. Yet there was something about the shop that always made her a little uneasy – the shop girls there never seemed happy, somehow. Isobel was not quite sure about the life of a shop girl. Was it better or worse than being in service? She should ask someone, some time. Perhaps her father would know: he talked to all kinds of people.

And then there were rumours of girls missing – girls who had worked in the shop, and then, somehow, disappeared. The rumours had even, recently, been reported in the *Edinburgh Courant*. Had Mr. Pillans somehow been delayed in connexion with this mystery?

She had her mouth open to try to make some reply to Mrs. Pillans, when Robbins appeared in the hallway, moving – well, one would not say with haste, for Robbins was in general a calm person, but somehow he could not quite hide the fact that something striking had happened, and he was eager to share it with Mr. Murray. Mrs. Pillans and Mrs. Skead, less familiar with Robbins' character, noticed nothing amiss, but Isobel's ears felt as if they were stretching out on stalks to catch any information. Could something terrible have happened with that icehouse excavation? She prayed not.

Then came the sound of a chair being pushed back in the dining room, then another, and in a moment her father appeared in his wheeled chair, propelled towards the ladies at the fire by Murray himself.

'More tea, then, Robbins,' Murray was saying, 'and brandy, if they've had a shock. No doubt you're already preparing a room for them.'

'Yes, sir, and the gig to bring them here. I'll get a cart down for their bags as soon as may be.' He spoke in a low voice, not one, quite properly, for sharing drama with guests.

'They won't have had dinner, either, I daresay.'

'I'm sure Mrs. Mack won't let them starve, sir.'

Murray grinned. Mrs. Mack would take such a thing as a challenge.

'We'll talk later, then, Robbins.' Robbins bowed and slid off to deal with – with what? Isobel was trying her best not to look as if she wanted to know, but Murray came at last to sit down with his guests.

'We have an unexpected extension to our party,' he said. 'Isobel, you'll know that we were expecting the Wedderburns?'

'Of course,' said Isobel. 'You were saying they would be staying nearby, and dining with us here over the summer.'

'That's right. A slight change of plan, though. They are here, with a broken axle, five minutes from the front gate.'

The advantage of taking one's tea in the entrance hall was that it was hard to miss anything. The disadvantage was a cold draught blowing across one's tea while the new guests came in in more of a state than Isobel had ever seen Deborah Scoggie before. She tried to quell an unworthy sense of satisfaction – Debs had always been rather superior.

'It has just been one thing after another, Mr. Murray,' she said. 'I almost wish I had never left Fife to start with, for since we went to Edinburgh for the season there has been nothing but misfortune. I thought we should be safe, back now in Fife, but whatever demons are pursuing us were clearly not daunted by crossing the Firth of Forth! Good heavens, how sorry I am that we are come to disturb your peace like this!'

Mr. Wedderburn, a shortish man with sandy whiskers and a ready smile, shook Murray's hand.

'More than good of you, sir, to take in such sudden waifs and strays. More than good of you.'

'Not at all,' said Murray. 'As you see, we are all camping in the entrance hall these days, so if you would like tea or brandy straightaway then it is very convenient, while the maids sort out room for you and your bags are fetched. No doubt Robbins will see to everything. Mrs. Wedderburn, may I present Mrs. Pillans and Mrs. Skead? Mrs. Wedderburn, and Mr. Wedderburn of Kineden, to the north west of here.'

'You will be wishing us to the north west of here,' said Deborah Wedderburn, when she had made her curtseys, greeting Isobel and Blair, and come close to flopping down in a corner of the sopha.

'Your axle broke?' asked Blair, always eager for details.

'Oh! That was the last of our troubles. Oh, I know I am babbling, Mr. Blair. It is everything at once. Wait now till I take a breath.'

Isobel poured her a cup of tea, and indeed after a moment of deep breathing she drank it in controlled sips. She was more plump than Isobel remembered, no doubt the consequence of the three children she had borne, but her fair hair showed no grey around her lace cap, and whatever misfortunes she had been suffering she still looked neat and fashionable. Mr. Wedderburn straightened his waistcoat and perched on a hard chair, and accepted a glass of brandy. Both of them seemed well on the road to recovery.

'Yes, Mr. Blair,' said Mrs. Wedderburn, 'the axle broke. We left Edinburgh earlier than we had intended – the house was broken into, and I was quite upset. But our friends in Cupar were happy to see us a week early, so we took the ferry and returned with relief to Fife. Then we had only stopped in North Queensferry and were sorting out the carriage – you know what it's like, when the horses have been on the ferry, they do like to be settled – when we received a note from our friends to say that the children had all come down with chicken pox and could we please not come to see them after all. So we thought we would come this way, for when we reach home it's really not so convenient to come and see you, and from Cupar it is not far anyway. And the inn here is perfectly adequate if it had been inconvenient for you: we could have rested there and gone on. But we never reached Letho inn – we had almost reached your gate when the wretched axle simply gave way, and we were flung against the wall of the carriage, and the poor groom was in the ditch! Well, by the time we had seen that he was all right, our coachman had headed off to walk up here for help, and then I realised how close we were to you anyway – but honestly, Mr. Murray, if you'd rather, we can go and stay at the inn until the axle is fixed.'

'I wouldn't hear of it,' said Murray, though Isobel thought he was trying to work something out in his head. 'Besides, I believe the inn is full at present. Now, can we find you something to eat? I'm afraid we've just finished dinner.'

'The Wedderburns,' said Robbins. 'Pleasant couple. We'll need to find space for the coachman and the groom – and the groom has an injured arm and his livery is entirely mud down one side. She has no maid – lost her, I gather from the coachman.'

'Jennet's away to make up the yellow room,' said Mrs. Mack, 'and she's William with her to do the heavy lifting. Jennet's tired, Mr. Robbins.'

'I know, I know. But it's a broken axle – they could be here a week, if the mend is awkward. I heard Mrs. Wedderburn saying they would stay at the inn if it wasn't convenient for us, but of course the master couldn't have that.'

'Anyway the inn is full,' said Iffy, helpfully. 'Full of housekeepers!'

Mrs. Mack looked at Robbins.

'You were talking of giving one of them a trial,' she said thoughtfully.

'Aye, but at a quiet time.'

'Aye, but if she came now, whichever of them, it would be a proper trial, would it no? And anyway, it'd be another pair of hands.'

'Maybe you should ask the two of them!' Iffy suggested.

'Oh, aye, that'd work,' said Mrs. Mack, heavy with sarcasm.

'But which, Mrs. Mack? There was little to choose between them, I thought. And I'd have to make sure the master was happy with the idea.'

Mrs. Mack nodded at that, then considered.

'There wasna much in it, it's true,' she said, 'but for my money I think I'd say Mrs. Gilmour. She was a bit more open than Mrs. Warner, I thought. But Mrs. Warner could just be shy, I suppose.'

'Well, we don't really want a shy housekeeper, do we?' Robbins sighed. 'That would be awkward with guests.' He had not thought her shy, though: he had had the impression that she was not entirely forthcoming. A different thing. 'We might not have a choice,' he said after a moment. 'One of them – or both of them – might say it doesn't suit them to stay for a trial period.'

'Then it's easy. Here, there's plenty left over from dinner, even for the servants as well. We have enough if all the Wedderburn party wants to eat. As for the groom ... maybe Miss Blair has medicines with her? For Mr. Blair and all?'

'Maybe so.' Robbins sighed again. He would not bother Miss Blair: his own wife Mary could tend to the groom in their own house, for she was an experienced nurse. Once the coachman, helped by Letho's own stable staff, had recovered horses and carriage from the main road, he too could be fed and then found accommodation either with the groom or at the stables. He had already sent one of the boys to the village for the smith to come in the morning to see to the axle. The baggage had been on a cart of its own behind the carriage, and once it was brought up to the house William and Daniel could deal with it. What else?

The housekeeper's parlour at least was in good order. He had made sure of that before the candidates had arrived. If either of the women was prepared to come up to the house for a while, at least it would not mean any more work for Jennet.

He hurried back into the main house to see if Daniel had finished clearing in the dining room. The master and his guests looked settled enough in the hall, and as long as Daniel remembered to use the servants' door into the dining room they would not be disturbed by the removal of plates and dishes. He himself used it now, and was pleasantly surprised to see that Daniel had made good progress.

'Just take everything out now that needs to go, and make sure the table's clean. Then lay a short cloth at this end and places for two.'

'What, has some of them not had enough?' asked Daniel in surprise.

'Unexpected guests,' said Robbins shortly. 'Mrs. Mack's preparing some of the leftovers for them. You'll serve: William's helping Jennet do their room.'

'Me, Mr. Robbins? Where will you be?'

'If it's any of your business, Daniel,' said Robbins, 'I'm off to find a housekeeper. Or a temporary one, at any rate.'

He felt uneasy leaving Daniel in charge of serving even so small a meal, but he did not feel that he could reasonably summon a temporary housekeeper by means of a note, and, since he could not be sure which one he was going to select, he needed to be able to think on his feet. So his feet took him by the shortcut to the village, and then down the slope of the village green to the inn at the bottom. In the main room, Ninian Jack was seated in a corner, quite at ease with a mug of ale and a pie, and a young man with blond hair and a gingery moustache stood in the middle of the room, waiting for something in mild agitation. The innkeeper was just coming back in from the parlour.

'I'm sorry, sir,' he said to the young man. 'We are only a small place. We have but the two rooms, and at present they are both occupied.'

'Then am I to sleep in a ditch?' demanded the man.

'Where is it you're heading?' asked the innkeeper. 'Maybe I can get someone to set you a bit further along your way?'

'I am bound for a house in this neighbourhood,' said the man. Robbins noted with surprise that his accent was not native – Germanic, perhaps? 'The name of the place is Collessie.'

'Then you'd likely be better off sleeping in the ditch,' remarked Ninian Jack, but fortunately the stranger did not appear to notice.

'It is possible that I have a solution,' said Robbins, diffidently joining the conversation. 'Am I right in thinking that your two rooms are occupied by Mrs. Warner and Mrs. Gilmour?'

'Aye, that's a fact,' said the innkeeper.

'Then could I perhaps have a word with – um, with Mrs. Gilmour, if she is available, and if not then with Mrs. Warner?'

'Aye, I suppose,' said the innkeeper, clearly not sure how this might help him. The serving girl was nearby, and he sent her up the stairs with a nod.

'How is this to help me?' asked the stranger. 'Are you from Collessie?'

'No, sir, I am from Letho House,' said Robbins, as if that explained everything. The room fell silent, and Robbins stood still, hands behind his back, steady and patient. He did not have to wait long. In a moment, after a little muffled conversation from upstairs, Mrs. Warner appeared.

'How may I be of assistance, Mr. Robbins?' she asked, her voice calm, though he could tell she was already trying to work out if this visit was a favourable sign or not. 'Mrs. Gilmour is not answering her door – perhaps she has already left.'

'Then you will receive the first offer,' said Robbins. 'We have had unexpected guests arrive at the house. Would you be willing to come for a week and regard it as a trial? You would of course be paid at the advertised rate.'

'A trial?' It did not take Mrs. Warner long to decide. 'Of course – yes, I'll come straightaway.'

Chapter Ten

Mrs. Warner quickly packed up her bags and was ready, leaving a very happy innkeeper and a fairly content stranger who no longer had to compare the relative merits of sleeping at Collessie or in a ditch. He was so grateful, indeed, that he shook hands with Robbins as though Robbins had personally brought him a bed for the night, and introduced himself.

'Markus Rieder, sir, at your service. Very much at your service, sir. You will find me – if all goes well – at Collessie.'

Ninian Jack observed the toing and froing with marked lack of interest. Mrs. Warner left her larger pack with the innkeeper, and allowed Robbins to carry her smaller bag back up through the village to the shortcut. Neither of them spoke much along the way. Mrs. Warner, thought Robbins, was not going to make Letho a noisy household.

They circumnavigated Letho House by the east side this time, round the back of Robbins' own house and in by a gate to the kitchen garden. This had not formed part of the tour when Mrs. Warner had visited previously, though she must have seen something of it through the windows of the servants' wing. Robbins slowed to let her admire the neat, raked beds, the new sprouts of growth in some of them, the herb garden with fresh shoots greening the shrubs.

'One would hardly need to send out for anything!' she remarked with pleasure.

'It's well established,' said Robbins. 'Our old housekeeper took great delight in it. You've seen her stillroom.'

'Yes, indeed.' She surveyed the garden for a moment longer, then turned brisk. 'Now, if your – our – guests are already here, show me what has been done and what still needs to be done, and I shall get to work.'

'She seems willing,' said Robbins to Murray later in the library. Supper had gone smoothly, the Wedderburns were pleased with their room, Mrs. Pillans and Mrs. Skead had returned to Collessie after Mrs. Pillans had played her violin quite nicely, and the Blairs were content as ever. The Wedderburns' servants had been accommodated, and their groom was recovering, and substantially cleaner than when he had arrived. All this, of course, had been achieved without the input of Mrs. Warner, but she had indeed seemed willing: she had gone about with Jennet having the whole place explained to her, had found out as much as was reasonable about the guests and their preferences, and had listened to Mrs. Mack, Daniel and William at supper telling her about themselves and how they came to be at Letho. She had taken it all in, Robbins noted, watching, but had not, in return, shared much about herself. 'She wants to know if we can get a second maid.'

'We were waiting until we had a housekeeper, weren't we?' said Murray. 'No reason why we shouldn't look for one now, though, even if she's only temporary – the summer seems bent on being busier than I had hoped. Is there anyone you can think of who might be available?'

For a while they discussed various local families who might want a daughter employed at Letho House, but no one seemed obvious.

'We can think about it,' said Murray. 'I can ask Mr. Helliwell if he knows of anyone in a neighbouring parish, perhaps. Or someone from Edinburgh – after all, Edinburgh seems to be supplying every vacancy in the place just at present.'

Robbins smiled slightly.

'Except for the engineers, sir.'

'Oh, yes: how are they getting on? Did Ninian Jack come up to talk to them?'

'Apparently so, sir. Mr. Thalland was present. He told them the spring had made the stonework very unstable as they were building the tunnel and after a couple of small collapses, I think, they decided it was not worth pursuing.'

'That's useful to know, anyway,' said Murray, nodding.

'I believe the engineers spent most of the rest of the day making drawings and measurements, sir. They came into the servants' wing for their dinner, then carried on until the light went. I think they collected their supper and took it back to their cottage.'

'Did they seem happy?'

'Mr. Kelly declared the day a very useful one, sir. He seemed to be content, except for one thing: Daniel's boys and some of the estate children kept trying to sneak into the structure when their backs were turned. Apparently Daniel's eldest has been putting it about that the icehouse is haunted by someone who was crushed in there, and so the boys are daring each other to get in.'

'For pity's sake,' Murray groaned.

'I've had a word with Daniel, sir – not for the first time - and he promises he will keep a better eye on them when he's at home, and remind Mrs. Hossack to do the same during the day. There are so many of them, though, sir, I'm sure Mrs. Hossack cannot possibly do it all herself.'

Mrs. Hossack, Daniel's wife – Murray always thought of her as Artemesia, the name he had known her by as his cook in Naples. That was before Daniel and she had found that they were going to be parents – an almost perpetual state for them ever since. Artemesia was responsible for Daniel's stately appearance: she was a very good cook.

'Besides that,' Robbins went on, 'Mr. Kelly has remarked several times on the convenience of the cottage for them. They are very pleased with it.'

'Well, that's good. I think Mr. Blair was out watching them for a couple of hours today: he'll probably do the same tomorrow, if he is not in their way. Though I suppose he could be almost anywhere: one never knows what will interest him next.' Murray sighed, thinking again of Daniel's boys. They were not old, but they were well advanced in mischief for their years. 'Do you know if the gate at the icehouse is properly locked for the night?'

'I'm told it is, sir. The keys are with the engineers and Mr. Thalland.'

'I might just take a walk around there and check. Just for my peace of mind.'

'Very well, sir. Shall I bring a lantern?'

'I'll go out by the door in the servants' wing, I think: it will be easier than unlocking and relocking the front door, won't it? And I can collect a lantern on the way.'

Picking up a sturdy walking stick from the hall, he led Robbins back across the hall to the door to the servants' wing, with Robbins followed in turn by the dogs, who knew that there was a fair chance of food if they went in that direction. They stopped at the outside door while Robbins lit and trimmed one of the lanterns that were always left there ready, but before he had finished, the spaniel's ears went up, the deerhound's head twitched, and in a moment all five dogs were barking.

'Someone outside,' said Murray unnecessarily. He took a firm grasp of the stick, and opened the door, and Robbins held the lantern as high as he could. 'Who's there?' Murray shouted.

For a moment they listened intently. A light breeze had risen, ruffling the trees on the rise above the icehouse, making it hard to hear anything else. Then Murray thought he caught just a patter of running footsteps in the distance, before there was a movement closer to hand.

'Um,' said someone, 'it's me, sir.'

'Daniel!' Robbins sounded exasperated. 'What are you doing out here?'

'You told me to make sure the boys behaved themselves, Mr. Robbins. Sir,' he added to Murray.

'Don't tell me they are out at this time of the night? It must be well past their bedtime!' Robbins and his wife ran a well-regulated home – no doubt their son and daughter were fast asleep.

'They slipped out, Mr. Robbins! I was letting the cat out, and I heard a noise and it distracted me, and the next I knew they were away!'

'And where are they now?' Murray asked quickly, for Robbins was looking dangerous.

'Ah, that I don't know, sir,' said Daniel pathetically. 'But I heard the dogs and thought maybe they were here and had disturbed them.'

'This one would disturb a saint,' came a woman's voice behind them. Murray turned, to find Mrs. Mack trotting along from the kitchen, finger and thumb firmly attached to the ear of a small dark-haired boy. 'In my kitchen again!'

'How did you get in here, Jackamo?' Daniel demanded, seizing his son by the shoulder. The boy, all of five years old, glanced up at Robbins, then at the impressive height of Murray, and decided to go quietly.

'The door was unlocked, Papa, honest!'

'Come away home with you,' said Daniel firmly, taking his opportunity to leave while he could. 'We can discuss it there.'

Holding firmly to the boy's upper arm, he marched off into the night, needing no lantern on the familiar path.

'One of these days,' muttered Robbins darkly.

'Oh, aye,' said Mrs. Mack, nodding, 'but the eldest is worse still, wherever he's got to. Good night to you, sir. Mr. Robbins.' She made a pointed, past-my-bedtime curtsey, and left them to it.

'Come on, then,' said Murray. 'Let's go and take a quick look.'

Robbins straightened the lantern and walked next to Murray along the muddy path to the ragged entrance to the old icehouse. Whether it would look better in the end or not, it certainly looked worse just now. Robbins went to the chain and padlock, and held the lantern close.

'It's open, sir,' he said, almost resigned. 'And the servants' wing door open, too. Surely that lad is not old enough yet to have learned how to work a lock with no key.'

'If he has, we should maybe put him as apprentice to Ninian Jack soon. Such promise should not go to waste, and it might keep him out of trouble.' Murray liked his staff and their families to be tidy.

'It would take more than an apprenticeship to keep that one out of trouble, I think, sir,' said Robbins.

'Well, we'd better get one of the keys and see that it's locked again,' said Murray. 'Assuming he hasn't broken it.'

'It looks all right. Shall I go and fetch Mr. Thalland, sir?'

'Mr. Thalland likes an early night,' said Murray. 'And the engineers' cottage is closer even than Thalland's front door. If you stay here and watch the gate, I'll step along and ask them to lend me the key.'

'You'll need the lantern, sir.'

'Well ... all right, thanks.' It was not that he did not know the path, but the uneven surface caused by all that ungoverned water made it an uncertain walk in the dark.

As he had suspected, the light was still on in the cottage allocated to the engineers for their stay. Mr. Kelly in particular had not struck Murray as one who feared burning the candle at both ends, thought he was a little surprised to find that Mr. Sweeney was also still awake. If anyone had suggested that this might be the case, he would then have expected Jo Sweeney to be sitting up late over his plans and drawings: he did not seem the type to enjoy leisure. But when Murray knocked on the door and it opened straight into the little parlour, he found that Mr. Kelly had just risen from the table where Mr. Sweeney still sat – though he rose when he saw who their visitor was – and in front of them were a jug, two cups, and a hand of cards, along with two small stacks of farthings.

'I am sorry to disturb you,' said Murray, 'but I find that someone has tampered with the padlock and chain on the gate. May I borrow your key to secure it?'

'Oh, aye, of course, sir,' said Kelly. He stepped across to where his coat was hung from one of a couple of hooks on the wall. 'I hope the lock is not damaged?'

'It doesn't seem to be,' said Murray. Kelly was rummaging in his coat pockets, and beginning to look perplexed.

'Jo, it was I who locked the gate, wasn't it?'

'You always take the key, Edward,' said Jo Sweeney, still standing by the table.

'Did you see what I did with the key?' He must have tried all the pockets by now. He stepped back, and ran his fingers over the front of his waistcoat, with no result.

'You put it in your coat pocket. The left one,' said Sweeney, with certainty.

'Well, it's not there now.'

Chapter Eleven

'Is there maybe a hole?' asked Jo Sweeney, but Kelly shook his head.

'Never a one,' he said. 'Mr. Murray, I'm sorry!'

'Has anyone been in here?' Murray asked. 'I heard you brought your supper back here with you – did anyone help you carry it?'

'That'd be – ah, one of the lads. Is it Daniel? William?'

'The fat one,' said Jo Sweeney without malice.

'Daniel,' said Murray. Could that be it? Had Daniel's boy followed him on his errand, and seen where the key was? It did not explain, though, how he had also managed to get into the servants' wing. 'Well, anyway, it's late, and for now I'll go and get Mr. Thalland's key and lock up.'

'Let me do it, sir,' said Kelly at once. 'I promise you I'll see it safely secured.' He was already fetching a lantern. 'Mr. Thalland's in the big house this side of the main house, is that right?'

'That's right, yes. Well, then, I'll leave you to it. Thank you.'

'We'll find the key tomorrow, sir, or I'll eat my hat.'

But Kelly looked genuinely worried as he pulled on his coat, and followed Murray outside.

Murray returned to the icehouse.

'Mr. Kelly will be along shortly. Let's leave it for now,' he said to Robbins. 'After all, the main culprit is presumably under Daniel's guard for the night.'

'You'd like to think so, sir.' Robbins shivered.

'Come on, you're getting cold.'

'It's not that, sir.' He paused. 'You'll think I'm fanciful –'

'You, Robbins? Never.'

'I kept thinking there was someone nearby, sir.'

'Oh?' Murray raised the lantern, glancing about. 'I don't see anyone.'

'No, I don't suppose so, sir.' But Robbins still sounded uneasy, as well he might be at that cursory search. 'And the door is still unlocked in the servants' wing.'

'Then let's get back inside, and lock it.'

Murray did not sleep well that night. Random thoughts pursued him in the darkness: Isobel, Blair's health, the Wedderburns and their broken axle – so many people arriving from Edinburgh! - the icehouse, the housekeeper, Miss George – Lady Rocheid – and her agitation, Isobel, Augusta, Isobel, the awful memory of the servants' wing collapsing, Isobel ... The sound of running footsteps in the distance – perhaps running because they thought they were far enough away to make a sound now without being followed. Robbins' impression that there had been someone near him, and near the icehouse, in the dark. The gate unlocked. The door unlocked. If young Master Hossack had got in, who else might have done so? What if there were an intruder in the house now? What if they were to attack Augusta? Or Isobel? Or Blair?

It was no use: he had to take a look.

He left his candle unlit on his bedside table: he knew the house better than any intruder, and could walk silently on floors where he had known every creaking board since he was a boy. He padded up to the nursery floor, down to the guest rooms, across the ground floor to the door of Blair's parlour-bedroom, to the library, to the dining room, to the door to the servants' wing, through it and along the stone-flagged passage to the kitchens. Nothing stirred, except for the spaniel, Belle, who followed him, claws clicking, from the entrance hall to the kitchen.

'Living in hope,' Murray said silently to her, rewarding her only with a rub of the ears. He did not want to venture further, for fear of disturbing the servants. No point in them having a bad night, too, though these days only Mrs. Mack, Iffy, Jennet and now the housekeeper – temporary housekeeper – would be sleeping in the main house. Smith, Blair's man, was in, too, but he had his own duties to attend to. They needed another manservant, as well as a maid or two.

He sighed, turned, and led the dog back up the passageway towards the entrance hall, passing the door to the cellars. He hesitated, and tried the handle. It was locked. Good, he thought, with a twist of his lips. Anyone who locked themselves in Letho's cellars deserved all they got.

He thought he might read the *Courant*, which would send him to sleep faster than any book, but he could not find the copy he was sure he had left unread in the drawing room. He went back to bed, only half-comforted, leaving the dogs in the hall. At least they might bark if anything disturbed them, but in any case, he lay awake until dawn.

'There's a note come, sir, from Collessie,' said Daniel, presenting it to Murray at the breakfast table.

'I pray it's not an invitation to dine,' said Isobel, when Daniel had left the room. 'Mrs. Pillans and her mother are very charming, and a change of scene is lovely, but that house is not the scene I should like to change to.'

'It's not an invitation to dinner,' Murray reassured her. He was enjoying breakfasting with her, though in the splendid setting of the dining room rather than the more intimate parlour which was usual when Blair was not sleeping in it. Was breakfast an appropriate time for a proposal of marriage? It felt slightly improper. 'No doubt that will come when her husband arrives from Edinburgh: they have mentioned it several times.'

'Oh, dear,' said Isobel, tucking in to rolls and butter. She had never been one for sitting in ladylike solitude in her room to sip chocolate for breakfast. She was wearing a gown in a practical, brownish check pattern which seemed to say that she had plans for the day, and they were not of the lingering-indoors kind.

'No, she is asking a favour. Apparently this long-expected musical tutor of hers has arrived from Edinburgh –'

'Where else? I expect to see the minister of the High Kirk and the Lord Provost skipping up the drive at any moment.'

'He is at the inn,' said Murray patiently, 'and she feels it expedient to meet him there first, but does not wish to go unescorted.'

'Surely she has a manservant?'

'I believe so, but she adds that as a man of musical taste myself I might be more interested in meeting him – and more capable of assessing his abilities – than any manservant she might take.'

'Oh, beware, Charles, such flattery! This sounds like a trap. Are you sure her husband really exists? She is not out to snap you up, and Letho with you?'

'You had better come with us, then, as chaperone, if you're so concerned for my welfare. And your musical sensitivities are, of course, second to none.'

She laughed at the joke.

'Then I shall be the level head. If the man plays music so brilliantly as to charm you both into blindness to whatever faults he might have, I shall be immune, and save you from yourselves.'

'It seems we cannot do without you, then. You had better come. I'll send a note back to tell her.' He rang for Daniel, and in a moment the note was on its way. And Murray was alone again with Isobel. Should he say something?

But at once there was a light cough from the hall.

'Good morning – I hope I am not interrupting?'

It was the unexpected guest, Richard Wedderburn, standing diffidently in the doorway.

'Come in, come in!' Murray stood to greet him. 'We are all in state today as the parlour is otherwise occupied, but come and help yourself. Daniel is about somewhere if you need to call for anything extra.'

Richard Wedderburn chose a seat and began to organise his breakfast.

'How is Mrs. Wedderburn this morning, sir?' Isobel asked.

'Debs? Oh, she is quite well. I must say, we were so relieved you could take us in. Aside from being in our own home with the children, it is the best place we could imagine just now.'

'Mrs. Wedderburn mentioned something about a bad time in Edinburgh?' Murray prompted, as Wedderburn seemed happy to talk about it.

'One thing after another! Good heavens, if I'd thought about it I should just have taken the axle off the carriage myself and had done with it, for it was bound to break. Almost everything else has gone wrong, and at least poor Robbie the groom would not be laid up with bruising.'

'I am half-scared to have you in the house!' Murray joked.

'And well you might be! Watch out for house-breakers, and illnesses, and having to move unexpectedly to a different part of the town, and routs where the meat is off at the supper, and twisted ankles at a ball, and … oh, if I never see Edinburgh again I shall be a happy man! Give me old age and my own fire and my grandchildren about my feet – well, I suppose I should at least wait until my own children grow up before I think about grandchildren. But really, what a season!' His rounded sandy eyebrows rose and fell as if they wanted a part in the story themselves. Despite his woes, a smile was never far from his lips.

'Most disagreeable,' said Murray, who generally preferred Letho to Edinburgh himself. 'But I hope the family are well?'

'By all reports, yes,' said Wedderburn cautiously.

'Whose was the twisted ankle?' asked Isobel sympathetically.

'My own,' he sighed. 'My dancing was a little over-ambitious.'

'And the house-breaking?' asked Murray. 'Was much lost?'

'Some jewels that had been Lady Scoggie's,' said Wedderburn, referring to his late mother-in-law. 'That was unpleasant. Debs' maid went off with them while we were out. The only mercy is that she could not carry much. Thank heavens for lazy thieves,' he added, eyebrows performing again, trying to make light of it though he looked upset at the servant's betrayal. Murray thought of his perambulations in the night, and hoped his own house had not been broken, nor his servants dishonest. Though it would add another chapter to Richard Wedderburn's story of disaster.

'I wonder, though, before we go down to the village,' said Mrs. Pillans later, 'if I might at last have a look at your icehouse? Mr. Blair told me so much about it yesterday, and it sounded quite picturesque!'

Murray ignored Isobel's look of disbelief.

'Of course,' he said. 'The engineers will no doubt be working on it this morning, and you may inspect it – though I should recommend keeping well back. I'm not wholly convinced that it is safe.'

As it turned out, the engineers had not started at the icehouse itself yet. As Murray and the ladies came round the corner of the house, they were emerging from their cottage with rolls of plans and pens behind their ears, hatless and busy. Mr. Kelly had the key.

'Thalland's?' Murray asked.

'Ah, no, sir, we were able to return that. This is our one – I found it under the window when I went back again last night to the cottage.'

'Inside or out?'

'Out,' said Kelly, shame-faced. 'I must have dropped it. It'll not happen again,' he said.

'It'll not indeed,' said Jo Sweeney grimly, setting his rolls of paper down on a convenient rock as they reached the gate.

'What's that in there?' asked Isobel, the first to look into the icehouse. 'Did you leave a coat there yesterday?'

Murray, alarmed, peered into the gloom. Could someone have been in there last night, perhaps locked in for the night in all the confusion? He could indeed see something, oddly shaped, towards the back of the hollow.

'It'll be something the lads have thrown in over the top of the gate,' said Kelly.

'There seem to be stones on top of it, though,' said Murray. 'And there's not much of a gap at the top of the gate. How could they have flung anything that far?' He was talking almost to himself, though Isobel and Mrs. Pillans were close behind him. Something was wrong here. A cold hand seemed to grip his spine as he tried to make out shapes and sizes. Whatever it was, it lay in the darkest part of the old tunnel. Kelly fumbled with the key, dropped it, and swore.

'Where's the thing gone?' he muttered, poking at the remaining weeds around the gate's foot.

'There it is.' Murray pointed, glancing down. Kelly swooped on the key and more carefully this time inserted it into the padlock. It clunked round dismally. The chain fell free, and Kelly eased the gate back out of their way, one eye on the roof, just in case. As soon as there was room, Murray edged round the gate, dipping his head under the stone roof. In only a few paces he could see the dark shape much more clearly.

'Oh,' he said, and Kelly, behind him, stopped sharply.

'What is it?'

'I'm afraid there's been an accident,' said Murray. 'And someone is dead.'

'What?' Somehow, Mrs. Pillans was beside him, and before he could stop her, she had stooped down to all that was visible – legs in dark breeches and boots, a hand flung out to one side. She gasped.

'Mrs. Pillans, please –'

'But that's Gordon! That's my husband!'

Chapter Twelve

Mrs. Pillans was struggling to breathe, her chest heaving with dry gasps. Murray crouched beside her, taking one of her hands in his, but she paid him no attention. Then Isobel was there, gently drawing Mrs. Pillans to her feet, easing her, in the cramped space, back out of the icehouse, away from whatever was under those rocks.

'I must – I must get him out of there,' Murray heard her as Isobel took her outside. 'I must not leave him.'

'Of course not, my dear,' said Isobel, 'but it will be difficult work, and we must give them space.'

'I would do it myself!'

'They will take great care of him, I'm convinced,' Isobel's voice was soothing, the tone she used when Augusta was cross about something. 'Whatever happened, I'm sure Mr. Pillans would not want you risking injury in there.'

'Oh!' cried Mrs. Pillans. 'But he is injured, isn't he?'

Murray looked down at the heap of stones that lay across the body. There was no doubt that Mr. Pillans was injured. It had not occurred to him to wonder, though, if the man was actually dead. It seemed obvious.

'Come,' he said quietly to Kelly, 'let us clear these rocks quickly, if there is the least chance that he lives.'

'I suppose,' said Kelly, who seemed as dubious as Murray was. The two men knelt by the legs, Kelly to the left where there was a narrower gap, and Murray to the right where there was more room for his own long legs. Swiftly they picked off rock after rock, most of them not so large that they could not be lifted in one hand. The man's chest was clear in a minute, but it was motionless. The cloth of his black coat and buff waistcoat was dusty, as you would expect, but not torn: even his buttons were in place and barely dented. Murray removed a glove and laid two fingers on the man's throat, just accessible now. He could not detect the least flutter. He glanced outside. Isobel had drawn Mrs. Pillans away as far as she could, and found a rock for her to sit on, but Mrs. Pillans' gaze was fixed steadily on the icehouse. Isobel's hands were on Mrs. Pillans' shoulders, part comfort, part restraint. Reluctantly, Murray turned back, and met Kelly's eye across the dead man's chest.

'And now the face,' he said. Kelly swallowed, and nodded.

Two rocks obscured the man's head, almost as if they had been laid there. Larger than most of the others, the one on Murray's side had almost to be rolled off, and he was glad he had replaced his glove when a pointed edge jabbed into his fingers. Kelly shoved at the one on his side, and pushed it clear.

What they had revealed was not a man any more. It was nothing more than pulp, bone, blood, flesh and, disturbingly, teeth. Kelly shoved himself to his feet, lurched out of the icehouse, and could be heard vomiting extravagantly outside. Murray pressed his forearm against his own face, letting the nausea settle, blocking the metallic smell, wondering, briefly, at the fragility of his own skull, seeing the one before him so easily shattered.

Then he considered, and once again felt the dead man's throat. It was quite cold. He had been there for some time.

But what was he doing in Murray's icehouse?

Murray had laid his handkerchief over what was left of the man's face so that, even though the dark blood was seeping through, diluted by the moisture on the floor, the gardeners could more comfortably bring in a hurdle, carefully, and slide him on to it, and carry him out of the tunnel.

'I'm watching the roof,' said Edward Kelly as they worked. 'I can't believe that happened. I was sure it was safe. Jo, what do you think?'

'It was safe,' said Jo Sweeney with certainty.

'That's right,' Kelly agreed. 'It had settled with the years, but it was solid. It would have needed a good poke with a big stick to shift anything – the roots, see, they had stabilised the rocks. For now, anyway. Fifty years more and they might bring the whole thing down, but for now I'd have said it was sound.'

'It was,' said Jo Sweeney.

'If I had even thought for a moment it would fall, I'd have had a whole scaffolding in there supporting it. I mean, we've been working in there ourselves. It wouldn't have been worth the risk, the whole thing.'

Murray tried to brush the grit from the tunnel's floor from his breeches.

'I'm not blaming either of you,' he said.

'Are you not?' Kelly looked surprised.

'No, of course not. I know you had taken care. But in any case, go now and look at the tunnel roof, and tell me what strikes you about it.'

Kelly and Sweeney looked at each other, confused.

'I doubt any more will fall now,' said Kelly.

'It might, if it's once started,' said Jo.

'Go and look, please,' said Murray, a little more sharply than he had meant. The two men frowned in unison, and ventured back into the tunnel.

A howl broke out behind him. He spun, alarmed, and found that Mrs. Pillans, breaking free from Isobel's hold, had snatched at the bloodied handkerchief and seen what was left of the man's head. Isobel, too, gasped.

'My dearest!' cried Mrs. Pillans, and sagged to her knees in the mud, the man's gloved hand clutched to her breast. She sobbed uncontrollably now, her face soaked, the front of her pale yellow pelisse showing the marks of pouring tears. Isobel once again went to her, doing her best to comfort her. The gardeners, still one each end of the hurdle, were starting to strain at the weight. Murray gestured to them to lower the hurdle to the ground. Mrs. Pillans was muddy enough already: she was unlikely to mind a little more.

He glanced back at the icehouse, and saw Kelly and Sweeney emerge, still frowning. He went over to them, distantly aware of the sound of hooves and carriage wheels coming from the drive at the front of the house. More unexpected guests? He dismissed the thought from his mind for now.

'Well?' he said to the engineers.

'It's a strange thing,' said Edward Kelly slowly, 'but if you'd asked me if that roof had fallen in, just going by the look of the roof, I'd have said no.'

'Mr. Sweeney?'

'No,' said Jo Sweeney, 'it has not fallen in. It is exactly as it was. I drew it yesterday – you can look.'

'I shall, but it's what I thought.' He considered for a moment, looking back at Mrs. Pillans kneeling in the mud by the body. 'But those stones were in there, weren't they?'

'There was a wee heap of stones in the corner, indeed,' said Kelly. 'I'd say they had been intended for the work but were never used. Mr. Jack – is that his name? – said that a load of the stone bought for the icehouse was used to build something at the manse, I think, but maybe these ones were surplus to requirements, or they just couldn't be bothered going all the way down that wee tunnel to bring them out.'

'So what were they doing on top of him?' Murray asked, not really expecting an answer. 'And what was he doing in there in the first place?'

'Has he been looking at it before?' Kelly asked, helpfully. 'I mean, I've maybe seen him, but ...'

'It would be hard to tell,' said Murray. 'I know. But as to his being here – I don't even know if he has been to Letho before. I've never met him, to my knowledge.'

'Then that's an awful strange thing to do,' said Kelly. 'To turn up at a stranger's home, work your way through a locked gate – if it was locked – and into a place like that, in the middle of the night, and cover yourself with rocks, and die in the corner.'

'That's a thought,' said Murray, and left them for a moment to return to the tunnel. One of the gardeners stopped him, apologetically.

'She'll no move, sir. What are we to do?'

Murray glanced back at where Mrs. Pillans and Isobel were still kneeling in the mud beside the hurdle. Two more gardeners stood by, one looking sick, the other happy enough to be taking a break from his usual work.

'Wait until Miss Blair gives you the word,' he said. 'Poor Mrs. Pillans has had a terrible shock, but you're right, she cannot stay there forever. The body will need to be taken to Collessie. Can you arrange a cart?'

'Aye, sir,' said the gardener smartly, and took his chance to head off to the stables. Murray sighed, and headed once more towards the icehouse.

At the back, by the scattered stones, he crouched once again by the place where the body had lain. The knees of his breeches felt soggy, tight against his skin. He hoped Isobel was not going to take any harm from her own sojourn in the mud. Someone should fetch brandy. And someone should go and tell the music tutor ... tell him what? And he needed to tell Blair, too, about this unfortunate event. It was the kind of puzzle Blair was good at. Or would Isobel think it too upsetting for him?

The ground before him was ill-lit from the icehouse's mouth, but still he could see, quite clearly, the dark stain where the man's head had lain, wet, too, because of the damp of the floor. A little ragged at the edges where the slight flow of water was starting to carry it away, but still, enough blood had spilled there to leave its mark. Enough blood to show, to Murray's reluctantly knowledgeable eye, that whatever Mr. Pillans had been doing in his icehouse, he had been alive when he went in, and had died there.

Murray stood carefully, avoiding hitting his own head on the ceiling. He was not sure what height Mr. Pillans had been when alive and standing, so he made a careful examination of the walls for several feet up and down, right round. It had seemed very unlikely that such injuries as he had could have been caused by his walking accidentally into the wall – he would have had to have been moving at speed, for one thing, for such an impact, and with the way the walls curved over to form an arch he would have been more likely to hit his brow, and not damage the lower half of his face at all. Those teeth ... And he had been lying feet first towards the entrance, flat on his back, almost at the back of the tunnel. He could hardly have picked up speed so quickly from there – and then, what would he have hit to end up on his back like that? It made no sense.

And who, when he had once gone inside and died, had locked the gate after him?

Had they themselves seen to its locking? When he and Robbins had stood out there last night, had Mr. Pillans already been lying dead inside? He shivered. Could he have been saved?

But no, surely not. Not with all that injury to his face. Never.

But Robbins had thought he felt someone near him. And then there had been that tantalising sound of running footsteps.

Murray shook his head hard. There was too much to take in. He needed to get outside again, and clear his head.

He emerged from the icehouse to find Isobel trying to coax Mrs. Pillans to her feet. The woman seemed to have aged a decade in the last ten minutes, and the front of her gown and spencer were soaked and filthy, but still she resisted, clinging to the dead man's hand. As he wondered how to help Isobel, a pony and cart came round from the stables, with a sheet ready to cover the body. The gardeners braced themselves to lift the hurdle again, and Isobel looked up at them, ready to give them the nod.

A figure appeared around the corner of the main house, a tall figure in a dark red morning gown and ostrich feather bonnet. Miss George – Lady Rocheid. Murray's heart sank. This was not a good moment for her to start again about her husband's absence. He stepped forward, intending to intercept her, but she too had paused, taking in the scene. Then, faster than any of them could believe, she hurtled towards them and flung herself down on the opposite side of the hurdle.

'Jacob!' she screamed, and the walls of the buildings, the trees on the hill, the icehouse itself, resounded with the sound. 'Jacob! My husband! What has become of you?'

Chapter Thirteen

'What?' Mrs. Pillans froze, then, awfully, sagged back into the mud. Lady Rocheid had seized the body and was trying to lift it into an embrace. The handkerchief fell from the man's face, and in shock Lady Rocheid dropped the body the few inches she had managed to lift it, and slapped her hands to her face, horrified. Isobel spun to find Murray, but he was already passing her and stepping round the hurdle to Lady Rocheid.

'Come, madam, this has been a terrible shock for you,' he said firmly. 'Let us go indoors and find some brandy.' I could do with a glass myself, he thought.

'Who is she?' demanded Mrs. Pillans. 'Who are you, madam? How dare you manhandle my husband like that?'

'Oh, dear,' said Isobel, to nobody in particular.

'Your husband? How could he be your husband?' Lady Rocheid's face, pale before, turned almost grey. 'He's my husband! My husband!'

'Right,' said Murray. 'Lady Rocheid, this is Mrs. Pillans. Mrs. Pillans, this is Lady Rocheid. Indoors, ladies, both of you.'

'I won't leave him,' said Mrs. Pillans, obstinate.

'I'll not leave him with her,' said Lady Rocheid, breathing heavily. Murray could see Isobel with her hand in her reticule, probably looking for smelling salts.

'Neither of you will leave him,' said Murray. 'We shall all go into the house, and these men will bring Mr. – the deceased gentleman in, too. At the very least he can go home cleaned – whichever home he goes to,' he added, more quietly.

Isobel guided Mrs. Pillans round the hurdle, and Murray took Lady Rocheid firmly by the elbow. He was struggling to think straight: all he could pinpoint in his mind was that he longed to change into clean breeches, but knew he would not have the chance for a while. Isobel's practical brown check skirts were dripping with mud, as she almost dragged Mrs. Pillans along. Mrs. Pillans barely took her eyes off the hurdle and its awful cargo. The two engineers, somehow now separated from the party, watched them go, but the dogs followed mournfully.

Murray was astonished to see by the hall clock that it was only ten o'clock – he felt as if he had been out at the icehouse for hours. He rang for Robbins, who appeared in the hallway in seconds. His pale eyes widened at the sight before him.

'A cloth for the dining room table, first, please, Robbins, then brandy … ah, here in the hall, I think. And have someone take some to the engineers, too.' The drawing room would have been more comfortable but the hall furniture was used to being knocked about and muddied by dogs. And he was not sure that they would be able to persuade either lady to go so far from the body. 'I'll light the fire.'

Murray often wondered if Robbins waited until he was behind the door to the servants' passage and then ran like the wind, for as usual it was within the blink of an eye, it seemed, that he was back with Daniel and a thick felted cloth, William and some warm rugs, and the brandy. The gardeners, tempering weariness with their task with mild excitement at seeing inside the big house for a change, heaved their burden into the dining room and the door closed, with both widows apparent barely taking their eyes off it. Isobel slipped over to Murray.

'How will this fadge?' she asked quietly.

'I have no idea. Who do you think is right?'

'I have no idea, either. As far as I know I have met neither of the gentlemen: have you?'

'Lord Rocheid but briefly, once. Mr. Pillans never at all.'

'Well, did either of them have a reason to be in your icehouse, being killed?'

'Not that they informed me about.' They fell silent, watching the women.

'My father will be out of his room soon,' said Isobel. Murray was not sure if she thought this was a good thing or not. Certainly it would be hard to hide the matter from him.

Mrs. Pillans was breathing heavily, but struggling to steady herself, eyeing Lady Rocheid now with a strange mixture of respect and horror.

'Lady – what was it, sorry?' she began.

'Rocheid,' said Lady Rocheid starchily. She seemed to have any tendency to hysteria under control. Mrs. Pillans had the weary, headachy look of one who has cried all she has to cry for now.

'Lady Rocheid, I am convinced that that is my husband.'

'And I am convinced that it is mine,' said Lady Rocheid.

'But you barely looked at him.'

'I just know. Instinctively.'

'But why would your husband have been there, in Mr. Murray's icehouse?'

'In the icehouse?' Lady Rocheid hesitated, clearly surprised.

'Well, why would yours? Is he some kind of engineer?'

'An engineer? No, no: he is a shop – he is a merchant.'

'Well, why would a merchant be in Mr. Murray's icehouse? Mr. Murray,' Lady Rocheid brought him into the conversation, perhaps in the hope that it might lead to some kind of progress, 'I thought your icehouse was down by the lake?'

'This was one that my grandfather started, but never finished. It turned out to be unstable.'

'And it is still unstable, then, clearly. Do you know what my husband was doing in your icehouse? Your aborted icehouse?'

'Whichever gentleman it is,' said Murray, 'I have no idea what he was doing there. It was not with my knowledge, or permission, and it came as a surprise to the engineers who are working on the site. Please, Lady Rocheid, take some brandy. This has been a terrible shock for all of us.'

Lady Rocheid took the glass, and emptied it in one swallow. Murray heard Isobel gasp softly.

'Of course we have only your word for that,' said Lady Rocheid.

Murray blinked.

'I beg your pardon?'

'My husband has been missing for some days, and now he turns up in your – your not icehouse. You denied all knowledge of him when I came here enquiring for him not two days ago. Yet here he is, dead.'

'But my husband was missing, too!' cried Mrs. Pillans. 'I have been expecting him every day from Edinburgh! He wrote me to say he would be there before the very letter he sent.'

'Did he?' For a moment Lady Rocheid looked put out: Lord Rocheid had not written such a letter to her. 'My husband, too, was to arrive from Edinburgh. Though he may have had to visit his estates in Haddingtonshire first, of course. That may have delayed him.'

'May still delay him, Lady Rocheid,' said Isobel. 'Surely there is a chance that that poor gentleman is not Lord Rocheid?'

'Certainly there is,' said Mrs. Pillans, 'for it is not Lord Rocheid, it is Mr. Pillans.'

'Is there a chance it is both?' Murray heard Isobel murmur, but for the moment he had no wish to entertain such a controversial idea. He hoped the ladies had not heard her.

'Mrs. Pillans,' he said, 'describe your husband for me.'

'He is – was – a well-made man. Elegant, you might say. Raven haired, and brown eyed. A very –' her voice broke on a sob, 'a very handsome man indeed.'

'And Lady Rocheid? I only met Lord Rocheid very briefly, you'll remember.'

'She could have been describing my own dear Jacob,' said Lady Rocheid.

'But my husband was quite a young man,' said Mrs. Pillans, glancing sideways to take in Lady Rocheid's more mature appearance. 'He was but thirty. No doubt we could tell – even as things are – whether the man in there is thirty or – or ...' She tailed away, realising the trap into which she was walking.

'My husband was no more than thirty-two!' snapped Lady Rocheid.

'Oh,' said Mrs. Pillans in a small voice. 'That makes it difficult.'

'Had either of them any distinguishing features?' Murray asked, adding quickly, 'that you would be prepared to indicate to us?'

Mrs. Pillans opened her mouth to reply, a little pink, when Lady Rocheid cut across her.

'Do not tell him, Mrs. Pillans! Why should this man adjudicate in our case? Remember that we cannot trust him. He may have kidnapped both our husbands – if this one is mine, be sure that your own will turn up in a day or two – in an icehouse or in a doocot, or somewhere else he hoped to hide them away!'

Murray rubbed his forehead. The day, which had started so pleasantly, had taken such a peculiar turn that he was beginning to wonder if he had been snatched by the fairies – though the stories always made that sound like quite a pleasant experience, when you were actually there. Now Mrs. Pillans was looking at him suspiciously.

'Lady Rocheid, you have known me all our lives. When do you imagine that I began a career of kidnapping men on their arrival from Edinburgh? And what do you think I intended to do with them?'

'More to the point,' said Isobel, 'if you will not allow Mr. Murray to adjudicate your case, then who would be acceptable? For you know this cannot continue: he is one man, or he is the other. You cannot both claim him.' She did not meet Murray's eye at this, so he knew she was still wondering if in fact he was both one man and the other. Despite everything, a bubble of unstable laughter rose in his throat, and he took a quick sip of brandy to quell it. The two ladies regarded each other, calculating.

'The minister? Mr. Helliwell?' said Mrs. Pillans.

'He and my brother do not get on,' said Lady Rocheid. 'He might be prejudiced.'

'Then perhaps the gentleman who was here at dinner last week?' Mrs. Pillans suggested again.

'That is my brother,' said Lady Rocheid. Murray saw Mrs. Pillans giving her another surprised look.

'Mr. Blair?' Mrs. Pillans tried again.

'A close friend of Mr. Murray.'

'Nevertheless, this is not about whether or not Mr. Murray has any culpability here,' said Isobel. 'It is simply a matter of determining which of your husbands has been discovered.'

Murray did not feel that was entirely helpful, from his own point of view, anyway. But Mrs. Pillans gave a rough smile.

'He seemed a very kind man! Miss Blair, do you think he would?'

'I'm sure he would,' said Isobel warmly. 'Lady Rocheid, shall we ask him?'

Lady Rocheid scowled, thinking hard, but she could evidently not come up with another name for a quick decision.

'I believe him to be a fair man,' she said at last. 'Yes, Miss Blair, go and see to it.'

Isobel curtseyed – if curtseys could be sardonic, this one was – and went across to the parlour door. She knocked, they heard a voice, and she disappeared inside.

Mrs. Pillans, suddenly aware of the state of her clothing, sat abruptly on the nearest seat and fiddled with her brandy glass. Lady Rocheid, brought up not to fidget, looked as if she might slap her. Murray would not have been surprised: it was that kind of day. He hoped that in some manner the engineers were able to sort out the mess inside the icehouse, and would not be put off. It was a minor concern, but he liked it: it felt like something that could be sorted out with relative ease.

The parlour door opened, and Isobel hurried out and back across the hall. Behind her, Blair appeared, propelled by Smith in the wheeled chair. They reached the others, and Blair bowed his head at their curtseys.

'I am so very sorry to hear this sad news,' he said at once. 'Terrible, terrible. But I understand that there is some confusion. Perhaps – if you are both able to, of course, for it is quite a dreadful thing but it really needs to be both of you, I believe – perhaps we could go into – the dining room, is it? and see what the situation is.'

'The situation,' said Lady Rocheid, 'is that my husband has been killed.'

'Dear me,' said Blair, eyeing her sideways and upwards – even standing on two legs he had never been a match for her height. 'Or perhaps Mrs. Pillans' husband. Well, well, it is no good to have both of you mourning if it should only be one, is it? Come – Smith, would you be so good?'

Chapter Fourteen

For so short a distance, the procession seemed suddenly a grand one, the wheeled chair at the front, Mrs. Pillans and Lady Rocheid next, attended by Isobel, and Murray, taking up the rear. In the dining room, Daniel stood reluctant guard over the body – presumably the gardeners had managed to work the hurdle through the servants' door, and had gone back outside. Robbins had been busy. The body lay on a thick felted blanket, not cleaned or prepared but at least straight and decent. A fresh cloth covered it, and Murray's bloody handkerchief had been removed, so that for anyone walking into the room unawares the sight was not too much of a shock. The dining chairs stood around the walls, out of the way. The table, usually central, had already been moved a little to one side so that Blair's wheeled chair could be manoeuvred in, but he now seized the two crutches that he kept tucked into the side of the chair, and, with Smith's help, swung out and stood, wig crooked, no more of a shambles than ever, next to the table. He looked back at Lady Rocheid and Mrs. Pillans for a long moment, very little in his face except a sorrowful kindness. Then he turned to Murray.

'Have you sent for Dr. Feilden? And the sheriff's man?'

'The sheriff's man?' repeated Mrs. Pillans in alarm.

'He will need to be sent for, whoever this is,' said Blair sadly.

'I have been remiss,' said Murray, who felt he had been running since the man was discovered. 'I shall send for both at once.' He nodded at Daniel, who, after a perplexed look, as if he had not quite been listening, fled gratefully from the room.

'See?' said Lady Rocheid. 'Mr. Murray is determined to prevent all discovery!'

'Lady Rocheid,' said Blair, 'let us have no more of that for now. There will be time to discover perpetrators, when we find the name of the victim.'

Once again, Murray felt this did not do quite enough to emphasise his own innocence, but Blair was right: this was not the time. And Blair was continuing.

'You may wish to consider, ladies, that as sufficient doubt has arisen between you, this poor fellow may in fact be the husband of neither of you.'

At that, Murray almost laughed: both women at once looked taken aback, then affronted, then, as they realised the implications, tentatively hopeful. It was as if they had practised the sequence in advance. Blair acknowledged their mixed emotions with a nod, and turned back to the body.

For a moment he was awkward, trying to support himself with the crutches and bend lower at the same time. Murray knew what he would normally have done: how many times had he watched Blair prop his fists on his knees, peering down for a better view of a plant, an animal, a footprint, a bloodstain? It was a wrench now to see him so unsteady – one of those sturdy knees was missing, and the other was weak. Now, instead, Blair gave Smith a brisk wave and lowered himself into the dining chair that Smith brought over. His head was thus at the level of the dead man's, when he hunched his shoulders. He gave the body a broad, general examination for a moment, and Murray followed his gaze: the man was indeed, as the women had both said, well made, well proportioned, not over-tall but a good size with broad shoulders and fine, strong, arms and legs. A suit of black clothes, a buff waistcoat and a pair of well-maintained black leather boots, meeting his breeches at the knee. Black gloves on the hands, and at the throat a glimpse of what had been a decent white linen shirt and neck cloth. No hat, and no cane. Either might still be in the icehouse.

Blair completed his general view, then began a more minute study, noting, presumably, the damp on the man's back where he had lain – all night, perhaps? – on the wet floor of the tunnel, the fragments and dust from the rocks that had been heaped upon him, the lack of damage to the clothing or the gloves or the boots. Then he propped the crutches against the side of the table, and reverently lifted the clean cloth from the man's face. Both possible widows gasped, though they had seen the sight before, and began to sob.

They had been too rushed, before. Finding the body, removing the stones, bringing it out, dealing with Mrs. Pillans, with the engineers, with Lady Rocheid, all had been a frantic leap from one thing to another – hence forgetting about sending for the doctor or the sheriff's man. Now, in the sudden stillness of the dining room, there was time to reflect – time to look again at the fragmented face – the teeth – time to smell the odours of the soiled clothing, the drying blood, the wet wool of his coat. Time to imagine what might have happened. What had he expected, whoever he was, when he walked into the icehouse? Was someone already with him, urging him forward? Had he arranged to meet someone? Was he – for some odd reason – passing by, and heard a noise, and went to investigate? Was he frightened, or bold? Determined, or careless? Did he suspect what was about to happen? Did he – even in the night – see it coming, or was he downed before he could even protest? Had he gone there innocent, or were the tables turned on him?

'Dr. Feilden will be able to tell us more about how this poor fellow died,' said Blair softly.

'But surely –' Lady Rocheid began, a half-finished gesture to the ruined face. Robbins, or someone he had directed, had made a kind of pad for the head, perhaps to soak up any – anything that still issued from the smashed skull. A pillow for a very strange bed.

'Certainly it looks as if – was it rocks, Charles? – as if rocks caused this damage. But it is possible that he was dead before the rocks fell. There may be another injury somewhere.'

'Then my husband's own physician should examine him,' said Lady Rocheid.

'Hm,' said Blair, 'and where is your husband's physician, Lady Rocheid?'

'In Edinburgh, of course.'

'Then may I suggest – should we conclude that this is in fact your husband – that the preliminary examination is carried out by someone more, ah, local?'

'Well,' said Lady Rocheid. 'Well, I suppose.'

'Mrs. Pillans, have you any objections to Dr. Feilden?' Murray asked, for the purposes of fairness.

'Oh, no, no. I have never met the man, but no, I am sure not.'

Blair cast upon her a bright, beaming smile of approval. Murray could see that Mrs. Pillans bloomed a little in that light, despite the circumstances. She was more used to the world's kindness than this grief. Blair's beam faded, and he turned solemn again.

'Now, can either of you tell me of any distinguishing marks your husband might have had?'

Mrs. Pillans gave Lady Rocheid a sharp look.

'My husband had a mole on his chin. Just a little one, just there.' She pointed to a spot on her own chin, then looked with dismay at the body. 'And that is almost certainly of no use to you, is it?' she finished, moving her fingers to cover her lips. Tears were very close.

'Lady Rocheid?'

Her ladyship shrugged.

'No more useful than that. A scar on his cheekbone, come upon in a riding accident when he was a boy.'

Everyone looked down again in silence at the body.

'There's nothing about the clothes, then ...' said Blair, still studying the corpse minutely. 'No doubt their tailors could tell, but they are both, I assume, in Edinburgh.'

'Edinburgh again,' muttered Isobel. 'Nothing but Edinburgh.'

'In just such a suit of clothes was my husband accustomed to be seen, in the daytime,' said Lady Rocheid.

'And I am sure they are exactly what my husband always wears,' said Mrs. Pillans. All hostility seemed to have leached from them in the presence of Blair. That, at least, was good, Murray thought.

'The choice of colour is, indeed, nothing out of the common,' Blair remarked, though he himself wore the most striking colours. Today it was a rose pink waistcoat, heavy with embroidery in all shades from peach to scarlet, with green breeches and a blue coat – he must already have been dressed before he was asked to help. Murray looked back at the corpse. The colours might have been common, but the quality of the material should have told them something. But Blair was too tactful to enquire just yet. 'And did they wear anything else about them? A pocket watch? Rings? Seal fobs?'

'Oh, of course!' said Lady Rocheid at once, brightening. 'My husband had all of those. His seal at his waist, and a watch that had belonged to his father – gold, of course – and a ring on his little finger. Of his right hand, that is.'

'Mrs. Pillans?' Blair was already shifting in his chair, trying to see further down the body than just the face and neck. Smith was promptly beside him, helping him to shift the chair.

'A watch, yes,' she said quietly, 'but silver. His fob was on the watch chain.'

'Then we have a distinction,' said Blair, beaming, and reached out to the dead man's waistcoat pocket.

It was empty.

'No watch?' Isobel asked, to make sure.

'Smith, please go about to the other side of the table, and make sure his watch has not simply slid down into his coat, will you? Thank you.'

'Yes, sir,' said Smith. It took only a moment.

'There's no sign of a watch, sir. No chain or anything.'

'Or a fob? A fob at his waist?'

Smith delicately turned back the front edges of the man's black coat.

'No, sir, nothing.'

'Then,' said Blair, 'let us remove the gloves. Smith, if you please, your side. Mrs. Pillans, did your husband wear a ring, at all?'

'Yes, yes, he did.' Here was a better chance for Mr. Pillans to match Lord Rocheid. 'A gold ring, on his left hand.'

'My side, then, Smith,' said Blair, though Smith was already removing the man's right glove. He held up a pale, uncertain hand, like something from underground. It was bare.

Lady Rocheid gave a little gasp.

Blair looked at her, concerned. Lady Rocheid straightened her back, and lifted her chin.

'And the left glove, Mr. Blair?' she asked. Blair peeled it back, then pulled it clear of the fingers.

On the third finger was a gold ring.

'Is it inscribed, Mrs. Pillans?' Blair asked.

'Yes,' she said, 'with his initials, on the inside. "G.P."'

'May I?'

Mrs. Pillans gave a quick, frantic nod. She was breathing quickly. With a little effort, Blair slid the ring up over the knuckle, and off the man's finger. Murray noted signs of work on the man's hands: the nails were well kept, but the flesh was rough and calloused, as if the dead man had started life in a harder station than he had ended it. It was not what he would expect from the hands of Lord Rocheid, for example. Blair seemed to be looking at the same thing. Then he flipped the ring on to his own palm, and studied it carefully. He looked up at all of them.

'"G.P.",' he said.

'Oh! Oh! Oh, Gordon!' cried Mrs. Pillans, and slumped to the floor. Isobel hurried to help her once again. She had not fainted, but sobs wracked her body as if a storm tossed it to and fro. Murray rubbed his own face, then headed for the hall to fetch the brandy.

'You are quite sure, Mr. Blair?' asked Lady Rocheid.

'See for yourself, my lady,' said Blair, holding the gold circle flat on his palm for her to see. She came very close, bending stiffly over his hand. She nodded, once, slowly.

'Then,' she said, in a low voice, 'I must acknowledge my mistake. This man is yours, Mrs. Pillans. I am most sorry for your loss.'

Chapter Fifteen

'Don't you think she gave up rather easily?' Isobel asked, as Murray stood at the door to see Miss George – Lady Rocheid – off. There was no sign yet of the physican or the sheriff's man, unsurprisingly, but Murray peered hopefully down the drive, just in case.

'Well, the ring seemed to prove it,' he said reasonably, turning back to her.

'Do you think she was really in the market for proof? I half expected her to say you had taken the ring from Mr. Pillans and placed it on Lord Rocheid, just to confuse the situation.'

Murray rubbed a hand through his hair, hard.

'I hope she finds Lord Rocheid soon,' he said, 'or she will be going about the countryside telling everyone that I kidnap men and kill them. It sounds like a joke, but just at the moment I do not much feel like laughing about it.'

'No ...' Isobel agreed. 'Mrs. Pillans!'

The widow, now confirmed in her status, was at the dining room doorway, clinging to the doorpost with one hand. She looked unutterably weary.

'Mr. Murray, may I then take my husband home?'

Isobel, anticipating the answer, hurried over to take Mrs. Pillans' hand.

'Might you not prefer, since they have been summoned here, to wait until the physician and the sheriff's man arrive? Until then there is little you can do,' said Murray, knowing that the doctor would not be keen to go to Collessie, and that the sheriff's man would rather see the scene of the death and the corpse close together.

'In the meantime,' said Isobel, 'let us find you some clean, dry clothes, and you will feel more comfortable. You know Mr. Pillans will not be left unattended.' She tugged gently at Mrs. Pillans' hand. 'Come, let us see what we can find that will fit you. We are not too dissimilar in height. I'll ring for my maid.'

She guided Mrs. Pillans towards the stairs and led her away, unresisting.

Murray sighed. It suddenly seemed very quiet. He wanted to change his own clothes, but there were other things to be done first.

In the dining room, Blair and Smith were still in attendance, awaiting the return of Daniel to take their place.

'What do you think, then?' Murray asked, pulling out another dining chair to sprawl on.

Blair pursed his loose lips and let his eyebrows rise up into the edges of his wig.

'Dreadful,' he said. 'And yet, not so dreadful as you would at first think, I believe. He was covered in rocks, was he?'

'Pretty much,' said Murray. 'His legs were visible, from about halfway down the thigh. But the rest was under a pile of rocks.'

'Not large ones, I'd warrant.' Blair waved at the corpse's chest, now once more covered by a sheet. 'Of course I have not meddled with anything that Dr. Feilden is likely to do, or the sheriff's man might want to see, but it seems to me – unless you disagree, of course, dear Charles – that there is nothing misshapen about his chest. The stomach, I admit, is harder to judge. But I should think that when Dr. Feilden examines him, there will be very little bruising or breakage. And that all that happened after he was dead.'

'Just to conceal him, you mean?' asked Murray. 'It seems hardly worth it – the engineers would be clearing that pile of stones very soon anyway. And besides, his legs were sticking out.'

'The killer could have been interrupted.'

'True, but what about the smell? The weather is growing warmer every day, even in that tunnel. It would not have given the killer much time to flee, or whatever they wished to use the time for.'

'Perhaps, though, concealment was not the intention,' said

Blair, bouncing a little on his dining chair. 'Perhaps it was intended to make us think that it was an accident.'

'That sounds more likely,' Murray agreed. 'For that is what we thought it was, at first. But Mr. Sweeney had made a most accurate drawing of the roof of the tunnel, and it was clear to see that everything was still in place – even without the drawing, it looks as sound as it did before.'

'A drawing?' said Blair, momentarily distracted. 'I must ask him if I may see it. He seems a great draughtsman, Mr. Sweeney.'

'That's all very well, but I hope between them there is at least one great engineer. I have had quite enough of falling masonry here. Well,' he said, pushing himself reluctantly to his feet, 'I had better go and have a word with Kelly and Sweeney, anyway. The tunnel will have to be cleaned, once the sheriff's man has seen it, and I need to find out properly when the gate was locked and when it wasn't.'

'It wasn't locked?'

'Not when Robbins and I went out to check last night. And at that time, Kelly could not lay his hands on the key.'

'Oh!' Blair's eyes widened.

'It turned up later, at his door. Not a place I think any of us would have missed it, but I could be wrong. Are you content to stay here, or shall I ring for someone?'

'No, no, I shall stay,' said Blair. 'I shall sit like a hermit – barring Smith, of course – in contemplation. Besides, you have few enough servants at present, Charles: I should not like to cause you to have one in here any longer than necessary.'

'Thank you,' said Murray with a smile. No doubt the contemplation would not go to waste, but he thought Blair would probably rather be coming out to the icehouse with him. But either on crutches or in the wheeled chair he would not have found it easy to reach the place where the body had been found. Where Mr. Pillans had been found. The body now had a name, even if it was that of someone he had never met.

He brushed the worst of the mud from his breeches and went outside again, round the house to the tunnel mouth. Gordon Pillans. What did he know about him? A warehouse owner, a business man, who, by his hands, started with less than he had now. An inhabitant of Edinburgh, though that might not have been where he came from.

Married, to a woman from the Borders. No children, as yet, of this marriage, and now never would be, presumably. Wealthy enough to take Collessie for the summer, though perhaps a man of more wealth, or more discretion, might have taken somewhere better. Around thirty years of age, and well made. And late, arriving at Letho.

Presumably Mrs. Pillans was used to his lateness, for she had not been half as concerned about him as Lady Rocheid had been – still was – about Lord Rocheid. Or was it simply that she trusted him more? That was something to find out, perhaps.

So, Gordon Pillans had finally arrived. But how? By his own carriage? By post? By ... some other means?

And then, even though he was at last here, he had not gone to Collessie. He had come to Letho House, and to the old icehouse. Why? And with whom?

Murray had walked slowly, thinking, but his thoughts had now taken him all the way round to the icehouse, and as he did not know any of the answers to the questions he had thought of – let alone the ones he had not yet thought of – he abandoned his efforts for now, and paid attention to what was before him.

The horse and cart had gone back to the stables, but Mr. Thalland had appeared, and was talking with the engineers. They saw Murray approaching, and went to meet him.

'Can I ask who it turned out to be?' asked Mr. Kelly at once. 'It's of no matter to me, I entirely admit, but I've never seen the like of that before.'

'It appears to be Mr. Pillans,' said Murray. 'The first lady's husband. The second lady's husband is still missing.'

Mr. Sweeney turned pale, and Mr. Kelly's jaw dropped.

'Does that mean we're looking for someone else, as well? Because, sir, these are not the conditions in which Jo Sweeney and I are used to working.'

Jo Sweeney laid a hand on Kelly's arm, ready to restrain him.

'It's all right, Edward,' he murmured.

'I don't suppose there is any connexion between Mr. Pillans and Lord Rocheid,' Murray said firmly, though the suggestion immediately played in his mind. Was there? Was Lord Rocheid soon to be found, too? 'Anyway, I came to ask you not to work in there any more today, until at least the sheriff's man has been and then it has been cleaned for you.'

'Cleaned, is it? Well then ...' Edward Kelly seemed surprised, and pleased.

'Good heavens, man,' Thalland squeaked, 'no one would expect you to work in there until that's been done! But the sheriff's man, sir? Is that necessary?'

'I believe so, Mr. Thalland,' said Murray. 'He might decide not, but it's best to leave things as they are until he has taken a look.'

'Of course, sir.'

'Is there other work you two can be doing, without going into the tunnel?' Murray asked.

'Oh, aye, we can go up the hill and take measurements, can we not, Jo?'

Sweeney nodded.

'Can you please leave the drawing of the tunnel roof, though?' Murray asked, suddenly thinking of it. 'I'm sure the sheriff's man will find it a useful thing.'

Sweeney went wordlessly over to where his bundle of rolled drawings still lay on a boulder, and began sorting through them. Kelly watched him for a moment.

'You'll look after it, though, won't you, sir? He doesn't like letting his drawings out of his hands until he's ready.'

'I'll bear it in mind,' said Murray. 'The sheriff's man is a bit of an artist himself: he'll realise its worth.'

'How long till he's here?' asked Mr. Kelly.

'It could be a while,' said Murray. 'He's to come from Cupar. The doctor will be here first, though he's unlikely to want to come out here.'

'The doctor? Surely it's a bit too late for that?'

But Mr. Thalland met Murray's eye.

'The sheriff's man and the doctor, sir? I'm guessing you don't think this is an accident, then?'

'Well,' said Murray, but before he could say one way or the other, he saw Edward Kelly's face. It was the colour of bleached linen.

Isobel stayed close by while Mrs. Pillans, aided by Isobel's maid, found petticoats and a skirt to fit, and some clean stockings. The maid gave her boots a good brush, and helped her to put them on again.

'I need to send word to my mother,' said Mrs. Pillans, not for the first time.

'It's all right, Mrs. Pillans, you sent her a note earlier.'

'I did? So I did. I'm so sorry, Miss Blair.'

'Not at all. You have a great deal to take in.'

'But my poor darling Gordon …' Tears ran again, as they had periodically all the time they had been in Isobel's chamber. The maid handed her a dry handkerchief, and removed the wet one. 'His face …'

Isobel swallowed. It was not something she much wanted to remember.

'What could have happened? Mr. Murray seemed to think someone had attacked him. Mr. Blair hinted at the same. And Lady Rocheid …'

'It did not seem to be an accident,' said Isobel briskly. 'That much is true.'

'A robbery, then? Where is his watch? Where is his fob? And was his pocketbook there? I don't believe so. He was robbed! So close to home, and he was robbed!'

'How were you expecting him to be travelling, Mrs. Pillans?' Isobel asked, trying to get her to focus on something straightforward. Anyway, surely she was not expecting her husband to arrive having walked past Letho House.

'He was to come by post,' Mrs. Pillans said, frowning as if it took an act of concentration. 'We have but the one carriage, and my mother and I have it at Collessie.'

Then Charles could make enquiries at the inn, Isobel thought. If Gordon Pillans had arrived by post, the innkeeper would not have missed him.

'But why was he here?' asked Mrs. Pillans. 'Why was he at Letho House?' She turned, and fixed Isobel with a look of desperation. 'What did Lady Rocheid mean? What has Mr. Murray done to these men?'

Chapter Sixteen

In the end, the sheriff's man arrived before the doctor, though he had ridden his mule from Cupar. His long legs almost trailed on the ground, and as he had always looked cadaverous, the few years since Murray had last seen him had made little difference to his appearance. Murray went out to the front step, now in clean breeches, and greeted him.

'Good day to you, Macduff. I hope you are well?'

'Aye, well enough, Mr. Murray,' said the man, lurching off the mule and handing the reins to a stable lad. He watched the boy lead the beast away, with a slightly wistful look about him. Then he bowed to Murray. 'Good day to you, sir. I hear you've a body for me.'

'Follow me,' said Murray, and led Macduff into the dining room. He had to remind himself to walk slowly: Macduff's limp had grown no better, either.

The man paused at the dining room door, in any case, and surveyed the body – and Blair, who struggled to his foot to greet him. Macduff looked down at the space where Blair's lower leg used to be, and nodded, as if he had always expected others to be reduced to his own level. But he did not comment, bowing again in greeting.

'So where was the fellow found, sirs? Who is he?'

'He has been identified by his ring,' said Blair eagerly, 'as Gordon Pillans.'

'The man who's taken Collessie for the summer?' Macduff wrinkled his lip slightly, presumably a response to the thought of Collessie rather than Mr. Pillans.

'That's the one. He was late joining his wife and mother-in-law here: I think he has been expected for several days. Then he turned up.'

'At Letho House?'

'I'll show you the place when you're ready,' said Murray. 'It's a place that was intended long ago as an icehouse, but it was never finished. There's some work going on there now, and he was found inside.'

'Who found him, sir?' Macduff liked to have the whole situation laid out before him before he did anything else.

'There were several of us there,' said Murray, 'including, at a little distance, his widow. The two engineers were there, and so was I.'

'I see. When?'

'About ten o'clock this morning. The engineers had been working elsewhere up to that point, but – oh, that's why we were there. Mrs. Pillans had asked to take a look at the place, as we had mentioned it at dinner yesterday.' Was that significant? Did it prove Mrs. Pillans' innocence, or did it somehow implicate her?

'I see. Now, you said, sir, that he was identified by his ring … I'm guessing there's a reason it wasna by his face?'

'There is,' said Murray, his tone warning. Macduff limped forward, round the dining table, and carefully folded back the cloth that covered Mr. Pillans' head. He considered what lay underneath for a long moment, then laid the cloth gently back down.

'I see what you mean,' he said. 'Where is the widow now?'

'My housekeeper gave her some tea to help her sleep,' said Murray. Isobel had reported that Mrs. Pillans had gone without much resistance to rest for a while, and that when she had looked in soon afterwards the widow was sound asleep. 'She did not want to leave him here, but I thought you would find it more convenient to examine him here than at Collessie.'

'Oh, aye, sir,' said Macduff. 'I should think anything would be more convenient here than at Collessie.' He stepped back, and considered the body, shrouded in its sheet. 'Have you sent word to the physician?'

'Yes, we're expecting him soon.'

'I'll wait for him. Can you have me shown to the icehouse thing, then, sir?'

'I'll take you myself,' said Murray, trying to ignore Blair's wistful look.

They walked slowly round the house to the muddy scene of their drama. Thalland had put one of the estate workers to guard the entrance, but he had elected to guard it from a safe distance – the other side of the laneway – and scrambled to his feet from his seat on a boulder when Murray appeared.

'Any problems?' Murray asked him.

'No, sir, none, sir,' said the lad.

'This, then, is the unfinished icehouse,' said Murray. 'You'll remember my problems with the servants' wing – the spring that caused those also prevented the completion of this building in my grandfather's time, we believe, and is still making the lane very damp and muddy, as you see. This place has been sealed up for years, but we opened it, found it empty and in better condition than we had expected – if wet – and then we put a gate on it to stop children going in to play and injuring themselves.'

'And you'll have put a lock on it, no doubt, sir,' said Macduff.

Murray did not choose to mention that locks might not be a problem for Daniel's young son. A sheriff's man might discover that himself in due course.

'We did, an old padlock and chain. Two keys, one to Mr. Thalland, and one into the care of the engineers.'

'Who are these engineers, then, sir?' Always the full story first. Murray looked about, and up the hill, but there was no sign of them.

'They came recommended by a friend in Wigtownshire,' he said. 'They are Irishmen, from Dublin.'

'Oh, aye,' said Macduff sourly. 'Politically inclined gentlemen, are they?'

'I don't believe so,' said Murray.

'Well ... so the gate was locked, then.'

'Well, that's it, no, it was not. Robbins and I went out to check it for the night last night, and the lock was open. The gate was closed.' He took a breath: he might as well say all. 'The door of the servants' wing, that one there, was also unlocked.'

'And did either of you look inside the tunnel thing, sir?'

'I don't think so. We didn't when we first found the gate open, and then I took the only lantern we had to go and ask the engineers for their key. They had lost it. They found it later, but at the time I instructed them to go and fetch Thalland's key and lock up. I went back to where Robbins was – just here, at the gate – and told him we might as well go home.'

'Leaving the gate unsecured?'

'That's right, yes. Probably only for a minute or two. Robbins ... thought he heard something. Someone, nearby.'

'Did he indeed? Aye, well, sir, I'd better have a word with Mr. Robbins, too, then. And these engineers.'

They paused and studied the icehouse's entrance for a moment, then Macduff nodded at the gate.

'I see it's unlocked the now.'

'Yes, but the lad's been keeping an eye on it.'

Macduff looked back at the boy who had been guarding the gate, assessing him.

'Aye, well, I suppose. I'll take a look inside, then.'

Almost as tall as Murray, he had to stoop to enter the tunnel, and stay mostly in the centre of the arch. He went slowly, careful, no doubt, of his gammy leg amongst the rocks that were now scattered over the wet stone floor.

'And these were all on the body, sir? Like they'd fallen?'

'That was what we thought, yes.'

'But they didna fall from the roof.' It was a statement: Macduff was inspecting the roof with the air of an expert.

'You'll be pleased to know that the engineers had prepared a sketch of the roof yesterday, and it matches what the roof looks like now.'

'Indeed? That's awful handy.' He turned his gaze down from the ceiling to the floor, to where the blood still stained the wet stone.

'There'll have been a gey lot of blood, then, if that's it washed away,' he remarked.

'There was. I suppose that means he was killed here, anyway.'

Macduff nodded.

'I think you have the right of it there, sir, aye.' He tutted, as if he had expected something more imaginative from the killer.

'Ah, there it is! We didn't look closely earlier.' Murray

stooped to point, but not pick up, a round black hat which must have belonged to Pillans. Macduff, after a moment's examination of distances and angles, leaned down and plucked it from the corner. There was a clink as he lifted it.

'What's that?' he asked. He bent again. 'A metal flask – tin, I suppose. Empty.'

'May I?' Murray took it. 'It smells sweet. Could it have been poison? Or a sleeping draught?'

'We can ask an apothecary,' said Macduff. 'Unless it was what your engineers bring their tea in.'

'I've never seen it before. And a draught would explain why he lay down so peaceably to be hit, if that's what happened.'

'So,' said Macduff, looking about him, 'not a rock fall, but made to look like a rock fall. Any idea why he might have come here?'

'I know very little about him, and had never met him. I have no idea why he might have come here. If he had, for some reason, needed to seek help in the middle of the night, for example, surely he would have gone to the front door, or to Thalland or Robbins? Or to the door in the servants' wing. He was not a tramp, to expect to have to find his own shelter. And most tramps I've met would rather sleep in a hedge than on that wet floor, I should have thought.' In fact he had not met many tramps - the parish system deterred begging – but Blair had talked of the ones he had met and chatted with. Macduff, who probably knew every tramp in the county, seemed to agree.

'It's clean, but I doubt it would be comfortable,' he said. 'I don't see any sign of his watch. Nor a pocketbook, nor fob. It's a wonder he was still wearing the ring.'

'I hadn't thought of that,' said Murray. 'Perhaps because he was wearing gloves?'

'Aye, maybe so ...'

'Unless they wanted to rob him, but wanted to make sure he could be identified.'

'Did you have any doubt it could be him?' asked Macduff, interested. Murray told him about Lady Rocheid, without going into the lady's emotional state. Just as he was finishing, he heard wheels on the drive.

'Oh, heavens, that's probably her back!' he said, then

paused, listening. 'No, I think that's something lighter than her carriage. And only one horse. It will be Dr. Feilden.'

Macduff seemed to have finished in the icehouse. He followed Murray back to the front of the house, where indeed Dr. Feilden was just descending from the seat of his gig. The same stable lad took the reins from him, rubbed the horse's nose and led the vehicle away.

'Good day to you,' said the physician, and bowed. 'And to you, Macduff. Not a straightforward matter, then?'

Murray led the way once again into the house and the dining room. Daniel, he noted, had returned, but Blair was still on his chair, waiting for the next visitor. He struggled to his feet and bowed when he saw Dr. Feilden.

'Now we shall know all there is to know!' he said excitedly. 'All the experts will have spoken.'

'Who is the individual?' Dr. Feilden asked, laying down his bag and removing his hat.

'Daniel, please fetch some hot water and a towel,' Murray said. 'It appears to be Gordon Pillans, who has taken Collessie for the summer.' And he explained once again the circumstances. Listening, Dr. Feilden removed the sheet from the body, and handed it to Macduff. Murray's description of the rocks must have prepared him for the shape of Pillans' head, for he faced it with some equanimity, considering. It was the first point of interest in his close examination.

'It seems to me that he was struck twice, and very hard,' he said, straightening his back. 'The rest of the skull ...' he felt delicately around, under the remains of the corpse's dark hair, 'is flattened, but that would correspond with heavy blows landing on the face as the man lay on a hard surface. Very heavy blows,' he added with emphasis. 'But not – if I may speculate – the blows of a furious man. Two, or perhaps three, controlled and heavy blows. Unless the body tells me differently, of course.'

Daniel returned with the water and towels, and set them on the sideboard, trying hard not to look at the body. But Dr. Feilden called him over.

'Here, help me to unfasten his clothing, would you?'

Daniel looked as if he was about to be sick. Macduff glanced at him, and used the sheet to cover Pillans' terrible face again.

Daniel shot him a grateful glance, and stepped forward, helping the doctor to strip all the clothes, piece by piece, from the body. It was not easy work, and it was a while before at last the poor man lay revealed – with not an injury to be seen from his neck down.

Chapter Seventeen

'So he did not even fall down?' said Murray after a moment.

'It seems not,' said Dr. Feilden. It had not been pleasant turning the body, and in the end they had used Robbins' makeshift pillow to form a kind of handle for supporting the head. But back and front, there was not a mark on the man.

'Can we put his clothes back on?' muttered Daniel, clearly not happy about the whole business.

'It will be harder than taking them off,' Dr. Feilden warned him. 'But you're right: we cannot return him to his widow like this, if possible. Where is she? At Collessie? Does she know?'

'She was here when he was found,' said Murray. 'She's asleep upstairs, I believe: our housekeeper gave her a draught.'

'Your housekeeper?'

'On trial,' said Murray. 'She has only been here ... a day and a night.' It felt like a week.

'And did I hear that Mr. and Mrs. Wedderburn have arrived on a visit? They are always so welcome in Letho.'

Murray had almost forgotten that Deborah and her husband were in the house. He had not forgotten, though, that Dr. Feilden did like to gossip.

'Yes, they are here,' he agreed. He hoped they had found ways to amuse themselves this morning. 'This is an unfortunate business to happen during their visit – though more unfortunate for poor Mrs. Pillans.'

'Should I see her, do you think?' asked Dr. Feilden. 'I don't believe we have met.'

'They have not been here very long. I'm not even sure that Mr. Pillans visited to view the house before he took it.' The conversation was desultory now, designed to cover the awkwardness of trying to reclothe the corpse.

'If he had he'd no have taken it,' Macduff put in.

'How do you think he finished on the floor of the tunnel, Dr. Feilden, if he didn't fall?' asked Blair.

'He lay down, perhaps?' suggested the physician. 'Or was lowered down?'

'Not sure why he would lie down on that wet floor,' said Macduff. 'Unless he was drunk.'

'Could he have been drugged, perhaps? Or could he have been drunk? We found this flask,' Murray added, withdrawing the tin flask from his pocket. Blair eyed it eagerly.

Dr. Feilden took it, sniffed it, and bit his lips in thought. He handed it back.

'It's hard to tell without a face to look at. Eyes, and so on. Breath to smell. I could open him up,' he went on, disregarding a yelp from Daniel, 'but I'd like to talk to Mrs. Pillans about that. There's no smell of alcohol from him, though, that I can detect.'

Murray agreed.

'Yet the idea of someone sober lying down on his back on a wet floor, and meekly allowing himself to be struck on the face … that is strange.'

'It was dark, though,' said Blair.

'Aye, but then it was a very accurate hit,' said Macduff. 'Whoever struck him must have been able to see him a bit, so he could probably see them.'

'Could he have been ill?' asked Murray. 'Too ill to be fussy about where he lay down?'

'Again, difficult to tell,' said Dr. Feilden. 'If you could find out how he got here, then you might find someone who saw him, saw what he was doing or eating or drinking.'

'Aye, I'll be trying that,' said Macduff sourly, quite able to do his own job without instruction from Dr. Feilden.

'There – that's very nearly respectable,' said Dr. Feilden. 'Just do up his waistcoat buttons there, Daniel.' He went to the sideboard and commenced a thorough wash of his hands. Macduff was just rearranging the sheet over the whole body when the door opened and Robbins entered, approaching Murray.

'Sir, a person has arrived, looking for Mrs. Pillans.'

'For Mrs. Pillans? What kind of person?'

'A German musician, sir. He is in the kitchen.'

'Oh, the tutor! I'm not sure he will be required now, but I'll need to ask Mrs. Pillans. I wonder if she is awake?'

'What kind of a man is he, Robbins?' Blair asked eagerly.

Robbins glanced at Dr. Feilden and Macduff.

'Polite enough, sir, but growing impatient. He has been at the inn since yesterday and not had word from Collessie.'

'No,' said Murray, 'Isobel and I were to go with Mrs. Pillans to meet him this morning, but we went out to view the icehouse first and – well,' he finished, gesturing to the table.

'He was to go to Collessie? And he was in the neighbourhood last night?' asked Macduff. 'Maybe I'd better go and have a word with him first.'

Murray glanced at the clock on the mantelpiece. It was very nearly three o'clock: half the day gone, and the servants would be wanting to know where dinner was to be served. For himself, looking at the dining table, he did not feel very hungry.

'I'll find out what state Mrs. Pillans is in: if she is up she will be wanting to take her husband home. Macduff, do you need to talk to her?'

'Aye, I do.'

'And I'd better tell her that her musical tutor has arrived. Why don't you go and talk to him – and Robbins, I believe Macduff would like a word with you, too.'

'Of course, sir.'

'Then take Macduff along to some suitable place in the servants' wing and have the tutor brought along to him. Can you send the housekeeper – what's her name again?'

'Mrs. Warner, sir.'

'Can you send her into the library? I should meet her anyway, but I'll need her to find out about Mrs. Pillans, unless Miss Blair appears. And the brandy, please.'

'Very good, sir,' said Robbins, and eased Macduff out of the room with him towards the kitchens.

'Dr. Feilden, thank you as always. Will you join us in the library for a glass of brandy?'

'Delighted, sir,' said the physician.

Blair waved away the option of the wheeled chair – it was awkward in the library anyway – and used his crutches to swing slowly across the hall, chattering to Dr. Feilden about his accident and his injuries as he went. Dr. Feilden, who had been too polite to ask, took it all in with interest. Murray ensured that Daniel knew he was to stay with the body, and followed them.

Robbins showed Macduff into his own pantry, then popped his head into the kitchen. 'Have you seen Mrs. Warner, Mrs. Mack?' he asked.

'Not for an hour or so,' said the cook. 'She's gone off with Jennet to look at – I don't know, something that housekeepers and maids look at.'

Robbins assessed the level of irritation in Mrs. Mack's tone, and decided she had not yet taken against the temporary housekeeper. It was just her usual mood as she began to prepare dinner for the household. William did not look any more hunted than usual.

'William, take brandy to the library, would you, for three, and then go and find Mrs. Warner, pay my respects and ask her to go to the library to meet the master.'

'Aye, sir,' said William, happy enough to be off and doing something. Robbins looked about the kitchen again. Seated well out of the way, by the scullery door, was the man who had arrived from the inn, Markus Rieder. What was it about Letho House at the moment? All waifs and strays seemed to be attracted to it like moths to a flame – though he hesitated to call the Wedderburns waifs and strays, this man certainly had a subdued look to him. But that might just have been the effect of spending an hour or so in a kitchen with Mrs. Mack and Iffy.

'Mr. Rieder, will you step this way, please?' he said. 'The sheriff's man would like a word with you.'

'The sheriff's man?' Rieder was on his feet in a flash. 'What? Why?'

'It's all right,' said Robbins, 'it's just about something that happened here last night. I think he'll be asking everyone what they might have seen or heard, but he wants to talk to you first in case Mrs. Pillans wants you to go back with her to Collessie soon.'

'I … I see,' said Rieder, though he looked a little quivery. 'Where is he?'

'He's in my pantry,' said Robbins. 'It's a more private place for an interview.'

Rieder considered, fingers twitching.

'May I bring my violin?' he asked.

Robbins was visited briefly by an image of Rieder playing his fiddle for Macduff and himself in his tiny pantry, amongst the accounts and the polishes.

'Of course,' he said.

He led the way back out of the kitchen and up the passage. But as they passed the outer door, he felt a shove in the small of his back and lurched forward. Behind him, the door was flung open, and Rieder, with a yelp, vanished through it.

'Oh, for goodness' sake,' muttered Robbins. He steadied himself and made for the door, but Rieder was a young man and evidently fit. He had already disappeared from view.

'Which way did he go?' he called out to Edward Kelly, just coming down from the hill above the icehouse.'

'Who?' asked Kelly.

'Never mind. Thank you, sir,' said Robbins, and trod wearily back along the passage to his pantry to explain himself to Macduff.

'Now that's no a good sign,' observed the sheriff's man, hitching one hip on to Robbins' desk. Robbins hoped he would not disturb any of the papers on it. 'On the other hand, it's no always a bad sign, either. The man might just have a guilty conscience.'

'It's true,' said Robbins. 'Perhaps he has had some trouble in the country, being a foreigner.'

'It would not be the first time for such a thing,' said Macduff.

'I suppose not.' Robbins sat in his desk chair, feeling he was entitled to. Then as a kind of apology, he offered Macduff a glass of claret, pouring it from an old decanter on a shelf. Macduff sipped, and smacked his lips.

'So, Mr. Robbins,' he said, not unfriendly, 'what happened last night?'

'The master wanted to make sure the gate on the icehouse was locked. The only keys are with Mr. Thalland and the engineers,' said Robbins. 'Mr. Murray and I came to this door and found it unlocked.'

'Had you locked it earlier?'

'I had not carried out my final checks for the night, of course,' said Robbins, 'but by that time of night – it was around eleven – I should have expected it to be locked. The household understands that outside doors are generally locked after dark, so anyone coming in that way, or passing the door after dark, should have turned the key.'

'Aye, can't be too careful,' Macduff agreed. Robbins nodded. 'Was there any sign of mischief?'

'The master thought he heard running footsteps. Some distance away, he said.'

'But you didn't?'

'I was more concerned about who had left the door unlocked.' He did not want to mention Daniel and the child, not if he did not have to. 'Anyway, we took a lantern and went to look at the gate. It was unlocked, too.'

'The padlock was unlocked.'

'That's right. The chain was hanging there, with the padlock at its end, obviously open,' said Robbins precisely.

'You had a lantern. Did you go into the icehouse, or use the lantern to look inside?'

'I've been trying to think,' Robbins admitted. 'We didn't deliberately look in, and we definitely didn't go in.' In his mind's eye, he did look in, and saw all manner of dark shapes awaiting them. But he was almost sure they had not, in fact, looked in at all. 'I would have thought that the engineers would have looked in, before they locked it again. Just in case they were locking anyone inside.'

'Aye, you'd hope so, wouldn't you? But I gather they're a couple of young men, and maybe not that thoughtful. Anyway, you found the padlock open.' He waved a hand, encouraging Robbins to continue.

'Mr. Murray said he would go and get the key from the engineers. He was going to leave the lantern with me, but then he took it – the path is very rough there just now with the mud.'

'Aye.'

'So I stayed by the gate in the dark.'

'Could you see anything?'

'Not really, no.'

'But you heard something?'

Robbins frowned.

'I think I did. Or not heard, exactly. I thought there was someone nearby, but how I thought that I am not sure.'

'Nothing beyond that? Footsteps? Breathing?'

Robbins wished he would not make suggestions. It only confused his memories. Had he maybe heard a footstep? Sensed someone trying not to breathe too heavily? He was not sure. He shook his head.

'I should not want to say anything definite.'

Macduff sighed.

'Aye, well. So Mr. Murray hears running footsteps, and you think there's someone close by. Someone who knows the place well enough to go running about in the dark, then, would you say?'

'You mean someone in the household? Someone who works in the gardens, or on the estate?'

'Aye, well, or a visitor who knows his way about. I'm thinking,' he said carefully, 'of the way you just told me yon man Rieder vanished just now. How long's he been around, and how well does he know the place, then? And where has he come from?'

Chapter Eighteen

Robbins took Macduff to the library to join the gentlemen, and as he turned away he almost bumped into Mrs. Warner.

'Is that the library?' she whispered to him.

'That's right, yes. There's a few of them in there – they want to ask about Mrs. Pillans.' It was always as well to be prepared. Mrs. Warner nodded acknowledgement. Though she straightened her lace shawl, she looked quietly self-assured as she approached the library door. If she was conscious of the fact that Robbins was lingering, perhaps to see how she managed, she did not show it.

Murray regarded her with interest as she stood a pace or two into the room.

'I believe you wished to speak to me, Mr. Murray. I am Alice Warner.'

Steady, was his first thought: she looked as if little would shake her. Just as well, at present. A heavy jaw, and a long, straight nose like a Greek sculpture, but not an unattractive woman.

'Good day to you, Mrs. Warner,' he said. 'I hope we shall have the opportunity of a proper talk at some point, though you will no doubt have all the directions you desire from Mr. Robbins. You have arrived at a difficult time, I'm afraid.'

'I hope I may be of assistance, sir.'

'I'm sure you will. For the moment, can you tell me, please, how things stand with Mrs. Pillans? I understand you gave her a draught and she was asleep.'

'I think she is likely to be awake now or very shortly, sir. It was not a strong draught: it was more to calm her than anything.'

'I should be interested some time to hear the details of your concoction,' said Dr. Feilden, in a friendly tone. 'I practise physic in the parish.'

'Sir,' she said, with a small curtsey. Murray could not tell if she were flattered or alarmed.

'The examination of Mr. Pillans' body is complete, and I think Mrs. Pillans will want to make arrangements to take him home. There is also the question of her proposed musical tutor, who is, I believe, in the kitchen. And before that, Macduff here, who is the sheriff's man, would like to speak with her about her husband.'

'In here, sir?' Mrs. Warner asked, taking in all four men – and no doubt the mildly eccentric appearance of Alester Blair.

'That was what I had intended, yes. Why?'

'I do not know Mrs. Pillans, sir, but if you will forgive me I should think that she would be happier in a – a less intimate surrounding.'

Murray took his turn to look around. The library was a little crowded, and no doubt Mrs. Pillans would want a chaperone, too.

'You are quite right, Mrs. Warner. Let us see Mrs. Pillans in the drawing room upstairs. We'll need Smith and one of the men to help Mr. Blair.'

The timings worked beautifully: at the moment that Blair settled and arranged himself on his favourite armchair in the drawing room, and Macduff and Murray had found themselves appropriate perches – Dr. Feilden had excused himself for the approach of his own dinner – Isobel swung round the drawing room door and ushered Mrs. Pillans into the room, and Macduff and Murray stood once more. Her borrowed skirts swept the floor a little too generously, and her bodice seemed a touch strained, but otherwise she was spruce and neat again. Her eyes, though, were red, and she clutched a handkerchief still.

'There, now, Mrs. Pillans. You know Mr. Murray and Mr. Blair. And this is Mr. Macduff, from the sheriff's office.'

'I'm not ...' said Mrs. Pillans, alarmed to be the focus of so much attention. Murray came forward, and showed her to a sopha. Isobel sat beside her, and took her hand.

'Remember what you said, Mrs. Pillans. If Mr. Pillans was unfortunate enough to meet with deliberate violence, you want to find out who did it, don't you?'

'Of course I do,' said Mrs. Pillans breathily.

'And Mr. Macduff is here to help. And my father and Mr. Murray, of course.'

Murray noted that Mrs. Pillans' gaze lingered on him a little longer than was necessary, her look more suspicious than anything. Surely she had not believed Lady Rocheid's wild accusations? If that was so, he would be better not contributing much to any questions she was asked, just in case. He hoped that Macduff and Blair between them would find out all that was needed.

Macduff, indeed, had assessed his interviewee and now took a lower seat than the one he had first selected, bringing his eye level down below hers.

'Permit me to say that I am very sorry for your loss, madam,' he said, somehow making his voice smoother than usual. 'I know it is very early to be thinking about such things, but this is the best time, believe me. When memories are fresh. Other thoughts will come back later and we may speak again, but for now, as Miss Blair says, we need to discover the what and the how and the why and the who, so fast as we can, if we can.'

'I … I see,' she said. A sob caught her for a moment, and then she appeared to try to take control of herself, with a deep breath, and a quick touch to her hair, and a final wipe of her nose. She sat up, and took another breath. 'Then how can I help, sir?'

'First of all, tell me when you last saw Mr. Pillans?'

'In Edinburgh, four weeks ago. He saw us off in our carriage, outside our house, and we came up here to stay at Collessie.'

'He took Collessie for the summer, did he not?'

'He did. A friend had mentioned it, some time ago, as being available for – for a reasonable price,' she finished, dropping her gaze to her own knees. Well, Murray thought, at least they were not being robbed over the house.

'Had he been up here himself?'

'No, I don't believe so. To Fife, I suppose, over the years he must have been, but not particularly to Collessie nor to Letho, no.'

'Does his friend – the one who mentioned Collessie – does he live nearby? Did your husband have any acquaintances nearby?'

'Not at all, no. We came here to see new places and make new acquaintances. It has been a true pleasure – until now.'

'Aye, well,' said Macduff. 'What is your husband's business?'

'He owns a warehouse.' She cleared her throat, and continued with a hint of pride, 'The Oriental Warehouse, on the South Bridge, in Edinburgh.'

'Cloth, and such?' Macduff queried.

'Mostly cloth, yes. Very beautiful cloth, too.'

'Oh, yes!' said Blair, growing a little excited. 'I know the Oriental Warehouse well. I have acquired some remarkable cloth there!'

Murray suppressed a smile. Blair's tastes did tend towards the exotic in his clothes and décor. But he himself knew the shop, too: it was quite a concern. Had the man in the icehouse really owned all that?

'Friends of his from his youth went to India and indulged in the country trade,' said Mrs. Pillans, 'and he stayed at home and sold what they sent him. That was the start of it, and he built all that up in – oh, ten years, perhaps.' Murray could see that now she had started, she was taking pleasure in telling them of her husband's achievements, and in truth, he had done well for a relatively young man. He glanced at Isobel. Why was she looking at him strangely?

'Had you heard anything from him since you saw him? Were you expecting him to join you here, madam?'

'I had had two – no, three letters. We write a good deal to each other when we are apart.' She blushed a little, and Macduff must have noticed it.

'Have you been married long?'

'A year and a half, sir.' Her voice faded. A year and a half would be all. Macduff paused a moment, respectful.

'Mrs. Pillans, were you expecting him to arrive?'

'Yes.'

'When?'

'I wasn't sure. He had written – oh, a day or two ago, to say he would probably be there before the letter. But he was not. I assumed he had been detained by his business. There's always something, in business.'

'Would he have come post?' asked Blair, jiggling in his chair. 'I wonder if his luggage is at the inn?'

Mrs. Pillans stared at him as if he had imparted strange and wonderful knowledge.

'His luggage? But of course – he must have had luggage!'

'And someone would have seen him,' Blair said. 'Someone on the coach, perhaps.'

And someone in the village, too, no doubt, thought Murray. The post coach came through in the early afternoon. Where had Pillans been between then and arriving at the icehouse?

'Someone like Rieder,' murmured Macduff.

'Like – what did you say?' asked Mrs. Pillans.

'That man Rieder,' said Macduff.

'The music tutor?' Murray asked. 'Oh, of course – he arrived yesterday, did he not? He would have been on the same coach. But we can ask him. Apparently, Mrs. Pillans, he arrived here earlier, when no one turned up to meet him.'

'Here?' This time, Mrs. Pillans turned very pink. 'What was he doing here?'

'Whatever it was, he has gone,' said Macduff sourly.

'Already? Has he gone on to Collessie?' asked Murray. 'Did you speak to him?'

'No,' said Macduff, 'I'm sorry to say my bad leg prevents me interviewing men moving at speed.'

'Oh!' said Blair. 'Did he abscond?'

'At a good pace, according to your man Robbins,' said Macduff. 'He could be settled at Collessie by now, for all I know. I'll have to ask about for him, though. For indeed, they could both have been in the same coach.' He sighed, and rose to his feet. 'Mrs. Pillans, I'll let you be for now.'

'Arrangements have been made to take you and Mr. Pillans back to Collessie,' said Murray, feeling it safe to contribute again. 'Would you like any of us to go with you?'

'My mother is there and expecting me,' said Mrs. Pillans, gathering herself up for the next challenge. 'I sent her a note earlier. I suppose I'll need to talk to the minister, and – and …' Her voice faded again, and Isobel, now standing beside her, squeezed her arm and helped her to her feet.

'There will be a great deal to think about,' she said, 'but you have the consolation of your mother there, and if there is anything I can help with please send at once. I'm sure the Helliwells, too, will help all they can.' Isobel knew the village well: the minister and his wife were both perfect, in their different ways, for this situation.

'I'll add my own offer to that,' said Murray, hoping she would trust him. 'And if Mr. Rieder appears –'

'If Mr. Rieder appears, I want to talk to him,' said Macduff sternly. 'I'll go down to the inn now, see what yon innkeeper knows, and see if I can get myself a room. It looks as if I might have to stay for a few days.'

Macduff was back on his mule and off down the drive to make for the village long before Isobel and Murray, and Blair in the doorway, had respectfully attended the departure of Mrs. Pillans, seated by the coachman in a gig. In front of her went a cart with the sides up, taking a gentle pace so as not to disturb, any more than necessary, the body of Mr. Pillans wrapped in sheets and covered with a blanket. They watched the entourage disappear on to the road, and Isobel turned back to the house. Once within hearing of her father as well as Murray, she said,

'Well! The Oriental Warehouse!'

'Yes,' said Murray, coming up behind her. In the hallway, they went to sit by the fire again, dogs joining them. 'Quite a concern, for a youngish man.'

'Have you not been reading your Edinburgh papers, Charles?' she asked in surprise.

'My – no, the last one vanished before I read it. Why? What should I know about the Oriental Warehouse?' He looked from one to the other of them. Neither father nor daughter missed an inch of the Edinburgh papers.

'There is beginning to be an outcry,' said Isobel, 'concerning that very place.'

'Go on.'

'An outcry about the number of girls who, having worked there, have now disappeared. If Mr. Pillans was detained longer than he had intended in Edinburgh, it is small wonder.'

Chapter Nineteen

Robbins, summoned, had brought the *Edinburgh Courant* with apologies.

'I had thought it finished with, sir.'

'Will all be ready for dinner?' Murray asked. Here in the hall, they could hear noises from the dining room as the place was tidied and cleaned.

'I believe so, sir.'

'Thank you. Oh, good day to you!'

He got to his feet as Mr. and Mrs. Wedderburn came down the stairs.

'Good day, Mr. Murray!' said Deborah Wedderburn. 'I hope we are not intruding? The maid came to tell me of the sad occurrence.'

'Mrs. Pillans has just taken the body back to Collessie,' said Murray, grateful for the Wedderburns' discretion through the day.

'Poor woman,' said Deborah.

'If you'll excuse me,' said Mr. Wedderburn, 'I'd just like to pop to the stables and see how things are going with that axle, before dinner.'

He headed out by the front door, and Deborah took a seat beside Isobel.

'What happened? I was not sure whether the maid was prone to exaggeration. She said something about an icehouse? I did not even think that Mr. Pillans was in Fife.'

'It looks as if no one knew,' said Murray. 'The sheriff's man is off to the inn to discover whether or not he was seen there.'

'I should have liked to have gone with him,' said Blair sadly. 'And to find out about Mr. Rieder. Could he be the killer, do you think?'

'Then he was killed? The maid did say, but of course ...'

'Yes, I'm afraid it looks like that,' said Murray. 'It seems impossible for it to have been an accident.' He described briefly what had happened.

'And who, then, is Mr. Rieder?'

'A music tutor, who seems to have arrived about the same time and has now absconded.'

'Then it seems to me that he is very likely to be the killer,' said Deborah Wedderburn. 'Why else abscond? Was Mr. Pillans robbed?'

'His watch and pocketbook are missing, certainly.'

'Then that is it. All your sheriff's man has to do is find him, and the matter is concluded.'

Deborah was generally a sensible woman, but she was used to having her opinions unchallenged these days.

'It may be as simple as that, yes,' said Murray, 'but I should be glad to hear the tutor's side of the story first. If he can be found.'

'Mr. Pillans owned a warehouse in Edinburgh,' said Isobel. Mrs. Wedderburn looked at her, eyebrows raised.

'A successful one, I assume: the women seemed prosperous. All the more reason to rob him, I suppose.'

'Yes, indeed, a successful warehouse,' said Isobel, who was clearly enjoying imparting this particular bit of news. 'The Oriental Warehouse on South Bridge.'

'Well, then,' said Mrs. Wedderburn. 'That's prosperous enough – wait – is that not where those girls worked? The ones who have gone missing?'

'I had not heard of it,' said Murray, 'but here it is in the *Courant* – so it must be true! I should judge by the wax on this page that the servants have been eagerly perusing this, too. It says here that three girls have disappeared since the end of March.'

'Three,' repeated Blair, pursing his lips. 'It is possible that that is a coincidence, I suppose.'

'I don't know about shop girls,' said Mrs. Wedderburn, 'but there is a certain class of maid in a town that disappears very readily. Usually just when you're organising a ball or a rout, and need everyone to hand. Have you found a new housekeeper yet, Mr. Murray?'

'We have one on trial this week,' said Murray, not wishing to mention that the Wedderburns' arrival had been the reason for this. 'This does not give names for the missing girls, only very vague descriptions. A red-haired girl, a girl of striking appearance, a widow.'

'I found their names, if you would like to know,' said Blair innocently. 'The red-haired girl is Mary Johnston, the widow is Jean Soutar, and the other one – I cannot make any comment on her appearance – must be Maggie Daniels. They all live – or lived – around the area of the South Bridge, and all were of good reputation, I gather. There was no indication that they might have left of their own accord. All disappeared on their way home from work on a Friday night. One was seen talking with a handsome, dark-haired man – not, I might add, their employer – but this was not the case with the others, so far as I have been able to ascertain.'

'Then that does sound like a little more than a coincidence,' said Murray. 'Not one every week, surely? No: that does not work, unless there are other missing girls not yet noticed.'

Blair made a face.

'I think the Fridays were scattered about,' he said. 'But of course, now the shop workers are more careful, if they can be. I spoke with several of them.'

Of course he did, thought Murray. The lack of a leg would not stop him entirely.

'I see, too, that Mr. Pillans is named in this report, though there is little information about him. Only that he is the owner of the business.'

'I wonder if he habitually takes country houses for the summer,' said Isobel suddenly. 'Or did he want his wife and mother-in-law out of the way while this was drawing interest in the press?'

'He would want to protect them, would he not?' Mrs. Wedderburn said.

'And they are not long married. Eighteen months, she says.'

'Poor woman,' said Mrs. Wedderburn.

'Well,' said Murray, 'I should like to know why a man who did not announce his arrival in Letho should wander into my icehouse in the middle of the night and be killed. I know it is selfish of me, but I could wish he had gone elsewhere.'

'It is selfish of you, Charles,' said Isobel. 'Where better? Who else is going to discover what happened here, if you do not?'

'Macduff is perfectly competent,' Murray objected.

'No doubt, but is he driven by the same sense of obligation as you? If poor Mr. Pillans had died at Collessie you would have left it to Macduff, who would no doubt follow Mr. Rieder – or whatever clear suspect presents himself – and, failing him, give the case up. You will track down the murderer like a dog on a scent, ignoring all perils and indignities, until you have him in your clutches.' She grinned at him, teasing.

'I should just leave the whole matter alone, to prove you wrong,' said Murray. 'I shall leave it to Macduff.'

'Mr. Murray cannot leave such matters alone, can he?' said Deborah Wedderburn. 'Miss Blair is right, Mr. Murray. You cannot possibly leave it to Macduff, whoever he is. The poor man died on your property. You must at least give some thought as to why.'

Murray shook his head, smiling, almost determined to forget the whole thing had happened. Almost. He knew, that on every level, that would be impossible.

The dining room was fragrant and clean by the time they had all assembled to eat, the table polished, and everyone seemed keen to pretend it had never been otherwise. The windows were slightly open, and pastille burners adorned the mantelpiece on either side of the clock. An épergne in the centre of the table was thick with lilac – not usually a flower one would choose for the dinner table, but the scent was refreshing this evening. And then the food arrived, and all was well, even if Murray caught each of his guests, at some time during the meal, grow silent and a little thoughtful, remembering that only yesterday Mrs. Pillans had sat with them and looked forward to her husband's arrival.

At the inn, Macduff was wiping his thin lips on his handkerchief and gazing with some regret at his now empty plate. It was a shame, he thought, that his work did not take him more frequently to Letho. The inn's cook knew what to do with a pair of mutton chops and some herbs. Nearer the fire, Ninian Jack was seated behind a similarly empty plate, contemplating a jug of ale and occasionally shooting suspicious glances at the sheriff's man. Macduff nodded to him, expressionless.

Markus Rieder's bag was still here at the inn: that was the first thing he had ascertained on his arrival. He had not been back to claim it, nor sent word that it was to be delivered to Collessie. Or anywhere else. It had taken five minutes to go through it – two clean shirts, spare hose, a decent suit of dark green, and about a half-hundredweight of sheet music. Macduff, not a musical man himself, went through the pages one by one but there was nothing on them that stood out as peculiar. Anything valuable or personal was presumably in his pockets when he ran. Macduff wondered if he should send word to the neighbouring counties to keep an eye open for Rieder. He would need to get a description, as he had never seen the man himself. It was a shame, for he had a good eye for faces, and some skill at rendering them on to paper for the use of others. It was not so easy if he were, so to speak, working blind.

The innkeeper came in to remove the dishes – more often the job of the maid, but the innkeeper was not above a bit of curiosity about the visit of the sheriff's man.

'So yon man Rieder has one of your rooms, and a woman the other?'

'That's right. But if what you tell me about Rieder is right, you can have his room.'

'Aye well,' said Macduff, who was not above sleeping by the fire in the main room, if he had to. 'Can you tell me what he looked like?'

'Have you not seen him yourself?'

'I have not had the good fortune,' said Macduff ironically. 'Wait now till I get a bit of paper out. Have you ink handy?'

'A thin creature,' said the innkeeper, reaching for ink from the dresser. 'Brown-haired, and kind of nervy, ken? Like a cat that's been kicked once too often.'

'Once is once too often,' muttered Macduff, who was fond of cats.

'Aye, but ken a cat, even a kicked cat, still has that air about them that says they're better than you? That was the man.'

Macduff eyed the innkeeper for a moment. He was proving more insightful than Macduff had expected.

'Is the woman aught to do with him?'

'No,' said the innkeeper, 'not at all. There were two women – they were here to be interviewed up at Letho House. Ken they've no had a housekeeper there for a while.'

The men met each other's eyes, both knowing the circumstances.

'Where's the other one gone, then?'

'Oh, there was some kind of emergency at the house, and Mr. Robbins came down on Friday – yesterday – to ask if one of them would go on a trial for a week to help out. The one went, but the other was out or not answering at the time. And she's still here.'

'What was the emergency?' Macduff asked, curious. It could not have been the discovery of the body.

'Some unexpected guests, I heard. Split an axle on the road and came to stay while it's fixed. And, ken, the Blairs are there just now.'

'Oh, aye.' Macduff drained his cup of ale, and told himself he would not ask for another until he had finished his business for the day. 'Have you a few sheets of paper, too? I want to send out some letters.'

'Oh, aye,' said the innkeeper. 'You'll be in good time for the post tomorrow, then.'

Macduff sighed. Should he make the outlay and send messengers? How much did he think that Rieder was the killer?

He spent the next couple of hours reluctantly arranging messengers, then ordered supper. A man needed sustenance. The innkeeper was still attentive.

'Yon Rieder, then, he came by the post?'

'Aye, he did. Yesterday, and all.'

'Busy day. Did anyone else alight here?'

'No, just him.'

'Are you sure?' It was a silly question. The arrival of the post was the highlight of the innkeeper's day.

'Aye, I'm sure. It's not like you get twa dozen folks getting off at Letho.'

It would be a challenge to fit two dozen people on to the mail coach, though Macduff had seen it attempted.

'Who are you looking for this time?' asked the innkeeper, not willing to let it go without more gossip.

'A well-made man in his early thirties, dark haired, dressed in a suit of black clothes with a buff waistcoat. Probably a silver watch and chain.'

'Oh, do you mean Mr. Pillans?'

Macduff blinked.

'What do you know about Mr. Pillans?'

Mrs. Pillans and her mother ate a desultory supper at Collessie.

'I must go back to him,' said Mrs. Pillans, when they had pushed away their plates.

'You need to get some sleep. The servants will be there all night.'

'I slept this afternoon. I can't leave him, Ma.'

Mrs. Skead sighed, and stood to go and hug her daughter, giving her silent permission. Mrs. Pillans rose, and left the parlour, crossing Collessie's dark hallway. Her mother watched her go, thinking of following her.

Then Mrs. Pillans screamed.

Chapter Twenty

'Aye, he introduced himself,' said the innkeeper simply. 'The fellow that's taken Collessie, for whatever reason. I've seen Mrs. Pillans about the place with – it's her mother, is it not?'

'How did he arrive? How did he get here?'

'He came in a gig. He had only the one kist with him, and it was the kind of gig with a shelf on the back so it fitted well enough.'

'His own gig? Where is it?'

'No, some other fellow set him down here, stopped for a draught of ale and a slice of bread, and headed on up the road.'

Macduff's mind scrambled, trying to think what to ask next.

'What time was that, then?'

The innkeeper considered.

'Well, it was after the mail coach had left, aye. But not yet when I'd be thinking of serving dinner to the woman upstairs and yon Mr. Rieder.'

'But they were both here? Would they have seen him?'

'I suppose. The woman – Mrs. Gilmour – she keeps to her room most of the time, but there's nothing to say she might not have seen him out the window, or she maybe came down for something. I canna mind. Yon Mr. Rieder was about the place, taking up space, most of the time. He was looking out for someone from Collessie to pick him up.'

'Did Mr. Pillans arrive before or after Mr. Robbins came from Letho for Mrs. – the other woman?'

The innkeeper thought again, using his fingers to enumerate something or other he was counting in his head.

'It must have been before. Yon Rieder was still hanging about. When Mr. Robbins took Mrs. Warner away, I told him he could have that room.'

'Did Mr. Rieder go out again at all, then?'

The innkeeper shrugged.

'I saw him head off yesterday morning. But I wasna watching him closely. The less I saw of him the better, quite honestly. He has a talent for being just where you don't want him to be. If you're cleaning or such, ken.'

'Right …' Macduff took in all the information, hoping he had not missed anything. 'Now, what did Mr. Pillans say to you?'

'Well, not that much,' the innkeeper admitted. 'He said who he was, and asked for directions to walk to Collessie. Then he asked if he could leave his box here.'

'He was walking to Collessie?'

'That's right. He said he wanted to surprise his wife.'

Macduff thought for a moment.

'If he was walking to Collessie from here, he'd go through Letho land, would he not?'

'That was the way I would have sent him, aye. It's shortest. I mean, once you get on to Collessie land it's maybe better if you've gone by the main road, for the drive is the only bit of Collessie that isn't – well, you ken what it's like. But he had a grand pair of boots on him, and his clothes were not so fancy that he might be worried about them, and even when I told him what the two routes were like he seemed to be opting for the Letho one. Said something about picturesque,' he added, unimpressed.

'You said you would have sent him?'

'Did I?' The innkeeper looked puzzled, reviewing what he had said.

'You did, aye.'

'Oh, aye, aye, I ken what you mean. He asked about walking to Collessie, and then I minded someone had left him a note. The name, see, it wasna that familiar to me.'

'A note?'

'It was on the table here when I came out to see who had arrived. It had his name on it, see, that's how I kent it was for him.'

Macduff opened his mouth, closed it again and counted to ten.

'Did you see who left it?'

'Naw.'

'Did he say a'thing about it?'

'Naw. Only that he wanted to know where Letho House was. So that was the way I sent him, see? I mean, I would have, anyway, because it's shortest, aye?'

Macduff had a sense of going round in circles.

'Did you see a'thing about the note? Did he seem pleased? Angry?'

'He frowned. Whatever it was, it wasna something he was expecting, like. I'd say he wasna too pleased, no.' Then he paused, and said, 'So is he the fellow they found in the icehouse?'

Macduff, resigned to the speed of village gossip, nodded.

'That's a shame,' said the innkeeper. 'It's hard enough to find tenants for Collessie.'

'I told them that lock was useless,' Ninian Jack put in suddenly from the corner. Macduff looked at him.

'When did you tell them that?'

'Yesterday. They asked me to go and look at the place. I told them the lock would barely last the night.'

Macduff pondered. No one had mentioned that the lock had been broken or forced.

'What like of a man did he seem?' Macduff asked.

'Pleasant enough. Not a gentleman, of course, but not the kind to get all high and mighty to make up for that. Asked me nicely to keep his box, and gave the stable lad just the right amount for helping him with it.'

'I'll need a look at that box,' said Macduff. 'What about the fellow who set him down here? Did you think they were friends?'

'No,' said the innkeeper at once, 'I had the idea they barely knew each other. There was no great farewell when the driver went, just thanks and good day and good wishes.'

'And did you know the driver, yourself?'

'No, not at all. Nor the gig, either, nor the horse. Strangers, the lot of them.'

'Did you happen to hear where he was going?'

'I had the impression it might have been St. Andrews. Now, why do I think that?' He frowned, straining his memory for an answer, then shrugged. 'No, I'm not sure. Maybe he looked the academic kind.'

Macduff made a face.

'So he went off one way, and your Mr. Pillans headed off the other. Did you see him talk to anyone else?'

The innkeeper shook his head.

'I couldna say I was really watching,' he said. 'Better things to do.'

'Aye, well, I suppose,' said Macduff. 'Right, then. Let's take a look at that box.'

The box was newish, maybe a couple of years old, and quite smart, with brass fixings. It measured around three feet by two, and about a foot and a half deep. It was, of course, locked.

'Had he no the key on him?' asked the innkeeper reasonably.

'It was most likely in his pocketbook,' said Macduff. He felt that swearing was beneath his dignity as an officer of the sheriff, but that did not prevent him from thinking some dark thoughts at this point. 'He left nothing else? A cloak, or coat?' The body had not, apart from the gloves, been particularly well clad for the out-of-doors.

'There's nothing else here that I know of,' said the innkeeper. 'Nothing at all.'

Macduff tapped his fingers abruptly on the box. He wanted to take it with him, away to safety. But safety from what? After all, it was locked. And how on earth would he take it anywhere? His mule would take one look at the size of that box, and bolt.

'I could maybe get that open for you,' said Ninian Jack.

The knock on the library door came as a surprise, late on Saturday evening. Murray was alone in the room, catching up on the correspondence and weekly paperwork that he had missed in the morning. The tin flask they had found in the icehouse stood on his desk, a reminder to him to return it to Macduff in the morning. The door opened, and a woman in grey walked in. The temporary housekeeper – Mrs. Warren? No, Warner.

'Good evening, Mrs. Warner,' he said. 'What brings you here at this time of night?'

'I am sorry to disturb you, sir, but I wanted to say that I do not wish to stay.'

'Oh?' How long had she been here? A day? Two? 'I hope

there has not been a particular reason why the position does not suit you.'

'Well, yes, there is, sir. The other staff have been very welcoming, and the house is delightful – if you'll excuse me saying so.'

'Happy to,' said Murray, who was very fond of Letho.

'It's about the size of establishment that I'm used to, though of course there are positions that need filling. Mr. Robbins is well aware of that, and he has told me that you've been waiting for the appointment of a housekeeper for that.'

Murray nodded. So far, it all sounded quite satisfactory to him.

'The stillroom is a joy,' she added, clearly wanting to make all her positive points first. 'But today – today, Mr. Murray, is not something I should wish to repeat. That poor man – that – in the dining room. And the mud everywhere. That was not – not what I am used to.'

'I should think not,' said Murray. 'And while I can't promise anything, I should not like it repeated myself. The mud – well, I think we are usually more careful than we were today, but in the circumstances ...'

'I should say, sir, that I should like to give in my notice, but as I understand it this was a week's trial anyway to be terminated by either side at will. So if you will allow me to remain tonight, I shall leave in the morning.'

'Of course you will be paid for your time.'

'Thank you, sir.'

A thought occurred to Murray.

'Where do you intend to go?'

'Back to Edinburgh, in the first instance, sir. Then wherever the opportunity presents itself.'

'I fear you will not be able to leave so quickly. The sheriff's man has not yet questioned you, I believe.'

'The sheriff's man? What has he to do with me, sir?' Yet she did not look entirely surprised, being a sensible woman.

'Well, you were here, in the house, last night. He'll want to speak with everyone in that position, I should think.'

'But I can't stay!'

'You could stay at the inn,' Murray suggested, but then

thought perhaps she did not have the money for that. 'It's possible that there might be room at the manse, if I asked the Helliwells.'

'The manse? But I don't want to stay anywhere around here! Not after today.'

Her agitation seemed strange: surely in the course of her life so far she had seen accidents and injuries, and dead bodies, too. And mud.

'Mrs. Warner, you said you intended to stay tonight, anyway. Why not see how you feel in the morning, and between you and the sheriff's man something can be worked out.'

And Robbins would have to go down to the inn to see if the other candidate could be persuaded to come and serve as housekeeper for at least a few days. He hoped the other woman had not already left Letho.

'Perhaps you might even be persuaded to stay. This is usually a peaceful place – today was definitely an exception.'

Even as he spoke he was vaguely aware of voices – or one voice – shouting, somewhere not too far off.

'What's that?' demanded Mrs. Warner. 'What's that now?'

'A good question.' Murray rang the bell for Robbins, and headed for the entrance hall. The shouting was growing louder. Robbins appeared.

'What's that, sir?' he asked.

'I thought you might know.'

The entrance hall windows had not yet been shuttered. Robbins crossed to one and shielded his eyes to peer out into the darkness. Whoever was shouting was just outside, though the shouts were growing hoarse.

'*Geisten!*' Murray could just make out the word, if he was right. '*Hexen!*'

'It's nonsense! Some kind of mad man!' Mrs Warner had followed Murray into the hall, though she kept well back from the door.

'It's not nonsense,' said Murray, 'or not strictly so.'

'There's just the one fellow,' said Robbins.

'*Gespenster!*' The word came almost as a scream.

'It's German,' said Murray. 'I think we've found Markus Rieder. And he seems to have seen a ghost.'

Chapter Twenty-One

Rieder was exhausted. It was no great job for Murray and Robbins between them to seize him by an arm each – one hand still clutched his violin case – and draw him, with calming words, into the entrance hall. When they could see him clearly in the candlelight it was obvious that Mrs. Warner had more mud to worry about. It looked as if Rieder had crawled to the door from wherever he had been hiding, and perhaps occasionally rolled in a ditch. His face, under the mud, was flushed, his gaze panicky.

'This is Rieder, is it?' Murray asked. He had not met the man before. Robbins squinted at the man.

'I believe so,' he said.

At the sound of his name, the man jerked and nodded.

'Rieder, *ja!*' he said, breathless.

'Hm,' said Murray, and turned to German, translating for Robbins' benefit as he went along. 'What has happened to you? Where have you been?'

'Ghouls!' whispered Rieder. 'They took him away!'

'Where have you been?'

'The house – the house Collessie. Here they wanted to question me, and I went to Collessie where I was supposed to go but no one came to meet me. They were supposed to come to meet me yesterday morning at the inn, but they never came. So I came here, and then I went there. But no one came to the door there, and I hid and watched. I thought it must be some kind of trick, to bring me all this way and not want me after all.'

'Maybe a glass of brandy?' Murray suggested, finishing the

translation of that piece.

'Sir,' said Robbins, moving quickly. Murray glanced round. Mrs. Warner was still standing at a safe distance, watching, a little frown on her face. It was probably the mud.

'So where did you hide?' Murray asked. There were plenty of options round about Collessie.

'In the trees. I watched from the trees. And then I saw a woman come to the house, in a gig, and a cart with a man's body on it. A dead man!' He waved a shaking hand at Murray. Was this what had unnerved him? Seeing Mr. Pillans' body being brought back to Collessie? And he had presumably only seen the corpse shrouded in sheets, not the awful mess of the face. Murray was beginning to feel he had seen too many dead bodies, if this was the effect they had on Rieder and Mrs. Warner.

'That must have been a while ago,' he said, remembering that Mrs. Pillans had left before dinner. Robbins reappeared with a tray. Rieder took the glass of brandy gratefully.

'Yes, yes,' said Rieder, nodding ferociously, 'and I thought to myself, I cannot go in there now with my applications to play and to teach. And I realised then why they had not come for me in the morning. Clearly there had been a tragedy in the house. I should go back to the inn, and wait.'

'And did you?'

Rieder paused.

'I was hungry,' he said. 'I had thought I would be having my dinner at Collessie, but I had brought with me a small refreshment in case the journey was a longer one than I had thought. I had bread, and cheese.'

Murray waited.

'And whisky,' Rieder added.

'Neat?' Murray queried in surprise.

'Oh, yes! The Scottish whisky is very fine. I bought it … but perhaps I should not say where I bought it. I understand there are strict laws here on such things.'

'Well, we'll leave that bit,' said Murray with a smile. Rieder must be stronger than he looked if he could manage whisky neat. 'I suppose you fell asleep?'

'I was very comfortable in my little nest,' said Rieder, a hint of a smile on his own face. 'And the sun was not on me, but it was warm. And then I woke and it was dark, and I was cold, and I wondered if I could find my way back to the inn or not, and whether or not they would let me in at that late hour.'

'I should think not,' muttered Mrs. Warner, when Murray had translated. 'It's a respectable inn!'

'But then I saw lights. Half-hidden lights.'

'In the house?'

'No,' Rieder shook his head slowly. 'On a cart. That at least was not a ghost. I could hear the wheels on the gravel, the horse's hooves. That was real enough.' He nodded, reassuring himself. 'There were two with it. And they were admitted to the house, by the front door, when I was not. I waited to see – I thought perhaps when they left I could follow them, using the lights to guide me. But in a few moments they came back out, carrying something. Is there a word in your language, sir, for *leichenräuber*?'

'Body snatcher?' Murray suggested, cold shivers up his spine. 'Is that what you mean?'

'I am certain it was a body. The body the woman brought to the house. They loaded it on to the cart – someone else helped them, I suppose someone from the household – and when it was done one of the men from the cart seemed to hand something to the one from the house – I suppose he was paying him.'

'Bribing a servant at Collessie. Not entirely surprising, sir,' said Robbins at that.

Murray nodded.

'A bribe,' said Rieder in English. 'Yes, that is what I thought. But why? Is it body robbers?'

'I've never heard of them taking a body straight out of a house,' said Murray, 'and we are far here from any anatomists, I should have thought. But you said ghosts? Witches?'

'It was my rational mind that came up with body robbers,' said Rieder, 'but when I was there and watching it, all I could think of, there in the dark, was ghosts and witches. I ran,' he said simply. 'Ran, and fell, and got up, and ran again, until I saw your lights and came here. And if you say there are no body robbers in Letho ...'

'Very few witches, either, though,' said Robbins firmly.

'But then who would do such a thing?' asked Mrs. Warner, casting a suspicious look at Rieder. 'If it really happened.'

'Oh, it happened, madam!' said Rieder at once. 'Believe me,

it happened! I swear it.' He laid a muddy hand on his heart, and swallowed the rest of his brandy.

'I'm definitely leaving,' Murray heard Mrs. Warner mutter. Robbins glanced at her with a frown.

'We can talk about that later,' said Murray. 'In the mean time, I think some hot water and perhaps a bed in the servants' wing for this person. Is there room? With the Wedderburns' staff there?'

'Yes, sir, we have space,' said Robbins.

'Mr. Rieder, we'll investigate this in the morning – oh, it's Sunday. Nevertheless, we shall have to make enquiries. Are you content to stay here tonight?'

'I should be most grateful, sir,' said Rieder, with a sharp bow. The brandy seemed to have revived him a little, but he was still tired and filthy.

'Mrs. Warner, perhaps you would see to that?'

Not wholly enthusiastic, Mrs. Warner led Mr. Rieder away. Robbins tidied the brandy tray, then went to close the shutters for the night and lock the front door. Murray stood, trying to remember what he had been doing when all this had begun, and to consider what had to be done in the morning.

'I don't think there's any point in sending to Dures tonight,' he said.

'You think that's where the body has gone, sir?'

'It's the most likely, isn't it? I'm afraid Lady Rocheid might still believe that the body is that of Lord Rocheid.'

'Do you think there's a chance it is, sir?'

Murray shrugged.

'It's her word against Mrs. Pillans. But the ring matched Mrs. Pillans' description. Unless someone took the ring from Gordon Pillans and put it on Lord Rocheid's body ... but why? And who would do such a thing?' He shook his head. 'I shall go and see Mr. George before church tomorrow, and see if we can sort this out without further embarrassment.'

Mr. George must have seen Murray riding up the drive to Dures House, for he was standing in the doorway when Murray dismounted, a puzzled smile on his face.

'This is early to call,' he called, by way of greeting. 'I hope you do not bring bad news.'

'I am glad to see I have not roused you, anyway,' said Murray. He had been pondering half the night and all the way here over what exactly to say to Mr. George. I think your sister is not well – she seems to have stolen a dead body from Collessie, and may I take a look about your house and see if I can find it?

'No,' said Mr. George, as he ushered Murray into the house. 'Come into the parlour. My sister has got it into her head to go back to Edinburgh today, heedless of the Sabbath. I think she has finally tired of waiting for Rocheid, and intends to go and discover him for herself. Heaven protect her when she does – and him, I suppose.'

'How do you mean?' Murray asked, feeling he had permission. And it was perhaps a path to what he wanted to talk about.

'I have to tell you, Murray: my brother-in-law is an atrocious man. The way he treats my sister is appalling. The company he keeps in her absence is shameful. Drinking, gambling, women – say nothing, Murray. I know my reputation, and it is well deserved. But if once I took a wife,' and Murray was surprised to note a faint flush around Mr. George's ears, 'I should be entirely faithful to her.'

Since Murray saw no danger of Mr. George ever marrying, he was able to nod sincerely at this.

'When does she plan to leave?' he asked.

'As soon as may be. Of course, this requires a shocking amount of preparation, but it seems she has been up since the small hours packing. Her carriage should be ready in half an hour, she tells me. Then of course there is the cart with her baggage. All her baggage.' He rolled his eyes and grinned, expecting sympathy or at least amusement. But Murray's thoughts were on the cart.

'Tell me,' he said, 'where is the cart to be found?'

Mr. George's grin slid sideways into confusion.

'Why on earth would you want to see my sister's cart?'

'Please, forgive me. Humour me, if you will. If nothing is amiss, you may ... take your choice of the pups when my spaniel has her next litter.'

Now Mr. George frowned.

'That is a serious offer,' he said. 'Your spaniel Belle?'

'That's the one. I hope to breed her next season. You may have your choice.'

'Well ...' Mr. George was clearly tempted. 'I'd need to

know the sire, of course.'

'My cousin's dog – you know Balfour. He has a good eye.'

'He does. Shake?'

They shook hands solemnly on the bargain.

'Go on, then,' said Mr. George. 'The cart is in the stableyard, I daresay. You're a very strange man, Murray, and I shall have a very fine spaniel next year.'

They walked together round the house to the stableyard at the back. Mr. George kept a good stable, much admired in the county. Even the cart standing in the centre of the yard was clean, well made, and painted a dark blue not quite to match, but certainly to echo, Lady Rocheid's carriage. Several boxes and baskets sat around the cart, waiting to be packed on to it. Several others were already on board. As they approached, Murray could see that one of the lowest of these boxes was a long, narrow one, its edges showing signs of recent manufacture.

'There, you see?' said Mr. George, rubbing his hands together. 'Nothing amiss. What shall I name the pup?'

'I should be obliged if I could look in that box there,' said Murray, pointing to the long box.

'Really?' Mr. George looked a little awkward. 'What if it contains some – I don't know – feminine accoutrement that men are not supposed to see?'

'I cannot think what feminine accoutrement might be that shape,' said Murray. 'It will take only a moment, I'm sure. Set my mind at rest. Think of the spaniel.'

'Oh ... Oh, very well.' Mr. George waved over one of the stable men, and issued instructions. The man returned with a light crowbar and a hammer.

It took a minute or two for the luggage on top of the long box to be removed. Then the man slipped the sharp end of the crowbar under the box lid, neatly and efficiently, tapping and turning. And in a minute or two more, they were in a position to shift the lid. Murray held his breath, and gave the nod.

Chapter Twenty-Two

'Who is that?' was all Mr. George could manage, as he surveyed the contents of the long box. He reached out a hand to pull the wrappings down from the man's face. Murray stopped him.

'You won't know by his face,' he said. 'It has been destroyed.' Then it occurred to him that it would be wise to make sure that this was indeed the same body – not a problem he remembered ever having to deal with before. He gently drew down the shroud from the head end, and Mr. George gave a little gasp, covering his mouth with his hand. Certainly this seemed to be the same body.

'But who is it, then? And why is it in my sister's cart?'

'You can't make a guess? You don't recognise ... well, his hair, perhaps? His ears?' Murray knew he was sounding desperate.

'His ears? Good heavens.' Mr. George stared at the back of the man's head, so far as he could see it. 'I can't say I often recognise people by their hair or their ears, certainly not people whom I do not often see without a hat.'

'You don't think it might be Lord Rocheid?'

'Lord Rocheid? Now, wait, Murray – what are you saying?'

'It has been suggested this might be Lord Rocheid. Would you agree?'

'What are you doing?' The shriek came from the gate of the stableyard. They had been discovered.

Lady Rocheid sped towards them, furious, shawls flying.

'Leave that alone! That's my business! Mine!'

'There's a dead body in your baggage, sister. That is

generally a concern for more than one person. Who is he?'

'Isn't it obvious?' Lady Rocheid stretched out a hand to caress a fold of the shroud. 'It is my husband, of course. Whom this man has cruelly murdered!'

Mr. George looked uncertainly at Murray, then at his sister, then at the corpse.

'What makes you think that this is Rocheid, my dear?' he began gently.

'Why do you need to ask? A woman knows her own husband.'

'Yes, but you see … I don't believe this is Rocheid.' Lady Rocheid drew breath, but her brother put out a steadying hand at once. 'Look at his ears. Remember, Rocheid has such neat little ears. I have often noted it.' He glanced at Murray as Lady Rocheid leaned forward, reluctantly, to look at the one visible ear. 'This man's ears are really quite large, aren't they?'

'It is an illusion, caused by – by what has happened to his face.'

'No, it really is not, my dear. And his hair, look at that. Straight, and a little thin. Rocheid's hair is thick and curly, isn't it? You have often remarked on it, how fine it is. My dear, I fear you are mistaken. I don't know who this gentleman is – or was – but he is not Rocheid.'

Lady Rocheid bit her lip, so hard it was white. Murray held his breath. Then Lady Rocheid collapsed against the cart, and sobbed.

'Then where is he? Where is my husband?'

Mr. George, after some consideration, sent his butler back with the cart to Collessie, wanting to reunite Mrs. Pillans with her husband as soon as possible. He sent a letter along with it, written while Lady Rocheid wiped her eyes and drank tea, and Murray sat with them in the parlour, wondering what to say. Mr. George seemed equally at a loss. In the end, silence produced the best results.

'I don't know where he is,' said Lady Rocheid at last, in a low, desperate voice.

'He'll have had to go to his estate for some business, no doubt,' Mr. George tried. Defending his brother-in-law did not seem to come naturally to him. Lady Rocheid shuddered.

'Oh, perhaps so, perhaps so. But with whom?'

Francis George glanced at Murray.

'Do you suspect him of something, my dear?'

'Suspect him? I know. I know very well that there is hardly a girl in Edinburgh who is not in danger from him. Only his own wife is ignored.' Her frantic mood seemed to have diminished: her voice was cold now. 'He promised me he was not far behind me, coming here to Dures. I should have known that his promises are worth nothing.' Her fingers tangled with each other. 'I thought, if I could take the body, and take it down to Edinburgh, then I could say he had died in Letho and I had brought him back for burial. And here I could tell people he had died in Edinburgh, and come back a widow, and forget all about him.'

Which would have been awkward, Murray thought, when Lord Rocheid did finally turn up. He might not take kindly to being declared dead, particularly since, as rumour had it, it was Miss George's fortune that financed his colourful habits. Murray wondered how much Lady Rocheid had thought this through, or was it all part of her desperate hunt for him?

Lady Rocheid heaved a deep sigh, as if as she breathed out she could rid herself of all of this.

'What is it come to? When that poor man was found – I did, I did honestly for a moment think it was Rocheid. And then, can you believe it? I was jealous of that little woman. Jealous of her, because she had her husband there, with her, even if he was dead. How can I have come to this?'

'When did all this happen?' asked Mr. George, as he walked Murray to the door. 'I had not heard, for once.'

'Lady Rocheid arranged for the body to be brought here last night,' said Murray as tactfully as he could. 'We think that Mr. Pillans was killed late on Friday night or early on Saturday. He was found on Saturday morning. Were you about the village? Have you seen anyone – well, doing anything odd? Arousing your suspicions?'

'I was in Cupar on Friday,' said Mr. George, 'well away from suspicion!' He looked unusually pleased with himself. Murray wondered what girl had taken him there.

'Well, we'd all better keep our eyes open. The sheriff's man was looking for a German music tutor who had acted suspiciously, but he has turned up.'

'No other particular suspects?'

'Not that I know of, no.'

'Had you ever met him?'

'Not to my knowledge – you?'

'No, indeed. Poor Mrs. Pillans. Sweet little woman, I thought.'

His tone was kind but uninterested. Mrs. Pillans was not his style.

Nevertheless, as Murray rode away, it struck him that Lord Rocheid seemed a much more likely victim than Mr. Pillans. If Lady Rocheid's portrayal of him was accurate, who knew what enemies he might have made – gambling enemies, irate fathers, brothers, husbands, perhaps. Irate brothers - like Mr. George? Avenging the wrong done to his sister? Except that Mr. George had been in Cupar, doing whatever he was doing on Friday night. And he had indeed seemed shocked at the sight of the body. But then anyone might feel shocked at a body turning up in one's own stableyard, and perhaps all the more so if it were someone one had killed elsewhere. And if he had killed Mr. Pillans - or whoever – in the dark, the sight of the body in daylight could have been very disturbing, the sudden realisation of what one had done. Yet he had made a good argument for the body not being that of Lord Rocheid, and Lady Rocheid had, eventually, accepted that. Murray wished that on the brief occasion he had met Lord Rocheid, he had taken the trouble to notice the man's ears. He wondered if Rocheid had ever had his portrait painted – almost certainly. It might come to it that someone would have to go to wherever Lord Rocheid's estate was, and take a look.

But no – the body was that of Gordon Pillans. That was that. Any thought of Lord Rocheid was no more than a distraction – and concern for poor Lady Rocheid. She had longed for a husband for so many years. Her belated success must have a bitter taste now.

Not far off the same time of the morning, Robbins paid a call at the inn once again. The innkeeper blinked and stared at him for a moment before apparently recognising him.

'Is it yon sheriff's man you want to talk to?' he asked. 'Or are you rearranging my guests again?'

'The latter, I fear,' said Robbins. 'Is Mrs. Gilmour in?'

'I canna think where else she would be at this hour on a Sabbath morning,' said the innkeeper. 'She said she would be down for her breakfast about now. I can set it in the parlour – your sheriff's man has had his. Do you want to wait in there?'

'That would be very suitable,' said Robbins. He had no wish to discuss a possible trial period with Mrs. Gilmour when he knew that Mrs. Warner was probably not far behind him, heading back to the inn in a cart with her bags. He was disappointed in her, he had to admit: he had thought her a sensible woman. But some innate sense of fairness in him was pleased that the other candidate was now to have her chance, too. He hoped she would accept, and would not turn tail at the thought of bodies in icehouses.

He had only been in the parlour for a few minutes when the door opened, and Mrs. Gilmour stepped in. The innkeeper must have warned her of his presence, for she smiled and dropped a curtsey to his bow.

'You'll want to leave the door ajar,' he said, letting her choose her seat.

'Are you going to make a run for it?' she asked, the smile lingering. Not, he thought, a flirtatious smile. Not that he expected it to be.

'I've come to ask if you would be ready to take up the position at Letho House,' he said, coming to the point. 'You'll know that Mrs. Warner has already worked there for a couple of days.'

'Yes,' she said, 'and now you're down to the second choice, is that it?'

'Not at all,' he said, with stiff honesty. 'It would have been hard to choose between the two of you, but she was the first I saw when I came to ask one of you, and you were not answering your door.'

'Oh, yes, that's right.' She did not seem in the least put out. 'Can I ask, though, why Mrs. Warner has not stayed in post? She was supposed to do a week, was she not?'

The innkeeper must have been talking.

'I'll tell you the reason,' said Robbins, 'for I should not like you to come to the house under false pretences. If you have heard anything of the village gossip yesterday you'll know that a man was found dead in – in a kind of old icehouse behind the servants' wing. He probably died on Friday night. He did not belong to Letho, neither village nor house – he is the tenant of Collessie, one of the other two large houses in the parish.'

'I heard he had been murdered,' she said, solemn now.

'He had been, yes.'

'Is anyone in the household suspected?'

'You can ask the sheriff's man – he is staying here for now, I believe – but I don't think he suspects anyone in the household.'

'I see,' said Mrs. Gilmour. 'Do you mind if I get on with my breakfast while we talk?'

Robbins went to the door to summon the maid with tea and bread and eggs. Mrs. Gilmour tucked in. She had a healthy appetite.

'Has anyone else died recently?' she asked, when her plate was partly cleared. 'I mean, is this part of something larger?'

'No, not that I've heard of,' said Robbins. 'Again, you can ask the sheriff's man. Or the minister, or the doctor. Anyone you like.' If she was going to come to Letho, he wanted her to settle and be easy. He felt Mrs. Warner had been a waste of time he could have employed more usefully elsewhere.

'And the household,' she said, pouring herself another cup of tea, 'how are they in themselves? How have they taken this tragedy?'

Chapter Twenty-Three

It was a good question. Robbins considered.

'Of course there will be different reactions, in a diverse group. Iffy the kitchenmaid had hysterics, but then she often does. Mrs. Mack turned grim and made sure twice that the servants' wing door was locked last night, and I'm told she took a rolling pin to bed with her for a weapon.' This woman made him almost chatty, he noticed. He felt familiar with her – in fact, he almost felt he knew her, somehow. 'Jennet the upstairs maid is a sensible soul, and carried on with all her duties, helping Mrs. Warner where she could. The serving men … William is the better of the two, though he is not as bright: he is steady enough. Daniel did not like having to clean up after the corpse – we had to lay the man in the dining room, you understand, in all the haste.' Mrs. Gilmour nodded, not shocked. 'Daniel is not steady. But in the end, well, I believe they all feel that Mr. Murray will do his best to protect them and to sort out any problems.'

'It's a close household, isn't it?' said Mrs. Gilmour. 'I noticed that. How will they take a newcomer?'

'They know that new people are needed. Another maid at least, probably two. A manservant to be trained up – we had one, but he left us for the university.'

'My!' she said, impressed.

'He's better suited there,' said Robbins. He must stop this chatter. He paused, then said, 'If you are calm, and sensible, and fair, and of a good humour,' – and not a witch, he added to himself – 'then likely they will be happy with you.'

'Calm and sensible and fair and of a good humour – goodness! All at once?' she asked, with a quizzical look. 'Or one at a time, by turns? I could try that.'

'Then you'll come?'

'A week's trial, you said.'

'A week's trial, indeed. Starting today – now, if you will. Or you'll want to go to the kirk, first: the household will be there in a little while, no doubt.'

'Ah … best I not meet them there, then.'

'You are not a church goer?' Witchcraft raised its head once again in Robbins' mind. He wondered how long it would be before he would stop thinking of it.

'I am … I am not … ah, you are a married man, I think, Mr. Robbins? You know that from time to time women are ill suited for long standing.'

'Oh, of course,' said Robbins, feeling himself redden. 'I understand. Now, you will not have to walk up to Letho House, though, because a cart has been sent to bring Mrs. Warner and her bags back here, where she must stay for now, and it will remain to take you and whatever you need to bring.'

'That is very kind. Thank you, Mr. Robbins.'

'Then I shall see you at the house, at your convenience.'

'I hope it will be to all our convenience, in the end,' she said, and smiled.

The Wedderburns used Murray's own carriage to go to the kirk, and with the Blairs in theirs and the servants following they made quite a procession for once. Mr. Helliwell, the minister, nodded in satisfaction to see them all turned out amongst the villagers, along with Mr. George from Dures. Miss George – Lady Rocheid – did not put in an appearance, and nor, of course, did the new tenants at Collessie. When he rose to leave the church at the end of the service, though, Murray did note another newcomer. Mrs. Warner had been at the back: clearly she had been prepared to stay in Letho at least for this length.

Outside the weather was mild enough for the parishioners to linger for a gossip, though with the news of what had happened on Friday night they might have been prepared to spend some time in the kirkyard even if it had been blowing a gale and raining. Quite a few villagers gathered around Blair's wheeled chair, eager to greet him after his long absence. Isobel moved away with the Wedderburns to greet Mrs. Helliwell. Mr. George, stopping a little distance from the church door so that he would not have to speak to Mr. Helliwell, had clearly been thinking since he had seen Murray a couple of hours earlier.

'Who was this Mr. Pillans, then?' he asked. 'I know Mrs. Pillans said something about him working in Edinburgh. What was he?'

'Have you heard of the Oriental Warehouse on South Bridge?'

Mr. George's expression was hard to read. Murray had not had him down as someone too precious to mix with tradesmen.

'I have, yes.'

'He was the owner, or the joint owner, perhaps.'

Mr. George raised his eyebrows.

'Really? What age of a man was he?'

'About thirty, I believe.'

'He can't have inherited it – that place has only been there half a dozen years, if it's the one I'm thinking of. Did he start it himself?'

'Apparently so, with a couple of friends in India to send him the goods.'

'Impressive. No wonder they can afford to take a place in the country for the summer, even if that place was Collessie. I hope that leaves the poor widow well provided for, at least.' He fell silent for a moment, watching the parishioners in their little groups, talking animatedly. Murray noticed Ninian Jack holding court, telling some story – probably about the inadequate lock on the icehouse gate. Isobel was laughing at something Mrs. Helliwell had said, and digging the point of her furled parasol between the stones of the path. Today she was wearing light blue, summery as the sky, and a white bonnet and pelisse with long tails. He tried not to be seen looking for too long, but it was not easy. He cleared his throat. Macduff, the sheriff's man, was not here, as far as Murray could see. It was possible that he was already at Letho House, talking to that man Rieder.

'I suppose it could be something to do with his business, then,' Mr. George said after a moment, rousing Murray from his speculations. Murray looked at him. Mr. George did not seem to have spotted the direction of his gaze.

'I suppose so. Though why follow him into Fife, if it is an Edinburgh matter?'

'Started following him, couldn't catch up till here?'

'Maybe … His wife could not think of any friends he had in Fife, anyway. Maybe you're right.' He shrugged. 'I hope the sheriff's man will come and report later. He was to make enquiries at the inn – it's unlikely that Pillans arrived in the village without the innkeeper knowing.'

'Then why did he go to Letho House and not to Collessie? That's a question.'

'Yes, it is. No one at Letho House seems to have known him.' Not that he had made much in the way of enquiry, so far. Yesterday seemed to pass in a flash, from discovery of the body to Rieder's arrival in the night. He had gone to bed after that and, despite all there was to think about, he had fallen asleep directly and not woken till almost six o'clock, well after dawn. Then the ride to Dures had been spent trying to work out how to handle the theft of the body. He needed time to think, at least to think of the questions that needed to be asked. The answers, he hoped, would come later. Perhaps once they were back at Letho House, he and Blair could take their old seats in the library and begin the process of working things out. Maybe Isobel would join them. She was talking with some of the village women now – old Lizzie Fenwick and some of her cronies.

'I hope Lady Rocheid is not too upset,' he said eventually. Mr. George did not seem disposed to a general gossip amongst the crowds, and still stood beside him, a little apart from the rest of the parishioners. He made a face.

'That man has been a disaster from the start,' he said. 'I believe he took one look at my sister, assessed her fortune and her weaknesses, and paid court to her from that moment. Of course she was going to fall for him – a handsome rascal, with a title for her, and so devoted, after so many years of nothing. I tried to talk her out of it, but there was nothing to be done. I don't know whether it is better or worse that she now sees him for what he is: I hate to my core seeing her so hurt.'

'Could she set up her own establishment? Keep away from

him?'

'It's the only thing, I believe. I should like her to stay here, with me – I should make sure she had company and protection, if nothing else - but I'm not sure she could bear being somewhere where everyone will be wondering where her husband is. I tell you, Murray: if that body had indeed been his, you could have had me as chief suspect. I could not deny that I've contemplated his death more than a few times.'

'Well, you are safe there, then,' said Murray, almost smiling, almost reassured. 'We have to find some other reason for the murder.'

'Does the wife know of nothing?'

'She seems not to,' said Murray. 'But there is a possible connexion. According to the *Courant* – and to Mr. Blair, who has spoken with some of their fellow workers – girls have been going missing from the Oriental Warehouse.'

Mr. George blinked in astonishment.

'Girls? You mean the girls who work there?'

'Well, two girls and a woman, a widow. Yes, people who work in the warehouse.'

'Do you think Pillans was involved? That that had something to do with his death?'

'I have no idea. Miss Blair mentioned it –' he managed not to glance at her as he said her name, '– and then Mr. Blair said he had taken an interest.'

Mr. George smiled, as if not at all surprised that Blair might have taken an interest, even now. It was easy to imagine him urging Smith on to push him through the Old Town, down the Bridges, to find shopgirls to question.

'I wonder where they've gone,' he said. 'The missing girls.'

'You've been down in Edinburgh a few times recently, have you not?' said Murray. 'I wonder that you had not heard the story. Or perhaps it has only come out in the last week or so.'

'Perhaps.'

'Charles!' He turned swiftly as Isobel came up. 'Oh, good day, Mr. George.' She curtseyed, and he bowed with a friendly smile. Isobel was not his style, either.

'Good day to you, Miss Blair. A fine day.'

'It is, isn't it? Almost like summer! I shall hope to make a drawing of the kirk if this sunshine continues. Charles, I'm sorry to interrupt, but I've just heard something I think you might find interesting.'

'Go on, then,' said Murray. 'Don't keep me waiting!'

Isobel grinned.

'Lizzie Fenwick and her friends were visiting another friend on Friday night, somewhere along the main road, but not very near the inn - to the left at the foot of the hill, they said?'

There were several cottages along there. Murray nodded: it should be easy to find out which one, if it mattered.

'They came out to walk home, they said, about midnight, and were surprised to hear a horse and wheels coming along the road. A light vehicle, they said, and moving fast. They pushed back into the hedge, and expected to see Mr. George,' she nodded to him, 'or you, go past, but it was a strange gig, they said – higher than either of yours, and unlit.'

'Unlit? That's bad,' said Murray.

'But they could see quite well – it was a starry night – and the driver was a man none of them knew. Moving fast, out of Letho.'

Chapter Twenty-Four

'Someone just passing along the main road?' Mr. George suggested. But Isobel shook her head.

'No, they are quite sure the gig was coming out of the village, out from the turning from the green.'

'No one living in the green has a gig, except for Dr. Feilden,' said Mr. George, with a frown. 'They would have known him – and I have never known him to go out unlit. It must have been a visitor. They could have been coming out of the inn.'

'Strange to leave the inn at that time of the night, with an unlit gig,' said Murray, and Isobel nodded.

'I suspect you'll find the innkeeper knew nothing of the man,' she said.

'That's easily checked, anyway,' Murray agreed. 'I think that Macduff will be interested enough to go and do that.'

'They are off just now to talk to him, if they can find him.'

'Did they see any details of the man in the starlight?'

'Not a large man,' Isobel said, 'and not tiny. There, that must eliminate someone!'

'Very helpful,' said Murray drily. 'Come on, we'd better go. I thought I should call at Collessie.'

'That was my intention, too,' said Isobel.

'So should I,' said Mr. George. 'I said in my letter that I would call later, in case they wanted some further explanation or apology.'

'Come with us, then, if you wish,' said Murray.

Blair was tired, after the excitement of meeting everyone at church, and elected to return to Letho House. The Wedderburns debated a little: Mr. Wedderburn felt it was not their place to call quite so early after Mr. Pillans' death, but Deborah argued that since they had met Mrs. Pillans not so long ago, it would be appropriate to make a quick call. In the end they decided to agree to disagree: Mr. Wedderburn would return with Blair, and Mrs. Wedderburn would visit Collessie. Then Mr. George had his horse, and some additional obligations, so it was settled at last that Mr. George should ride ahead with his explanations – somehow trying to excuse or explain his sister's behaviour - and Murray, Isobel, and Deborah Wedderburn would walk, as the day was so fine.

Murray held back for a moment or two to give instructions to servants and coachmen, and Isobel set off with Mrs. Wedderburn.

She had known Deborah Wedderburn for years, though Deborah was rather older. They had much in common: they had both, for different reasons, managed their household from a relatively early age, and dealt with fathers who were by most measures of society thoroughly eccentric. They were both intelligent, sensible, well-informed persons with a not incompatible sense of humour. For the most part the two women were friendly, having no reason not to be. Almost no reason, anyway.

'Little Augusta is charming, is she not?' Mrs. Wedderburn started. 'Just precocious enough for that age, and very pretty.'

'She is a delight,' Isobel agreed, wholeheartedly.

'Which is very fortunate,' Mrs. Wedderburn lowered her voice, though they were already some distance from anyone else, 'when you consider her mother. You knew Lady Agostinella, I believe?'

'Of course,' said Isobel. Mrs. Wedderburn shuddered expressively.

'Extraordinary woman. But she died, what, four years ago now?'

'Augusta is four, yes.' Lady Agostinella had died in childbirth.

'And Augusta is a daughter. He will be wanting to marry again soon, I should think. It's not as if he could have missed Lady Agostinella, after all.'

Isobel did not think it her place to comment. Deborah, too,

paused, adjusting the stem of her parasol.

'What you might not realise,' Deborah continued, 'is that Charles will always want to do his duty.'

Hence Augusta, Isobel thought, but wisely did not say.

'You might think that he is content here, in his bachelor state, but I know Charles. When he worked at Scoggie Castle, I quite believe he would have offered for me, had his situation been only a little different. And then there was Beatrix Pirrie, of course – much more his level, if you understand me, at that time.'

'Oh, I know about Beatrix Pirrie,' said Isobel, a little more quickly than she had intended.

'You do?' Deborah turned and raised an eyebrow at her, still managing to imply that she knew a great deal more about Beatrix Pirrie and Charles Murray than Isobel did. Somehow Isobel doubted that, but still Deborah's constant hints at her deep acquaintance with Charles were annoying. She was not even sure that Deborah, whom she otherwise liked, was even aware of what she was doing. But Isobel did her very best to ignore her remarks. She had heard Charles' stories of his days at Scoggie Castle, and felt she did not need a comparative version.

'Well,' said Deborah, kindly, 'do let me know if you need any further information. Before you – commit yourself to anything.'

'I can't think to what I could possibly commit myself,' said Isobel with a smile, and was relieved when at that point Murray caught up with them. Deborah at once linked an arm in his.

'So, Mr. Murray, have you ever visited Pillans' Oriental Warehouse?' she asked.

'I'm not sure that I have,' said Murray. 'Have you? You are not so much in Edinburgh these days, I believe.'

'No,' said Deborah, 'but of course I have been there, during our recent stay. It is the place to go for Indian chintzes and paisleys and the lighter silks for summer – quite lovely. And it always seems very well run. I was surprised to hear that the owner was such a young man.'

'I think I had heard that,' said Isobel, 'but I had no idea of the name. He has hidden very successfully behind the name of the warehouse. Perhaps that is because it is owned not just by him but by the three men – is that not what Mrs. Pillans said? Two in India and one here?'

'Do you suppose there could have been a quarrel,' said Deborah, 'and one of them came from India to kill him?'

'That's a long journey to settle a quarrel,' Murray remarked, having done that very journey. 'Unless they had come back to Edinburgh and found some irregularity ... but then, why kill him here? Why not in Edinburgh?'

'So many questions!' said Deborah. 'I do not understand how any business like this is ever reasoned out. But then, Mr. Murray, you have done such things before – perhaps it comes with practice?'

'Practice and exigency,' said Murray with a smile. 'Necessity is always the mother of some kind of reasoning out. If no one cared about the dead, or about those left behind, then no one would ever have to puzzle out anything.'

'Unless,' said Isobel, 'one feared that the killer might strike again.'

There was a pause.

'Yes,' said Murray. 'There is that.'

They had gone by the public road rather than through the woods, a path that at the Collessie end was never well maintained enough to be safe for ladies in their Sabbath finery. It was not long before they passed the end of the drive to Letho House, where the carriages would shortly turn in, and carried on past well-maintained sandstone walls for some time, talking a little more idly about the Wedderburn children and their prospects. Where Letho land ended, the walls at once became more ramshackle: branches, untrimmed, had pressed on them and crumbled the coping over many years, unscrupulous locals had probably removed a few for their own purposes, and only the necessity to keep the road clear really made sure a border was marked at all. Murray wondered now if Mrs. Pillans would keep on the lease, or indeed would be financially able to keep on the lease. If she did, she might need some advice about upkeep. If not, when would Collessie find a tenant again?

The gates, when they reached them, stood open and unguarded, but the drive itself must have been well-laid in the past and had always stayed relatively clear, luring unsuspecting people up to the unkempt house. As they turned in through the gateway, Mr. George appeared, riding towards them.

'I have made my apologies,' he said, almost before he was close enough, 'and I have been forgiven, or obtained forgiveness for my poor sister. But I thought it better not to linger: you will be more welcome, no doubt. And I have business to attend to, I'm afraid.'

'On a Sunday? Nothing serious, I hope,' said Murray.

'Weighty, perhaps, but not grave!' was Mr. George's enigmatic reply. 'I hope to see you soon!' He nodded to the ladies, and rode past them. Murray, glancing back, noted that he turned right at the road. His business was not in Letho, or at home at Dures, then: something in Cupar, perhaps? Hadn't he said that he had been there on Friday night, too? A girl, no doubt, he thought, and grinned to himself. Mr. George was not grown old yet.

Ahead, the ground floor of Collessie had blinds over the windows, while upstairs only one or two were still shuttered. A proper state of affairs for a house in mourning, and Mrs. Pillans must be receiving visitors, or Mr. George would have said.

'I don't think we should stay long,' he suggested. 'Just ensure that they have all they need.'

'It must be strange to have someone die in an unfamiliar place,' said Deborah, as if the thought had struck her for the first time. 'Not to know who lays out, not to be much acquainted with the minister, or a carpenter.'

'And the Collessie servants cannot be much help. Poor Mrs. Pillans,' said Isobel. 'At least she has her mother with her. And we must make sure that she does not feel she has to be alone.'

But Mrs. Pillans seemed to be more organised than they had expected. The door was opened with some efficiency by a maid with a clean apron, and the Letho House party was shown upstairs and into the drawing room at once. Mrs. Pillans and her mother, crisp in smart new black, rose to greet them, quite as if no one had ever absconded with a corpse from the house the previous night. Mrs. Pillans even rang for tea, as if she were quite sure that some would be brought. Murray could see Isobel glancing about discreetly. The drawing room was freshly aired, dusted and clean, and the furniture had either been replaced or repaired.

'My husband lies in the next room,' said Mrs. Pillans. 'We had a little difficulty last night, and I decided he would be safer upstairs.'

'We heard about the difficulty, Mrs. Pillans. I'm sorry you

should have been so distressed.'

'I understand the lady in question is unwell,' said Mrs. Skead. She was pink about the eyes, but otherwise in control. 'I feel very sorry for her. After all, at least I know what has happened to my daughter's husband.'

'So dreadful! So dreadful!' Mrs. Pillans was seized with sobbing, into a handkerchief she must have borrowed from her husband for its size. 'To think we shall never see him alive again – never hear all his eager talk! Who could have done such a thing? I'm sure poor Gordon never hurt anyone in his life!'

'Oh, my dear Annie,' said Mrs. Skead, and put her arm about her daughter's shoulders. 'We must be strong. Gordon would have wanted us to manage, would he not?'

'But you are not without friends, too,' said Isobel. 'If there is anything you need – any help, or local advice – you have only to ask, you know.'

'You are more than kind,' said Mrs. Skead. 'Thank you. No doubt there will be something - if it had happened when we were at home in Edinburgh, with our friends about us – our old friends … The minister is to come this afternoon and help us with arrangements, and that will bring us a stage further on.' She nodded, as if they had a long journey to make but had taken the first steps. Which, Murray thought, was not inaccurate.

Chapter Twenty-Five

Blair was indeed tired by the time church was over, and not much better when he arrived back at Letho House, even though the drive was a smooth one and his own carriage had been rendered more comfortable by several inventions of his own, over the years. He found he was almost more tired at the thought of what he used to do, the energy he used to have to examine and investigate and question, not necessarily with respect to crimes but with respect to anything remotely interesting he might happen to come across, than he was at the thought of doing anything now. As if someone might expect him to go back to where he had been, to pull himself out of his chair and hirple along on his crutches, to tolerate the nagging pain in his stump, the occasional vagueness in the back of his head, the anxiety in Isobel's face ... exhausting even to contemplate. What he needed to do was to find a way to make the interesting things come to him, and to be patient with him, and let him examine and investigate and question them in his own time.

The stableyard cats had already discovered that he had taken up residence on the ground floor, which made things easier for them, too. Smith tried to encourage them to leave when he found them, but Blair suspected that Smith had a soft spot for cats, too, and he was now quietly leaving the window open to allow them in. Blair noted when they returned from church that his parlour-bedroom door had been left ajar, and when he chose to settle himself in the hall, cosy under a rug against the draughts, a ginger and black cat slipped discreetly from the doorway and settled herself, swift as you like, on his comfortable lap. Content, he tickled her head and stroked her ears. And waited until someone interesting should happen to go past.

The first person, once Smith had left him, was Richard Wedderburn, who had been slower returning from the church than Blair. The stableyard cat eyed him with interest, but not concern.

'Will you take some refreshment, Wedderburn?' asked Blair, indicating the tray that Smith had brought for him. There was more than one cup on it.

'Aye, that I will!' said Wedderburn, casting aside his hat and gloves. 'I find village churches overwhelming: everyone knows everyone else and you are the novelty, and so they pounce. Like that cat, I daresay!'

'Oh, dear, I had not thought ... I should not have left you to come back last ...'

'Not at all, not at all.' Wedderburn was at once alarmed that he should have been thought to be criticising. 'The minister's wife engaged me in some talk about her garden. A very nice woman, I thought.'

'She is indeed,' said Blair sincerely. 'The lynchpin on which the village functions, I think. You are not one for village life, then?'

'For my own village, yes indeed,' said Wedderburn. 'I should much rather be there than anywhere else – though of course Letho is charming, and we are more than grateful that Murray was able to put us up. But I was just looking forward to escaping Edinburgh and getting home.'

'More than usual, I gather?' asked Blair, innocently.

'Good heavens, yes!' He settled back in his seat, ready for a gossip. 'I mean, I suppose we usually go down to see a few friends, keep in touch – useful when we're looking for husbands and wives for our own three, though that's a few years off yet – and of course Debs does some shopping, making sure we are all in good style!' He grinned, then turned more solemn. 'I hear that man that has been killed was something to do with the Oriental Warehouse. That's one of the places she goes. Terrible, is it not?' It was not wholly clear, thought Blair, whether he was referring to the murder or to his wife's association with the shop.

'Did you know him at all?' Blair was interested in how people moved up and down the social scale, particularly in Edinburgh. Had Gordon Pillans been prominent enough yet to dine with the daughter of Lord Scoggie and her husband? But it seemed not. Wedderburn shook his head.

'I didn't even know the name of the shopkeeper,' he said. 'It was completely unfamiliar to me. The wife seems a decent soul.'

'She does indeed,' Blair agreed, unable to prevent a slight sigh. Then he drained his tea cup with a noisy slurp, and refilled it. 'So tell me what went wrong with your visit? I heard tales of all kinds of disasters!'

'Oh, it would be tedious in the extreme to listen to all my woes!' Wedderburn protested. 'It began when we found there had been a mistake with our accommodation. My man had gone ahead to prepare the house – we rent, of course, for the season – and there was another family already installed. And of course by then everywhere else was taken, and we ended up in a new place in Newington. Plaster hardly dry on the walls! But I suppose it was clean.'

'Newington is interesting,' said Blair, 'almost a town on its own.'

'Yes, it made entertaining our friends awkward, and we spent half our time travelling.'

'But once you were out then it must have been much the same as ever?' asked Blair, who would doubtless have spent his days interrogating his neighbours about living in Newington.

'Oh, it just went on from there. Suffice to say that I slid on a grape – fallen from the supper table – at a rout, and turned my ankle and had to be carried to a chair to be taken home, with Debs fussing along behind. Then she and half the servants came down with a terrible cold, and we had to cancel our own party. Debs could barely think for a week, and the cook could not cook. Meat that should have been cooked a week before was forgotten, and accidentally served up for dinner. And then we were robbed.'

'I thought it was house breaking? Were you robbed on the journey back?'

'No, no: we reserved a rough crossing and a broken axle for that. No, you could not say it was house breaking, for the maid herself went off with the jewellery.'

'She absconded?'

'She did indeed, the ungrateful brat. We had brought her from our home at Kineden: I think the big town turned her head. What I shall say to her father I do not know – I've written, of course, but now I'll have to talk to him.'

'Did she leave a note?'

'She did, yes. I have it with me to give to her father, though much comfort that will be. I daresay he'll be down to Edinburgh to beat her back home.' His sandy face sagged: he clearly felt he had failed. It was possible that the maid's father would see things the same way, too.

'And then a rough crossing?'

'The Forth was as bad as I've ever seen it at this time of year,' said Wedderburn, dragging himself back from thoughts of irate fathers. 'One of those times when you want the ferry to sail so that you can get home, but at the same time you want it not to sail – maybe just so that you know you are not being pathetic, and even the ferrymen think it is bad. I was half-tempted to turn the carriage and go up by Stirling, but then who knows where we might have been when the axle broke?'

'Well,' said Blair, 'you might have been somewhere where a man was not murdered in an old icehouse, I suppose.'

'Ah, well, that much is true.' Wedderburn looked uncomfortable. 'You believe, then, that our run of bad luck is not yet over? Perhaps we should not go home until it is, lest we take it with us?'

Blair looked at him with interest: it was a curious thought, staying away until one had worn through one's bad luck, like an infection. He had not credited Richard Wedderburn with anything like that level of individual thought before.

'Mr. Blair!' The shriek of delight came from somewhere upstairs, and in a moment light steps pattered on the staircase.

'Careful, Augusta!' came a more adult voice, following.

'Miss Fizz says I have to be careful,' said Augusta, attempting, for a few steps, a dignified pace, before rattling on down to the hall. 'See, Miss Fizz? I'm quite safe. Now you must be careful, too!'

Miss Fitzsimmons descended the stairs with a good deal more grace than her charge, and curtseyed to the gentlemen.

'I am sorry to have disturbed you, sir,' she said to Blair, but he shook his head violently so that his wig jiggled.

'Miss Augusta could never disturb me!' he said. 'But Augusta, you might disturb the cat, so you need to be peaceable if you're going to sit here. Miss Fitzsimmons, pray, do take a cup of tea with us! If you are not too busy.'

A little uncomfortably, Miss Fitzsimmons perched and took a cup and saucer from the tray. Augusta calmed herself sufficiently to talk to the cat, still proprietorially on Blair's lap.

'You see, Miss Fitzsimmons, I sit here in the hall seeking to be disturbed: it would be very dull to sit in my room, and I find it hard to wander about as I used to. So I come here and hope to be entertained – it is very selfish of me!'

'I'm sure it is not, sir,' said Miss Fitzsimmons. 'It seems to me very sensible.'

He saw that her gaze flickered quickly towards Wedderburn and away again, then back to Augusta.

'Well done, Augusta! You are very gentle with the cat – exactly what they like.'

'Thank you, Miss Fizz!' Augusta beamed at the praise.

Wedderburn stretched his legs, and stood up.

'If you'll excuse me,' he said, 'I had promised myself a turn in the gardens before the afternoon service. Take a few ideas for my own gardens, you know?'

He bowed, chiefly to Blair, and Miss Fitzsimmons rose and curtseyed. When he had gone, she glanced back at Blair before sensing she had permission to sit again. Governesses, secretaries and tutors – stuck in the awkward interstices between family and servants. But they held no fear for Blair.

'So tell me, Miss Fitzsimmons,' he said, 'are you quite well? Has this upset you, this business?' He made an elaborate shrug, presumably intended to indicate the general area of the icehouse. Miss Fitzsimmons did not flinch.

'It is not the kind of thing one expects, certainly,' she said, 'and it is most unpleasant, particularly for Mrs. Pillans and her family. And for those who had to deal with – with the body.'

'Yes, yes, most – unpleasant, as you say. But you are not inclined to abandon your charge and run for the hills?'

She looked briefly affronted, he saw, before she realised he was making a kind of joke.

'Not unless things grow worse!' she said. There was a pause, but something about Blair invited people to talk. 'It is no small matter to me, though it might be to some, to find and settle in a new home, with new people. The idea of leaving now, when I am only lately arrived, is not appealing, particularly when all I have seen so far so suits me, I believe. Mr. Murray has been most considerate, as has Mr. Robbins. My accommodation is delightful, and my charge …' Her face softened as her gaze fell on Augusta, 'my charge is tremendous fun!'

The best answer he could expect, Blair thought, as he too watched Augusta play with the cat. Then the door from the servants' corridor opened, and Robbins appeared.

'Mr. Blair, sir, Mr. Macduff is here. In the absence of Mr. Murray he asked if you would like him to speak with you?'

'Oh, oh, yes please!' said Blair, almost bouncing in his chair. 'That would be excellent!'

Robbins, used to Blair's ways, bowed and went to fetch the sheriff's man. Miss Fitzsimmons rose discreetly and took Augusta's hand as the cat, sensing change, jumped down and slipped back into Blair's parlour bedroom, presumably to avail herself of the window exit. Miss Fitzsimmons curtseyed, encouraged Augusta to do the same, and took her over to the side of the hall to fix on her bonnet and shawl for their walk. They had already disappeared, Augusta chattering happily, by the time Robbins returned with Macduff. The man limped into the hall, gave a disappointed glance at the empty hearth, and stood thoughtfully where Blair would be able to see him clearly without having to move.

'Well, now, Macduff, how are matters progressing?'

'Well, sir,' said Macduff, 'if anybody knows who drove an unlit gig through the village after dark last night, they're no telling me. For all I could discover, it might as well have been a ghost.'

Chapter Twenty-Six

'No one saw it at all?'

'Only the women who reported it, sir. But I ken those women: if they made it up they'd have good reason for it,' he said, a little sourly. 'And I canna think what the good reason might be, and,' he sighed, 'I don't believe they made it up.'

Blair pursed his lips, and drummed a hand on the arm of the chair.

'It's a foolish man who drives an unlit gig about the roads at night,' he said.

'It's a quiet road,' countered Macduff. 'Maybe his lamps had run out of oil.'

'Maybe … But where was he going? Where had he come from?'

'He was heading from Cupar, sir, and towards St. Andrews.'

'But his journey could have been a longer one than that – or indeed, for we must consider all possibilities, a shorter.'

Macduff nodded, for it would be hard to disagree.

'I've spoke to yon foreign fellow, sir. I've heard his story from last night. That's a rare one, eh?'

'Oh, Mr. Rieder? The musician? How is he this morning? I believe he was quite upset last night!'

'That he was, sir: bodies being carted around the parish in the middle of the night. No wonder he was upset. And then, I gather, Mr. Murray went to find out where the body had gone, and …'

'And all has ended well, I believe,' said Blair. 'Or as well as it can be, when one man is dead and the other is still missing.'

'Aye, it's an unco' thing, that's fair to say,' said Macduff, and for a moment they fell silent in contemplation of the odd and unsatisfactory nature of the situation.

Silence had also been dominant at Collessie for some time. It was not, Murray knew, unnatural, but it had an uneasy feel to it that he could not quite place. The soft murmuration of Mrs. Skead's sobs into her handkerchief continued, and the occasional chink of cup on saucer. Murray had tried, gently, the conversational horse of 'Who could have done this terrible deed? Did Mr. Pillans have enemies?' but it had trotted off at once into the long grass of 'accidents' and 'mistaken for someone else', which, in the circumstances, was reasonable. After all, who was to say that a murderer lurking in an unfinished icehouse might not mistake one passing victim for another? Though why on earth any of them should have been in the icehouse in the first place was beyond Murray.

They had established that there was no other family to inform: Pillans' parents were long dead, and a sister had gone out on the fishing fleet to Calcutta on the hunt for a husband and never been heard of since.

'His business partners, though, in India – they will have to be told,' said Mrs. Pillans, as if writing herself a note.

'Were you much involved in his business?' asked Isobel. 'Do you know the staff in the warehouse? This will materially affect them, I should think.'

'Materially affect ...' For a moment Mrs. Pillans' apparent serenity faltered. She seemed confused. 'Oh, the people in the shop?'

'Did you know them? Did you visit often?'

'Oh, no. Gordon would bring me whatever he thought I would like. There was no need for me to go there.'

'Did he have a manager? Someone, presumably, would be there to take care of things while he was up here.'

Murray loved the gentle, interested tone Isobel was using – concerned, caring. Not at all interrogatory. He tried not to look at her face, but allowed himself a sideways glance at her gloved hands, folded neatly in her lap. Clever hands, skilled at drawing and painting ...

But Mrs. Pillans was answering.

'There's a woman who oversees the basics,' she said vaguely. 'I know he has spoken of her.'

'Could I be of service and contact her for you?' asked Murray, trying to sound just as concerned and caring. 'If you wish I could send a manservant down – or I could go myself, if you would prefer.'

'Would you do that?' asked Mrs. Pillans, a little breathless, taken aback. 'We have no manservant here,' she said, with a slight emphasis on 'here' that made Murray wonder if they had a manservant at all. 'I could send a letter, of course, but if someone told her, in person … a man would give it much more authority, don't you think? She would listen then. I don't think she would listen to me.'

'Then allow me to be your messenger,' said Murray. 'I can be in Edinburgh by Tuesday evening, speak to her on Wednesday, and return perhaps on Thursday, if no complications arise.'

'Oh, you are too kind, Mr. Murray! To take you away from your lovely home for so long!'

'Not at all,' said Murray, though truth be told he would sooner stay at Letho. But he was curious about this Oriental Warehouse. 'Perhaps we should leave you now in peace, and I shall make preparations. If you think of anything else, any other message I can convey for you in town, you can send word before … nine tomorrow morning?'

He stood, and Mrs. Wedderburn and Isobel rose, too. Mrs. Pillans and Mrs. Skead pulled themselves to their feet to bid them goodbye.

'You're a kind man, Mr. Murray,' said Mrs. Wedderburn, once they were safely on the driveway again. 'I should not like to pop down to Edinburgh and back in four days.'

'Maybe five,' said Murray. 'But not long. I hope you will excuse me, when I have guests, but Blair will no doubt be happy to act as host until my return.'

'He'll love it,' said Isobel. 'And I shall look forward to finding out your impressions of the Oriental Warehouse and its manager – if there are any staff left by now.'

'She speaks oddly of it, don't you think?' asked Murray. 'A

little superior, a little – what, afraid?'

'Not used to being the owner's wife,' said Isobel succinctly. 'No habit of command. She doesn't know where she stands with the staff, I should say. I wonder if she was one of them before she married?'

Deborah Wedderburn managed to look shocked, and disappointed that she had not thought of it first, at the same time. Then she smiled, gently mocking.

'No doubt Mr. Murray will discover all that there is to know about the Pillans, the Oriental Warehouse and even the missing girls. How long did you say you were staying in Edinburgh, Mr. Murray?'

The missing girls – yes. What could he find out about them? And what, if anything, did they have to do with Gordon Pillans' murder?

Recognising that he might, indeed, have to stay a little longer in Edinburgh, Murray began to gather a list of useful things to do. He would go and see Macduff before he left, he thought, and talk to Blair, of course. And perhaps he would have another talk with Mr. George, and see if there were any questions he might usefully ask, somewhere, as to the whereabouts of the elusive Lord Rocheid. He was pleased to find that his first two objectives were already in the entrance hall at Letho when he and the ladies arrived back from Collessie.

'Mr. Macduff can't find the owner of the unlit gig,' said Blair at once, not troubling with a greeting, as they came in. 'The innkeeper knew nothing of it.'

'Well, if the innkeeper knew nothing ...' said Murray, reaching out to ring for more tea. Mrs. Wedderburn and Isobel sank on to a sopha, and began to fiddle with bonnets and gloves. It was a very mild day. Along with the tea Isobel's maid appeared, removed anything the ladies did not want, and vanished again, no doubt finding this socialising in the entrance hall inconvenient, neither coming nor going. But Murray noticed that it seemed to suit Blair quite well.

'I plan to go briefly to Edinburgh tomorrow,' he told Macduff, 'to take the news of Mr. Pillans' death to his business associates – well, his staff. His partners are in India. Is there anything I can do for you there? I plan,' he added, smiling, 'to discover as much as possible while I am there.'

Macduff was pleased.

'That'd be what I'd say, sir. I'll give you a note, if you won't take it amiss, to some of the sergeants there and maybe you could get a look at their house and all?'

'I could – and one can rarely have too many introductions, thank you. I have the direction to their house – not far from the warehouse, in Newington, I believe. If you think of anything else before I leave tomorrow, you can let me know.'

'Aye, sir, I'll do that.'

'Any news? Or have you told all to Mr. Blair?'

'There's not much, sir. Yon gig is the only sign I've heard of a stranger about the place, and while you know and I know it doesn't take a stranger to commit a murder, I don't believe anybody around here knew Mr. Pillans apart from his own household, so why would anybody up and kill him?'

'On the other hand,' said Murray, reluctantly, 'how did a stranger know about the icehouse?'

'How did Mr. Pillans know about the icehouse?' added Blair eagerly. Deborah Wedderburn looked a little disconcerted.

'Is this how you manage such things?' she asked. 'Sitting about and drinking tea and going into every little detail?'

'The details are terribly important, Mrs. Wedderburn,' said Blair – and indeed, they seemed to be reviving Blair himself tremendously. Murray met Isobel's eye, and saw that she had noticed, too. But she was not solely considering her father's health.

'It seems to me we have two obvious suspects,' she said, drawing another shocked look from Deborah Wedderburn. 'Your two Irish engineers, Kelly and Sweeney. They are comparative strangers, and may well have known Mr. Pillans somehow. And they certainly knew about the icehouse.'

'They came very well recommended,' said Murray, in his own defence.

'I'm sure they did,' said Isobel, 'with regard to their engineering skills, and perhaps to their general behaviour. But I imagine you did not enquire as to the likelihood of their harbouring murderous intentions?'

Murray tutted.

'I knew there was something I had forgotten,' he said.

160

'They say, miss, that they've never been to Edinburgh, either of them,' put in Macduff. 'I'll be asking Mrs. Pillans if she knew them at all, or thought her husband might.'

'And then there's that musician, isn't there?'

'Aye, we're finding out more about him and all,' said Macduff. 'Och, there's plenty to be done.'

'Well,' said Murray, 'we shouldn't keep you. But thank you for coming and telling us what is happening. You're staying on at the inn?'

'Oh, aye,' said Macduff, without enthusiasm. 'I'll be there a while yet, I daresay. Though I'm away up to Collessie just now: I want a likeness of the dead man, if I can get one.'

Macduff was a skilled artist: if Mrs. Pillans had a portrait of her husband, Macduff could take a copy of it quickly and competently. Murray thought it was probably his favourite part of his work.

'Well, and I shall go to the afternoon service,' he said. 'Though I suspect we heard all the gossip there was to hear this morning.'

In truth, he went to the service in the hope of catching Mr. George there, but his neighbour did not attend.

Then Murray remembered that Mr. George had last been seen heading off in the direction of Cupar earlier, and might well not yet be back. He wondered again what business Francis George might have in the market town on the Sabbath, and went home to consider dinner.

After dinner, with full daylight still warming the sky, he decided again to try for Mr. George, this time at Dures. Mindful of the fact he would be riding for a good part of the next two days, he headed over to Dures on foot, enjoying the early evening air scented with gorse and hawthorn, the chirrups of goldfinches and yellowhammers, the lambs in the fields he crossed on his way.

Mr. George was at home, though he had the look of a man with his mind too much on business, or at least something similarly worrisome. Murray found him seated in his library by an unlit hearth, with no candles, and a glass of brandy by his side. It was too dim for him to have been reading.

'I'm off to Edinburgh in the morning,' Murray explained,

not wishing to keep him long, 'and I wondered if you had any commands for me? News of Lord Rocheid, perhaps?'

Mr. George sighed.

'My sister left this morning for Edinburgh.'

'Oh! I thought ...'

'That if we took the body back to Collessie, she might change her mind? No, alas: she has gone. She has perhaps found him herself by now.'

The silence that followed was broken by a door slamming. Mr. George rose to his feet, frowning, as the library door in turn shot open.

A man was in the room at once, confident, brisk, angry.

'Where is she? Where's my wife?'

Lord Rocheid had appeared.

Chapter Twenty-Seven

'Edinburgh? Don't be ridiculous,' said Lord Rocheid. 'I've just come from there.' He flung his gloves down on the library table.

'She only left this morning,' said Mr. George, who was clearly clinging on to his temper with both hands. 'Looking for you.'

'I told her to wait here until I came.'

'I believe she was anxious that the delay meant that something had happened to you. No doubt she will be gratified to find that you are unharmed.'

'Ridiculous,' muttered Lord Rocheid. He was a slim man, and favoured a coat tight-nipped at the waist in the new fashion, with wide lapels to give breadth to his shoulders. He made Murray feel very old-fashioned.

'Perhaps it would be best if you went after her,' suggested Mr. George gently.

'Go after her? When I've only just arrived? Talk sense, man!' Lord Rocheid flung himself into an armchair. Murray was visited briefly by a wish that he would burst his buttons. 'She can come back here, if she's that eager to see me. Though granted, if she is not here to meet me I shan't linger long in this forsaken spot. I only came because she wanted to.' He did his best to sound martyred, but came across as petulant. Though to be fair, Murray thought, he was not going out of his way in any direction to be likeable.

'I'll not keep you, Murray,' said Mr. George, with an apologetic look. 'Here, let me walk you to the door.'

They left Rocheid sprawled by the empty fireplace, and

crossed the hall.

'I'll find her,' said Murray, 'and make sure she's all right, if I can.'

'Will you?' Mr. George frowned. 'I should go myself ...'

'I daresay you don't want much to leave Dures at the moment, though,' said Murray, thinking that he himself would not care to think that Lord Rocheid was in his house unsupervised. Mr. George shot him an odd, surprised look.

'No ... no, for various reasons,' he agreed. 'But I need to know she's safe. She is ... well, you know what she is, Murray, of course. But she is my sister. She may be married, but I still feel responsible for her. For her happiness, and for her safety.'

'Of course. Give me her direction, and I'll call.'

An early departure in the morning would mean that he could stay the night in North Queensferry, and take the first boat at dawn, as long as he could change horses on the way. Murray spoke with Robbins before supper, aware that Robbins would not be wholly pleased with his decision.

'Who will you take with you, sir?' was his first question.

'I thought I'd go on my own,' said Murray. 'There's plenty to keep everyone occupied here. I'll travel post, and stay at the Tontine in Princes Street.'

'Not the Queen Street house, sir?'

'Hardly worth opening it for a few days, do you think?'

'What if you're delayed, sir? Or need more shirts than you can carry in a saddlebag?'

That was a fair point. If he had to call on Miss George – Lady Rocheid – he would need to look respectable. He knew that Robbins could see he was wavering.

'We left Nathaniel at Queen Street, sir. He's young, but he's beginning to know what he's doing. He could open up even a room or two, and see to it that you're provided for. It would give him some much needed practice,' Robbins added, as if all this was to be for Nathaniel's benefit. 'And you would be sure the beds were clean.'

Murray had wanted to stay at an inn to reassure himself that it was only a flying visit. Opening the Queen Street house felt like moving back, and at this time of year – almost always – he wanted to be at Letho. But Robbins was right, as ever. It made more sense to use Queen Street.

So, taking his own horse as far as Cupar, he left early on Monday morning, and arrived in Edinburgh late on the morning of Tuesday, grubby from the journey and looking forward to a hot bath when poor Nathaniel had recovered from the shock of his arrival and remembered how to heat the water. It was not the first time that Murray had had to manage with only Nathaniel in the town house, but each time had worked better than the last.

'You can bring hot food in for the morning, Nathaniel,' Murray told him, 'and have some fresh milk about the place, and a loaf of bread and some cheese. Open a bottle of brandy to breathe. That should do me, besides whatever you usually provide for yourself: I'll dine out, I daresay, and I hope not to be here more than a couple of nights. All well here? No leaks or house-breakings or infestations of vermin?'

Nathaniel looked alarmed at that, but quickly recovered.

'I go round the house every day, sir,' he said, 'just like Mr. Robbins told me to.'

'Have there been any deliveries?'

'All sent on to Letho, sir.'

'Well done. Thank you, Nathaniel – now, if you see to the water I'll go and turn down my bed myself to air for later.' Life as Lord Scoggie's tutor, long ago, had taught Murray a degree of independence.

He saw to his bedchamber, made sure there were indeed clean shirts and neck cloths in the press, and went to the window to stare out over the Forth to Fife. He had left Blair in charge at Letho, with Robbins' help. And Isobel as hostess. Isobel as mistress of Letho ... would she take that post? Would she take him? They had known each other for so long – she could have no illusions about him, anyway.

His thoughts drifted for what may have been some time, then he pulled them back reluctantly. After all, the faster he dealt with matters here, the sooner he would be back with her.

The morning would probably be a better time for visiting the Oriental Warehouse, he thought, and the afternoon for visiting Lady Rocheid. Would Lady Rocheid have arrived in Edinburgh yet? He had travelled quickly, but he imagined that she would not have been lingering on the road either, so even though she might have been slower in her carriage she would have taken the route he had taken, and she had started a day earlier. But perhaps he should allow her to recover from her journey first – or was that an excuse? There was the Pillans' house to visit, and no particular time better than another there ... that's where he would go, once he was bathed and changed. With luck, he would be done there before dinner time.

It was good, after riding so far, to cross North Bridge on foot and walk up to Newington. Situated south beyond the old town, Newington was airy and modern, and growing steadily, but without the staid planning of the New Town to the north. Here instead the villas of prosperous merchants were beginning to appear, each different, most with a little patch of garden, an economical compromise between sedate town houses and country estates, and not too far from the owner's warehouse or factory or brewery, without the ignominy of living behind the shop. It was exactly what Murray would have expected Gordon Pillans to own, though again he was probably a decade younger than most of his neighbours. A successful merchant, newly rich – perhaps, if he had gone on at the same rate, he would have bought himself that country estate in another twenty years, sold the warehouse, and gone in for cattle breeding.

The house was shut up, but Macduff had somehow persuaded Mrs. Pillans to give him a key, which he had passed on to Murray along with his note for the local sergeant. Murray decided to reserve the note: the sergeants did not often wander as far as Newington unless called, and he preferred to look about on his own.

Still, it felt a terrible intrusion to slip the key into the lock and enter someone else's house in the absence even of their servants. The little front garden seemed terribly exposed as he tried to look as if he ought to be there, and turned the key.

The house did not smell stale, but then it had not been locked up for more than a few days, presumably. He made a note in his head to ask the neighbours when Gordon Pillans had left. Someone had likely noticed: this was not like the New Town, where the houses faced ostentatiously forward and never looked from side to side. This was more like a village.

The hallway was pokey and dark, with all its doors closed. He tried the first door on his right, and entered a drawing room, also dark, with the shutters closed. Deciding that there was no point in tiptoeing round and not being able to see anything, he went to the window and opened one shutter with a startling creak. Light from a fine May morning spilled into the room, and it glowed.

Every surface that could be covered with a cloth was rich with colour: furniture, floor, a small box piano. The walls were white, but that made the curtains seem all the brighter. Swirls of dizzying paisley patterns, dazzling stripes, floral prints and embroideries, swirling crewelwork - the effect was like an Indian bazaar, so much so that Murray found himself sniffing for the spices to go with it. If Mr. Pillans intended in his home to advertise his business, he had certainly done it thoroughly.

Once Murray's eyes had recovered, he looked about him for anything out of place, but this room was clearly for show and entertainment. No papers lay about, nor any trace of recent occupation. He closed the shutter and retreated. Across the hallway, the dining room offered a similar spectacle, and was similarly uninformative. The furniture, where he could see it clearly, was good, but not extravagant – nothing, he suspected, that would draw attention away from the fabrics.

The public rooms were clearly that – intended to be public. Would he have to venture upstairs to try to find anything concerning Gordon Pillans' recent activities? He had a horrible feeling that he would have to, and decided it was best to get it over with. He shut up the dining room, and made for the stairs.

Once again, upstairs all the doors were shut. He noted that dust sheets had not been spread in the rooms: it must not have been Mr. Pillans' intention to spend the whole summer at Collessie. Probably his business would require him to return fairly frequently, so the house had only been partially shut up. That might mean there was more chance of finding information here, unless everything was in the mysterious box that Macduff had found at the inn – if they could ever open it.

There were four doors off the landing, two to the front of the house and two more towards the back. The first at the front was a bedchamber, the decor a little less flamboyant than that in the downstairs rooms. Murray scanned it quickly, but there was more evidence of Mrs. Pillans here than of her husband. The other front room seemed to be that of Mrs. Skead, and contained one or two items of quite humble furniture that she had perhaps brought from her own home when she came to live with her daughter: a plain wooden chair, and a cheap clock. It was the closest thing Murray had seen to a personal touch in the house.

He left the front rooms, and went to the back of the house. A small door to the side gave access to a servants' stair, probably leading from the kitchens to the attics. Murray left it for now, and tried the next door.

A desk, and papers, and one or two ledgers. He had found Gordon Pillans' office.

And just at that, there came a shriek behind him, and a ringing blow to the top of his head.

Chapter Twenty-Eight

Isobel would not have admitted to it, not even to her father, but she felt a certain thrill at being, however temporarily, mistress of Letho.

In some ways, of course, it was just work, only on a larger scale, with more servants and rooms and variety of duties than she would have had in her father's Edinburgh house, and had had since she was sixteen. Her father had no gardener, nor factor, nor stillroom, nor dairy. Nor indeed farm nor grounds nor woods, nor all the other complications which she would not need to worry about, like the engineers in the old icehouse. They were none of her concern.

But she had known Letho all her life, and loved it, and though she knew she might be busy over the days of Charles' absence, she was rather looking forward to seeing more intimately how everything worked, and to being, just for a little while, the lady of this lovely house.

Monday started smoothly. Charles had ridden off early, and Isobel had summoned the stand-in housekeeper (the second stand-in housekeeper – this would be interesting) to meet her after breakfast and talk over the week to come.

Mrs. Gilmour, reporting to the drawing room for want of the downstairs parlour, was fair and stocky, neatly turned out in a fresh white cap and grey gown, with an air of knowing what she was about that was more inclined to inspire confidence than to intimidate. She stood at just the right distance from the desk where Isobel had established herself with pen and paper, and notes of what she wanted to ask or say: Mrs. Gilmour folded her hands neatly in front of her, but also had a notebook and pen ready with her keys at her waist. She was the picture of the perfect housekeeper. Nevertheless, Isobel wanted to step off on the right foot: as a visitor to Letho (if nothing else, added a quiet voice at the back of her head), it was possible she might have to get along with this woman for years ahead.

'I am Miss Blair,' she explained, not sure how well the poor woman had managed to take account of the household yet. 'My father and I are to be in charge in Mr. Murray's absence, though of course we shall depend upon you and Mr. Robbins. We are well acquainted with the household, but I should like to know a little of your background, Mrs. Gilmour.'

'Of course, ma'am. I have been working up to recently in Edinburgh, in the Old Town but in a fair-sized establishment, with two manservants and a coachman and carriage.'

'Oh really? Where was that?' Blair's own house was a fair-sized one in the Old Town, in George's Square.

Mrs. Gilmour looked taken aback at the question.

'In ... in Brown Square, near the College.'

'I know it well,' said Isobel with a smile. 'Who was your master?'

'The family were Reid, ma'am.'

'Reid ... I cannot call anyone of that name to mind.'

'My master entertained a good deal in the way of business – he was a brewer – but the children were up and away and when he died six months ago the mistress wanted to move to a smaller place. I could have stayed, but I thought perhaps it was time to make a change. We parted on good terms and she has made me a recommendation which, I believe, Mr. Robbins has taken a copy of.'

'How long were you there?'

'Half a dozen years, ma'am.'

'And before that?'

'In London, ma'am, but I tired of it, and wanted to return to Scotland.'

'If Mr. Robbins is satisfied with your recommendations then there is no need for me to examine them. Do I detect a hint of Fife in your voice? Have you come close to home?'

Mrs. Gilmour blushed.

'I have a bad habit, ma'am, of picking up the accents of those around me. No doubt in London no one would have taken me for a Scotswoman at all. Forgive me, ma'am: I try not to, and it is not intended to cause offence.'

She seemed anxious on the point, and Isobel decided to leave it.

'Are you finding your way with the other servants?'

'Yes, ma'am, I believe so.'

'I know we are a little short-staffed: if you happened to know of someone seeking a position as a maid, I'm sure Mr. Robbins would be glad to hear of it.'

'He has said as much, ma'am.'

'Good. If you do have any problems during this week, feel free to come to me if you wish, or consult with Mr. Robbins as you feel appropriate. Now, to the menus.'

She spoke with Mrs. Gilmour for a good hour, all told: there was much to discuss when it came to what was to be ordered from Cupar and what was becoming available in the garden, and what was in the stillroom and the pantries that needed to be used up. Isobel enjoyed the way her mind needed to stretch just a little to take it all in – good practice, she thought, in case one day – one day – she might really have charge of such a place.

She dismissed Mrs. Gilmour at last, and watched her go, then turned to scribble a little picture of her on the back of the copious notes she had made. Mrs. Gilmour, who had lived half a dozen years only round the corner from where she herself had lived. It was not impossible: Edinburgh was a busy place, and Isobel and her father spent a good deal of time elsewhere. But was she wrong? Had she been mistaken, or was Mrs. Gilmour uneasy about something – something in that Edinburgh part of her life, perhaps, or at Isobel's questioning her about it? She hoped it was nothing bad: Letho had been without a housekeeper for too long, and she found herself liking Mrs. Gilmour. She hoped that the woman would be able to stay.

'Ouch!' cried Murray, snatching off his hat to rub his head even as he spun to see his attacker. In the centre of the landing stood a small person, waving a copper saucepan and squealing like an agitated pig.

'Hush!' he said, trying to modulate his own voice. 'Hush.

Mrs. Pillans gave me a key, look?'

He waved the key as close to the girl as he could get without being dunted again by the saucepan. She was not very efficient at wielding it, but she did persist – with both that and the squealing.

'Please be quiet,' said Murray, as soothing as he could be. The squeaks continued. 'BE QUIET!' he bellowed, and the girl, shocked, sat on the floor with a thud. 'Thank you. Now, please listen. Mrs. Pillans in Fife gave me a key so that I could look round the house. She thought there was no one here.'

'There isna, sir,' said the girl, who appeared, now he could see clearly, to be wearing a maid's apron. 'The house is empty till Mr. Pillans comes back for his work, sir.'

He reached out a hand, but she scrambled to her feet unaided.

'If there is no one here,' said Murray, 'who are you?'

'I'm no here, sir – dinna say I was!' she added in sudden alarm.

'Well … but you look as if you are here,' he pointed out. 'What's your name?'

She hesitated, but despite her evident wariness she did not seem to be able to resist instructions.

'Annie, sir. Oh, dinna tell him!'

'Is he a good master, Annie?'

'Well, aye, he's no bad, sir. But he tellt us all to go home till he called for us, and the cook and the housemaid went, sir. But my mother has died and my da's marrit again and she disna like me, so I've no home to go to.'

The hurt was recent: he could hear a catch in her voice.

'And Mr. Pillans didn't know?'

'No, sir. So I thought there would be no harm if I stayed and – and looked after the place, sir. In case of intruders.'

She had evidently forgotten that he was an intruder.

'Did Mr. Pillans get to Fife all right, sir?'

It was Murray's turn to hesitate.

'He's there now,' he said. 'When did he leave here?'

'Last Thursday, sir. He said it would take the best part of two days to get to where he was going. The housemaid told me. That's a gey long way.'

'It can feel a long way, certainly,' Murray agreed. 'You're local, then?'

172

'Och, no, sir. I was born in the Grassmarket.'

Of course – perhaps a quarter-hour's walk away.

'And are you the kitchenmaid?'

'Yes, sir.'

'Have you worked here for long?'

'Since Mr. Pillans was married, sir.'

'That's about eighteen months, isn't it?' She nodded. 'It must be a good place to work, if you're here so long.' It was not very long, but he thought that perhaps in her young life it seemed so.

'It's no bad, sir,' she decided. 'Cook says there's lots worse.'

'It'll be different, though, I daresay, when Mrs. Pillans and her mother are here, and when they go away?' He smiled, making a joke of it, and she took it that way.

'Oh, aye, sir! Mrs. Pillans keeps everything in order, and she can be awful strict. Cook says it's because she never had a household before, but I canna see how that could be. Ordering people around is ordering people around – what could be difficult about that?'

Murray remembered what Isobel had said about Mrs. Pillans being unused to command.

'Do you know anything about Mrs. Pillans before she married Mr. Pillans?'

'Aye, sir, well, her name would have been Skead, would it no? For that's Mrs. Skead's name. Her mother.'

Murray smiled.

'Very true.' Perhaps. 'But anything else? She comes from somewhere down in the Borders, does she not?'

'Aye, that's right, sir.'

'What brought her to Edinburgh?'

'To work, sir, same as many.'

'What kind of thing did she work at, then?'

'Cook says she worked in the shop.'

'Actually in the Oriental Warehouse? Did she work for Mr. Pillans?'

'Aye, sir, I think she did.'

Isobel would win a prize for this.

'Would you like to work in a shop? Do you think that would be better than working in a household?'

'Oh, no, sir! Cook says it's much better to work for people you know, not have all those strangers about every day.'

'But Mr. Pillans still works in a shop, doesn't he?'

'Oh, aye, sir, but he's the owner. He's in charge.' It was said with some pride. Blair would be interested in this girl and all she had to say about her station in life.

'So when Mrs. Pillans and Mrs. Skead are away, the household is a little more relaxed?'

'Well ...'

'Is he strict, too?'

'Oh no, sir, not so much at all. But we're much busier when he's here without them. There's hardly a night without guests, ken, and they're – Cook says they're the noisy kind, they liven up the place.'

'The cook likes it?'

'Yes, sir, but the housemaid doesna. She has to deal with them. Cook just has to feed them.'

This sounded like the echo of an argument she had witnessed many times. Murray could picture the scene even in those few words, but he tried not to jump to conclusions.

'So these guests – men, I suppose?'

'Oh, aye, sir.'

'They come to dine? To drink?'

'Not to dinner, sir, no. Later than dinner – supper, usually.'

'And drinking?'

'A bit, sir, aye.'

'And what else – singing?' It sounded like one of the drinking clubs that used to be common in the Old Town, with their strange customs and secretive ways. Newington did not seem the place for one of those.

'No singing, sir, no. Drinking, aye.'

'Then what?'

'Well, cards, sir. That's why they come. They play cards.'

Chapter Twenty-Nine

And when the maid finally left Murray in peace to look properly into Mr. Pillans' office, he found ample evidence of what she had said. Whether Mrs. Pillans knew of it or not, it was clear that Mr. Pillans, in her absence, hosted a serious gambling club.

Instead of the ledgers connected with the Oriental Warehouse, which Murray had expected to find, there were quite different records. A collection of four leatherbound volumes recorded games of various kinds: one was for piquet, one for whist, one for faro, and the last for loo. The dates and the players were listed in each match, but not the location, making Murray think that generally the games were played in this house. In another set of books, debts and payments were meticulously laid out, and he could, had he wished, have cross-referenced the entries here to the games recorded in the first books. And if those were the papers of a serious gambling club, one volume was given over to the frivolities: 'A.F. bet J.R. that the raindrop on the left hand pane of the parlour window would reach the frame before the raindrop on the right hand pane. J.R. accepted. One guinea placed. A.F. won. Verified E.F. and G.P.' And only initials appeared – in none of the books could Murray find anywhere a full or even partial name was given, and no book in which there was a key to the initials. This was a discreet business indeed – and apparently, very rigorously run. If this was an example of Gordon Pillans' efficient work, then it was much less surprising that he owned a successful business at so young an age.

Gordon Pillans was presumably G.P., Murray thought, verifying that A.F.'s raindrop had reached the frame first. Murray could think of nothing less dull than betting on something like that. Gambling might be fashionable, but he could find better ways of spending his money – and if he did bet, he preferred there to be some skill involved, somewhere in the process. But some could not help it, he knew. He wondered if Pillans' club catered to men like that, or if it were simply social.

Could Pillans afford to gamble?

He could find no record of personal finances here, no letters from the bank or bundles of paid vouchers. Pillans must have kept such papers elsewhere, perhaps at the warehouse. He took the latest book of debts and payments with him, and headed downstairs – he had asked the maid to make him a pot of coffee, which she seemed to think was within her powers.

He found her in the kitchen, something which seemed to alarm her.

'I'll bring the pot to the back parlour, sir,' she said urgently, though he wondered how often she served anything to guests. He retreated, though, and found a room behind the drawing room, shuttered and still like the rest of the public rooms. He pulled open two of the shutters, and found that this room, at least, had the air of being lived in. A workbox stood by the fire, with some needlework in progress laid on the top. A newspaper, neatly folded, lay on the table – the date was the previous Tuesday, two days before Pillans was supposed to have left Edinburgh. The furnishings were comfortable, but not brand new, not an advertisement for the Oriental Warehouse. There were no books, but there was a desk, a davenport against a wall away from the fireplace, where the light from the window would illuminate a morning's correspondence. He listened for the maid coming with the coffee, and slipped over to take a closer look.

Here, at least, were the most recent domestic bills, paid and neatly stacked. Here were one or two letters from the bank on the Mound, with nothing untoward to say about the household finances. It looked as if Pillans' organisation extended to his domestic affairs – or that Mrs. Pillans was given liberty to pay these vouchers for ... he glanced through a few ... groceries, tobacco, wine, seeds for the garden – without reference to her husband. He opened the gambling record book and compared the writing there with the labels on the outside of the vouchers, and it was not the same. Mrs. Pillans dealt with the house, and it seemed well-run and not in financial difficulties. He was glad, in a way: he did not feel in the least comfortable poking around like this, and to find embarrassment would make it worse. He could only tell himself that if it helped to find Gordon Pillans' murderer, his intrusion would be justified.

He was seated at the parlour table, innocently looking around him, when the maid appeared with a tray, the coffee pot, a coffee can and saucer, and a slightly elderly biscuit. There were no spoons, and no sugar.

'Oh!' she said. 'And there's no milk anyway.'

'That's all right,' said Murray, who had not expected there to be any, 'but sugar and a spoon would help.'

She scuttled off, and reappeared with both. She was about to go again when he stopped her.

'This cook of yours seems a sensible woman,' he said, applying sugar to his coffee. 'What does she have to say about the food and drink she has to work with here?'

'What do you mean, sir?' The maid looked bewildered, as well as edgy.

'Does she complain about the quality? Comment on the extravagance? Remark on the numbers she has to cater for, or say that the poulterer is asking for his bill to be paid? Anything like that?'

The choice seemed to confuse the maid even further. She took a moment or two to unpick the list.

'The poulterer's a she, sir. I don't remember Cook saying anything about bills to be paid. She gets what she wants from the people – I've heard her say that's a good cut of beef, or the lettuces are fresh, or things like that. There's never very many people here, not when the mistress is here, and only the men I told you about when she's not. I don't know, sir! She seems happy enough. We're all happy enough. It's all right, working here. Please don't tell Mr. Pillans I came back!'

Servants, thought Isobel.

Well, people in general, but servants were the ones you were responsible for.

Her early-morning visit on Tuesday to the nursery found a subdued Augusta and a Miss Fitzsimmons who had clearly been crying. Quiet conversation, while Augusta was sent off to busy herself at the nursery box piano, elicited Miss Fitzsimmons' unpleasant encounter with, apparently, a gentleman, on the far side of the village when she was taking a walk: the gentleman had insulted her, but not physically, fortunately. Isobel did her best to comfort her, and made dark mutterings about Mr. George who had a reputation for approaching girls, though this did not sound quite like him, somehow.

Her father had not yet appeared, so Isobel had then arranged with Mrs. Gilmour to take a tour around the kitchen quarters, and was a little surprised to find, on meeting Mrs. Gilmour in the entrance hall, that the housekeeper was cross.

'What's the matter?' she asked.

'There's a man in the kitchen,' said Mrs. Gilmour.

'A man? You mean Daniel or William?'

'No!' said Mrs. Gilmour dismissively – she had clearly assessed the two servants well – 'not a servant. A foreign person.'

'A foreign person?' Isobel repeated, feeling idiotic. She was not sure what Mrs. Gilmour would count as foreign. 'Not one of the Irish engineers?'

'No, not them. This is a musical person, ma'am. A foreign musical person, and he refuses to leave.'

Struggling to dismiss the image of some kind of lifesize musical box on the kitchen table, Isobel thought hard.

'Oh! Do you mean the German who went to Collessie? Mr., um, Rieder?'

'That's him, ma'am.'

'And why is he refusing to leave? I know it must be awkward to take up a place at Collessie just at the moment, but –'

'He says he's too scared, ma'am.'

'Goodness! Scared of what?'

'Ah, well, then he goes all foreign,' said Mrs. Gilmour, tight-lipped. 'I daresay, though,' she conceded, 'that I'd be the same in foreign lands, if something had scared me. I doubt I'd be able to say much in another language to explain myself.'

'I know a little German,' said Isobel, and instantly regretted it. Her German was bookish, learned only for reading. She had never had a conversation in German with an actual German, only with friends with similarly limited vocabularies, and never for very long.

Her father was resting. Where was Charles when one needed him? 'Let's go and see him.'

She had not been down to the kitchens for years, but they had not changed much. Mrs. Mack had a few more grey hairs, perhaps, as had Iffy. The men were not around. Jennet, too, was presumably off upstairs making beds. Any time Isobel had glimpsed her in the last week she had been moving at speed and frowning. Isobel had asked her own maid to make their beds and tidy, in the hope that Jennet would not actually collapse before the household found a new maid to help her.

The kitchen led off a long corridor that also gave access to the stillroom and pantries, and, to the other side, the kitchen garden. As so often, the kitchen garden door was open, to ease the heat of the kitchen itself, though it was milder at this time of the day. Mrs. Mack was sitting at the broad fir table, picking precisely through a batch of radishes, usually a task for the kitchen maid. It was possible that she did not trust Iffy to remove the less satisfactory roots. Iffy, anyway, was battering the breakfast dishes in the scullery, and singing in an anxious little voice, which presumably prevented her from hearing when Isobel and Mrs. Gilmour came into the kitchen. Mrs. Mack, however, rose and curtseyed.

'Aye, it's grand to see someone in charge for a change, miss!' she said with a grin.

'Oh, Mrs. Mack, you're always in charge!' said Isobel, smiling back. 'But I hear you have a lodger?'

Mrs. Mack made a face and nodded to the corner. This individual in the dark clothes, trying to make himself as inconspicuous as possible to the extent of actually facing the wall, must be Mr. Rieder.

'*Guten Tag*,' said Isobel, cleared her throat, and tried it again. '*Guten Tag* – Herr Rieder, *n'est-ce pas*? I mean – oh, goodness.' Every word of German she had ever learned absented itself from her mind, with the exception, when she scrabbled around a bit, for *Für Elise*, the only piece of piano music she had ever, eventually, mastered. That was not going to help here.

The man, however, had scrambled to his feet, looking alarmed.

'Mr. Rieder,' Isobel began again, a little too loudly. The man was not, presumably, deaf. 'Mr. Rieder, I am told that you are scared? Frightened?'

'Afraid,' the man said. 'Yes, madam, I am afraid. I do not wish to leave here. I will not go!'

At his raised voice, Iffy's singing broke off. She stuck her head around the pantry door, looked in dismay at the scene, and apparently dropped the dish she was holding. Regardless, she wriggled her skinny self back into the kitchen, raised her arms as if she might ward off some attack, surged forward, tripped on something only she could see and fell at their feet.

Murray left the Newington house to a profound impression of the maid's relief – and indeed his own. He carried with him the latest account book from the gambling club, hoping that perhaps Mrs. Pillans would be able to identify some of the participants by their initials, but if the events only happened when she was not there it seemed less likely.

He called, tentatively, at a couple of the neighbouring houses, but no one there seemed to know the Pillans well: recent arrivals, with no family and a lively social life which, nevertheless, had not been particularly disruptive to anyone else. One couple had been invited to dinner, and had found the furnishings overwhelming: their impression of their hosts was less definite.

It would have made sense to visit the Oriental Warehouse, source of those furnishings, next, as it lay on his route back to the New Town, but he felt he should make sure of Lady Rocheid's safety first. That way, if she had not already done so, he could send a note to Mr. George to reassure him. Lord Rocheid, he felt, needed no such reassurance. Murray wondered if a thought of his wife had even crossed his mind since their conversation on Sunday evening.

He did pass the warehouse, though, on his route back, and noted the elaborate hanging sign outside, the windows full of bright cloth, the widened doorway inviting customers inside. He thought he detected a hint of spice in the air, too, though whether the warehouse stocked spices, or the cloths brought the scent back, or Pillans scattered the spices about to lend an air of the exotic to his stock, he was not sure.

It was enticing, but he left the place for now, and strode back down the North Bridge to the New Town, skirted the imposing walls of the General Register House and the less ambitious modern tenements of St. James' Square round the corner. Already here, with the wind in the right direction, one could catch the salt air of Leith, whipping up from the harbour. But the direction Murray had been given for Lady Rocheid's town house was in the more sheltered and salubrious Picardy Place, with its back to those harbour winds and its face towards Queen Street.

Chapter Thirty

He looked up when he was close to the house. The shutters and some of the windows on the main floor were open, but curtains above that were closed; the house, at least, did not look shut up, but perhaps the servants were taking the chance of Lord Rocheid's departure to give the place a thorough clean and airing. No proof that Lady Rocheid was in residence. He crossed the street, and gave the risp a good rattle.

A smart but unhappy-looking manservant answered the door after a minute, and gave Murray a quick inspection.

'Lord Rocheid is from home, sir,' he said.

'It is not Lord Rocheid I have come to see,' said Murray. 'It is Lady Rocheid.'

Suitably surprised, the manservant reassessed Murray. It was just possible, Murray thought, that he had risen in the servant's estimation.

'Mr. ... George?' the manservant tried.

'A friend of Mr. George, from Letho. From Fife.' He had given the man his card. It did not look as if Mr. George often visited his sister here, nor that Lady Rocheid often had any callers. 'Is Lady Rocheid at home?'

The man's eyes flickered, as if he could look behind him and see Lady Rocheid.

'She is not receiving visitors, sir.'

'But she is here? She is in residence?'

The man looked increasingly uncomfortable.

'She said not to say, sir.'

'Look,' said Murray, 'I am come from her brother Mr. George, in an effort to assure him of her safety and wellbeing. And I have some news she will, I am sure, want to hear as soon as possible. Could she could perhaps even send me down a note? Something like that? Could I speak with her maid, perhaps?'

'Her maid? Oh!' The man's fingers were twitching as he stared over Murray's shoulder, trying to think what to do.

'Look,' said Murray again, more gently, 'you're clearly worried about her, too. Please let me help.'

The manservant came to a decision.

'Please to come in, sir, and wait in the …' he tried to think what was suitable for a strange gentleman waiting for a lady, 'in the master's study here.' He pushed open a door, and ushered Murray inside. 'I shall see …'

He hurried off, leaving Murray in a small room with a fireplace and two easy chairs, a table that might pass for a desk and a hard chair to it. There was little sign of any studying, but it was a comfortable enough retreat for a gentleman, or a place for him to entertain one or two close friends. It had the air of being used: a couple of illustrated books had been well-thumbed, and the ceiling was yellowed with tobacco smoke. On the wall were prints of horses, dogs and pugilists.

He had little chance to see anything more, for in a moment or two the manservant returned, looking calmer.

'Please to step upstairs, sir.'

He guided Murray up the stone stairs, and into a drawing room. It formed the entire face of the house at this level, with three tall windows, and the full light fell on a room furnished with all the taste and expense Murray would have expected from Miss George. Every chair, every curtain, every ornament sat in harmony with its neighbours and was a delight to the eye. But by contrast with the study downstairs, it looked as if it had never been used.

Lady Rocheid was seated by the far window, as if she wanted him to have to walk as far as possible to reach her, revealed by the nearer windows. The light that fell on her was merciless enough. The Georges were older than Murray, sufficiently older that he had never known Miss George well, though he had grown closer to Mr. George over the years of being near neighbours, fellow landlords. Miss George had always been that bit distant, the difference in age more felt. And that age showed now, more than he had ever noticed before.

She watched him approach, watched him bow, nodded stiffly in response. Was she actually going to speak? He was already wondering when, at last, she said,

'Mr. Murray, good day to you.'

'Good day, Lady Rocheid.'

It seemed to be an effort for her to talk.

'I had thought to have left you at Letho.'

'Indeed, Lady Rocheid, but a business matter brought me back to town for a few days. I thought I would take the liberty of calling to pay my respects.'

'Well – I should thank you, I suppose,' she said. 'You are the first guest in this drawing room almost since it was decorated. But I imagine my brother sent you?'

Murray hesitated.

'I volunteered. You left at such short notice and so swiftly that those of us who knew of it were concerned.'

'Those who knew of it? Half the parish, you mean, and all the village.'

'I don't believe so,' he countered.

'And that woman, Mrs. Pillans?'

'I should not think so at all. She is more concerned with her own problems.'

'To feel envious of a widow!' The theme she had touched on at Dures seemed to be lingering in her mind. 'That he should have brought me to that!'

Not her brother, Murray was sure. This 'he' was Lord Rocheid.

'Lord Rocheid had arrived at Dures by the time I left. Not long after you left, in fact.'

She straightened.

'He did?'

'I met him myself.'

She frowned.

'But how?'

'I don't know how he travelled –'

'I mean how could he have arrived and not passed me? I went by the most direct route. What way did he go?'

'I believe he also said that he went by the most direct route, my lady,' said Murray. Perhaps they had each been so involved in their own thoughts that they had not noticed the other – or one had stopped at an inn and the other, unknowing, had passed by. Anything could have happened. Not every direct route was obvious to every traveller.

'I suppose he expects me to turn around and go back to Dures,' said Lady Rocheid, pursing her thin lips. Murray opted to remain silent. 'Well, he can wait. Perhaps I shall enjoy a few days here, visit some friends, spend some money. There's a cloth warehouse on South Bridge I favour – I might just go there, and see what I fancy. After all,' she muttered, half to herself, 'it was my money.'

'May I send to Mr. George to reassure him that you have reached here safely? No doubt you yourself will write to him, but I should be happy to let him know immediately.'

She looked at him with weary eyes.

'No doubt he is congratulating himself on having been quite right about Jacob Rocheid. A fortune hunter, he said. He must be very pleased with himself.'

'More concerned, I believe, for your welfare.'

'Well then. Yes, tell him. Tell him I am safely arrived. Tell him I am comfortably established. Tell him I am glorying in my position at the head of Edinburgh society, invitations from all sides, callers morning, noon and night.' She made a faint, hopeless gesture about the empty drawing room. 'Tell him all that, if you will, Mr. Murray. And tell him,' she swallowed, audibly, 'tell him I shall soon be home.'

Mr. Rieder had leapt back in fright as Iffy had lunged towards him, but when she fell he sagged back on to the stool he had adopted, and quivered as Mrs. Mack and Mrs. Gilmour picked Iffy up, applied cold cloths to her bleeding nose, and checked for bruises where she had hit the corner of the table on her way down. She had broken a rib, and yelped with pain when they pressed it.

'What did you think you were doing, girl?' Mrs. Mack demanded. 'Did the dishes leap out and chase you?'

'I thought you were going to – to –' Between her ribs and the cloth over her nose, Iffy struggled to catch her breath. 'To send him away.'

'Who?' asked Mrs. Mack, but Isobel could see that Iffy's longing eyes were firmly fixed on Mr. Rieder. Oh, dear, she thought: poor Iffy. Her twin sister was married years ago – to William, who was at least better than Daniel – but Iffy had been scarred in a fire and had never yet succeeded in finding a beau of her own. And by the look on Mr. Rieder's face, she had not found one now.

'She is mad. She follows me everywhere,' he said firmly.

'I want to make sure you are happy!' Iffy told him, trying to smile, though as her nose continued to gush the effect was not appealing.

'Happy? In this place? How could any man be happy here? One cannot sleep easy in one's bed!'

'Iffy?' said Mrs. Mack, suspiciously.

'No, Mrs. Mack! Not me!'

'In any case, I do not stay in my bed, in case I am trapped.' said Rieder. 'I sleep here, by the fire, under the table. With my knife out, in case of attack,' he added darkly.

'Mr. Rieder, what is it you are afraid of?'

'Have you not heard? Heard of the moving of bodies in the night, of murders, of attacks, of disappearing men? I, I am a man,' he said, thumbing his own chest to make the point. 'I could be disappeared too!'

'But you cannot just stay here, Mr. Rieder,' said Isobel, trying to sound reasonable. 'Surely there must be somewhere else you should be?'

'At Collessie, yes,' he said, nodding ferociously. 'I should be at Collessie. I give up all my Edinburgh work – all my profitable engagements, all my generous patrons – and I come to Collessie, and I find it is a wreck, and like some Gothic novel of your Horace Walpole they drag dead bodies out of it at night and make off with them! I cannot stay there. Even if they would have me, with the master dead and his body taken who knows where!'

'The body has been returned,' said Isobel, but even as she said it she knew it was not as reassuring as she had hoped. She glanced at Iffy, who had never taken her eyes off Mr. Rieder, who had never so much as looked at her since she had fallen. The body … Poor Lady Rocheid, so desperate for a husband she would take a dead one. Goodness, the world was an unhappy place sometimes.

Head full of Lady Rocheid and Mr. George, Murray elected now to go home to the Queen Street house and write to Francis George at once. It took him the length of Queen Street, walking (for him) quite slowly, and including a pause to buy an evening paper, to compose the letter. How much concern should he raise? How desperate was Lady Rocheid? By 'home' did she mean Dures? Or something more terrible, more final? Was her manservant unhappy because he also feared that something bad was going to happen? Should Murray have seen to it that she packed herself up and set off straight away back to Fife? But that would presumably mean meeting her husband, and just at present that did not seem calculated to cheer her at all.

Turning it all over in his mind, he decided at last to write as full a description as he could of his meeting with Lady Rocheid, and to send it express to Mr. George. Mr. George knew his sister better than anyone. He would know whether or not to worry – and if Murray added that he would follow any instruction Mr. George might send, he would be as much help as he could be. If Mr. George was worried, he would send an express back.

He did his best with the letter, then called Nathaniel and sent him out to the express office, with a further message to deliver on his way back. Then he helped himself to bread and cheese and a draught of ale in the kitchen, ignored the slightly guilty feeling of independence it caused in him, and settled down upstairs to wait.

Chapter Thirty-One

About two hours passed. Murray read the more interesting articles in the *Courant*, and hunted unsuccessfully for any mention of more missing girls, or indeed discovery of any of those already missing, whether dead or alive. At least, he thought, they were not finding bodies, not yet. Thinking of bodies, he scanned the notices of births, deaths and marriages, and saw that Gordon Pillans' death had not yet been announced: perhaps it might be considered bad for business.

Then he heard, distantly, a sound at the back of the house, below his window. The yard door was opened and shut again. Then there was silence, as presumably Nathaniel gained the kitchen and cleaned his boots – he was a particular sort of lad – before heading upstairs to look for his master. Murray at last heard, as he had hoped, two pairs of feet outside the parlour door, and a pause before the door opened, and Nathaniel appeared.

'Sergeant Clyne, sir,' he announced, pleased with himself, and bowed.

'Some ale, please, for the sergeant, Nathaniel,' said Murray. Nathaniel bowed again, and the sergeant looked gratified.

'Good day to you, Clyne, and thank you for coming.'

'Your man showed me the note from Fife, sir,' said Clyne. 'Of course I mind you and I worked together before, with some success.'

It was not quite how Murray remembered the story, but he was content to leave that be – and he was pleased to note that the sergeant had, in the intervening half-dozen years, gone so far towards self-improvement that his waistcoat buttons now strained over muscle, rather than fat. His thick black hair was neatly cut, his face recently shaved, and he stood straight with a poise that was due less to self-satisfaction and more to a confidence that looked as if it had been built on experience. And anyway, Sergeant Clyne was in charge of the police office nearest to the Oriental Warehouse. If Murray were to show Macduff's note to anyone in Edinburgh, it really had to be Clyne.

'I'm afraid that this matter, too, might take all our ingenuity to sort out, Sergeant. Part of the story seems to have happened in Fife, and part here in Edinburgh.'

'And it involves the Oriental Warehouse, sir?'

'It does, yes. What do you know of the women who have gone missing from there?'

'Well,' said Clyne, and was at once interrupted as Nathaniel returned with a cup of ale for him. Murray gestured to Clyne to sit at the table, thinking that any tale the sergeant had to tell might be eased by taking the weight off his feet. It seemed to work.

'The first I heard of it, sir, was when one of the reporters from the *Courant* turned up at the police office last week, asking what we were doing about it. Of course, that was a wee bit embarrassing, to be asked about a matter I knew nothing of, so I told him to come back next day and I did a bit of asking about, quick as I could. It seems that three women who were working in the warehouse – shop girls, all of them – have disappeared in the last wee while. A couple of months, at most, that we know of. No one told us,' he added, sounding a little hurt.

'Well, then, it would have been difficult for you to have known to do anything,' said Murray sympathetically.

'Exactly, sir. That's what I thought.'

'What do you know about them? I only know what I have read in the *Courant*.' He gestured to the paper by his chair. Sergeant Clyne straightened his waistcoat, as though it would order his recollection, and leaned one arm on his broad thigh, ticking off the numbers with his other hand.

'The first was Johnston, Mary Johnston. A redhead, with the temper to go with it. She had a row with the woman that manages the shop one Friday evening, and left. When she did not appear for work on Saturday morning, it was assumed that she had decided to quit the place and seek other employment.'

'What was the row about, do you know?'

'The manager claimed that she had spoiled the end of a bolt of cloth, so that she could take it home as scrap. Mary Johnston was furious, and said that the manager was as good as accusing her of theft, destroying her good reputation.'

'And had she a good reputation?'

'She had, sir,' admitted Sergeant Clyne reluctantly. 'Apart from the temper, no one had a word to say against her. Honest and respectable.'

'So if they did not miss her at the warehouse, who did?'

'Her parents: she lived with them in a flat not far from the shop. They say she never appeared home on Friday night. They asked all the neighbours on Saturday, and asked again at church the next day, but no one had seen her. They thought perhaps she was staying with a friend, but they were worried, all the same. They contacted one of our officers, but he – and I've had words with him – made no note of where it was she worked.

'So when the next woman disappeared, a fortnight later, we had no idea there was a connexion.'

'Which one was that, then?'

'Maggie Daniels.'

'The *Courant*, I think, said that she was a handsome girl?'

'Oh, aye – she was a fine-looking lass. Lots of admirers, but she kept herself to herself – or rather, to one young man. She was engaged to be married to a Robert Ellis. That Friday she said to the other lasses in the warehouse that she was away out to meet him, and then she never came home. He says he waited for her and she never showed up. He's the nervous type, assumed she had met someone better, never thought he deserved her.'

'Poor fellow. No thought that perhaps he had something to do with her disappearance?'

'Aye, indeed, sir. That was our main idea, and we were only looking for some clue as to what he had done with her – for he was not out of sight for very long any time that evening, from one person to another. Anyway, that was what we were working on. And then three weeks after that, another woman gone.'

'This is the widow, then? Jean Soutar?'

'Aye, that's the one, sir. A young woman, husband was a

soldier, died not long after he came back from Waterloo. She was lodging in a very respectable house in Potterrow – the kind where the landlady keeps an eye out for trouble, but isn't too nosy.'

'Fortunate for Mrs. Soutar, no doubt – until that night.'

'Aye, she left work as usual, said she was away straight home. Which was what she usually did. Never appeared. The landlady sent word to us about midnight, and we took a good look around for her between the warehouse and Potterrow. I suppose because we were after Robert Ellis for Maggie Daniels' disappearance, we didna put two and two together. But when the reporter came around asking questions, and pointed out that Mary Johnston had worked there, too, well, that was when we started to think there might be something bigger going on.'

He nodded importantly. Murray waited, but had at last to ask,

'So what happened next?'

'I went to talk to the ones at the warehouse. It's a Mrs. Miller that does the running of the place, and there are usually about a dozen girls working there – they have twa-three in the back room, sewing for customers' orders, and eight or nine at the front of the place helping the customers, taking the money, writing the orders, cutting cloth and so on. Aye, it's a grand place, bigger than you would think. Not that I fancy that kind of thing myself, you understand,' he added. 'I telt the wife that I go home to rest, not to have all they bright colours shouting at me.'

Murray blinked at this unexpected revelation of poetic domesticity.

'And what did they have to say about the missing women?' he asked.

'Oh, aye, well, they said they hadna seen them. I spoke to Mrs. Miller,' he began a count on his fingers again but it faltered, 'and to one of the back room girls and two of the front ones. All the missing women had worked at the front, no in the back.'

Where they would be on public display, as it were, Murray thought. More likely to catch the eye of any predator.

'Did anyone have any idea where they might have gone? Had anyone been seen lingering about the shop, watching the women?'

'None of them mentioned anything like that,' the sergeant

admitted. Murray wondered if he had asked. 'The women are all gey bonny, see. They likely have a few men watching them.'

That was interesting. A deliberate decision on the part of Gordon Pillans, or whoever employed the women? Or just chance?

'And what is Mrs. Miller like?'

'Oh, she would scare off anyone not behaving himself!' said Sergeant Clyne with certainty. He shivered. 'She's only a wee body, but she has a face on her that would make a wasp think twice. Aye, if anything would protect those girls, it'd be her.'

But she had not protected them, not once they had left the warehouse, anyway.

'And what about the owner? Gordon Pillans, did you speak to him?'

'Och, he's no there awful much, by all accounts. I doubt he would know anything.'

'Well, it's too late to ask him now, anyway.'

'Has another lassie gone?' asked the sergeant, his face mournful in expectation.

'As to that, I have no idea,' said Murray. 'But Gordon Pillans himself is dead.'

He described the situation to Sergeant Clyne as they walked back through the New Town, along the broad ridge of George Street, across St. Andrew's Square and down by back lanes to the North Bridge. The sergeant was heading back to his police office in the Old Town anyway, and Murray thought it might not be a bad idea to have him present when he spoke to whoever he could find at the warehouse. Though whether the staff there would necessarily take the sergeant seriously, he was not sure. He did not seem to have found out much from them before.

'That's a gey strange way to go, so far from home,' the sergeant remarked. 'And you say nobody in the village had seen him before?'

'Not that we know of. Apart from his wife and his mother-in-law, of course, but he seems not to have made it that far.'

'And no knowing what's in the kist?'

'Not yet. One of the villagers is clever with locks: he's working on it.'

'Aye, the answer'll be in there, nae doubt,' said Sergeant

Clyne sagely. 'But aye, that's gey peculiar. Your own icehouse, and all?'

'Not quite an icehouse, but yes. It had only just been opened up again, as I said. Was it chance, or did someone know of the place? I have no idea.'

'So do you reckon, if Mr. Pillans is dead, that the girls are all dead, too?' asked the sergeant, trying to work it out.

'I don't think it's a logical conclusion,' said Murray. 'Mr. Pillans did not disappear as the girls did, and he was not hidden even when he was dead. No one has found a body yet for any of the missing women, have they?'

'Aye, well, not that we know. But they could all have gone into the Water of Leith and we'd be none the wiser,' he said lugubriously.

'That's a happy thought,' said Murray. 'But I do think there is a good chance that Mr. Pillans' death has something to do with the missing women. Perhaps,' he added, thinking about the gambling club. Had Pillans fallen into debt? The account book should tell. 'Perhaps he has got himself tangled in something that was more dangerous than he expected.'

Chapter Thirty-Two

Isobel looked at Rieder, and at Iffy, and tried not to sigh. Two days – two days Charles had been away. Well, she had not been left alone, and she was not above seeking help when she needed it – usually. She resolved to talk to her father about Rieder, and possibly Robbins, too. Robbins was a sensible man.

She had just decided that when Robbins himself appeared in the kitchen, blinked once at Iffy – everyone in the household was well used to Iffy's combats with inanimate objects – and bowed to Isobel.

'Miss Blair, Mrs. Warner – the person who kept house briefly – has asked if she might speak with you. She is waiting in the entrance hall.'

A careful grading. Robbins must have been disappointed in Mrs. Warner, or he might have put her somewhere more welcoming. He would probably sooner she was gone.

'Very well, Robbins. I shall see what she has to say.' At least it was an excuse to leave the kitchen: she would speak with her father when he was ready, and then with Robbins later. Her tour of the kitchens could wait.

She led the way back towards the main house, pausing before she reached the door to lean back to Robbins. 'Were there any problems with her? Why did she leave?'

'She was not keen on being in a household where there had been a murder, ma'am.'

'But she's still in Letho? Oh, I suppose Macduff will not have wanted her to go yet.'

'I think that would be her only reason for staying, ma'am.'

He made the presentation in the entrance hall, and left, though Isobel had the impression he had not gone far. She crossed to the chairs by the dark fireplace, and sat down. Mrs. Warner curtseyed, and waited.

Isobel had barely seen her in the short time she had served here, and was not sure she would have recognised her.

'Mrs. Warner, you wanted to see me,' she said, allowing the other woman to speak.

'Yes, miss. Mr. Robbins said that Mr. Murray was away and you were – it was you I maybe needed to see.'

She had been a pretty woman, Isobel thought, waiting for her to go on. A pretty woman who had had a hard life, for whatever reason – illness or poverty or ill-treatment or anxiety of all kinds. Yet she must have overcome some of it, at least: she had at least temporarily taken the position of housekeeper in a good household, and no doubt would find another position soon.

'How can I help you, Mrs. Warner?' she prompted.

'Well, Mr. Macduff, the sheriff's man – he wants me to stay here. In the village, I mean.' She caught the tail of her shawl, began to twist it between her fingers, then made herself stop. 'So I'm at the inn. And I don't know how long I'll be there …'

'Had you somewhere you intended to go? Family somewhere, perhaps?' Isobel knew as little about her as she had about Mrs. Gilmour.

'Not family as such, ma'am,' said the woman. 'Friends – and a better chance of perhaps finding another place. Would there be anywhere else near here in need of a housekeeper, miss? I've heard that Dures House is well run.'

'It is, indeed, though I have not heard that they are in need of anyone. Collessie probably is, but I warn you that you would have a great deal of work to do there to bring things up to the standard of Letho or Dures.'

'But if I do not stay, then I suppose I shall return to the place I came from.' She sighed, as if it were all too much effort. Isobel was not particularly curious, but felt she had to ask.

'And where would that be?'

'My last position was in Edinburgh, ma'am.'

Another one, thought Isobel.

'Where in Edinburgh?'

'In the New Town, down where the new houses are north of Queen Street, if you know it, ma'am.'

'But you're not from Edinburgh yourself?'

'No, ma'am, I'm from Sussex. Near Chichester.'

Of course – her father had found the recommendation when they were in Sussex themselves, and followed it up when they came north.

'Well, I cannot say how much longer Mr. Macduff might want you to stay in the area,' Isobel said, 'but I can ask for you if anyone in the village might be willing to take you in as a lodger, at a cheaper rate than the inn. Would that help?'

'Yes, ma'am,' said Mrs. Warner after a moment. 'Yes, I suppose it would.'

'Then I'll be in touch, as soon as I can,' said Isobel, making a note. Her notepad was busy today. Mrs. Warner curtseyed, and withdrew to the door to the servants' quarters, presumably intending to leave by the servants' door. No doubt Robbins would ensure that she left.

Isobel wondered who might take her in. She was not sure that it was the answer that Mrs. Warner had hoped for. But Isobel could not offer Charles' money to pay for Mrs. Warner to stay indefinitely at the inn, and she could certainly not tell Macduff to let the woman go. And no other possibility seemed to present itself.

The doorway might have been widened in welcome, but it was still rather low for someone of Murray's height. He stooped to enter, breathing in the spice-tinted air, allowing his eyes to adjust to the lamplit interior, hung with every colour of silk and gauze, fine woollens from Cashmere in the north of India, floral printed cottons with complex repeated figures, cool and fresh. The famous paisley pattern was there in every possible variation, but there were all kinds of other shapes and twists and turns, too. The warehouse was warm, and he could almost – almost – imagine himself back in Delhi or Calcutta in some dark stall at the market, negotiating prices with some bright-eyed Indian.

But the girl behind the nearest counter was so obviously a red-headed Scot – and a startlingly pretty one at that - that for a moment he was shocked out of his vision. He smiled awkwardly at her, and then said, more seriously, 'I wonder if I might speak to the manager of this business?'

She was well-trained. With a brief curtsey, she said,

'Of course. One moment, please, sir,' and vanished into the darkness at the back of the shop.

Sergeant Clyne was behind him, staring about at the cloth.

'See, that's no restful, is it?' he whispered. 'Give me a nice bit of heather plaid any day.'

Murray was struggling to think of an occasion on which he might find himself giving Sergeant Clyne a nice bit of heather plaid when the girl returned, and curtseyed to him.

'Mrs. Miller says she will see you in her office, sir,' she said. 'Please to come this way.'

Murray and the sergeant followed her through a set of heavy silk curtains and into the plainer apartments at the back of the building. They were small and cramped, the priority clearly being to give space to the shop. Stairs led up and down at odd angles, and Murray assumed that part of the property reached into the strange rooms that had been created when the Bridges were built, down apparently into the depths of the earth, like the troglodyte accommodation that existed under buildings on the High Street. But the girl did not venture either up or down: she led the way to an even lower door quite close to the curtains, knocked, and waved them inside.

The office had possibly started life as a cupboard, and then had a bit taken off it for some other purpose.There was no natural light, and it was barely possible for Murray to fit into it with its present occupant and her table and chair. Sergeant Clyne gave a brief, hollow laugh, and took up his position in the hallway outside. The woman in the office, a gnome in her cave, looked up, scowled ferociously, and waved Murray back out of the space with sharp little flaps of both hands. Once he was outside in the hall she stood and came to the doorway, and they could at last look at each other properly.

Her reassessment was swift, and her face softened as she dropped a curtsey.

'I beg your pardon, sir – the accommodation is a little cramped.' She ignored Clyne. 'How may I be of service, sir?'

She was indeed short, as Clyne had reported, but looked

muscular, as if she could carry several bales of cloth over each shoulder and barely notice.

'My name is Charles Murray of Letho,' he began, 'and I have come with a message from Mrs. Pillans to Mrs. Miller, if that is you.'

'It is, sir.' She curtseyed again, just to be sure. 'But a message from Annie Pillans? It's a while since she sent any kind of word to me.'

'She used to work here, did she not?'

'Oh, aye, she did that. Until she caught Mr. Pillans' eye.' A hint of bitterness – had Mrs. Miller had intentions towards Mr. Pillans? Or was it jealousy of anyone lifted out of the need for paid employment?

'In the shop, or in the back room?'

'In the shop, sir. Mr. Pillans likes to have handsome girls in the shop. I said why bother, sir, when it's mostly women who come in to buy the goods? But he said that pretty girls sell well to women, too, because they think if they buy the goods they'll be pretty, too. Seems strange to me, sir, but it does work.'

Murray wondered if it worked on Isobel when she shopped here – or indeed on Blair. Blair often seemed oblivious to people's looks. He was much more interested in what went on in their heads.

'Mrs. Pillans must be gratified to have been chosen over the other handsome girls, then?' he said lightly, wondering if Mrs. Miller would deign to respond to such a remark. But she shook her head quickly.

'No, he never took any interest in any of the others, sir. He's always been very business-like here. You hear of some businessmen, some employers, who behave badly, think they have rights, but not Mr. Pillans. Takes an interest in their abilities in the shop, aye, but that is all through me. We work closely together, sir. He places a great deal of trust in me.'

Murray cleared his throat.

'I'm afraid I have some bad news for you, Mrs. Miller. Mr. Pillans is, unfortunately, dead.'

The woman gave an odd squawk, and slapped her hands to her chest, eyes bulging. For a moment Murray thought she was having some kind of seizure, but in a moment she began to breathe again, two or three heavy gasps, before she managed to pull herself under control.

'Who did you say you were?'

'Charles Murray of Letho, in Fife.'

'He was going to Fife.' She pointed a finger at him, making the connexion.

'My estate is next to the one he had taken for the summer. Mrs. Pillans and her mother are already there.'

'He was to join them. He left here on Tuesday.' The finger was pointing again.

'He died on Friday night.'

'And that's – that's the message Annie Pillans had for me?'

'She did not want you to find out from a letter.'

She seemed to stop to imagine what that might have been like, staring past him, pointing finger forgotten. Then she nodded.

'Aye, aye. You came down here just to tell me?'

He smiled.

'That and a few other things. Mrs. Pillans had not seen him for some time, of course, and though he had written she wanted to know more of what he was doing, what he was thinking or how he was feeling before he left. He left here on Tuesday, you said?'

'That's right. The warehouse, I mean. I understood he was to set out on Wednesday morning.'

'And what was he like? Was he behaving in any way strangely? Out of character?'

But Mrs. Miller was puzzled.

'What way did he die? Did he take a stroke or something?'

'No, nothing like that.'

'How is it she didn't see what he was like himself before he died? Was she no in Fife – in this place, whatever it's called?'

'She was – anxiously awaiting him. But he died before he could reach her.'

'Oh!' cried Mrs. Miller, as if suddenly remembering. 'The gig! It was the gig, was it no? Was it overset? Oh, I should have stopped him! The gig!'

Chapter Thirty-Three

'Did he leave here in a gig?'

'That's what he told me he was to do. He said that someone was to take him up to Fife in his gig. I knew it – I knew it would be overset. Oh, why did he not listen to me, the poor man? I told him – I said to him straight that gigs are deathtraps!'

'Did you see the gig at all?' asked Murray, breaking across her outburst.

'Me? No. He'd have been going from his house, I daresay, or from the other man's.'

'Did you see the man? Or did Mr. Pillans mention his name at all?'

'No ... no, I don't believe he did. He said 'my friend', but not like it was really his friend. Do you know what I mean, sir? Like when someone says "Now listen, my friend".'

'Yet whoever it was was to carry him and his luggage all the way to the north of Fife – a friendly gesture, indeed.'

'Unless Mr. Pillans was paying him,' put in Sergeant Clyne wisely. Mrs. Miller jumped: she had forgotten he was there.

'Aye, aye, maybe,' she acknowledged, but she did not sound entirely convinced. Murray considered for a moment, then tried another question.

'Speaking of money,' he began, 'Mrs. Pillans asked if the business was generally on a good footing.'

Mrs. Miller's jaw snapped shut, and her eyes took on a dangerous light.

'Meaning what?'

'Meaning, I suppose, should she be concerned about anything?' He allowed a count of ten for that to sink in, then added, charitably, 'Or will she be able to concentrate on other matters while you look after what's here?'

'Is she minded to come and look after it herself?'

'I have no idea. I should imagine that she is more than grateful for your expertise and your steady hand, for now.'

Mrs. Miller folded her arms, as if she were locking a chest with all the business's papers safely inside it. Her mouth was like a fortress in miniature. It was a moment before she was even capable of speech.

'The business is in a grand way. I see the books myself, and there is no doubt about it. She can take that worry off her plate. For now.'

'I'm sure she'll be much relieved.'

Mrs. Miller's hands, temporarily trapped when she folded her arms, made a kind of bid for freedom.

'Is he to be – to be buried up yonder? In Fife?' She made it sound like Newfoundland.

'I believe so, yes.'

'When?'

'I'm not sure. Does – did he have a desk here? An office to himself?'

'No, he did not,' she said, willing to be distracted from the thought of her employer's burial. 'He left all the papers with me. There's a press with the ledgers, over yonder.' He could hear her teeth grind briefly. 'She can look at them when she comes. Nothing secret here.'

'No, indeed. Now … I wonder if I might be allowed to speak with some of your employees, some of those who knew the missing women?'

Now her hands were off on their own, fingers fluttering. She caught them before her and folded them together at her waist.

'The missing women?'

'Aye, Mrs. Miller,' said Sergeant Clyne, 'you ken how I was asking about them, eh? Well, Mrs. Pillans …' He faltered in his fiction, not having met the woman.

'Mrs. Pillans wants to know if there has been any progress in finding them,' said Murray smooth as could be.

'Well, I haven't heard anything,' said Mrs. Miller tartly. 'Surely if anybody would know, it would be him.' She jerked her head towards Sergeant Clyne's waistcoat, which was about her head height.

'I thought you'd be the first to hear a'thing,' said Clyne, in his own defence. 'I heard you tell the girls to tell you first if they remembered a'thing, or heard some news.'

It was Mrs. Miller's turn to look sheepish.

'It's my job to look after them, sir,' she said primly.

'Of course it is, Mrs. Miller,' said Murray, soothing. 'And I'm sure you've done your best – you can't account for girls after they leave the warehouse, can you?'

'Well, exactly,' she said, with a poisonous glance at Clyne. 'Yon woman – Mrs. Soutar, I mean, sir. She's a widow woman. She could look after herself.'

'Did she have a particular friend here? Is there someone I could talk to, who might know of any news of her?'

'Oh, aye, I suppose,' said Mrs. Miller, presumably selecting whoever it was that she had allowed Clyne to talk to before. 'And I daresay, sir, you'll want a word with the friends of the other two, and all.'

'I should be very much obliged,' Murray agreed, and to his surprise Mrs. Miller was quick to summon the three women and clear a bit of space in one of the workrooms, pushing aside folds of silks and cottons to make room. Murray noted the three: the red-headed girl he had spoken to on the way in, a rounded, happy-looking girl with blond ringlets, and a tall, solemn creature of unusual elegance. They were not introduced, nor did Mrs. Miller explain who he was, though they obviously recognised Sergeant Clyne. Murray sighed, and tried to think of something useful to ask in spite of Mrs. Miller's presence.

'Are you ready to face the first problem of the day, Father?' Isobel asked Blair, when Smith wheeled him out of his parlour bedroom and into the entrance hall. She went over and kissed him good morning.

'A problem? Oh, dear me!' But he looked quite pleased at the idea, and she told him about Mrs. Warner first.

'Can you think of anyone in the village who might be

prepared to put her up for a lower price?' she asked.

'Oh, I should think there might be several,' said Blair, pursing his lips in thought. He named three or four, and turned to Smith. 'I daresay you'd like a walk and a little fresh air, would you not?'

'I would, sir, if you can spare me,' said Smith. He was not a great one for smiling, but he did look pleased at the prospect. 'I'll fetch my hat.'

'Oh, and Smith,' said Blair, quickly, 'should you see Mr. Macduff, the sheriff's man, ask him to step up and give us his news, would you?'

'Of course, sir,' said Smith, and made his bid for freedom.

'That was not much of a problem,' said Blair. 'Was there more to it than that?'

'I think she would rather have left altogether, and gone to find herself another place,' said Isobel. 'It must be like being pickled in aspic – she cannot get on with the next thing while she's tied up with this one.'

'Pickled in aspic,' Blair repeated, nodding enthusiastically. Isobel glanced at his wheelchair, and thought he might well be sympathetic.

'Anyway, then there's the roving German musician – only that he's not roving enough,' she added, and told him about Mr. Rieder. 'I thought perhaps I should consult Mr. Robbins on that one. It's flattering when they think you'll know what to do, but it does make me feel very stupid when I haven't a clue.'

'It's probably best to hold on to him for a while,' said Blair. 'I don't think that Mr. Macduff has quite finished with him, yet, either. But by all means talk with Robbins – no doubt Mrs. Mack would prefer it if he did not sleep under her kitchen table.'

'With a knife in his hand – no, that way accidents happen. Particularly if Iffy is about the place.' She sighed. 'Iffy has broken a rib, or perhaps two.'

'Um,' said Blair.

'I wonder if Mrs. Wedderburn might know of anyone around their way looking for a situation.'

'Oh, but they'll need to replace the maid who left them in Edinburgh,' said Blair, with an awful frown.

'Oh, of course. I wonder how close they are to having their

axle mended? Or will they want to stay and see Charles and say goodbye?'

Blair shrugged.

'I'll call Robbins,' said Isobel, and rang the bell.

Robbins had one of his hunted looks. It was never a good sign.

'Accommodation for Mr. Rieder? Aye, Miss Blair, I'll try and persuade him back somewhere – somewhere he can feel secure, if I can.'

'Thank you, Robbins.' She told him what Mrs. Warner had wanted, and what Smith had gone to the village to look for. Robbins seemed happy enough with that.

'I'm surprised, ma'am, that she has stayed in the village even as long as this, even at Macduff's instigation.'

'You thought she was keen to be away?'

'That was my impression, yes, ma'am.'

'Mine, too. Well, she is best to do what Macduff tells her, all the same.'

'Is something else the matter, Robbins?' asked Blair, bouncing a little in his seat. Robbins gave him a look of resignation.

'Well, sir ...'

'Go on, go on! Better out than in!'

Robbins gave him a look that seemed to disagree with that, but he swallowed, and after a moment found the words to begin.

'It's the engineers. They're complaining that their cottage is haunted.'

'Haunted? By – oh, by poor Mr. Pillans, perhaps?'

'That's what they're saying, sir, yes.'

'Oh, please – Mr. Robbins,' said Isobel, a sudden dread clutching her heart, 'please don't tell me they are threatening to leave!'

'Well, ma'am,' said Robbins, 'well, as to that ...'

'Oh, no! If Charles finds out they've gone –'

'What did you say to them, Robbins?' asked Blair, waving a hand at Isobel that was somewhere between restraint and reassurance.

'I've asked them to stay on till the master gets back,' said Robbins, 'but I'm not sure they will. Mr. Sweeney seemed particularly nervous, and neither looked as if he had slept well, sir.'

'Then we had better do something about it, had we not, Robbins?' asked Blair, and Isobel was alarmed to see the light of excitement in her father's eyes.

The conversation with the shop girls, as far as Murray was concerned, was a failure. Mrs. Miller remained steadfastly present, and it was clear that in front of her the women were not going to say anything to the remotest detriment of the business, nor of the missing women. Their responses were monosyllabic, and they glanced to Mrs. Miller for approval each time. Murray sighed, thanked them, and asked at what hour the warehouse closed.

'In an hour, sir,' said Mrs. Miller, looking pleased with herself.

'Then I shall make a purchase before I go,' he said.

'I shall attend to you myself, sir,' she replied, making it sound like an honour.

In the shop, Murray chose a bright yellow embroidered silk and bought a length of it as a present for Blair, and gave directions for it to be taken to the Queen Street house. He and Sergeant Clyne left, and walked up South Bridge, unhurried.

'Would that colour no give you indigestion, sir?' Clyne asked.

'It's not for me, Sergeant. Now, how long till the warehouse shuts?'

'About twenty minutes, sir.' Clyne turned to glance at the clock on the Tron Kirk.

'Let us step into this lane,' said Murray. 'Do you think the shop girls come out by the front door?'

'I saw no other door when I was in there, sir.'

'Yes, but if the building goes down into the chambers below the Bridge – well, we'll just have to hope. Three girls – surely one of them will head in this direction?'

A smile spread over Sergeant Clyne's broad face.

'Oh, aye, sir! I see what you're up to!'

He was a bright man, Sergeant Clyne, thought Murray with a smile. He drew out his own watch and opened it, then settled back to wait.

About ten minutes after the warehouse was due to close, a familiar figure bobbed along the street next to them. Murray swung out, and said,

'Excuse me, may we have another word?'

The happy girl with the ringlets closed her eyes tight, and shrieked at the top of her voice.

Chapter Thirty-Four

'Abduction!' she screamed, and even on South Bridge in the evening light one or two people stopped and stared. 'Kidnap!'

Murray stepped back, and kept his distance, holding Sergeant Clyne away, too.

'I'm sorry, I did not hear your name when we spoke in the warehouse,' he said, trying to keep his voice calm while making himself heard between the screams. Something about their unthreatening stance must have communicated itself to passersby – that and Sergeant Clyne's uniform – and they kept walking. After a minute the girl herself, realising that she had been neither abducted nor rescued, opened her eyes and gave them a closer look.

'Oh! It's you, sir!'

'Charles Murray of Letho,' said Murray, bowing. 'May I ask your name?'

'Susan Knox, sir,' she said after a moment, and curtseyed, blond curls bobbing. 'I – I'm sorry, sir. I thought I was to be the next to go.'

'Didn't they all vanish on Fridays?' asked Murray with a smile he hoped was reassuring.

'Aye, well, habits can change, can they not, sir? If I thought I was to be kidnapped I'd no be standing there saying, "Do you no ken it's only Wednesday? Away home and come back at the week's end." Would you, sir?'

'Well, no,' Murray agreed. 'Which of the missing women were you particularly friendly with?'

'Och,' she shrugged, 'I was friends with all of them. We all get along well enough in there. United against a common enemy,' she added, with a wink.

'Mr. Pillans? Your employer?'

'No, of course not. There's nothing wrong with him – we dinna see him that much since he married, anyway. No, it's yon witch, Mrs. Miller.'

Sergeant Clyne nodded his head in satisfaction that someone agreed with him.

'Tellt ye,' he remarked sagely.

'Did you know Mrs. Pillans? Before they married, I mean – didn't she work there, too?'

'Aye, she did. She's no bad, Annie Skead. Doesna talk much about herself – she's no very open, you might say – but I think she said once she was from the Borders. Just an ordinary lass like the rest of us, but she caught Mr. Pillans' eye. And she was no in it for the money, if you ask me. She really likes him. Like, himself, ken? See, he used to be around a good bit in the shop and we all saw him every day – he worked hard in yon days. Maybe he still does, but we dinna see it so much.'

Evidently they had not yet been told of Gordon Pillans' death. Murray decided to leave it for now.

'So have you any news of the missing women? Something you did not want to say in front of, ah, yon witch?'

She giggled, but shook her head.

'I havena heard a single thing since they went. I dinna like it, ken. I mean, why our warehouse?'

'And there hasn't been anyone gone since?'

'Since Jean Soutar? No, not a bit of it. So maybe he's found somewhere else to hunt. But that's no good for wherever else he might be hunting, is it?'

'No, indeed. Have you heard anything of other disappearances?'

'How would you know? It's a big town,' she said sensibly. 'If they three hadna all disappeared from here, would a'body have noticed?'

Sergeant Clyne cleared his throat.

'I think we'd have noticed, mind, miss.'

'Only if someone had told you,' she retorted. 'How could you know if someone's disappeared if no one misses them and tells you?'

Clyne frowned, but the point was well made.

'And the women who have gone – was there anything they had in common? They didn't live in the same area, though they were all near here, is that right?'

'Aye, sir,' said Miss Knox. 'It's hard to think of a'thing beyond working at the Oriental. One single, one as good as affianced, one a widow. Two living with their families, one in lodgings. A redhead, a blond and a dark-haired woman. All accounted pretty, if that's something.'

'It may indeed be a factor. There was no hint beforehand with any of them – nothing they said had made them nervous? Afraid to walk home alone?'

'Not a bit of it. In fact, Maggie had some plans to leave for a better place, and she was looking forward to it.'

'Did she say where?'

'No, I dinna think so.' She considered for a moment. 'Do you know, I have a notion that Mary said something similar? She left that day in a rage, you'll have heard, and we werena surprised when she didn't appear on the Saturday. And I think someone said well, she's gone to that new place where she said she might – she'd had an offer, or something. Now, if I could mind who said that …' She frowned, but shook her head. 'It'll no come. See, the middle of the night that'll likely wake me and I'll remember straight off.'

'Here's my card,' said Murray. 'If it does come back to you, will you let me know?'

'Oh, aye, a' course.' She looked absently at the card. 'And then, of course, Jean Soutar, she was looking gey pleased with herself the days before she left. We all thought something was up, that she'd be telling us she was to be married again. We were all looking forward to it. She's lovely, Jean: she's so kind to a'body. Aye, we miss her. When we heard she'd gone … well, I suppose we all still hope she's off somewhere with a good man, so happy she's just forgotten to write and let us know.' She sighed, and her eyes moistened. 'I was just getting more friendly with her, too – see, my best friend left a while ago, and she hasna been in touch either.'

'Left the warehouse?'

'Aye, that's right. It was a wee while ago now – the beginning of March. The second, it was.'

There was a pause, and they all considered.

'That's not really that long ago, is it?' said Miss Knox slowly. 'Oh, my.'

'Could she be the first one?'

'Could she?' Miss Knox echoed. Sergeant Clyne gave a grunt.

'Och, come on, now! You'll be saying next that half the women who've ever disappeared in Edinburgh were part of this thing!'

'Tell me more about her,' said Murray.

'Well, d'you know, she did sort of hint to me that she had something better to go to. She was kind of excited, ken?'

'Where did she live? Had she any family?'

'She did – she had her mother. They didna live together, because her mother was in service, a widow herself, and Sarah lived in lodgings. In fact, she was the other end of Potterrow from Jean Soutar.'

'Did she see much of her mother? Did you ask her mother where she was?'

'I did. I didna ken where she was in service, but I happened to meet her in the town one day, and I asked her how Sarah was getting on. And she said she'd tell me when she found her. I suppose I thought maybe they'd had a falling out or something. But they always got on well, ken?' Susan Knox, suddenly struck by the possibility of her friend's abduction, went white. 'I should have said something, should I no? I should have asked her if I could help. I should have done something. Sarah was my friend. Now what? What can I do? I still dinna ken where her mother worked.' She stared past Murray and Clyne, hand passing over her mouth, picturing all that could have happened. It was clearly not pretty.

Then she snatched her hand away, straightened her shoulders, and said,

'Right, sir, you're looking into this. Tell me how I can help you.'

Murray was taken aback, but ready.

'Did you have the impression, putting these people together, that they would be leaving town? Or staying in Edinburgh?'

Miss Knox gave it more consideration, thinking back.

'I would have thought so,' she said. 'I mean, with Mary –

the first one, the one that left in a rage – it could have been anywhere, and I'd think she'd have thought the further the better. But Maggie, she had Robert. If she didna tell Robert – you have spoken to Robert, have you no?' she demanded, turning on Sergeant Clyne again.

'Of course we have,' he said, affronted. He did not mention that they had suspected him.

'She'd have told Robert if she was leaving the town, would she no?'

'That would make sense, yes. So wherever she went, she must have thought she would not be going far.'

'Wherever she went,' echoed Susan Knox dolefully. 'Wherever they all went.'

Despite the fact that it was not Friday, Susan Knox was pleased enough to be walked to her door by a gentleman and a sergeant of police, and waved them goodbye. But before they went, she made Murray promise to take down her name and address, so that if he needed her to do anything, he could contact her. Murray dutifully drew out his pocketbook, and took down every detail before they left.

Then, back on the main road, he bade good evening to Sergeant Clyne.

'Will you send to me at Letho if you hear anything new?' he asked.

'Aye, sir, I will.'

'And I'll do the same. I doubt I shall be in Edinburgh for much longer on this occasion.'

An inn on the Lawnmarket, he knew, offered a very good dinner to late-working lawyers, and he decided to stop there, eat and think.

What had he learned? That all three missing women were pretty, and had hopes of some improvement in their lives? The second seemed vague but somehow promising. Could it be that none of them had been violently abducted, as everyone imagined, but had in fact been lured away? Persuaded to go? But not to go far, as Miss Knox had pointed out. Maggie Daniels, the second – or was she the third? – girl, would not have abandoned her poor suitor, or presumably taken any position that might have threatened their

211

relationship. He would have to take Susan Knox's word for it that Maggie valued her suitor above her career. But of course, what the girls were offered was not necessarily what was actually in store for them, wherever they were. Otherwise, surely, at least one of them would have been in touch – at the very least Maggie would have sent word to her young man. If nothing else, they would have asked for their things to be sent on.

What else had he learned? Mrs. Miller was strict – any supervisor of a body of young people like that had to be, he imagined – and Mr. Pillans, though liked, was less often seen about the place than he had been before his marriage. Mrs. Pillans was all right – no wild enthusiasm for her, but no sense of hostility, either. No jealousy that she had captivated their employer. Had he missed something? Or was it genuinely a friendly, relatively content workplace?

Prosperous, anyway, according to Mrs. Miller. She seemed to have no concerns about the business, and she would be in a position to know if it were in trouble. In trouble, for example, because of the owner's habit of gambling …

The gambling club … He had left the account book back in the Queen Street house, but he would have to give it a closer look. Not that the carefully anonymised lines were likely to tell him much. Anonymised for secrecy, or just for convenience, quicker to write initials than the whole name? Probably the latter: Pillans would not have expected anyone else to be looking at the books.

He paused in his thoughts for a few minutes, while the potboy brought to his quiet alcove a bowl of broth and a jug of claret, and agreed further to furnish him with a pair of chops and potatoes when the broth was done.

Why had he been killed? Why? Was it connected to gambling? Or the missing girls? How could it possibly be the latter?

Then what else could it be? There had been no hint that there was any unhappiness in the marriage. Were there any beneficiaries of his will that might have ventured to Fife to kill him? That would be easily discovered, if so. But then - why had he been killed in Murray's own abandoned icehouse? Had he or the murderer accidentally come upon it at that moment, or had one of them known about it before the murder? Not many people had known, surely. And even if they had known, why go there? Not far from the servants' door, nor from the engineers' cottage. Not far from the house. Did it mean that the murderer was someone who felt comfortable there, knew it well? That was not a happy thought.

The broth dish was removed and the chops brought. He ate them absent-mindedly, looking forward to Mrs. Mack's cooking again in his own home. How would Mrs. Mack feel if Isobel were mistress of Letho? He knew that sometimes cooks and mistresses did not shake down well together, and Mrs. Mack was a strong-minded woman.

If Isobel were mistress of Letho …

He finished the chops and poured the last glass of claret to wash them down. Did he have any other reason to stay in Edinburgh, or could he go back to Fife? He had visited Lady Rocheid and sent word to Mr. George. He had been to the Oriental Warehouse and spoken with the manager, and with one or two of the staff. He had gone to Mr. Pillans' Newington house, and spoken with his maid. He had talked with Sergeant Clyne about the missing girls. That was the list of all he had come to do, and it was done. Was there anything else, following on from anything he had learned, that he should do while he was here?

He finished the claret, paid, and left, taking the steep route past the bank and down the Mound to Prince's Street. The New Town was quiet: many would be away, as he would soon be, to their estates for the summer. The rest were at home or with their neighbours eating dinner. During the season, it would have been so much busier: the Assembly Rooms on George Street would have held dances and musical events, carriages and chairs would have been hurrying back and forth, ladies in splendid evening gowns, attended by maids and beaux, would step with care on muddy cobbles, every house would be lit up and glittering.

But somewhere here in Edinburgh, unless he was very wrong, something had happened to cause Gordon Pillans to be struck down and killed far away in Fife. And someone prepared to go to those lengths was very dangerous indeed.

And they were probably still at Letho.

Chapter Thirty-Five

Isobel, being her father's daughter, would have liked to go straight out and talk to the engineers on the spot, and take the opportunity, too, to see what progress they were making. She could take Robbins with her for the appropriate level of respectability. But it would be even more appropriate to take her father, who was itching for a chance to see the work done so far around the old icehouse, and so instead Robbins was pressed into service pushing Blair's chair, no easy or quick task on the gravel at the front of the house. Robbins was not a large man – Daniel was a good bit larger, but more in terms of the weight he could have brought to bear – but he was determined, and as he had been the one to whom the engineers had made their complaint, it seemed right that he should also be present.

Both the engineers were already at work on their site, though as Robbins had suggested, neither looked as if they had slept for a week. Jo Sweeney saw them coming around the corner (or heard the effort of the wheels), and nudged his more outgoing colleague. Edward Kelly froze, then came forward to greet them, a smile found from somewhere and plastered on.

'Good morning, madam! Good morning, sir! Are you come to see what we have been up to? You might find it disappointing as yet, for we are still at the measuring and drawing stage: no great holes have been dug nor walls raised, I'm afraid.'

He was on the point of babbling, Isobel thought, caught himself, and stopped with a bow.

'Good day to you, good day to you!' Blair looked as if he

would have leapt from his chair. 'Measuring and drawing are of great interest to me, if I might be allowed to see what you have accomplished so far?'

Talk grew technical very quickly. Blair had, of course (Isobel would have expected nothing less) the ability to draw out even quiet Jo Sweeney to explain and point and wave papers around, to encourage the engineers to measure again to show him how it was done, to describe their tentative plans for water control and the redesign of the road between the old icehouse and the servants' quarters. Edward Kelly held back a little, though he seemed to enjoy the conversation, allowing Sweeney to take the leading role for a change.

'Now,' said Blair at last, when they had finally exhausted everything to do with the project in hand, 'Mr. Robbins here says you're suffering from some disturbance at night. Ghosts! Tell me all about it!'

And of course they did, because that was what people did when they met Blair.

'It began with footsteps outside,' said Kelly, 'late at night. I mean, footsteps, right? This is a farm, or at least the edges of one, and I thought nothing of it. Someone tending a sick calf, or an injured horse, or … or …'

'We weren't brought up in the country,' added Jo Sweeney, 'but when we discussed it the next day we could think of a few things that might mean people were around at night.'

'Of course,' said Blair, 'very sensible.'

'But then there was the noise at the windows,' said Jo Sweeney, and he shuddered. Blair waited. Tapping, thought Isobel. That was the usual thing. She glanced over at the cottage the engineers were using: there were no trees about it, nor other plants that might be blown against the glass. But many things could tap.

'A kind of scraping,' said Kelly, looking pale. 'But not scraping.'

'As if,' added Sweeney, 'someone was dragging their fingers down the glass, if you know what I mean.'

'Not their nails?' Blair wanted clarification. 'Just the tips of their fingers, to make that squeaking noise?'

Both the engineers nodded.

'It sounds like nothing, when you say it. In the daylight, and all.'

'But you had the shutters closed on the inside?' asked Blair.

'Oh, aye, we did. It was late,' said Edward Kelly, looking at Sweeney, 'we were away to our beds.'

'So,' said Blair, 'footsteps and fingers on the windows. Anything else?'

The two engineers exchanged looks again.

'It sounds awful stupid,' Edward Kelly admitted. 'But that's all. Only ...'

'Only what?' asked Blair kindly.

'It seems to get worse each night,' said Kelly. 'And it's only been since we found yon fellow – the gentleman – there in the icehouse.'

'Worse each night,' Jo Sweeney emphasised. 'Definitely worse. So what's it going to be tonight? That's what we're asking ourselves, sir.'

Blair considered the matter for a moment, eyes closed, chin in the air. Isobel and Robbins waited patiently.

'Leave it with us,' said Blair. 'Do what you would usually do tonight. Go to bed at your usual time, close the shutters, whatever you would do. Leave it with us.'

'Well ... all right, then, sir,' said Edward Kelly. 'We'll do that.'

But it was clear that he did not like the idea. And Isobel was not so sure that she liked it herself. What did her father have in mind?

As soon as Murray reached the Queen Street house, he instructed Nathaniel to organise a horse for him for the early morning, to South Queensferry. Then he packed all he could of the few things he had brought with him, and when Nathaniel came back he gave instructions for their supper. He was sure, he told himself, that everyone at Letho was quite safe, but still, it was time to go back.

Nevertheless, when he had done as much as he could for the next day, he settled down in the silent parlour with a single candle and the gambling club's account book, in case something appeared there that might require following up here in the town. He could always send a note to Sergeant Clyne.

He had selected what seemed to be the latest of the account books to bring with him: he could not have taken many others without the maid noticing and, perhaps, querying, and he had not felt confident enough in his incursion to come up with excuses. If necessary, Macduff or Sergeant Clyne could go back for them. But this volume, at least, would give him some slight picture of the recent activities of the club, and perhaps show him its financial state. And that, he thought, might possibly have a bearing on Gordon Pillans' murder.

The volume was small, for an account book, measuring perhaps ten inches tall by eight inches wide, with a spine of only an inch or so. The binding was of ordinary brown leather, a little scuffed at the corners from handling. The only decoration on the spine was a single embossed figure, 'V', and he had seen the run in the Newington house of 'I' to 'IV'. The first had started a couple of years before, some time in 1819. Flicking through, he saw again that this volume was almost complete, and that soon the club members would require a 'VI'. Assuming that the club survived the death of its – what was he? Host? Accountant? Business manager? He wondered if they met at other houses, too, and only at Pillans' house when his wife and mother-in-law were absent. He began to make a list of questions in a notebook of his own. Did Mrs. Pillans know about this club? Was that why the meetings in Newington only happened when she was away?

This book listed dates, money owed, money paid, the man who paid and the man who received, always with initials. Man? He supposed so: in London and other places, maybe forty years ago, some ladies took to the tables and the cards, but in Edinburgh it was less common. And the maid at Newington had only mentioned men. But initials could tell very little. J.R. T.A. A.B. Who might that be? Alexander Bain? Andrew Balneavis? Archibald Badenoch? It could be anybody. None of the initials included anything as useful as an X (Xavier?) or a Z (Zachariah? Zebedee?) or a Q (Quentin? Quintus?) It was hopeless.

J.R. did appear quite often, though. J.R. – that could be so many things. John Robertson? James Richie? Josiah Raeburn?

Lord Rocheid – was he not Jacob?

A foolish idea. Had he not already shown to himself that there were endless possibilities for J.R.?

He went back through the accountancy pages of the book, looking for G.P. That, at least was a less common combination. George Porter, Graham Porteous, Gavin Primrose. Or Gordon Pillans, the one person he could be fairly sure had some connexion with this gambling club.

Each transaction was laid out in much the same way here: this was just the financial side of what appeared in the records of the bets. There were six columns, containing the date, the person owing money, the person owed, the amount, the date it was paid and the initials of a witness. Most usually, G.P. appeared in the witness column. In some instances he appeared in the column for those owing money – usually a small amount, paid on the same day, to various different other sets of initials. Then, further on in the book, he appeared just a few times in the column for those owed money. Each time it was a substantial amount – several guineas – and in every case the person owing the sum was listed as J.R.

It looked as if Gordon Pillans, who had begun as a cautious, conservative gambler, had suddenly gone for something with much higher stakes. So far he had won. Could he afford to lose?

Murray felt suddenly tired, and anxious. Was everything all right at Letho? Was Isobel safe? Robbins would send an express if anything happened – but even expresses took time. He needed to get back. And he needed to start early tomorrow.

He took the account book to his room and tucked it safely into his bag for the next day. Then he went in search of his supper. He would make an early night, and do his best to rise refreshed. Maybe, when he got back to Letho, some of his questions would already be answered.

'I don't suppose you really think it is the ghost of poor Mr. Pillans,' said Isobel, when Robbins had managed to wheel Blair back to the entrance hall.

'I should be very much surprised,' Blair admitted. 'But I should like to know, nevertheless, who it actually is. For it is possible, I believe, to see a pattern of sorts here. The engineers have not been here for long, and as far as I am aware they know no one locally. It seems unlikely, therefore, to be a personal attack on them. But if they were deterred from staying at Letho, then work on the icehouse would again stop. Is there someone, I wonder, to whose advantage that would be?'

Isobel glanced at Robbins.

'Father, you're not saying that Mr. Pillans was killed just to stop work on the icehouse!'

'Well,' said Blair, 'well, that would be excessive, I admit. But what if all this is actually to do directly with the icehouse? What if … I know! What if someone was using it for something, and all this is now effectively stopping that something from happening?'

'Something illicit, you mean, sir?' asked Robbins.

'Yes, yes, that's it!'

'Almost directly outside the door to the servants' wing?' Robbins asked again, respectfully.

'Ah, well,' said Blair, and his face drooped. 'Ah, well, there is that.'

'Well, anyway,' said Isobel briskly, not liking to see him sad, 'what is it that you think should happen tonight?'

'Ah!' Blair brightened again. 'Yes, tonight.'

The plan was simple: discreet observation.

Blair had himself wheeled over to the factor Thalland's house after supper, and Thalland helped him establish himself at the window of a small pantry at the back of the house. Robbins and William were outside, well bundled up in dark clothes, to each end of the cottage. Isobel, who had not been asked to participate in what might, possibly, be a dangerous exercise, had changed into a dull-coloured wool dress that made hardly any noise, wrapped a grey shawl about her head, and persuaded the dogs to stay in the entrance hall while she slipped out and quietly round the corner of the house to watch from the shadow of Thalland's house.

The cottage lay in darkness, shutters closed, no chink of light apparent. Or was there? Isobel squinted. She was not sure. She tightened the shawl around her shoulders, feeling the cold.

The night was quiet: there was a very slight breeze, enough just to lift the fresh leaves on the trees above them on the hill. Owls hooted back and forth, and small nocturnal animals went about their business.

And then she heard it.

A footstep, the least sound, on the rough stones of the road, and another – coming along past the servants' wing, towards the cottage. Toward them.

She shrank into the shadow, hoping that the folds of the shawl hid her face. What could she see? She stared so hard she was not even sure there was anything there at all – but no – what was that white thing? Dangling in the air, shifting with the breeze, light and floating, coming closer ...

Then she could see the outline against the paler stone wall of the cottage. A figure – or was it two? Yes, one short, one taller, in dark cloth. The pale thing, whatever it was, still moved between them. The short figure went to the nearer window, reached up, and began slowly drawing fingers down the glass, just as the engineers had described. The taller hesitated, Isobel would have said, then the smaller gestured, and the taller moved away, going to the cottage door. There was some movement with the pale thing, and then Isobel jumped. The figure knocked, loudly, on the cottage door.

And then there was chaos.

Chapter Thirty-Six

Murray's early crossing of the Forth was mercifully smooth – it was about as far as he could travel by water without being nauseous, so he enjoyed it while he could, and landed at North Queensferry feeling more refreshed than anything. The new steam crossing from Newhaven to the saltpans of Dysart might have cut quite a corner off the journey, but Murray preferred the short ferry and more time on land.

The popularity of the new ferry meant that North Queensferry was quieter than it used to be. Still, arriving early as he did, he had a reasonable choice of horses at the inn and took the one he had hired from Cupar on Monday: the innkeeper was pleased not to have to return it himself. He availed himself of a swift breakfast, and headed off, happier with every pace he drew nearer to Letho. Surely everything would be well there. The Blairs and Robbins were far too sensible to allow danger to threaten.

Robbins, sensible as he was, would very much have preferred the interview to happen in the servants' quarters. The entrance hall, in the company of the Blairs, whom he respected very much, was not the ideal place for the dressing down of a junior servant. But then Mr. Blair and Miss Blair (unexpectedly) had been present at the incident – incident? Chain of incidents – and were therefore due a full explanation, he supposed. And he had to take some responsibility himself. This should not have happened in a well-run household. He had turned a blind eye – well, not entirely, but he had not been strict enough. It was at least partly his own fault, and for that he would have to answer, if not now to the Blairs, temporarily in charge, then later to Mr. Murray.

'It's no my fault!'

Daniel, however, was less inclined to take responsibility. There was a giggle from near the staircase, and Robbins shot a look that would have frozen lava. The giggle, for once, subsided.

'It's no my fault either,' added another voice, pitched somewhere between Daniel and the giggle.

'It's Dandy, isn't it?' asked Blair. A boy stepped forward from the shadow, awkward and probably over-tall for his age. 'Your mother works at Collessie, is that not so?'

'Aye, sir,' said the boy.

'Why don't you tell us what happened? Step forward here, so that I can see you,' said Blair, friendly. Where he was asking Dandy to stand, Dandy would not be able to see the giggler in the corner.

'Well, sir, it was to be a kind of a joke, see?'

'I do see, indeed. Go on.'

'Janny said that the men in the cottage was up for a good laugh, and we would give them one, and all.'

'Janny said that, did he?'

'Did not!' came a cry, that was at once muffled. Daniel had seized the giggler – his son – by the ear, and turned his face into the folds of Daniel's coat.

'Be quiet, you!' Daniel muttered.

'So the other night – the Saturday, aye – we started a bit of a shuffle outside the cottage, and a few noises, ken. Then the next night, the Sabbath, we did a bit more. And so on. Last night Janny said he'd had a rare notion, and when we met outside he had yon clout with the blood on it – he telt me it had come from a pig.'

He pointed to the red-stained cloth that lay on the table in the midst of them – the cloth that had featured in their escapade last night.

'An' I was to drape it over my head, and chap at the cottage door. So that's what I did.'

'And if Janny told you to jump in the garden pond,' said Robbins dangerously, 'would you do that, too?'

'Naw!' said Dandy. 'I canna swim!'

'At least you have that much wit,' Robbins murmured.

'So tell me,' said Blair, with a sympathetic glance at Robbins, 'how came you to be out and about so late at night? You're – what age? Twelve? Fourteen?'

'Thirteen, my ma tells me, sir,' said Dandy.

'And what age is Janny?'

'Six!' cried Janny proudly, breaking free briefly from his father's clutches.

'Six,' repeated Blair faintly. 'My word.'

'It's not a good start, sir, is it?' asked Robbins.

'Does he often wander about at night?' Blair asked.

'All the time, sir,' said Daniel, helpless. 'We canna seem to keep him in the house.'

'But anything could happen to him.'

'The gallows, sooner or later,' said Robbins in a low voice. Daniel did not hear.

'He could suffer an accident,' Blair pursued.

'Oh, aye, sir. I daresay, but we canna stop him!'

'Do you lock the door?'

'Aye, but he kens where the key's kept.'

'Hide it.'

'He finds it.'

'Hide it better.'

'Then he climbs out the window!'

Blair abandoned this game of conversational tag.

'Something will have to be done,' said Robbins, grimly. 'Too much licence has been allowed already.'

'I canna help it, sir,' said Daniel. 'See, Janny? See the trouble you get your poor father into?' He drew the child out from his coat tails, and shook his shoulders. Janny stuck his tongue out at his father.

'Dandy, at least, can be dismissed,' said Blair, with a judicious nod. Dandy did not wait: he fled at once, his face flushed with relief.

'Are the engineers all right?' Isobel asked, since they were making no progress at all in any other direction.

'Yes, miss,' said Robbins, drawing in a deep breath. 'They are back at work this morning, and quite content.'

'That, at least, is something,' she said.

Isobel considered going back to her room and asking her maid to bring her breakfast to her, just so that she could forget about the rest of the house for a while. But she decided that that was pointless and lazy: she was up and dressed anyway, and it was easier for the servants to lay the food in one room and clear up afterwards in there, instead of gathering crumbs from distant bedchambers.

Thursday, she thought, as she sat in solitary splendour in the dining room, toying with a couple of cooling eggs. Was there any chance that Charles might be back today? He had said he would be as quick as he could, not inclined to linger in town any longer than necessary once he had moved to Letho. But could he be back? She counted – not for the first time. To North Queensferry on Monday. To Edinburgh early on Tuesday, ferry permitting (and horseshoes, and muddy roads, and so on). To the Oriental Warehouse, and to wherever the Pillans lived – somewhere on the south side? To the police office, to ask about the missing girls. Could he achieve all that on Tuesday, or would some of it have fallen into Wednesday? Would some eager friend, still in town, insist on his company at a dinner, or a rout, or a picnic?

Her mind dwelled on that idea for a moment, until she shrugged herself free and worked on. If he finished on Tuesday, or even by the middle of Wednesday, then he could get back to South Queensferry and spend the night again in the south of Fife, and be back by this evening. He could. But would he?

And then, what would she say to him? That his engineers had almost been frightened off the premises by a couple of lads with a bloody handkerchief and no sense of decent behaviour?

Despite his aversions to travelling on it, Murray liked to see the sea and selected the coast road for his onward journey, through Inverkeithing and Burntisland and towards Kirkcaldy. At Kinghorn, though, following in the footsteps of the late Alexander III, his horse cast a shoe and he had to stop, though fortunately he was able to dismount in good order, and not be thrown.

'Aye, well,' said the local blacksmith, 'you'll have to wait a wee while, sir, if you'll forgive me – I've this team to do for this evening, and I'm behind.'

A stunning team of black carriage horses clacked and whinnied by his smithy, two bored grooms nattering as they stood with them, three horses each.

'Someone likes a good turn-out,' Murray remarked, admiringly. He only aspired to four horses to his own carriage, and it was hard enough to match those in looks. Six smart blacks would have taken some time to find.

'It's for the local laird – the Earl,' the smith explained, happy enough to chat as he worked. He raised his voice over the hissing metal. 'Beauties, eh?'

'You'll see some good horses along this road, no doubt,' said Murray, 'up and down to the ferry.'

'Aye, in both directions now – some to Dysart for the steam boat, and some to North Queensferry for the old run. I'd say we see most of the traffic here. The road inland – well, it doesna appeal to everyone, unless you're heading for Dunfermline.'

'An acquaintance of mine – his wife came through last Sunday, I think. That would have been a good enough carriage. Dark blue, with a nice set of bays.'

'I mind them, aye,' said the smith. 'Wait now till I hammer.'

He filled his lips with nails, and began to whip them one by one through the new shoe and into the first horse's hoof. One done, twenty-three to go. The smith was quick, but Murray was still going to be here for a while.

'There was a wee shield on the door, arms and whatnot,' he went on as if they had not been interrupted.

'That's right. Lady Rocheid. By chance, her husband Lord Rocheid was heading the other way about the same time, but somehow they missed each other.'

'Huh,' said the smith, though it was hard to know what he meant by it.

'He might have taken the inland road, though,' Murray conceded. 'I'm not sure which he favours.'

The smith tutted for a moment, but it seemed to be a necessary accompaniment to the fiddly business of fitting the second shoe, easing and tweaking it round. The powerful horse was docile, content with the attention. The sun dazzled on his coal-black flanks and his oiled mane and tail.

'Would he have been driving a gig?' asked the smith at last.

'I'm not sure. He might well have been.' Murray's mind leapt to Mr. Pillans and his mysterious friend. He should have asked the neighbours in Newington if they had seen the gig, if they knew the driver. He should have gone back.

'Dark haired man? Navy coat? Bit of a –' the smith hesitated, looking at Murray, remembering perhaps that Murray had claimed the acquaintance of this man. 'Very fashionably attired? Handsome, if not very tall?'

'That could be him, yes. Well then – was he here before or after his wife?' asked Murray with a grin, as if a small wager depended upon it. The smith tutted again, and was at last satisfied with the shoe. It was pressed into place, and he refilled his mouth with nails. Murray had to wait. The shoe was fastened, and the horse let his foot down with a sharp tap, as if testing the fit. The groom backed the horse a little, and the smith picked up the third hoof.

'The wife – Lady whoever,'

'Lady Rocheid,'

'Aye, Lady Rocheid. She came through Sunday, maybe dinner time. Aye, for I saw her through the window there.' He nodded to the cottage beside the smithy. 'It might have been the Sabbath, but a smith always has to watch out for work to be done.'

'Dinner time – yes, that would probably be right.' Not fast, but not too slow, either, from Letho. 'So Lord Rocheid would have passed through before that, then.'

'If it's the gentleman I'm thinking of, then aye, he was through before her.'

'They must have passed each other further down the road, then,' said Murray.

'As to that,' said the smith, casting the horse's old shoe on to a clanging heap of scrap, 'I've no notion. But he was definitely through here before. Well before – he came through Friday morning.'

Chapter Thirty-Seven

The door of the dining room opened, and Isobel glanced up, half-expecting to see that she had summoned Murray just by thinking about him. But it was Mr. and Mrs. Wedderburn, edging into the dining room with a shared, anxious look.

'I hope we are not disturbing anything,' said Mrs. Wedderburn, looking about the room.

'As you see,' said Isobel, 'there is nothing here to disturb! I am sorry if you were bothered by the noise earlier. My father was intent on seeing the business through, and that meant that the most convenient place to do it was the entrance hall.'

'I see …' said Debs Wedderburn, though presumably she did not, unless she had been sitting listening on the landing. Isobel had pity on her and told them briefly what had happened in the night.

'Goodness, if it's not servants, it's their families!' exclaimed Richard Wedderburn, meeting his wife's eye.

'This is Daniel who married the Neapolitan girl, isn't it?' asked Debs, familiar with Murray's household to a point.

'That's right. And has children. This eldest is but six, but shows exceptional promise,' said Isobel, provoked by fatigue and annoyance into indiscretion. She resolved to say nothing more on the subject – nor to mention Mrs. Warner's accommodation, either. Nor to ask if Mrs. Wedderburn knew of any maids looking for a position. Nor to make any remarks that might sound as if she were over-anxious for Charles' return. For a moment she could think of nothing else to say.

'Indeed – a very inventive child,' said Debs.

'I wondered if you might care to accompany me to Collessie this morning,' Isobel began again. 'I should like to make sure that Mrs. Pillans is still all right, and to find out when the funeral is to be. We should offer to help, I daresay.'

'I had hoped to go and chivvy the smith,' said Mr. Wedderburn in mild alarm. Visiting mourning strangers clearly did not appeal.

'Why don't you do that, my dear,' said Debs, 'and see if that axle is ever to be mended. I am sure that Isobel is longing to have at least one of her responsibilities lifted from her!'

'Not at all,' said Isobel politely. 'And indeed, aside from last night there is little to worry about.' She crossed her fingers under the table. Was that for luck, or because she feared that what she had said was untrue? There was Mrs. Warner, and Mr. Rieder. And Iffy, as usual. And an inexperienced housekeeper, and a dearth of maids. And the small additional matter of an unsolved murder, that had happened only yards away from this very house. No, nothing to worry about at all.

'Friday morning?' asked Murray. Could it be so? Then where had he been?

Then another thought struck him. A gig heading to Letho on Friday?

'Was he on his own?'

'On his own in the gig?' asked the smith, whose mind was now on the start of a new shoe, and not entirely focussed on Murray's questions. 'Let me think ...' He hammered away for a moment, his bare arms a spattering of burns of different sizes and ages pale against weathered skin. 'I saw him over yonder at the inn,' he began, peering more closely at the hot iron. The red curl reflected glinting in his eyes. 'He was out of the gig then – must have been in for breakfast, maybe. It's a bigger gig, eh? One with a shelf at the back for a box.'

'It could be,' said Murray. That was what the innkeeper at Letho had described, anyway. Not as Rocheid's gig, not then – but as the gig that had brought Gordon Pillans, yes. Room for that box that was causing puzzlement at the inn.

'That's how I saw he wasna very tall,' said the smith, pleased with himself. 'He was standing at the horse's head. A nice cob, it was, sensible choice for the work, but a fine head for all its solid body. Light bay, with a touch of white about the fetlocks. Stood well – there was a bit of breeding in there somewhere, I'd say.'

The smith would know the horse again, anyway. Murray hoped he was right about the man.

'Anyway, he stood there maybe five minutes, and you could see he was getting impatient – the foot was tapping, and he kept looking in at the inn door. Then what?' He stopped his tale to tut again. For a moment the groom broke off from his gossip and made much of holding the horse steady, but actually the horse was perfectly happy to stand there and watch the world go by. The groom gave a nod, as if he had settled the beast, and returned to his talk. The smith did his trick with the nails for the third time, and at last moved on to the horse's last hoof.

'I think I must have missed a bit – was that when the fellow came up with the grey for me to look at? Nothing wrong with the shoe, but a tight tendon on the nearside back. I got him the bits for a poultice. That grey's forever putting her feet down rabbit holes – I think she goes out looking for them. Anyway, when I came back and looked again, the cob was ready to go, and ... let me think ... aye, there were two of them up in the gig. The gentleman with the smart coat, and another man with him.'

'What did he look like?'

'Well,' said the smith, with a shrug, 'not unlike, when it came down to it. I remember half-thinking they might well be brothers. But the other fellow – aye, now I come to think of it, there was a difference. He was not so smartly dressed as the first. But then, sometimes one brother prospers while the other falls on harder times.' He nodded, pleased with this observation.

'And did you see them set off? Which way did they go?'

'Oh, towards Kirkcaldy. Same way as you're going, sir, if I ever get to your horse.'

That, indeed, was the question. Murray decided that the smith might make faster progress if he were not there talking with him, and leaving the horse in the queue, as it were, he went to find something to eat.

'But might I not go with you, too?' Blair's face was dejected, as if he expected a refusal.

'I can manage it, miss,' said Smith. 'The drive here, a good road, and then a reasonable drive at Collessie, if I remember right.'

'It's a long way to push,' said Isobel, uncertain.

'Not so long when you've had practice,' said Smith. Isobel was not sure whether or not she had caught bitterness in his voice. After all, this was not the job he had signed up to, years ago. On the other hand, working for Alester Blair had never been predictable. Smith had not resigned his place yet.

'I'm not even sure why I'm going,' said Isobel, 'only that I want to find out when the funeral is – which Mr. Helliwell could tell us – and to offer help, which I could do with a note and which we've done before anyway.'

'Perhaps you feel there is more to learn from her?' Blair suggested, which was probably his own motive for joining the party.

'I'm not even sure about that,' Isobel admitted. 'I don't even know what questions to ask. Maybe when Charles comes back from Edinburgh we'll have a better idea.'

'But if he is delayed ... she might be gone, if it is after the funeral.'

'Gone?'

'Mr. Macduff must let her go, some time. And I daresay she would rather be in Edinburgh, with her friends, than here with only her mother a familiar face.' Blair's own face was sympathetically mournful. But they were interrupted by Robbins appearing at Blair's parlour door.

'Mr. Macduff to see you, sir. I have him in the entrance hall.'

'Oh, excellent!' Blair cheered at once. 'He must have heard his name! I hope he has come to see us with lots and lots of lovely information.'

And already, knowing his eagerness, Smith was pushing him out of the parlour into the entrance hall, where indeed Macduff was ready and waiting. He bowed.

'Please to sit, Mr. Macduff, if your leg pains you,' said Blair. 'And tell me,' he added, unable to hold back, 'what news you have brought for us?'

'Well, then,' said Macduff, perching on a hard chair. Isobel almost thought she could hear his bones clunking against the wood. 'I suppose Mr. Murray's no back from Edinburgh yet?'

'Not till this evening at the earliest,' said Isobel, then

regretted sounding quite so specific.

'That's what I thought.' Macduff nodded lugubriously. 'Well, there has been a little progress,' he eyed Blair's excited bounce with misgiving, 'and almost all of it of a negative nature.'

'How so?' asked Blair, not willing to give up on the chance of a little pleasure.

'We canna find out who brought Mr. Pillans to Letho. We canna discover who the fellow was that drove his unlit gig through the village on Saturday night. We can find no one in the parish that admits to having met him before, or corresponded with him – you'll know the agent for Collessie bides in Cupar, so even they have not met. We can find no one in the parish who admits to seeing anything suspicious on Friday night, nor any other time, apart from that gig.'

'I daresay Mr. Pillans did not spend much time in the village,' offered Blair. Macduff came close to ignoring him.

'There is nothing to say that he and Mr. Rieder knew each other or had had anything to do with each other before. It was Mrs. Pillans and her mother who looked to engage him.'

'Mrs. Pillans is determined that her husband had no enemy to his name, that he had never offended a friend or a colleague or a business rival, that he owed no money and had not recently seemed to have less – or more – money than usual, and that, most of all, and here she is quite definite, he knew nothing about any missing women.'

'Well,' said Blair, after a moment's furious lip-pursing and a hard stare directed at the ceiling, 'well, that is something, I suppose.'

'It's not something that is getting us too far,' said Macduff sourly. 'I could add that she had no knowledge of Mr. Pillans ever being in Letho before, let alone knowing anything about a disused and recently reopened icehouse.'

'Well, no, why would he?' said Isobel, without enthusiasm. 'But wait – you said that almost all of the progress was of a negative nature. What was the positive? There must have been something!'

'Aye, miss, there is. Though even that …' He hesitated. 'May I call in Ninian Jack?'

'Ninian Jack?' asked Isobel.

'Oh, his luggage?' The words burst from Blair.

'The box he left at the inn.'

Even from her own seat, Isobel could see now that Ninian Jack was standing outside on the gravel drive, still as a statue, with a box at his feet.

'Did you find a key?' she asked.

'No, miss. Yon Ninian Jack is a rare one,' said Macduff. 'He studied the lock like a book for maybe the third part of an hour, near and far, and I'd swear he even listened to it and smelled it. Then off he goes and gets a roll of tools – wee tiny ones, that you could lose in your pocket and never know – and he comes back with them and hauls the box up on to the table, wouldn't take any help, cradles it like a prize calf. Then in he goes, with things you could near sew with, and in about three minutes the lock's wide open.'

'And what's inside?' asked Isobel, before her father could leap to his surviving foot in his excitement. 'You've looked, of course?'

'Oh, aye, I've looked,' said Macduff dismally. 'Here, you can look, and all.'

And he rose stiffly, and went to the front door.

Chapter Thirty-Eight

At last on his way, Murray considered what he had learned. If the smith had been correct, then it was Lord Rocheid who had brought Gordon Pillans to Letho. And that meant that Lord Rocheid was around Letho two days earlier than they had thought – in time, in fact, to murder Pillans. Why, if he had brought Pillans from Edinburgh, he should wait until they had reached Letho to do that was just one more mystery.

In fact, there were still plenty of questions. Had it really been Lord Rocheid who had, by prior arrangement, brought Pillans all the way from Newington? He should really have gone back to talk more thoroughly to the neighbours. It was possible that something had happened to the gig Pillans had started out in, gigs being gigs, and by chance he had met a stranger going in the same direction.

If not, if it had been by prior arrangement, then Pillans and Rocheid must have been acquainted, unlikely as that sounded. And what might bring together a prosperous trader and an arrogant peer? Well, what about a gambling club? There had been a J.R., after all. If Murray had proof that that J.R. was indeed Jacob Rocheid, then that account book would bear a second examination. Could there have been a dispute between them – an unpaid debt, perhaps?

An acquaintance with Rocheid might explain why Pillans, with little knowledge of Fife, would happen to light on Letho to spend his summer. Had it just been because he had heard of it, or had the two of them made some arrangement together? Starting a local gambling club, perhaps, or just continuing their activities over the summer? To be honest, Letho did not seem a likely place to set

233

up a new club, even for a few months.

And then, if Lord Rocheid had arrived at Letho on Friday, why had he not gone straight to Dures and his impatient wife?

Murray thought that perhaps there he had answered his own question. Lord Rocheid was not much attached to his wife. Perhaps he had found somewhere more entertaining for another few days, just to postpone the moment of reunion. But where? Could he prove where he had been? Would he?

The first thing to do, though, was to see if he could verify, to some extent, what the smith had said. And in Kirkcaldy, the last town on the coast before he would turn inland, he set about doing just that.

Ninian Jack carried the box solemnly into the house, laid it on a chair, and removed his woollen hat.

Macduff sighed, snatched up the box, and laid it on a different chair in front of Blair's wheeled chair. Then he looked to Blair for the next move.

'Go on, then, open it!'

Macduff flicked the latches, stood behind the chair out of the way, and opened the box, then paused as the servants' door opened. Isobel looked over, but it was only Mrs. Gilmour, who glanced quickly at Macduff and Jack and disappeared again, soundless, as if she had never been there. Isobel made a note to remind the housekeeper that she was perfectly entitled to walk into the entrance hall, whatever was going on, then looked back at the box.

'It seems wrong that we should see this before Mrs. Pillans,' she said suddenly.

'Aye, miss,' said Macduff, 'but if her husband's been murdered, and something in here might help us to find who did it, then, well ...'

Help us, thought Isobel. How odd, that her father and Charles – and by extension she herself – should be considered somehow allies with the sheriff's man, part of some kind of team. She was sure that none of her friends in Edinburgh did anything so outlandish.

But the box was open, and wrong or not, she was eager to see what was inside.

The harbour at Kirkcaldy was massive, compared with the others he had ridden by, and activity seemed centred around a whaling ship docked and unloading – barrel after barrel of oil, the whole ship glinting with grease, the crew weathered and beaming. Even away from the harbour the town was busy and industrious: in any street one could hear looms working, see carts of goods hauled along over the cobbles. The toll road ran north here to Newport, where you could take another ferry across the Firth of Tay: it was the best road in Fife, even if one had to pay to use it. Murray would almost have made a wager on Lord Rocheid taking it, whenever he had travelled. On the same principle, he headed for the best inn in the town, and made his enquiries.

'Lord Rocheid? Aye, he always stops here,' said the landlord, happy to boast about his guests.

'I'm sure he does – it's a fine inn,' said Murray dutifully. 'Has he been here recently?'

'Well, it's only recently he's started coming through,' the landlord admitted. 'He has some business up in the north of Fife, I hear tell.'

Some business – well, a wife. But since it was said he had married her for her money, then perhaps business was the best word for it.

'Have you seen him in the last week or so?'

'Oh, aye.' The landlord frowned, then consulted a book on his table. 'I always note when the gentry and nobility call.' He made it sound as if he had several of each staying every night. 'Like yourself, sir,' he added.

'Indeed.'

'So it was – last Friday, he was here. Just for a meal. He would have been here early dinner time, as I recall.'

'In a gig?'

'His usual gig, aye, sir. He had the stable lad wash it down, for it was dusty.'

'Was he here on his own?'

'On his own?' The landlord glanced down at the open page in front of him, as if for reassurance. 'On his own? Let me think … there's nothing here.'

No, Gordon Pillans would not have registered as gentry or nobility.

'A servant, perhaps?'

'Oh! There was a man with his lordship, aye, you're right, sir. I didna notice him, but I mind there were two dinners on the voucher. So I suppose he was not a servant, if he dined with his lordship.'

'Probably not, no. And this was definitely Friday?'

'Oh, aye, yes. Friday it was, near a week ago.'

'Thank you.'

Murray did not want to linger for a meal, but he had a cup of ale and made sure his horse was watered, and went on his way.

Definitely Friday, definitely Lord Rocheid. Probably Pillans. Unless there had been two gigs heading from Edinburgh to Letho that day. He should really, really have gone back to Newington, and spoken again with the neighbours. If he wrote to Sergeant Clyne, could he do it? Instinctively he felt that it was not the kind of enquiry that Sergeant Clyne would manage well. He had friends still in Edinburgh, but he was not sure that any of them was the right person to go asking questions in Newington. Who could he ask? Or would he have to go back down himself?

'A clean shirt,' said Macduff, lifting it out, 'and hose.' He laid them to one side. 'A decent pair of shoes – he was wearing boots, you'll remember. No doubt he had more clothes sent to Collessie for his arrival. Shaving things. A tinder box.' He removed the articles as he named them, as if any of the company would argue with his identification of them. Ninian Jack had removed himself to a space near the doorway and stood solemn, staring into space.

'What's that little thing? The size of a pack of cards,' Blair asked, pointing.

'It's a pack of cards,' said Macduff, without irony. He held them up for Blair to see. 'Tax paid. You couldna fault the man on anything.'

'But then there are books!' cried Blair. 'What are they? May I – forgive me, for books are always interesting, don't you find? And these ones more than many, I am quite sure. What are they?'

'This one,' Macduff opened it, closed it again and handed it to Blair, 'is just a notebook. Like a kind of reminder thing, ken, sir?'

'A novel,' said Macduff, dismissively, 'and a petty cash book. He was a careful man.'

'How long have I got?' asked Blair. 'To look at these, I mean. Petty cash? Has he made a proper list of his expenditure, or is it just the money? And a notebook - how much more useful could it be?' He jiggled in his chair, making the wheels squeak. 'Oh, how long do I have?'

Macduff looked at the clock on the hall mantelpiece, then drew out a pewter-cased watch, much dented, from his own waistcoat pocket, and compared them.

'Can I say two hours, sir? I want to take them on to Mrs. Pillans tonight, for the funeral is tomorrow. And I'll want to take a good look at the things myself, ken.'

'Oh, is the funeral tomorrow? Thank you,' said Isobel, ticking that off her list of things to do.

'But if you could take a look at these, I would indeed be grateful, sir. No doubt Mr. Pillans was an educated man, and I doubt it would take another educated man to make the most of what is here.'

'Two hours ... Smith,' said Blair, 'bring me to a table, and find me paper and a pen and ink. I must work fast. Isobel, my dear, would you like to take a look at the cash book while I look at the notebook? And then we can exchange.'

'I'll come back for them, then,' said Macduff, 'at three, if that is suitable, sir.'

'Three, yes, three, three,' muttered Blair, eager to get going. 'Isobel, ring for Robbins. We shall need some brandy, too, and I hope he will allow us to use the dining table. Three, three. Two hours. What shall we find? What shall we find?'

Halfway to Cupar. Murray's head worked away. He should have gone back to Newington – he had just been in such a rush to return to Letho, to his home and to Isobel. Isobel ... Had he any hope? He had asked her before, long ago, and she had turned him down, but circumstances had been different then. They had probably been different. He had not loved her then, he knew, as he loved her now. And she had certainly not loved him. Could she, now?

But he should have gone to Newington. Sergeant Clyne would be useless – he would terrify the Pillans' maid, anyway. To talk to a maid, you really needed someone who understood them, who had something in common with them – who would not be seen as a threat. Another girl, perhaps. But what girls did he know in Edinburgh? He had met some shop girls, certainly. But he could not say that he knew them, or even where they lived to contact them.

Except, of course, for Susan Knox. He knew where she lived. Would she do it?

She might, he thought. She was a bright girl, and sensible. And she looked as if she might be prepared to do something to rescue her friends. Particularly – was it Sarah? – if she could.

At the next village, he dismounted at the inn, asked for pen and paper, and wrote to her, leaving it with the mail to be sent back to Edinburgh, and hoped she had enough to pay for the postage when it reached her.

The petty cash book had yielded little of interest – Gordon Pillans had kept it meticulously, though, and they could trace his route from Edinburgh to Cupar, at least. No transport expenses were recorded, Isobel had noticed – no oats nor smithing nor stabling – but meals, and a bed for the night on Thursday, and sixpence for the maid who attended him. The old ferry was noted, not the steamboat. At Cupar some ale was mentioned, and money for a newspaper. That was the last entry.

Before his journey there had been the usual casual expenditure of a man in town: a drink here, some food there, a book in one shop, a ribbon in another. All small items, bought in places he must not have had an account for the purchase to be added to.

She had not been able to see the notebook yet. Her father was working his way through it, lips pursed ferociously, making occasional notes and flicking back and forth. She sighed, and picked up the book Macduff had dismissed as a novel, to see what it was.

The Bride of Lammermoor, one of the Waverley novels. She had read it when it came out, and enjoyed it. Who had mentioned it recently? Had it been Charles? She turned the pages absently, then went to the front of the book to see if it belonged to Mr. Pillans or his wife.

In a neat black hand, across the title page, was written, 'A memento mori.'

And below it, a simple sketch of a gallows.

Chapter Thirty-Nine

The Wedderburns, abandoned by Isobel and Blair, returned in time for dinner.

'She is so brave,' said Debs Wedderburn. 'There is a resilience to both Mrs. Pillans and her mother, as if they have seen tragedy before and know that they can face it.'

'Did you find out about your axle?' Isobel asked Mr. Wedderburn. 'Not that I am eager to see you both leave!'

'It should be ready on Saturday,' said Mr. Wedderburn.

'Which is just as well,' said Debs, 'as Mr. Pillans' funeral is tomorrow, and I feel we should go.' It was not clear that Mr. Wedderburn felt the same way, but he did not protest.

'Yes, I heard it was to be tomorrow. Did she need anything? The services of a good cook, perhaps?'

'She said that all was well and they were entirely prepared,' said Debs. 'She does seem to have some parts of that house organised, though I still have my suspicions about the staff. Any servant who will take money to allow his master's corpse to be stolen from the house ... well. Actually,' she added honestly, 'I don't believe I have ever come across that situation before.'

'I hope none of us shall again,' said Isobel. At least that had not happened at Letho. It was enough to have a nervous housekeeper, a frightened governess, a manservant who could not keep his children under control, and a stray German musician hiding in the kitchen. And no sign of Charles yet.

'Did the sheriff's man bring any interesting news?' asked Richard Wedderburn. Isobel saw her father look up eagerly, and hoped that he was not going to talk about the contents of the box for the rest of dinner. She had so many things in her head at the moment that all she really wanted to think about was the soup, and then the main courses, and then the puddings, and then Debs could play the fortepiano for them in the entrance hall and she could think of nothing at all for ten minutes.

'He has not made much progress, he says,' she told the Wedderburns. 'But we did find out what route Mr. Pillans took on Friday to reach Letho.'

'They say someone brought him in a gig?' said Mr. Wedderburn.

'The innkeeper says that is how he arrived, but no one knows who the driver was.'

'A real mystery,' said Debs. 'Now, I was thinking – my friend in Cupar, the one we were intending to stay with – I think her maid has a sister who might perhaps venture as far as Letho. If I were to find out more, do you think Mr. Murray would be interested?'

'It's possible. I don't even know if he's keeping this housekeeper yet, and no doubt if she stays she will want some say in the appointment of maids.'

'Is that the fair-haired woman, stocky build?' asked Mr. Wedderburn.

'That's the one,' said Isobel.

'Oh, yes. I saw her in the village when I went to call on the smith,' he said. 'I thought she looked familiar. She didn't look too happy, mind you.'

'Really?' Isobel stared at him.

'Now, now, dear: don't bring problems on poor Isobel,' said Debs at once. 'I'm sure it was nothing more significant than a stone in the woman's shoe, or something. Nothing more than that, I'm sure.'

Isobel was grateful for Debs' efforts. But Mrs. Gilmour had seemed nervous earlier. And then she had fled from the entrance hall when she saw Macduff there. So was it nothing more than a stone in her shoe? No, really – what could it be?

In fact Debs' playing, though perfectly good, was not enough to distract Isobel from her thoughts, particularly when Mrs.

Gilmour's activities were added in. Debs played on, though, clearly enjoying herself, and Miss Fitzsimmons and Augusta came to hear the music before bedtime. Miss Fitzsimmons … Isobel would have to ask Charles to have a word with Mr. George. Really, the man should be old enough now to behave himself.

Augusta danced for them for a little while, making Debs laugh, then crawled up on to Blair's lap and demanded to see what he had in his pockets. It was an old game with them, and kept her pleasantly occupied for some time, until a noise outside on the drive distracted her.

'Papa!' she cried, and sure enough, the front door opened, and there was Murray.

A change from travel-stained clothes, and then he could go back down to the company, and relax. Food, and wine, and eager greetings from the dogs, and chatter – an enthusiastic embrace from his daughter, a handshake from Blair, a glare from Isobel – he would no doubt find out later what that was about. The Wedderburns told him they planned to leave on Saturday, and that Mr. Pillans' funeral was tomorrow. Blair told him that the engineers, despite some unspecified hiccough, were still hard at work. Isobel told him that they still, for the moment, had a housekeeper.

Then Miss Fitzsimmons bade Augusta say good night to her father, and took her away upstairs, and the Wedderburns took themselves off to sort out dark clothes for the next day from their luggage. And the Blairs and Murray were left in the entrance hall, and Isobel had a chance to tell Murray all her woes: Miss Fitzsimmons' upset, and Janny's mischief, and Mrs. Gilmour's odd behaviour, and Mr. Rieder's continued sojourn under the kitchen table.

'I am sorry,' was all he could think of to say when she had finished. Had he put her off Letho forever? 'I thought I was leaving you a simple task, but it seems that everything was just waiting for me to go before causing trouble.'

'Oh, it was – it was fine, really,' said Isobel. 'I mean, the rest of the time everything was fine. And I like Mrs. Gilmour, really. I just wonder what's troubling her.''

'The matter of Francis George, at least, I can deal with first thing in the morning,' said Murray. 'I want to go and make sure he knows his sister is well, as well as tell him to stop insulting my governess. And I want to talk to Lord Rocheid.'

'Oh, yes?' said Blair, sensing possible progress.

'Yes. I want to find out why he was in Letho as early as Friday, and why he brought Gordon Pillan here in his gig. And where he was between then and Sunday evening.'

By midnight the Blairs knew all he had found out, and he had heard from them all that Macduff had had to say, and seen the notes they had both taken of the volumes Macduff had allowed them to see in Pillans' box. He went to bed thinking that from having too little information, he now felt they had too much – and still no idea of who might have murdered Pillans, or why.

Gordon Pillans' funeral was to begin around eleven – late enough in the day to allow plenty of activity beforehand. Murray spoke at length with Robbins, exchanged some words with Mr. Thalland the factor, and even managed to call at the icehouse and have a word with the engineers.

'We're coming up with some ideas now,' said Edward Kelly cheerfully.

'I'm sorry to hear you've had a bit of trouble with some of the local children,' Murray said. 'I hope there was nothing last night.'

'Not a bit of it,' said Kelly. 'I slept like a child, and I believe my colleague did the same. The food you get in that kitchen is tremendous,' he added, evidently intent on being placatory. Murray was reassured: they were not about to leave.

'Let's see what you have in mind, then,' he said, and the next half hour was spent poring over diagrams and elevations and plans, none of which, he was pleased to see, looked impossibly difficult or expensive. Blair was no doubt delighted with them, and Murray was relieved.

Then he went and changed his coat, gathered a couple of the dogs, and headed off on foot to Dures, to catch Mr. George before the funeral.

The manservant at the door directed Murray to the gardens at the rear of the house, where Mr. George, already in funeral black like Murray, was pacing the paths with his hands behind his back and, before he noticed Murray, a broad smile on his face. Not that the smile vanished entirely – Mr. George was too friendly for that – but it certainly changed quality. Murray wondered what girl he had been dwelling on, and hoped it was not his governess.

'Good day to you, Murray!' They bowed as soon as they were close enough. 'Do you want to go inside?'

'Not if you don't,' said Murray. 'It's a fine morning, and this place is looking well.'

'It's coming to the best time of the year,' said Mr. George, and Murray thought he was still looking very pleased with himself. 'The roses in particular are promising well for the next week, I think. Yes, it will look very fine.'

'Have you something in mind?' asked Murray. Mr. George looked puzzled, and he clarified. 'Are you expecting guests?'

'Guests? No! No, not at all. In fact … Oh, I must thank you, mustn't I? Your express. Very thoughtful of you. My sister is a fool, but at least you were able to reassure me that she was safe.'

'A pleasure,' said Murray. 'I was happy to be able to call and see her.'

They walked a pace or two. Mr. George's mind may have been on his sister, but Murray's was on how he was to approach a tricky matter.

'I wonder if you have by chance met my new governess? Miss Fitzsimmons?'

Mr. George frowned.

'The name is not familiar. Oh, but I believe I may have seen her at church. A handsome enough woman, well-bred, with dark hair?'

The words were enough to reassure Murray, oddly. Of course Mr. George had noticed her: he would notice any handsome woman in the county within a week. But the casual way he had added 'well-bred', oddly, was what proved him innocent. Mr. George had no record of being attracted to women of his own class – probably the reason he had never married. All his dalliances – and there had been many – were with servants and the like. To Murray's knowledge he had treated them all well, and at least in this parish he had built up little resentment. But Murray was sure that Miss Fitzsimmons was safe.

'Did you happen to meet her – oh, when was it – on

Tuesday? It would have been on the road into Letho from here.'

'On Tuesday? No, I can be sure of that. I was in Cupar on Tuesday, on business.' The memory of the business seemed to distract him for a moment, and then he asked, 'Why?'

'Oh, nothing of note. She is new to the area, as I say, and mentioned the people she thought she had seen on her walk. You were a name she listed, but I had a feeling she was mistaken.'

'Well, she is, I'm afraid – some other handsome old man!' Mr. George joked.

'I wonder who?' said Murray. He tried to make it sound casual, for if he now said that the man had insulted Miss Fitzsimmons, Mr. George would realise that Murray had suspected him. But it would bear investigation. What other dark-haired gentlemen were there about Letho, apart from Mr. George and himself?

They had reached a rustic summerhouse in the corner of the garden. At this time of day it looked murky, rather than invitingly cool. They turned, and faced the house again.

'Is there any word from that sheriff's man yet? Have they found a likely killer?' Mr George asked. But Murray was distracted by a movement at the French doors that opened on to the garden. Two figures appeared, one heading, smiling, into the garden, the other releasing the first from a passionate embrace. Lady Rocheid, draped only in a loose, wide-sleeved gown, pale fingers sliding reluctantly from the dark-clad arm of her husband, Lord Rocheid.

Chapter Forty

Lady Rocheid disappeared into the dimness of the parlour as Lord Rocheid scanned the garden and spotted Mr. George and Murray. He raised a hand, and started towards them.

'As I say,' muttered Mr. George, 'my sister is a fool.'

She must have left Edinburgh almost when Murray left, he thought. She had changed her mind.

'Good day to you, George,' said his lordship with a nod. 'And to you, sir.'

Murray was fairly sure that Rocheid had forgotten his name.

'Good day,' he replied mildly, his own bow not particularly deep. 'I wonder if I might have a word with you, my lord, concerning an acquaintance of yours.' How much could he assume, he wondered – which end would he start at? Of course he had not yet heard from Susan Knox, if he ever would.

'An acquaintance of mine?' Lord Rocheid looked Murray up and down, as if wondering what acquaintance they could possibly share. It did not entirely help him that he was a good six inches shorter than Murray. Presumably Pillans had been, too.

'The man you brought with you in your gig to Letho,' said Murray. 'Being a prominent person, you were of course noticed on your journey in several places, in the company of a man of similar appearance.'

He hoped this flattery would prevent Rocheid denying everything before they had got anywhere. It worked, to an extent.

'Oh, that fellow! I'd hardly call him an acquaintance. I met

245

him on the ferry, found he was making for Letho, and offered him a lift. He was going to hire a horse in North Queensferry – can you imagine?' he added to Mr. George. Perhaps he thought that Murray would not have to imagine such a circumstance.

'What was his name, my lord?' asked Murray.

'His name? Did he even tell me?' Lord Rocheid affected a bad memory, pressing a finger to his brow. 'I don't know that he did. He didn't say much at all, in fact.'

'I see. Of course, that makes it awkward to become acquainted.'

'It does indeed!' said Rocheid, with a sigh, as if he had hoped that he and his passenger might have become the closest of friends.

'Where did you leave him, my lord?'

'Leave him?'

'I daresay his destination was not Dures!'

'No, of course not. No, I left him at the inn. He had a box and someone came out to help him with it, and then I left him there.'

'On Friday, this was?'

'On –' Lord Rocheid stopped. He had seen the trap. 'No, it cannot have been Friday. It must have been Sunday, of course. The day I arrived here.'

'Unfortunately not, my lord. It was Friday.'

Murray sensed Mr. George tensing beside him. Had his brother-in-law really arrived two days earlier? And not communicated with Lady Rocheid?

'I cannot think it was Friday. George, when did I come here? It was Sunday, was it not? Sunday evening.'

'That's when I first saw you, yes,' said Mr. George carefully.

'There you are, you see?' said Lord Rocheid, satisfied. 'I arrived on Sunday. So whatever the fellow says – whoever he is – he could not have arrived at the village on Friday.'

'But he did, my lord,' said Murray, 'for he was murdered near there on Friday night.'

'He was not!' Lord Rocheid was two steps back before even he realised it.

'He was, I'm afraid.'

'Wait,' said Mr. George, 'you mean that this – that Rocheid here – was the man who brought poor Pillans to Letho?'

'By all accounts, yes,' said Murray.

'Not by my account!' cried Rocheid. 'Not by me! Murdered? Don't be ridiculous! Who are you, anyway? Who are you to come here, to this house, and accuse me?'

'Accuse you of what, my lord?' asked Murray.

'Of – of – of whatever has happened!' Lord Rocheid was doing a good impression of outrage and shock. How sincere he was Murray was not sure.

'I think just now all I have said is that you arrived at Letho on Friday, rather than Sunday, in the company of a man you say you did not know. And what interests me just now, my lord,' he decided to see how far he could push it, 'is where exactly you were between leaving the man at the inn in the village, and walking into this house on Sunday evening.'

'Well!' sputtered Lord Rocheid. 'Well! I don't see why I should answer you! You haven't even told me who you are!'

'Well,' Mr. George echoed, 'you know who I am, and besides being your brother-in-law and your host, I am one of the Justices of the Peace for the area. Perhaps you could tell me where you were?'

Lord Rocheid regarded him for a moment with loathing.

'I was in Newport,' he said at last, sulkily.

'In Newport, on the Tay,' said Mr. George, just in case. There were other, more distant, Newports. 'What were you doing there?'

Rocheid gave Mr. George a little sideways glance.

'I was with a woman, of course. You know all about that kind of thing.'

'Not as a married man,' said Mr. George. 'But you, by contrast, were betraying my sister. And not for the first time, I should think.'

'Betraying her? That's not –'

'Have you anyone who can vouch for you in Newport?' asked Murray swiftly. The two of them could discuss betrayal later: his concern was Gordon Pillans.

'Vouch for me? I have told you I was there: that should be sufficient.'

'Yes, but you also told me a moment ago that you did not arrive at Letho on Friday. And that now proves to be the case.'

'Oh, damn you!' snapped Rocheid. 'Damn you to hell. You

247

are an impudent fellow!'

'Perhaps so, but I am not at least suspected of murder,' said Murray.

'I have committed no murder!' shouted Rocheid. 'Why would I murder someone I had only just met? And go all the way to some icehouse to do it?'

As smoothly as he could, Murray said,

'An icehouse? Where?'

Rocheid fell quiet, and his mouth turned petulant.

'Someone told me it was an icehouse.'

'Did they, indeed? And who was that, then?'

Rocheid thought for a moment.

'I'm not telling you,' he said, drawing himself up, but only managing to look like a sulky schoolboy. He struck Murray as a spoilt bully, full of himself until he was told he could not have his own way.

'Why shouldn't you tell me?' asked Mr. George. 'No harm in a conversation, picking up a little gossip, is there?'

'Maybe I don't even know who I heard it from,' said Rocheid. 'Maybe I just overheard it somewhere.'

'Maybe you did. Where?'

'Well, in Newport, I should think. Now, I'm going to go and get ready for this funeral. My dear wife says we have to go and pay our respects – even if I never knew the fellow,' he finished with emphasis, and turned on his heel.

'Well, that was fun,' said Mr. George, watching Rocheid return to the house.

'One or two interesting points, too,' Murray agreed.

'Vile man. Well, Murray, I shall see you at the funeral, no doubt.'

They bowed, and Murray headed back home, going over what they had learned.

'We could do with proof that it was Lord Rocheid's gig that picked up Mr. Pillans. Ideally from someone who knew both of them, but at least from someone who knew Pillans,' said Isobel. She and her father were in the entrance hall when Murray returned, dressed in black, and waiting for the Wedderburns. Murray had given them an account of his meeting at Dures.

'I have written to someone who might be able to help,' Murray said. 'One of the shop girls, eager to find her friend.'

'A shop girl?' asked Isobel.

'Her name is Susan Knox. I've asked her, if she will, to go to Newington and ask the maid and perhaps the neighbours' servants, too.'

'But can a shop girl afford to gad about like that? And receive letters, and send word back?' Isobel seemed in a mood to object.

'I enclosed a draft on my bank,' said Murray.

'Then she'll rob you,' said Isobel simply. 'She'll be off to buy herself something fancy, and not darken the doors of Newington at all.'

'Newington?'

Mrs. Wedderburn and her husband were just descending the stairs.

'Where the Pillans lived,' Murray explained, without going in to detail.

'That's where we had to spend the winter!' said Debs. 'How funny – we were perhaps very close. I must speak with Mrs. Pillans about it. Of course we were cut off from much of society – and could not possibly entertain there – but it was really quite airy and pleasant. Almost like staying in a different town altogether.'

'There are the carriages!' cried Blair, who was straining to look through the window, though the noise of the wheels on the gravel had alerted everyone. 'Shall we go?'

From what he knew of Collessie, Murray thought that Mrs. Pillans or her mother had been quite clever. They had formed, as it were, an apartment within the house: the funeral guests were funnelled from the door to the dead room to the drawing room, with access to two reasonable privies, and by the use of screens and curtains and judiciously-placed furnishings they could not wander into any part of the house that was – well, typical of Collessie. The accessible rooms had quickly been disguised with cloth from the Oriental Warehouse, and looked, at first glance anyway, very splendid. Only one or two servants appeared but they, too, seemed spruced up for the occasion and on their very best behaviour, casting occasional terrified glances at Mrs. Skead, Mrs. Pillans' mother.

Murray was impressed and, catching Isobel's eye, saw that she was struggling not to giggle at the transformation.

They were the first to arrive apart from the minister and his wife, the Helliwells, and not long after them came the Feildens, the doctor and his wife. It was a large enough company for gentle chatter to begin, and Murray even heard Debs Wedderburn settle down with Mrs. Pillans to talk of Newington, though they seemed to have no mutual acquaintance there. Isobel joined the conversation smoothly, and Murray knew she would be collecting any information she could. Blair had had himself settled beside Mrs. Skead, her eyes still red with weeping and fatigue, and gently eased her into conversation apparently about the décor. Mrs. Skead, no more resistant to Blair's company than anyone else, was soon telling him all about it.

It was not going to be a large company, Murray realised, glancing about. No one in Letho had known Gordon Pillans or had to their knowledge met him: the lower orders would not take time from their work to come, even for a free meal. The next time the drawing room door shifted it was to allow in Mr. Thalland, Murray's factor, and the two Irish engineers. Murray went to speak to them when they had paid their respects.

'We thought it only right, sir,' said Edward Kelly, 'and I hope you will not think it amiss, sir. When we were there at the finding of the poor man, and him without a friend in the village.'

'Of course,' said Murray. 'It seems entirely right.'

'A good thing they had the man in his coffin already, though,' added Kelly in a much lower voice. 'I'd no wish to see that again. Those teeth!'

Murray nodded, then turned as the door opened once again. Lady Rocheid entered, followed by her husband and brother. Mrs. Pillans, gone quite white, rose from her chair, unconsciously steadying herself on Isobel's ready arm. Lady Rocheid stepped forward, not a good colour herself. She was in the very latest black, a gold necklace set with pearls about her thin neck, and everything perfect, except for her face. She swallowed hard, and curtsied.

'Mrs. Pillans,' she said, 'I come to offer my deepest condolences on your loss.'

'That is – very good of you,' said Mrs. Pillans, clutching hard at Isobel's arm. 'Please be welcome. Here – here is a chair, if you will.'

Lady Rocheid advanced, and took the chair, just beside Debs Wedderburn. Debs turned to smile at her, made a little squeak of surprise, and her teacup smashed on the floor.

Chapter Forty-One

'Oh! Oh, how careless of me!' cried Debs. 'And tea on the carpet! Mrs. Pillans, I am so sorry.'

Mrs. Skead flashed a look at one of the servants, who stared at her helplessly for a moment.

'A cloth, dear,' said Mrs. Skead, and the servant hurried off.

Mr. Wedderburn was already flourishing his handkerchief, and plucking pieces of china from the carpet, as if he were well trained in minor domestic crises. By the time the maid returned, most of the tea had been wiped away, and the ladies were in their seats, Mrs. Pillans beside a sopha on which perched Isobel and Lady Rocheid, with Debs Wedderburn on her other side.

'Unfortunate,' said Murray to Wedderburn, when he had shaken out his handkerchief into the maid's bucket, and retired to stand with Murray and Mr. George. 'Something must have knocked her arm, I suppose.'

'I don't know,' said Wedderburn. 'She did look a bit surprised, didn't she?'

'They've met before, haven't they?' asked Mr. George. 'Mrs. Wedderburn has been visiting Letho for years.'

'I'm sure they've met,' said Wedderburn. 'I've met both of you, and I haven't been visiting for so long.'

'Oh, who knows?' said Murray. He glanced at Lord Rocheid, who was standing by the fireplace as though he had been chilled by his journey from Dures. 'I assume his lordship went in to pay his respects to the corpse,' he said to Mr. George.

'Of course,' said Mr. George. 'The way they have the rooms

set up, it would have been very awkward for him to have refused.'

'Oh!' Wedderburn, half-listening, turned in surprise. 'You don't think – not his lordship?' he finished in a low hiss that shrieked conspiracy. Murray saw Isobel glance over. He and Mr. George made sure they were looking nowhere near Lord Rocheid.

'Good gracious, no,' said Mr. George comfortably, but Murray could see a gleam in his eye. It would be a scandal, yes, but a certain way to be rid of his loathed brother-in-law. Murray made a note to himself: if Mr. George did provide any evidence against Rocheid, it would be a good idea to verify it: it might be nothing more malicious than wishful thinking, but it did make Mr. George an unreliable witness.

'Well, is there anyone that the sheriff's man does have his eye on?' asked Wedderburn reasonably.

'I haven't seen Macduff since I came back from Edinburgh,' said Murray.

'I heard he had brought in poor Pillans' luggage,' said Wedderburn. Mr. George raised an eyebrow.

'I heard no one could open that,' he countered.

'Ninian Jack,' said Murray simply. Both men nodded – even Wedderburn had heard of Jack's powers.

'Anything interesting revealed?' asked Mr. George.

'Clean linen and a few books,' said Murray. 'A cash book, a notebook and a Waverley novel.'

'Which one?' asked Mr. Wedderburn, idly.

'*The Bride of Lammermoor*, apparently,' said Murray. 'I didn't see it myself.'

'Ha!' said Mr. George, and the other two looked at him. '*The Bride of Lammermoor* – near enough my foolish sister!'

Murray turned the plot over in his mind, reluctant to draw any comparisons, but Mr. Wedderburn was more direct.

'How so?' he asked.

'Him,' said Mr. George, with a jerk of the head in the direction of Rocheid, 'that's where he comes from, or thereabouts. Not that he ever takes her there.'

Isobel, allowing Mrs. Pillans to use her as a support and helping her to settle once again in her armchair, could not for a moment take a proper look at either Debs Wedderburn or Lady

Rocheid. When she did, she saw nothing very remarkable, except that Debs kept flashing glances at Lady Rocheid as if too frightened to look at her directly. Yet she was sure that whatever had caused Debs to drop her teacup, it had been something she saw when she looked at Lady Rocheid. True, Miss George had always been a slightly alarming person – most often when she came across an eligible man – but it was nothing to cause shock in an otherwise sensible woman with a teacup.

She put the matter aside for now, and tried to take the tone of the conversation back to what it had been before the Rocheids appeared. It was not easy. Debs' thoughts appeared to be elsewhere, and Lady Rocheid was perhaps embarrassed, as well she might be, at the memory of how she had behaved towards Mrs. Pillans on their last encounter. Mrs. Pillans had been perfectly gracious, Isobel thought: Mr. George must have defended his sister well, but it did not make for easy exchanges, either. Mrs. Helliwell, one of whose many talents was the diminishing of social awkwardnesses, sensed the problem and came over casually, as if there were nothing whatever the matter. She drew up a low stool and perched amidst them, expression absolutely apt for friendliness on a sad occasion.

'Dear Mrs. Pillans,' she said, 'you have made such a wonderful place here! You must have quite the eye for such things.'

'Thank you, Mrs. Helliwell,' said Mrs. Pillans, the words bursting out as if she were relieved to have anything to say. 'My mother and I have worked hard to achieve it – we wanted to make it look its best.'

'I have never seen Collessie look so well,' Isobel put in. 'I imagine your Edinburgh house is an absolute delight.'

'My husband gave me free rein,' said Mrs. Pillans, blushing faintly. 'He was so good to me. And after all, I could order whatever I chose from the warehouse. After all the time I had – had been acquainted with the goods there, to be able to make use of them was so – such a privilege.' Her voice faded a little. Perhaps in front of Lady Rocheid she felt some embarrassment at admitting she had been a shop girl. Both the Rocheids, Isobel thought, had a knack of making one feel defensive about one's place in society. Lord Rocheid stood still by the fireplace, too far from any other mourner to engage in conversation without shouting. Mr. Helliwell was chatting with the Feildens by the richly curtained windows, and Mr.

Thalland and the engineers remained close to the door, as if not quite sure of their welcome. Charles stood with Mr. George and Mr. Wedderburn, talking in low voices. They made a handsome trio, Isobel thought, Mr. George retaining his looks even as he aged, Mr. Wedderburn affable, and Charles … Well, he was always a fine man. She had always thought so.

Mrs. Helliwell was still hard at work.

'Lady Rocheid, perhaps you have visited – the Oriental Warehouse, is it not, Mrs. Pillans?'

'Indeed I have, madam,' said Lady Rocheid, who was also putting in some effort. 'On the South Bridge, is it not? My husband has been kind enough to bring me some charming silks from there, and some pieces of crewel work for cushions. Our house in Picardy Place is very much à la mode, you understand, for the circles we are required to move in when in town.'

'I'm very gratified to know that my husband's merchandise has been favoured with your attention,' said Mrs. Pillans, though a tear crept from her eye. What would happen to the warehouse now, Isobel wondered. Would the widow keep it on?

'We are so rarely in Edinburgh,' said Mrs. Helliwell, 'only for the General Assembly, but I shall make a point next year of going to see this wonderful place. It sounds an absolute treasure trove! You may yet see the minister of Letho parish clad in apricot silks!'

It was a completely ridiculous idea, but it punctured the tension nicely. All four women allowed themselves a little chuckle, and Isobel could see Lady Rocheid and Mrs. Pillans relax their fingers very slightly. Good work, Mrs. Helliwell.

But Debs Wedderburn was still not quite calm, though now she was making a point of not looking at Lady Rocheid at all. What on earth was the matter with her? Now she was trying to catch her husband's eye, like a guest who thought it was past their bedtime. Mr. Wedderburn, however, who with Charles and Mr. George had moved across to talk with the factor and the engineers, was describing some event to them and had his back half towards his wife, waving his arms about to aid the narrative. What did his wife want to tell him about Lady Rocheid? It did not look like good news, anyway.

'So that was how the axle broke, I believe,' Mr. Wedderburn

was finishing his account. 'The smith in the village here is taking his time over the mending of it: he's telling me it might be better altogether to make a new one.'

'Now that could well be, sir,' said Edward Kelly. 'There could be a weakness at the mend that might easily go again – and you'll have no wish to repeat that experience, I should think.'

'No, not at all! All I want to do is to get home to my own hearth – with respect to you, Murray – and not stir till the summer is done. And maybe not then. Our girls need no husbands just yet: I see no sense in going to town for the season until they are at least thirty-five.' He stopped, and shot a quick, embarrassed glance at Mr. George, but Mr. George paid it no attention.

Murray was only half-listening to Richard Wedderburn's story, having heard it before. He glanced about the room, and noticed that Blair was trying to attract his attention. He went over.

'Excuse me, Mrs. Skead,' said Blair at once, 'but I must ask my friend here to take me out for a moment.'

'Oh, of course, sir!' said Mrs. Skead at once. Murray, surprised, helped Blair from his chair and supported him out of the drawing room. Once they were out of sight of anyone in the room, Blair stopped.

'I thought you wanted –' said Murray.

'I think someone wants to talk to me,' said Blair at the same moment. 'I hope she has noticed my departure.'

'She?'

At that moment, one of the servants came out on to the landing, looked to left and right, and spotted them at once. She hurried over, and dropped a curtsey.

'Mr. Blair, sir, it is you, is it not?'

'It is – I'm sorry, I don't know your name?'

'It's of no matter, sir, and I don't have much time, for Mrs. Skead is that strict! But I have a son, sir, Dandy, and you were kind to him the other day. He feared he would be in terrible trouble – as he well deserved – but he's an innocent, sir, as I believe you realised.'

'Oh, Janny's friend?'

'I wish that were not so, sir!'

'Well, it was clear that the whole thing was Janny's fault,' said Blair.

'Aye, sir … look, there's something else, as you've been good to us, sir. They say – well, they say that you always look into any mysteries and so on, and you're like to be finding out about poor Mr. Pillans' death – not that I ever met him, but from all they say he sounds a fine man.'

'And you have something to tell me, have you?'

'I think so, sir, and if it will be of any help to you I should be pleased to make you a present of the information.'

'Go on, then,' said Blair, while Murray stood quiet beside him.

'The night that Mr. Pillans is said to have died, well, there was a strange horse in the stable and a strange gig in the yard, and, from all I saw, a strange man in the hayloft.'

'Is that so?' asked Blair. 'Did you see any of these?'

'I did, sir. I was not the one paid to turn a blind eye, and I chanced to be in the stableyard early on Saturday morning. I thought one of the other maids was in the hayloft – it's been known afore, sir, with one of the lads, but this time she was with grander company, if the gig was aught to go by. A dark one, sir, and a dark cob to it.'

'Do you know when they arrived?'

'The lass was missing all night from her bed.'

'And when did they go?'

'Not all Saturday, I believe, sir. Then all three were off, and the lass was back in her own bed.'

'Thank you very much!' said Blair. 'That indeed is most interesting! But you did not actually see the man?'

'No, sir, sorry.'

'That's fine, that's fine. No, that's very interesting indeed.'

'And now I'd better be off, sir, if you please.'

'Of course.' Coins changed hands quietly, though she looked reluctant to take them.

'If I find out more, sir, I'll be sure to let you know.' She curtseyed and fled. Murray and Blair met each other's eyes.

'Left here in time to drive to the village on Saturday night?' Murray asked. 'Our mysterious dark gig?'

'Perhaps he found somewhere to visit there, too,' said Blair. 'And didn't you say he knew about the body in the icehouse? That may be where he found out about it.'

'He, here, being our friend Rocheid?'

'Of course.'

'So he arrives in Letho on Friday, with Pillans. He comes here for Friday evening. Pillans dies that night. Rocheid leaves here the next day, Saturday ...'

'And drives his gig into the village and out again.'

'Hm. And perhaps then ... but this assumes that he did not kill Pillans?'

'I need to cogitate, Charles,' said Blair sadly. 'I need to apply my mind. It is so much slower than it ever was!'

'Then you need to exercise it. We can do nothing here: let us go back in and try to find a chance later, before he goes back to Dures.'

Back in the drawing room, the conversations were dragging.

'I wonder if we are expecting anyone else?' Mr. George asked. 'Surely everyone is here now: Helliwell could lead the prayers and get on with it. The poor fellow is already in his coffin, after all, and with so few of us here it could grow awkward.' He took a helping of teabread from the servant who was passing, and added it to his plate. 'I'm sure my sister and Mrs. Pillans do not have much to say to each other.'

They did not, but Mrs. Helliwell and Isobel were still determined.

'Tell us a little about Mr. Pillans, madam,' said Isobel. 'If you will, if it will not give you pain.'

'It pleases me to talk about him,' Mrs. Pillans said. 'Thank you, Miss Blair. He was a good man, a lovely man. A very generous man, and kind.'

Isobel tried not to make a face.

'Did he have interests outside the business? Was he, for example, a great reader?'

'No, not really. We did not have much interest in books.'

'Did you talk much together? Did he have many friends?'

'He had the men he was in business with, though of course they are in India. He talked to me about the business, of course: he knew I was interested in that, and all they were sending him, and how it sold, and who had been in the shop, and who was working there ... I liked all that.'

'Did you go often to the shop?'

'No, not at all. No. He brought me things, and told me the news.'

'Oh, but you must be interested in music!' said Mrs. Helliwell. 'Had you not arranged for a music tutor to come here?'

'Oh, yes,' said Mrs. Pillans, 'but that was for me. I ... other ladies play so nicely in company, when we go out. I wanted to learn how to improve, so that ...' She tailed away. So that she would not let her husband down, thought Isobel.

'Excuse me,' said Debs Wedderburn suddenly, and rose from her place. She almost tripped in her haste, then righted herself, and left the room fast. Mrs. Helliwell and Isobel looked at each other.

'Shall I?' asked Isobel.

'Will you, Miss Blair?'

Isobel stood and followed Debs. She found her out on the landing, at the door of the dead room, at a loss for where to go.

'Are you quite all right, Mrs. Wedderburn? Is something the matter?'

'It's – I don't quite know what to say,' said Debs, for once unsure of herself. Her hand drifted, unconsciously, to her own throat. 'But to you I can say something, I think. I believe you know that while we were in Edinburgh – in Newington – one of the misfortunes that occurred to us was that our maid absconded with some of my jewellery?'

'Yes, indeed. It must have been very distressing.'

'The more so,' said Debs, 'in that some of the pieces were my grandmother's, and of great sentimental value to me, as well as of some material worth.'

'I'm very sorry to hear it.'

'Pieces, you understand,' said Debs, pulling at her gloves, 'that I would know anywhere.'

'Of course.' Isobel was beginning to form an idea as to what the story might be.

'Even,' said Debs, 'when it is my grandmother's gold and pearl necklace, around the throat of Lady Rocheid.'

Chapter Forty-Two

'That's … surprising,' said Isobel, though she was sure that Debs Wedderburn was not mistaken. 'How do you think that can have happened?'

'I cannot say,' said Debs. She was clearly very upset. 'And does she have the rest? How could this be?'

'We need to find out where she got it from,' said Isobel. 'Let me be clear: you were staying in Newington, and your maid – wasn't she from your husband's home?'

'That's right: her family live in the village. A good girl, though excited by the thought of visiting Edinburgh. She had not been before.'

'So she could not have had friends there, or none of long standing.'

'No, but she knew where the key to my jewel case was kept, and she took, I think, five items, and left us while we were out at a rout. My first thought was that she was taking them to finance a life in Edinburgh, or even further afield – London, perhaps? But Richard told me I was too fanciful, and that she would be back with them before we had done anything about it. I had not thought her so untrustworthy, I really had not. Her family is very respectable.'

Isobel had never seen Debs Wedderburn knocked so sideways. She was almost gabbling. Isobel had always felt ambivalent about her: she was rather older, and always seemed so competent, so much in charge, that Isobel swung between resentment and admiration. But this was a new Debs, and Isobel felt so confident as to be able to give her a comforting hug, for which

Debs actually seemed grateful.

'Perhaps she sold them, and Lady Rocheid in all good faith bought this piece. Would you like me to ask her?'

'Would you? I don't think – if she denied it could be mine, if she refuses to say – I'm not sure I could be courteous. And that would be most unfair on poor Mrs. Pillans.'

'It would. Please forgive me, but are you absolutely sure it is yours?'

'I know you have to ask,' said Debs, nodding. She dabbed her eyes with her handkerchief, and pulled her shoulders back like a soldier facing the enemy. 'Look, it's quite old-fashioned, really. The clusters of pearls are set in gold, with short chains linking them. I played with it on my grandmother's lap when I was tiny, counting the links. They were just right for little fingers, like a shiny abacus. There is one chain on the right hand side – as you wear it, not as you look at it – which has only six links, instead of seven. Surely that is distinctive enough?'

'I should think so,' said Isobel, making a mental note of it. 'Are you ready to go back, or shall I go ahead?'

But before they could move, the rest of the company appeared on the landing with them, and Mr. Wedderburn naturally gravitated towards his wife. It was time for the minister to say prayers over the coffin, and for the other men then to escort Mr. Pillans to his burial place.

They assembled in the dead room. Isobel tried to make sure she was on the other side of the coffin from Lady Rocheid, so that she could see the necklace clearly, but Lady Rocheid must have been feeling a chill. She had pulled her shawl up about her shoulders, obscuring half the necklace. Isobel scowled, then noticed Murray looking at her, a hint of a smile at the corner of his mouth. She made a face at him, and turned her attention to the prayers.

Murray wondered why Isobel was scowling at Lady Rocheid. It was brave enough of the woman to come to this funeral, and face Mrs. Pillans – she could have pleaded any kind of illness or fatigue, any malaise, and remained at home: after all, she had not known Mr. Pillans any more than any of the rest of them had. But no, she had come. Perhaps she intended only to keep an eye on her wandering husband.

Mr. Helliwell kept the prayers to the point, and did not linger too long over them. He would be remaining behind, as was the custom, while the others took turns to carry the coffin into the village and up to the kirkyard. Murray wondered if Mrs. Pillans had been tempted to take her husband's body back to Edinburgh, where she might feel he was closer to her, rather than to leave him here where he had never even spent a night alive. Maybe Mrs. Pillans planned to stay on at Collessie.

He, Mr. George, Mr. Thalland and Edward Kelly took the first turn at carrying the coffin, awkwardly, out of the room and down the stairs. A few of Collessie's outdoor servants, smartened up for the occasion, were waiting to take their turn along with Jo Sweeney as the coffin progressed. Blair, pushed slowly along by Smith, could obviously not join in. Lord Rocheid avoided everyone's eye when carrying was discussed – it appeared such labours were beneath him.

Poor Pillans, thought Murray, as he struggled to walk while trying not to stretch to his full height, keeping the coffin level. Poor Pillans, just arrived for his holiday, with his new wife. What had his plans been for the summer? Why had he chosen Letho, and Collessie? How, leaving the inn for Collessie, had he found himself, hours later, in Murray's icehouse? What had he been doing all that time?

It was something he had not thought about much, though no doubt Macduff had made enquiries. Had he gone to see friends? Met his murderer, and spent the evening with him?

Reached Collessie, and left again?

But if he had done that, then why had Mrs. Pillans not said so? Nor anyone at Collessie, presumably?

He needed to talk to Macduff again. And he wanted to know more about that box, the one that the Blairs had seen and he had not. He needed to look at their notes again. People were rarely killed at random. So what was it about Pillans that had caused him to be killed? Revenge, greed, love, hate – what had he inspired?

Every funeral was different. Sometimes, when the men headed off for the interment, there was a feeling of let-down, as if the women, left behind with the minister, were missing the action. Sometimes it was a relief: the body had gone, and it was time to make fresh tea and have a gossip. Or now: the body had finally left Collessie, and the next stage of mourning could begin.

For ten minutes or so, Mrs. Pillans and Mrs. Skead, her mother, sobbed quietly together, while the others, with nowhere to go, conversed in low voices at the other end of the drawing room. But it was restful, somehow: it was not the time, despite Debs' grim face, to start a casual chat with Lady Rocheid about where her necklace had come from.

At last the sobs eased, and Mrs. Pillans and Mrs. Skead excused themselves – as perhaps they should have done earlier – and went to wash their faces. The other ladies took a moment to walk about the drawing room, stretching their legs – funerals were lengthy businesses – and adjusting crumpled skirts and shawls. Lady Rocheid pulled her shawl off altogether, and began to rearrange it.

'Oh, Lady Rocheid, what a pretty necklace!' cried Isobel. 'I don't believe I have seen you wear that before – is it a recent acquisition?'

'A gift from my husband,' Lady Rocheid simpered unbecomingly. 'On his return from Edinburgh.'

'May I look more closely?' asked Isobel, aware of Debs close behind her. 'The setting is charming, is it not? And the pearls are beautifully matched.'

The necklace was indeed exquisite, like something from an old portrait. Lady Rocheid stood poised, chin in the air, while Isobel examined it. Seven links in each chain – except for that one on the left hand side as she looked at it. Only six in it. A charming counting lesson for a little girl.

'I wonder where he found it. Is it perhaps an old family piece of his? Or has he come across a jeweller in Edinburgh who has such things? I confess I should love to know – but he certainly has a good eye!'

'I believe he did buy it, yes,' said Lady Rocheid, flattered on her husband's behalf. 'But I'm afraid I have no idea where.'

'A splendid gift,' said Isobel heartily. She wanted to ask if it had come on its own, but felt she would be pushing the point. But another witness would be useful. 'Is it not, Mrs. Helliwell?'

Mrs. Helliwell had not the least interest in jewellery, but was polite enough to come and see what Isobel was enthusing about, and observant enough that she would no doubt give a good account of it later. Isobel, for her part, would tell her father and Charles what they had found, and no doubt they and Mr. Wedderburn would deal with it. Isobel did not want to be there when Lady Rocheid, whose moods were volatile at the best of times, had to hand back her new necklace. But still it was an odd coincidence – that Debs Wedderburn's jewel should appear beside her in Fife, having gone missing in Edinburgh, with a maid.

A missing maid. Was that in any way the same as a missing shop girl?

The Wedderburns had been staying in Newington, where the Pillans lived. And it was Mr. Pillans' shop girls who were going missing.

Hm.

Isobel stored the thought away in her mind, ready to come back to it later, but before she could entirely lock it away, another piece of the puzzle fell resoundingly into place.

Mr. Pillans and the girls. Mr. Pillans came north with Lord Rocheid. And Lady Rocheid had the necklace.

It had to be significant, had it not? Now, what could she do about it here, or would she have to wait until she was away from Collessie and able to discuss it with her father and Charles?

Before she could make any decisions, head whirling with ideas, Mrs. Pillans and her mother returned, looking calmer. Mrs. Helliwell crossed the room and took Mrs. Pillans' arm, and led her back to her seat.

'I've asked for more tea,' she said, 'I hope you don't mind. What wonders you have wrought with the staff!'

'That's my mother's doing,' said Mrs. Pillans at once, giving her mother a smile. 'She cannot bear idleness.'

'And they were very idle, I'm afraid,' said Mrs. Skead. Again, Isobel thought what a strong woman she looked – resolute, perhaps even tough. As if she had faced all kinds of difficulties in her life, and dealt with them.

'Oh, the box,' said Mrs. Pillans suddenly. Everyone glanced to where she was looking. Isobel wondered that she herself had not noticed it before, but it was tucked under a table with a bright cloth over it – the box that Macduff had had Ninian Jack open, the box that Gordon Pillans had left at the inn. Mrs. Pillans, of course, did not expect anyone to recognise it. 'My husband's box, that he was

bringing here. I've taken out of it his – his shirts and, and so on.'
Tears threatened briefly. 'But I think there were some books inside
it. I wonder if perhaps I should return them to the warehouse.'

'Are they business books, then?' asked Isobel, knowing they
were not but curious to see what Mrs. Pillans would say.

'I don't know,' said the widow. 'I didn't look at them – they
are just books, after all.'

Isobel restrained herself from response.

'But you're right,' said her mother, 'they may belong with
the business. And as yet you don't know what is to happen to the
business, of course – the other partners are in India, and will not
know yet of Mr. Pillans' death,' she explained generally.

'Let me look,' said Mrs. Pillans. 'It must be done some
time.'

She went and knelt on the floor by the box, pulled it out, and
opened it. The three volumes Isobel remembered were still at the
bottom, and Mrs. Pillans lifted them out one by one.

'His cash book,' she said, 'of course. He was always so
careful. Some notes – that, I think, is personal, too. I shall go through
it at leisure.' She closed the notebook, fingers lingering on the
leather cover for a moment. Isobel hoped she would find nothing in
it to disturb her. 'And then what is this?'

She set aside the first two books, and lifted out the novel.
She opened it, gave a little cry, and sagged into a faint.

Chapter Forty-Three

It was not more than a moment before Mrs. Pillans came round, aided by the swift application of Mrs. Helliwell's smelling salts.

'What a horrible thing!' she exclaimed, when she had her breath back. She showed the inner leaf of the book to the others, with its little gallows.

'Is it Mr. Pillans' book? Perhaps someone lent it to him,' suggested Isobel.

'I have never seen it before in my life,' said Mrs. Pillans definitely.

'"A memento mori" – isn't that something to do with death?' asked Debs Wedderburn, sufficiently distracted from Lady Rocheid and the necklace. 'A memento of death, no doubt. Well, there is death in the book, is there not? Perhaps someone was just commenting on the story.'

'No hangings, though, to my recollection,' said Isobel. 'Well, I'm sure that if this is not Mr. Pillans' book, whatever is inside has nothing to do with him, Mrs. Pillans.'

'I shall throw it in the fire,' said Mrs. Pillans.

'Oh, never a book!' cried Isobel, involuntarily. 'If you like, may I take it away? I cannot see a book burn!'

'Then please take it out of my sight, Miss Blair,' said Mrs. Pillans with feeling. 'I cannot bear it.'

Isobel slipped the book inside her generous reticule – it was always large enough to contain a pad of drawing paper – and fastened the top.

'When do you think the gentlemen will be back?' asked Lady Rocheid, pulling her shawl round her again.

Soon, Isobel hoped. But was there more she could do while she was here? More she could discover about Mr. Pillans, or why he might have died? Her head was full of thoughts of the Wedderburns' maid and the shop girls – she could not ask about them, surely. And if Lord Rocheid and Mr. Pillans had been acquainted, clearly their wives were not aware of the fact. What could she ask?

But no ideas came to her before they heard footsteps and voices, muffled on the stairs, then clear as the men returned to the drawing room. The traditional whisky had clearly been taken: Mr. Wedderburn was rather pink about the ears, and Jo Sweeney looked queasy. Mr. George, brushed and neat as if he had just emerged from his own dressing room, bowed to Mrs. Pillans.

'I hope you will excuse me, madam: I have business to attend to in Cupar, and must leave straightaway.'

'Oh, of course, Mr. George,' said Mrs. Pillans. 'I quite understand. No doubt most of you gentlemen have matters to be busy with ...'

Whether this was intended as a general dismissal or not, it had that effect. Servants were called for horses and carriages, and before Mr. George was halfway down the drive, the rest of the party were already gathered on the front doorstep, preparing to leave. Mrs. Pillans looked somewhere between relieved and abandoned, and at the upstairs windows Isobel could see the indoor servants already pulling back the blinds and the dark coverings. The funeral was over.

'So you've linked Pillans and his missing shop girls to Pillans and the Wedderburns' missing maid, and the Wedderburns' missing maid to Lord Rocheid and his wife's jewellery?' Murray was impressed.

'And if you're right, and Lord Rocheid brought Mr. Pillans to Letho,' Isobel added, looking pleased with herself, 'then we have quite a pattern, do we not?'

They were in the garden: the fresh air was irresistible after a long morning swathed in mourning drapes at Collessie. Lilac sweetened the sunny air, and across in the orchard the branches were laden with blossom. Swallows chittered high up, promising more good weather to come.

'We do. And Lord Rocheid does admit to bringing Pillans here – he just says he didn't know the man. I hope that Susan Knox writes soon.'

'She could hardly write yet,' said Blair, though he jiggled with impatience at the thought. 'When did you write her?'

'Yesterday, from Cupar,' said Murray. 'She would not have received it till this morning at the earliest, and if she had to go to Newington – probably after she had worked at the warehouse all day, then maybe had her supper - if she replies as soon as she finds anything it's likely not to go with the carrier until tomorrow morning, again at the earliest. It won't be here till Monday.'

'Yet we need to find out about that necklace,' said Isobel. 'Mrs. Wedderburn is very upset.'

'For that, I think, we might need Macduff. I wonder if he is still at the inn? He came to the interment, just quietly in the background. I didn't have the chance to do more than nod a greeting to him.'

'You had better send for him, Charles, my boy,' said Blair. 'Or to be faster, collect him on your way to Dures. I should like to find out more about that necklace, oh, yes!'

'Mr. George is gone to Cupar on business,' Isobel remarked.

'Yes ...' said Murray. 'That must be the third time in a week. I wonder what he has found to entertain him?'

'He was looking very smart,' said Isobel, 'though funereal, of course.'

'If it was not he who insulted Miss Fitzsimmons, then who?' asked Blair. 'Or could it be that the answer is obvious?'

'A dark-haired gentleman? Apart from the late Mr. Pillans, Mr. George and me, I think there is only one in the parish,' said Murray, smiling.

'Lord Rocheid,' said Isobel, nodding. 'Of course. Is it me, or are more and more facts pointing towards him? He brought Mr. Pillans here, he knew the area better than Mr. Pillans did ...'

'But what could his reason be?' asked Blair. 'I agree he is a most unpleasant young man, but that does not make him a murderer.'

'I still think there might be something to do with the missing girls,' said Murray. 'And the missing maid from Newington is connected with the jewellery which Rocheid gave his wife.'

'Again, it does not make him a murderer,' said Blair sadly. 'Unless, perhaps – oh! That might work! Lord Rocheid has been stealing the girls, not Mr. Pillans, but Mr. Pillans realised it was him, and Lord Rocheid killed him to stop him telling anyone!'

Murray and Isobel were silent, considering.

'Why bring him to Fife?' asked Murray. 'It would have been easier to kill him in Edinburgh, surely.'

'Perhaps he did not know that Mr. Pillans knew until they came here. A conversation on the way,' said Blair, damp eyes wide.

'It's possible … Mrs. Miller, the shop manager, said that Mr. Pillans engaged handsome girls to work in the warehouse to attract custom. Perhaps they attracted the wrong kind?'

'Where has he taken the girls?' asked Isobel. 'Where have they gone?'

'His house south of Edinburgh?' Murray suggested. 'Or even sold on – it is not a nice thought, I know, but we must recognise the probable reason he has them.'

'Where is his house, anyway?' asked Isobel, frowning at the fate of the girls.

'Somewhere near Haddington, I believe,' said Blair.

'Haddington?' Isobel turned sharply to her father. 'Is that not near the Lammermuir Hills?'

'*The Bride of Lammermoor*,' Murray said, making the connexion. 'But does that mean the book belonged to Rocheid? Or that it was given to him as a warning, and somehow ended up in Pillans' box?'

'Or Pillans intended it as a warning, but did not have the chance to give it to him?' Blair countered.

'I'm stuck,' Isobel admitted. 'My head is full of facts, and there are so many possible connexions between them that I don't know what the real ones are.'

'I know what you mean,' said Murray. 'I want to write everything out on a large piece of paper, like the engineers' charts, and see how it all fits together. If it does.'

'The engineers,' said Isobel, 'the only people in Letho, it seems, who have not come here straight from Edinburgh.'

'Unless you count Lord Rocheid's travels, to Newport and back – if he's telling the truth,' said Murray. 'I'd better go and see if I can find Macduff, and take him with me to Dures. You say you and Mrs. Helliwell can vouch for the description of the necklace?'

'Indeed,' said Isobel. 'Maybe Mr. Wedderburn would want to go too? And he can tell them what Debs' necklace looked like.'

'Sensible thought,' said Murray, and grinned at her.

'But I should not want to be there when Lady Rocheid discovers her new jewel is stolen property,' said Isobel. 'Not at all.'

It was probably fortunate, then, that when the three men reached Dures, Lord Rocheid told them that his wife was resting. He eyed Macduff with disdain.

'Now what?' he said, when Murray explained who he was. 'Another feeble attempt to link me with that man's murder, I suppose?'

'Not at all,' said Murray, sure that was not exactly a lie. 'No, we are here because of a question over a recent purchase of yours.'

'Purchase? What? What do you mean, man?'

'The necklace Lady Rocheid was wearing this morning.'

Lord Rocheid looked bewildered.

'A necklace? Look, I daresay my brother-in-law George allows you to flit around the houses of the parish making strange accusations – he probably joins you himself – but you are making no sense to me.'

'Lady Rocheid said that the necklace she was wearing this morning was a recent gift from you. An old-fashioned setting, gold and pearls.'

'Oh, that thing? I mean, yes – valuable, I daresay. I – I bought it in Edinburgh.' He frowned again, this time as though he was trying to remember the circumstances – or arrange his story. 'A month or two ago, I think it was, but I did not give it to her until yesterday.'

A month or two would, thought Murray, be before the necklace disappeared with the Wedderburns' maid.

'Do you remember where you purchased it?'

'Oh, one of the luckenbooths up on the Lawnmarket, I think. I like to browse around there, picking up trifles. One never knows what one might see!' He was pleased with his version of events, anyway.

'A couple of months ago?' Murray repeated. Lord Rocheid

cast him a suspicious glance.

'That would be right. Let me think – early March, perhaps?'

'Hm,' said Murray, 'there's a problem with that, I'm afraid. You see, the necklace was in the possession of Mrs. Wedderburn – Mr. Wedderburn's wife,' he added, gesturing to Wedderburn, 'as late as – when did it disappear, Wedderburn?'

'The first week in May,' said Wedderburn apologetically. 'Just before we left town to come back to Fife. One of the reasons why we did, really.'

'Nonsense,' said Lord Rocheid after a moment. 'That cannot possibly be true. It's clearly a different necklace. The booth I bought it at had several, very much the same.'

'It was my wife's grandmother's,' said Wedderburn. 'We have never seen one like it.'

'Can we see the necklace just the now, my lord?' asked Macduff. 'Just so as we all ken what we're talking about. Mr. Wedderburn here, he says there's a discrepancy in the chains.'

'A what? No, why should I show it to you? You're obviously wrong. How do I know you won't snatch it as soon as you see it?'

'I've never had much inclination to jewel theft,' said Macduff. 'Just have the necklace fetched, my lord, would you? It would be a shame to disturb Lady Rocheid.'

Murray blinked. He had never heard Macduff sound so stern before – and clearly unimpressed with this particular example of the nobility.

'A shame to disturb …' Lord Rocheid took a second or two, then stepped back and rang the bell. 'I suppose you can have a quick look at it.'

He instructed Mr. George's manservant, and in a few minutes the man was back with a long box, which he handed with a bow to Lord Rocheid. Bows could take many forms: Murray thought this one contained a good deal of distaste.

'Here,' said Lord Rocheid, and turned the box towards them, and opened it.

Chapter Forty-Four

'My wife's necklace,' Wedderburn confirmed. 'See? This chain here has six links, while the rest have seven.'

'I'm afraid you've been unlucky enough to purchase stolen property, my lord,' said Macduff. 'Was there any more with this, or is that all you bought?'

'I don't go picking all kinds of rubbish from the luckenbooths,' said Lord Rocheid, changing tack again. 'This piece caught my eye, that is all.'

'Would you be able to find the booth again?' Macduff asked.

'I shouldn't think so,' said Rocheid. 'Look, take the damned thing. It's only an old piece of tat anyway. Take it back to your wife, and have done with it.' He snapped the box shut, and handed it ungraciously to Wedderburn. Wedderburn had the sense to take it at once.

'Very good of you, my lord. I'm most grateful,' he said. Murray wondered if he believed Rocheid's story.

'I shall send word to the police office in the Old Town,' said Macduff with great formality, 'and alert them to the case. Perhaps we may recover more of the stolen jewellery that way. Thank you, my lord.'

'You're most welcome,' said Rocheid, with just a hint of sarcasm. 'Now, if there's nothing else?'

'There is, though,' said Murray. He and Blair had agreed Murray should approach this.

'Oh, what now?'

'Where did you spend last Friday night?'

'In Newport, I told you,' said Rocheid, after a second. Murray said nothing. 'Why?'

'I was giving you a chance to revise your geography,' said Murray. 'You weren't in Newport. You were at Collessie.'

'Collessie? That hovel?'

'Yes – the hayloft, to be precise.'

Rocheid scowled.

'I knew she was untrustworthy,' he muttered. Murray breathed a silent sigh of relief that they had been right.

'How long were you there? And why Collessie?'

Lord Rocheid sighed, abruptly and angrily.

'I was following Gordon Pillans. I wanted to see what he was going to do.'

Murray looked at Macduff, who nodded very slightly. Both of them stayed silent. Wedderburn, confused, at least had the wit to keep quiet.

'We had had a difference of opinion, on our journey,' Rocheid admitted, then went on as though he was relieved at last to tell his story. 'I left him at the inn down in the village, but I wanted to know what he would do. The quarrel – the difference of opinion – it was connected to – to his wife. I wanted to see what he would do when he joined her.'

'What did you expect him to do?' asked Murray, trying to imitate Isobel's gentle tones, in case it might draw Rocheid out. Rocheid looked puzzled.

'I thought ... I wondered if they might make some move to leave, to go somewhere else. To remove themselves ... But he never appeared. I left the next evening, after dark, and – and I found out that he was dead. So I left the place – and went to Newport. But I knew I had to come back, so I returned on Sunday evening, as you saw. Now, is that enough for you?' His tone snapped back to defiant authority.

'For now, I daresay,' said Murray, 'if Mr. Macduff is satisfied.'

'For now,' Macduff agreed.

'Well, then. Good day to you, my lord,' said Murray, and bowed.

'Thank you so much, both of you,' said Wedderburn, as they

walked back to the village. He held the jewel box tightly in both hands. 'I have no idea about all that at the end, but Debs will be thrilled. What a coincidence! And very good of Lord Rocheid to hand it over like that – I'm sure it cost him a deal of money. He says it's tat but it really isn't, you know. It's a lovely piece.'

'It is indeed,' Murray agreed. 'Perhaps we ought to get some idea from you of the other pieces that went missing at the same time. Who knows where they might turn up?'

'Such a shame he could not tell us more about the booth he bought this at,' said Wedderburn.

If it existed, thought Murray.

'I'll get the Edinburgh police on to it,' said Macduff, 'and aye, if you can tell me what else is missing I'll pass that on, and all.'

'We told the Newington police at the time,' said Wedderburn.

'Best to have it twice, sir,' said Macduff. 'What's heard only the once can go out the other ear with great ease.'

'Do you think this could help us to find the maid, too?' asked Wedderburn. 'I should like to be able to tell her father that she is safe, at least.'

'You never know, sir,' said Macduff, and Murray could hear his effort to sound optimistic. 'If she was fit to sell jewellery, she may be fine. What was the date she went on? When did all this happen?'

'It would have been the evening of the twelfth, she went. I went to the police office the next day, but of course it was Saturday and they were busy, and then it was Sunday and there was hardly anybody there, so I had to go back on Monday.'

'So she disappeared on a Friday evening?' said Murray. Just like the shop girls. It looked as if Isobel was right.

Back at Letho, he went to his library and drew out some paper, listing, from memory, the dates the shop girls had disappeared. Mary Johnston, the first, had gone on the thirtieth of March. A fortnight later, Maggie Daniels had gone on the thirteenth of April. Then there was a three-week gap, then Jean Soutar, the widow, had disappeared on the fourth of May – and just a week later the Wedderburns' maid had vanished with the jewellery. What about Susan Knox's friend? That had been before Mary Johnston … he thought Susan had said the second of March. So the gaps were irregular, but every disappearance had happened on a Friday evening. He wished he could take a look at the notebook and cashbook that Isobel and Blair had seen, in case either of them covered those dates. Would anything unusual show up? Would Pillans have made a note, or some cash payments that would follow the same pattern? Blair was resting, and Isobel was probably dressing for dinner. He could ask them later if they had noticed anything that might help.

Pillans, he thought. Could he really be abducting the pretty girls he employed? And had he then branched out – perhaps feeling that the warehouse was receiving too much attention – and taken a neighbour's maid instead? And if he was abducting girls, where were they going? Or was Sergeant Clyne right – were they murdered, and dumped in the Water of Leith, or some equally convenient place?

And had Mrs. Pillans, steadfastly grieving at Collessie, any idea of what her husband had been up to?

In fact, he even wondered if she had known about the gambling club.

He reached back into the drawer of his desk, and drew out the account book he had brought back from Edinburgh, flicking through it for inspiration. Then a thought struck him.

Mary Johnston had gone missing on the thirtieth of March. Murray turned through the book to the entries for the end of March. There was nothing on that day, but three days later, on the second of April, the first of the high stakes was paid, from J.R. to G.P.

He turned a few pages, and came to the thirteenth of April, when Maggie Daniels had disappeared, leaving her poor fiancé behind. Nothing, but three days later, on the Monday, J.R. had paid G.P. four guineas.

Excited, he referred back to his list of dates.

When was the next disappearance? Jean Soutar, on the fourth of May. He turned pages, but another payment caught his eye – three guineas on the twenty-third of April. No girl had vanished on the twentieth, not from the Oriental Warehouse. Perhaps Pillans had made a mistake? Or was Murray wrong?

It looked as if he was. There was no payment two days after Jean Soutar's disappearance.

Dejected now, he thought he had better just check the last date he had, the date that the Wedderburns' maid had gone – the eleventh of May. And there, on the fourteenth, was a payment from J.R. to G.P of five guineas. Did that, he wondered, cover the price of the jewellery, too?

Dinner was good-humoured, for Debs, in high spirits, was wearing her necklace, and giving full credit to everyone who had helped her to recover it. Murray was impatient, though, to share what he had discovered with Isobel and Blair. The opportunity did not arise until the Wedderburns decided to take an evening stroll in the garden before supper, and Murray could convene with the Blairs in the entrance hall. He fetched the account book from the library.

'See?' he said. 'Three dates match, but not the fourth – and there's a payment that matches no date.'

'No date that we have been given,' said Isobel precisely. 'If they took the Wedderburns' maid, who is to say that they did not snatch some other girl?'

'That's true,' said Murray, 'but then what about Jean Soutar? Why is there no payment for her?'

The discussion went round and about, with no positive conclusion, until supper time. Murray expressed his regret again that he had not returned to Newington before he left Edinburgh. Blair reassured him that it was good to have him back at Letho. Isobel said nothing. Was she pleased to see him back? She had not enjoyed her time as mistress of Letho, anyway. Would that be key, if he proposed marriage to her?

The Wedderburns came in for supper, and the company was relaxed, and retired early, leaving Murray to go to his own bed and carry on thinking, just as pointlessly, long into the night.

Nevertheless, he woke at six on Saturday, and could not persuade himself to fall asleep again. Forgoing a shave until he felt he could reasonably summon a servant, he washed in cold water and dressed, and headed downstairs. The day looked fine, and the choice between a slump in the library or a stroll in the garden was an easy one. He headed outside.

The air was mild, indeed, but fresh enough this early to

brighten his mood a little. After all, it was a new day – another day towards the possibility of hearing from Susan Knox (though why he felt such faith in her he was not sure) and another day with no engagements in particular – except for the probable departure of the Wedderburns – which might allow him to catch up on one or two things. He wanted to go and talk to the musician Rieder in the servants' quarters and find out why he would not leave. He wanted to see if the engineers had come to a final decision. And he ought, though he was not sure he wanted, to find some way of dealing with Daniel and his wretched son Janny. Another day of wondering how and when he could propose marriage to Isobel. None of these tasks could be done properly, he realised, without a shave and some breakfast. But it was so pleasant, crunching slowly along the pale gravel paths between dew-damp leaves and nodding flowers, the swallows already flying high above, goldfinches and yellowhammers warming up for the day's song. Another quarter of an hour of fresh air, and then he would go in and prepare for the day.

'Miss Blair says that the musician Rieder is refusing to leave the house, Robbins,' said Murray, in between Robbins' razor sweeps. 'Is he causing a problem?'

'Not really, sir: he does his best not to get in the way, but Mrs. Mack does not like knowing there is someone in the kitchen before her in the mornings, who is not under her command.'

'And Iffy is smitten?'

'That's true. But I doubt Rieder takes much notice of that. He's too worried about himself.'

'May I go and interview him there?'

Robbins considered.

'I'll try and get him into my pantry. It's not that far, and it would be more private for you.'

Murray chose to wait in the pantry, a small room as neat and orderly as any human could make it. The closest there was to a personal touch was a small wooden elephant, perched on a shelf by some account books. Murray smiled. Robbins had encountered elephants in India, and had never been quite the same again.

He had been there some ten minutes when there was a light step in the stone corridor outside, a tap on the door, and an anxious face appearing around it. It was Rieder.

'Come in, then,' said Murray, in German. 'You may sit, if you wish. Would you care for a glass of wine?' He thought it might help the man to relax and communicate, but Rieder shook his head sharply.

'I wish to be alert, sir,' he said.

'In case of alarms?'

'Indeed, sir.' Rieder had already scanned the room for any sign of threat.

'I know you had a disturbing experience that night at Collessie,' Murray began, and saw Rieder shudder. 'A most unpleasant thing to happen.'

'Unnatural,' muttered Rieder darkly.

'But the matter is resolved, you know: is there something else that is causing you distress?'

'There are many things, in this strange place,' said Rieder.

'Can you tell me, perhaps, what the worst are? It is possible that we might be able to help you to sort out some other threats, that may not be quite so bad as they seem.'

'How can you resolve things that are not of this world?' demanded Rieder.

'We can consult the minister at the church,' Murray suggested. 'But what are these things? I have no more wish to have threats around my home than you do.'

'The night that man – that poor man whose body was taken from place to place like – like stolen goods – the night that he was killed. He was killed near here, was he not? The servants say he was found in some kind of cave?'

'An icehouse, yes.'

'With a gate? I saw a place with a gate.'

'When you fled here after Collessie?'

'No, no,' said Rieder, impatient. 'No, I was here the night that man was killed.'

Chapter Forty-Five

At least that confirmed Macduff's suspicions. Murray wanted to ask him what he was doing there, but thought the man might take it badly. And anyway, he had other questions.

'What did you see?'

Rieder turned pale.

'There was light, at the windows of the servants' hall – though I knew not what it was then.'

'So you could see, perhaps a little?'

'Enough,' said Rieder, shivering. 'I could see enough.' He drew a deep breath. 'I have lived for several years in your country. I know that many of your old houses, your castles, are haunted. You have a Green Lady there, a Grey Lady here, a weeping child, a headless man, a distant drumming boy … I know of these. I thought them stories to frighten the children. But you, sir, you have a haunted house, too. That night, I saw – I saw enough to prove the stories to be true.'

'What did you see, then?'

'I saw your Grey Lady, and I saw a phantom, white as mist, open the gate of that ice cave, and vanish inside.'

'A phantom in the icehouse? That is serious indeed,' said Murray. 'Do you know what time this was?'

'It was midnight, of course,' said the German. 'The witching hour they call it, do they not? The time when all things uncanny walk the paths of this strange land.'

'Can you tell me more about the phantom?' Murray asked. 'White as mist, you say?'

'It opened the gate, and went inside. I took my chance, and fled.'

'So you did not see it come out again?'

Rieder hesitated.

'Well,' he said, 'I found it difficult to move. And after a few moments it came back, and closed the gate behind it. It had found that which it sought,' he added.

'That which it sought? What do you mean?'

'It had found the dead man, of course, and taken his soul.'

'How do you work that out?' Murray asked, after a brief struggle to work out which legends Rieder was mixing here.

'The phantom was carrying it. A small, shining thing. His soul.'

Murray considered this extraordinary phenomenon, then asked,

'Did you hear anything?'

'Phantoms make no sound, do they? And anyway, there was a breeze.'

'And it was definitely a phantom? You were close enough to see that – I don't know – that it was not a man?'

'No! It was the size of a child. And what child would be abroad at midnight, walking into ice caves?'

'It's not like the Irish fellows were asleep anyway,' said Janny, entirely undaunted at being summoned for interview by the laird. Murray had decided to move his enquiry to the library, hoping to overawe the boy, particularly as Robbins was also present. The effect was negligible. 'They were up playing cards. We could see through the crack in the shutters.'

'Say "sir", Janny,' muttered his father ineffectually. Both Janny and Murray glanced at him, and looked away. Daniel was always a bit disappointing.

'Hardly the point, Gianni,' said Murray. The boy regarded him uncertainly.

'Only my ma says that properly,' he commented, though Murray was not sure if he was being praised, or warned not to step over a line. The child was – well, precocious was probably the kindest word.

'You dressed in sheets,' Murray went on, 'with the purpose

of frightening people who had done you no harm, innocently going about their business.'

'They wouldna let me see what they were working on,' said Janny reasonably.

'And then there's the matter of the pocketbook and the watch.'

'What's that, sir?' Janny was suddenly respectful, his eyes wide in alarm.

'The pocketbook and the watch you took from the dead body.'

'Janny!' yelped Daniel.

'Where have you put them?'

'He has a hidey-place, sir,' said Daniel, eager to help. 'I can look there.'

Janny's face fell. Perhaps for once his father was one step ahead of him.

'Maybe yon fellow Dandy put them in there to make me look bad,' he said, more in hope than in expectation.

'Yon fellow Dandy is not a small lad. You were seen,' said Murray.

'Oh,' said the boy, sadly, 'that's a pity.'

'What were you intending to do with the pocketbook and the watch?'

'Sell them,' said Janny promptly.

'And what would you use the money for?'

'Going to Edinburgh.'

'Why Edinburgh?'

'Less boring than here. Has to be. Everyone knows me here.'

Yes, that would not help him in his trouble-making – far too easily identified. He was clever, undoubtedly. Murray thought it must be from his Neapolitan mother's side. Daniel had never been the least bit bright.

'What do you want to do with your life, Gianni?'

'Well, I don't want to be a servant,' said the boy at once.

'There isn't a respectable household that would employ you,' Murray agreed. For a moment Janny looked taken aback. 'So what do you want?'

'I think I'd like to be a soldier. Or to join the navy.'

Murray looked across at Daniel, who, as usual, was much at

a loss.

'What do you think, Daniel?'

'He's gey young, sir,' said Daniel, wretchedly.

'In body, perhaps,' said Murray. He sighed. He would have paid for Janny's commission on the spot if anyone would have taken him. 'I think you're too young yet to enlist, and too short for the army, anyway. And these days, now that the war is over, I think you'll find they might prefer boys of good character, when they can pick and choose. No one wants to employ a thief.'

'I'm not a thief!'

'You took the pocketbook and the watch, intending to sell them.'

'From a dead man! The pocketbook wasna even in his pocket, it was on the ground!'

'Even the property of a dead man belongs to someone, Gianni,' said Murray. 'And I can tell you that the hangman will not concern himself with your age, or your height – not except for his own calculations.'

'What?' Janny gasped. Daniel had turned white. About time, thought Murray: the man had never properly faced the consequences of his own foolish behaviour over the years.

'Did you undo the lock on the gate yourself?' Murray asked after a moment. Janny blinked at the turn of the conversation – the image of the gallows seemed to have made some impact at last.

'Aye, sir, it was useless.'

'Without breaking it?'

'Aye.'

'Are you interested in locks, and mechanical things?'

'Aye, sir, well enough. I like fine to see how they work.'

'Could you build a lock, do you think?'

Janny considered.

'I'd like to learn how to. I canna shape the metal yet.'

Murray pondered. Would it work? Would it keep him occupied enough to distract him from mischief – or worse?

'Do you know Ninian Jack?'

'Aye, I know him to see. He makes all that kind of thing. They say he's gey clever, do they not?'

'He is. I wonder … if he were willing to accept an apprentice – and bear in mind you have not generally made yourself popular about Letho – would it interest you, at all? Bear in mind, too, that he is old, and stern, and grumpy, and will make you work hard. And that an apprenticeship is a binding agreement. But it would not mean that you could not join the army later, if you still wished.'

Janny did not take long to consider it – in fact, when Murray had said 'work hard' his face had even brightened.

'Aye, sir, I think I might!'

'But only if you behave yourself – and don't lead others into mischief, either.'

A problem postponed, he thought to himself, as he led Daniel, Robbins, and Janny out of the library on an expedition to retrieve the stolen goods. Stolen goods – that was what Rieder had called Gordon Pillans' body – *diebesgut*. Rieder had not wondered that his phantom had needed to open the gate, rather than walking straight through, though the effect on the padlock had been just as magical.

He hoped he had not raised the lad's hopes: Ninian Jack had never taken an apprentice, and Murray wondered if he could really be persuaded to now. He would have to think how to approach the old man – and pray that if he did take Janny on, he would live long enough to see the apprenticeship through, and not regret it.

Daniel and his wife had a cottage, overflowing with children and delicious smells, along the road from the servants' wing, the road that filled with mud from the spring behind the icehouse. Artemesia, Daniel's wife, curtseyed when she saw their visitors, and glanced at Janny in alarm – she was under no illusion as to her eldest child's behaviour.

'Gianni! What you done now?'

'We're just here to look for something, Mrs. Hossack,' Murray explained. 'Where is this hidey-hole, Daniel?'

'It's round the back, outside,' said Daniel. Janny looked very cross, arms folded in disgust.

At the back of the house, under a window, there was a protruding stone, and beneath it a hollow had been formed in the mortar between two other stones. It was not huge but it was eminently accessible to someone of Janny's stature. Murray knew his long hands would not fit in, and waved at Daniel to retrieve all that was to be retrieved. Several hens pecked uncuriously at his feet as he inserted his comparatively small hand into the hole. The look on his face suggested he was not over-keen on spiders.

The first thing he drew out was dusty from the sandstone and threaded with spiders' webs. Daniel handled it with care. It was a small bag of money, mostly farthings and halfpennies, which was unlikely to have been carried by Mr. Pillans – Janny had probably collected it over a period of time. Then there was a brown leather pocketbook, with 'G.P.' stamped on it. Murray flicked it open to find that it contained some coins, amounting to a decent sum for a journey, a key, probably to the box that Ninian Jack had opened, and a small card with Pillans' name and address on it, in case the pocketbook was lost. The watch was next, silver and unassuming.

'He had probably had this for a while,' he remarked to Robbins, 'and not thought to replace it when he grew wealthier. Perhaps it had some sentimental value.'

'Still going, sir,' said Robbins, opening it when Murray handed it to him. 'It's not far off the like of my own one.'

'Is there anything else in there?' Murray asked. Daniel poked around a little, and shook his head, but at that moment Murray caught a look of satisfaction on Janny's face. 'Just give it one more sweep, Daniel,' he said. 'Make sure you've searched thoroughly.'

Daniel grunted – the position of the stone meant that he had to bend down to reach behind it, and that, for a man so fond of his wife's excellent cooking, was not a comfortable position. Artemesia, who had followed them to the back of the cottage, watched anxiously. Daniel scowled, then frowned in surprise. He could clearly touch something, but it was just out of reach.

'*Gancio a bottone!*' cried Artemesia, with a click of her fingers, and trotted off. In a moment she was back, with a long-handled, white metal buttonhook.

'Of course!' said Murray, and Artemesia dropped him a pleased curtsey. Daniel manoeuvred the hook into the hole, while Janny looked on in disgust. In a moment, there was a flash and a tinkle, and Daniel drew out, with care, something that shone in the sunlight. A woman's bracelet, gold, with stones of red and white.

'Where did you find this, Gianni?' Murray asked.

'Same place,' Janny sighed. 'It was in the fellow's pocket.'

'A present for Mrs. Pillans?' Robbins speculated.

'Was it in a box?' Murray asked.

'No, it wasna,' said Janny definitely. 'It was just there. Is it worth anything?'

'Hm,' said Murray, 'as to that, we'd better ask the owner.'

'Mrs. Pillans?' asked Robbins.

'Maybe not,' said Murray. 'Maybe not. I've a feeling, that if we're quick, we might find that the owner of this bracelet is rather nearer than Collessie.'

Chapter Forty-Six

Murray and Robbins between them gathered the pocketbook, watch and bracelet together. Robbins turned to Daniel.

'Settle things here, then I expect to see you back for duty.'

Daniel gave a scrappy bow. Robbins looked him up and down, as if wondering if there was any hope, and turned to follow Murray away from the cottage.

'I wonder if Mrs. Pillans has plans to leave Collessie?' said Murray. 'Have you heard anything?'

'Nothing yet, sir. But you know the Collessie servants don't speak much to anybody outside Collessie.'

'I'd better see that the watch and pocketbook are returned soon. As for the bracelet …'

'Aye, sir, that requires even more haste. Though I doubt they'll leave without saying goodbye.'

Indeed, Debs Wedderburn was just coming down the stairs with Isobel when Murray and Robbins arrived in the entrance hall. Mr. Wedderburn was seated at the hearth, gossiping with Blair. They all looked around in surprise at Murray's arrival. He wiped his muddy boots on the mat.

'I'm glad to catch you, Mrs. Wedderburn,' he said.

'We'd never have sneaked off!' said Debs with a smile. 'Miss Blair and I were just checking to see we'd left nothing behind.'

'Just as well,' said her husband. 'That would be the next in our chain of misfortunes. My watch, or spectacles, or your keys.'

'Did you by any chance lose a watch when your maid absconded?' Murray asked.

'A watch?' Mr. Wedderburn looked puzzled. 'No, no watches.'

'Do you mind, Mrs. Wedderburn, giving me some idea of what else went missing?'

'You've found something, haven't you?' said Debs at once, her face lighting up. 'What have you found?'

'I need to be sure,' said Murray. 'If I am to go to Macduff, or some man of law, I need to be sure that I did not lead you into a false description.'

'That's you told, Debs,' said her husband. 'No trying to trick Murray into handing over something that isn't yours, eh?'

Everyone laughed, but shortly, impatient to see what Murray was talking about.

'Go on, then, Mrs. Wedderburn,' said Blair, unable to contain himself. 'Tell us all!'

'If you want to,' Isobel added.

'Well,' said Debs, 'what we lost might have been personal, but it was not private, if you see the distinction. Of course I'll tell, Mr. Blair – if it means that Mr. Murray might be able to return another piece of my jewellery, that would be wonderful!'

'There wasn't so much, was there, my dear?' said Mr. Wedderburn.

'Not really. I had the impression she just grabbed what she could manage, and shoved it into some kind of small bag. The necklace – oh, my lovely necklace! – that would have been in its old box, but some of the pieces were loose. I had some things just mixed together in the one chest, for convenience when travelling, you know? She must just have taken a handful or two.'

'And what do you know you are missing, then?' Murray pursued. The others seemed to be holding their breaths.

'There was a ring with a cabochon turquoise in it, and another with three garnets. They were both gone.' She glanced hopefully at Murray, but he did not respond. 'A pair of buckles, silver, engraved. Pretty, more than valuable.' Again, no response from Murray. 'Ah, well: alas for my evening slippers. Let me think: we made a list for the police office, but they might never have looked at it.'

'Brooches? Bracelets?' Isobel suggested.

'Well, yes,' said Debs. 'There were three little brooches – two were a pair, you know, with little rubies – so small they were almost invisible! But I had been given them as a child, and I like to wear them with a morning dress, for they are not too elaborate. The third had garnets again, and had been my grandfather's. The boys – my brothers – thought it too feminine, these days.' She looked at Murray. 'Oh, for pity's sake, Mr. Murray, have mercy on me! Have you found anything I have mentioned?'

Murray shook his head very slightly, and then Mr. Wedderburn said, gently,

'The bracelet, my dear.'

'Oh, my dear, the bracelet,' she reflected him, her face pale. 'Oh, my dear.' She gathered herself together. 'When we married, Richard gave me a pair of bracelets. I could not believe she could have taken them. Well, one of them.' They each reached out a hand, catching the other. 'She knew how much they meant to me, the little minx,' said Debs. 'She knew.'

'What were they like?' asked Isobel, her voice soft, coaxing. Murray felt a shiver run pleasurably up his spine.

'They were gold – well, wouldn't it be quicker if I showed you? For however much in haste she was, in the end she took only the one.'

Her dressing case was beside her – the last thing to be packed into the carriage, to be set at her feet rather than on the back with the trunks. She took a key from her reticule and unlocked it. Murray's hand slipped into his pocket, touching the bracelet Daniel had hooked from the hiding place in the cottage wall. Would Debs' bracelet be a match?

'Rubies and diamonds,' said Debs, drawing out a thread of gold from the dressing case. She laid it across her hand, showing them all. Murray pulled the other bracelet from his pocket.

'Rubies and diamonds,' he echoed. 'I think we have a pair.'

'Oh!' said Debs, and tears coursed down her pretty cheeks. Mr. Wedderburn turned to her and held her, and managed even to find an efficient handkerchief for her. The others stared down at the pair of bracelets, as if some conclusion could be drawn from them. There had to be an answer there.

Even if a question had to be asked first.

'Where did this come from?' asked Isobel.

'From a stash of various items hidden by Gianni Hossack,' said Murray. 'Not all of them came from his investigations in the pockets of the late Mr. Pillans –'

'He's a delightful child,' said Isobel, with a shiver.

'Quite. To be fair, he was working in the dark: he went into the icehouse to see what devilment he could cause in there, tripped over the corpse and felt about to empty the pockets. He would not have seen Pillans' injuries. But there was a pocketbook and a watch – Robbins?' Robbins, at the ready, laid them on the table for all to see. 'Thank you, Robbins. Perhaps you could send in some tea?' Robbins bowed and left. 'Both of these seem to be clearly associated with Gordon Pillans – his name is in the pocketbook, which was on the ground, incidentally, and his initials are on the watch case. And the boy claims that this bracelet came from the same place.'

'From Mr. Pillans' pocket?' asked Debs Wedderburn, easing away from her husband's embrace. 'But … what was he doing with it? It was Lady Rocheid – Lord Rocheid – who had the necklace.'

'Well, exactly,' said Murray.

'Oh!' said Blair. 'Another link between them!'

'I suggest we keep this quiet for now,' said Murray. 'If Lord Rocheid gets wind of it, he'll no doubt change his story and claim that his passenger, whom he had never met before, managed to sneak the necklace into Lord Rocheid's luggage.'

Blair's eyebrows rose, wrinkling his high forehead, and he nodded enthusiastically.

'He might well, indeed. But do you think that perhaps it was the other way around? That Lord Rocheid – who does not indeed seem to be a very pleasant character, either – that Lord Rocheid might have slipped the bracelet into Mr. Pillans' luggage?'

'Why would he do that if he didn't know him?' asked Mr. Wedderburn, confused.

'To rid himself of anything incriminating?' Debs suggested.

'That doesn't work,' said Isobel, 'if he was quite prepared for his wife to wear the necklace in public.'

'Of course,' Debs acknowledged. Murray, particularly conscious of Isobel, thought he detected a slight change between the two women. He thought that Debs had always thought herself somewhat superior to Isobel.

'So we have four possibilities,' said Blair, excitedly enumerating them on his fingers. 'The first is that for some reason Lord Rocheid passed the bracelet to Mr. Pillans. The second is that Mr. Pillans passed the necklace to Lord Rocheid. The third is that, for whatever reason, they each had a piece of jewellery in their own right, if that's the right way to say it.'

'It shouldn't be,' said Debs, 'when it's my jewellery. But I know what you mean, Mr. Blair.' She took a seat on the sopha, drawing her husband down to sit beside her. It looked as if they were not so eager to leave as before – the puzzle was intriguing them both. Particularly if the solution might lead to Debs recovering all her jewellery.

'And the fourth possibility?' Mr. Wedderburn reminded him.

'Is that someone else passed the pieces on to each of these men,' said Blair happily.

'Of course.'

'The first two and the last still indicate a connexion between the men,' said Isobel after a moment. 'The third does not prove anything. For example, each of them could have bought a piece of jewellery at the same stall in the Luckenbooths on the Lawnmarket. They were both in Edinburgh after your jewellery was stolen, Mrs. Wedderburn.'

'And presumably Mr. Pillans was in Newington when my jewellery was stolen,' said Debs sharply. 'Could he have been a thief? Persuading my maid to help him? But then where is she?'

'Where are all the missing girls?' asked Isobel.

'And why did Lord Rocheid make a payment to Gordon Pillans after almost every disappearance?' added her father.

'If indeed Lord Rocheid is the same person as the J.R. in the account book,' said Murray. Pillans is dead,' he went on. 'There is a good chance that Lord Rocheid was here in Letho, or close by, when that happened. We cannot prove a connexion between Rocheid and Pillans, though it's seeming more and more likely.'

'I think you are being too cautious, Mr. Murray,' said Debs Wedderburn. 'Both men had a piece of my stolen jewellery. Lord Rocheid admits he brought Mr. Pillans to Letho. J.R. are common initials, indeed, but they still match. I think we could assume a connexion. And that takes us even further, does it not?'

'You mean,' said Isobel, 'to at least a strong suspicion that Lord Rocheid, having brought Mr. Pillans here, having presumably known him in Edinburgh, having perhaps even connived at the stealing of jewellery by your maid, should then bring him to the unfinished icehouse, and murder him?'

'A falling out amongst thieves?' Mr. Wedderburn suggested, after a moment.

'Lord Rocheid said they had had a difference of opinion. Something to do with Mrs. Pillans,' Murray reminded him. 'He could, I suppose, have come here and killed him, then hidden at Collessie.'

'It's possible,' Debs agreed. 'But I still want to know what has happened to the girls.'

'I doubt they're at Collessie,' said Murray, 'and the Newington house was too small. Mr. George would know if Lord Rocheid had taken them to Dures.'

'What about Lord Rocheid's own house?'

'Lady Rocheid was staying alone with the staff at the Edinburgh house. Surely he could not have hidden them there,' said Murray.

'No, his estate,' said Isobel. 'That would make sense. And that's not far from Edinburgh, is it?'

'No,' said Blair, eagerly, 'it's not far at all! Do you think he could, Charles? Could he have the girls there?'

'Lady Rocheid said her husband never took her there,' said Murray, slowly. 'If it really is Rocheid conspiring with Pillans to abduct the girls, then that is indeed the obvious place to hide them.'

Into the silence that followed, the sound came of hooves on the gravel outside, and a man's voice calling to the stable lad to take his horse. Footsteps approached. Robbins turned to answer the door, no doubt taking the caller by surprise.

'Mr. George, sir,' he announced, opening the door wide. Mr. George hurried in, glanced around, and approached Murray.

'Good day to you, sir,' he said, with a swift bow. 'I am sorry to disturb you, but I wonder – have you seen Lord Rocheid today?'

'Today? No, I don't believe so.' Murray looked about the company. 'Has anyone seen him today?' He watched everyone shake their head. 'Why? Has he returned to Edinburgh, do you think? Or gone – to Newport?'

Mr. George made a face.

'No, his horse is still in my stable. We don't know where he is. He has vanished entirely.'

Chapter Forty-Seven

'You'll understand,' said Mr. George, 'that for myself I should not care if he vanished for good, but I do not want a repeat of my sister's behaviour the last time she went looking for him. I hope I speak amongst friends here – forgive me, but the man has tried my patience long enough. I have better things to be doing than pursuing him about the parish.'

'Could he have taken the mail coach to somewhere?' asked Debs Wedderburn.

'It has not passed in the time he has been missing,' said Mr. George. 'I have told the innkeeper to watch for him and let me know – not to stop him, of course.'

'Could he have gone with someone else?'

'No one saw him leave. I have asked all the servants – they are good people. I doubt he could bribe any one of them to keep silent for his benefit against me, or indeed against my sister. And anyway,' he took a deep breath, as though he were struggling to stay calm, 'apparently he has taken his gloves and his hat, but no cloak or coat, and only his second-best boots. It does not look as if he intended to go far, certainly not late in the evening.'

'Come, sit with us if you can and tell us more,' said Murray. It was very strange that Lord Rocheid's disappearance should be announced, just when they were speculating on Lord Rocheid's guilt.

'I shall,' said Mr. George with a sigh, 'for I am chasing my tail here. I have no idea where to go, only that I should go. Would he darken the doors of Collessie again? He did not seem impressed with it at the funeral yesterday. Is he on his knees in the church? That would take me very much aback. Is he visiting Dr. Feilden? All night? An abuse of the good physician's hospitality, surely. Has he had some kind of accident somewhere? All these questions, Murray, and no answers. Is there tea in that urn?'

'That, at least, we can answer, Mr. George,' said Isobel, and poured him a cup. He took it gratefully.

'When was he last seen, and by whom?' asked Murray, fixing on more easy answers.

'He was with us at supper time,' said Mr. George, making a face. 'There was a good deal of flirting going on between them – I left, pleading business to attend to in my bookroom. I assumed they had retired for the night, but I was just enjoying a last brandy before bed when my sister appeared, asking if I had seen him. Apparently she had retired, but he had not, saying he would see her in a little while. She thought that he was similarly engaged, taking a last refreshment before bed, but she waited and he did not appear. You can imagine her mood.'

Now that Mr. George had decided to speak of his brother-in-law openly, it seemed he did not much care what he revealed.

'Let me summon Robbins,' said Murray, 'and ask him to enquire amongst the servants. My factor, too, might know or have seen something.'

The indoor servants were quickly interrogated. Mr. Thalland, called to pop into the busy entrance hall, admitted that it would take a good deal longer to enquire amongst the outdoor staff, who were substantially more numerous and much more widely dispersed. Nevertheless the matter was put in train, and as Mr. Thalland bowed and made his exit, Murray looked to Mr. George.

'How else can we help you?' he asked. 'Would you like me to enquire at the manse?' Mr. George and the minister generally avoided speaking to each other. Mr. George gave a tight smile.

'No, I am sure that if he were in the village, we should have heard by now. I thought to head north a little, see if there was any trace of him thinking of Newport, however unprepared for a journey he might have seemed. I wondered if perhaps you might go to Collessie? I still feel somewhat embarrassed speaking with Mrs. Pillans after what my sister did.'

'By all means,' said Murray. 'I can go now and be back by

dinner, I believe.'

'Thank you – I should be much obliged. I had not thought of my brother-in-law as much of a pedestrian: I'm sure we shall not find him too far from home. In fact, perhaps I shall go home first and take a look at his things, in case there is some clue there.'

Mr. George finished his tea, and was about to take his leave.

'Husband,' said Debs Wedderburn, 'do you wish to help in this search? Should we postpone our departure? I confess I am anxious to know how this ends.'

'And you might recover more jewellery,' added Mr. Wedderburn, practically. 'It seems that it has followed us here, somehow. Murray, do you mind if we stay longer?'

'Not at all,' said Murray. 'I'll tell Robbins to tell Mrs. Gilmour.'

'I can tell Mrs. Gilmour, if you like, Charles,' said Isobel, 'and let you get off to Collessie. Remember to take these with you, though!'

She pointed to the pocketbook and watch, then stopped.

'May I just check? I'm sure you've already looked inside, but … may I reassure myself?'

'It's just money,' said Murray, 'but by all means look.'

Isobel opened the pocket book, and with her slim, clever fingers worked down into each section, a look of resignation on her face.

'No, of course there's nothing – oh, wait!'

One flap of the fine brown leather concealed a very discreet pocket within the wallet. Inside it was a small piece of rough paper. Isobel drew it out, and unfolded it.

'"I know about Sarah O'Rourke",' she read aloud. 'That's not a name I'm familiar with. Does anyone else know anyone of that name?'

There were shrugs.

'An Irish name, by the sound of it,' said Debs.

'What else does it say?' asked Murray.

'I think we may have the answer to one of our many questions,' said Isobel. 'Listen: "If you wish to discover what I know, come to Letho House at midnight." Then there are directions to the icehouse.'

'The note that the innkeeper mentioned!' Blair realised at

once.

'I suppose it's too much to ask that it might be signed,' said Mr. George, as Murray went to lean over Isobel's shoulder.

'Of course,' said Murray. 'But it's not a bad hand, is it? The paper is cheap, but the writer is educated.'

'A wonder the killer did not remove the note, though,' said Mr. George.

'No, no,' said Blair at once, 'it would have been dark. He might not have been able to find it. Did either of them have a light? Was a lantern found?'

'No,' said Murray, 'and surely at least one of them must have needed one, unless Mr. Pillans came here before dark and hid himself somewhere.'

'That might be the case,' said Isobel, 'and might also explain why he did not go straight to Collessie. It must have been latish when he arrived, and he thought he needed to deal with this first, rather than go to his wife and then explain why he had to go out again.'

'May I see the note?' asked Mr. George suddenly. Isobel took it over to him. He examined it closely. 'Ah, it is not my missing brother-in-law's hand. Of course, he may have asked someone to write it for him – it does have the look of a woman's hand. Or is that my imagination?'

He handed the note back, and Isobel squinted at it, then passed it to Murray who showed it to Blair. The Wedderburns eagerly awaited their turn.

'Maybe,' said Murray.

'Certainly,' said Debs, when she had sight of it. 'That's a woman's hand.'

'But not my sister's!' Mr. George clarified hastily. 'Of that I can be sure.'

'But why, again, would Lord Rocheid lure Gordon Pillans to my icehouse to kill him?' asked Murray. 'He had enjoyed his company all the way at least from Queensferry. He could have killed him anywhere. And if some quarrel arose that meant he had no motive to kill him until they reached Letho, it is still very odd to slip him a faked note like this. Via the innkeeper, who says he never met him.'

'Dammit, you're probably right,' sighed Mr. George. 'My

apologies, ladies. And I had better go on looking for him.'

'I'll go with you to the village first,' said Murray, 'and hand these to Macduff. I think he should see them before they go back to Mrs. Pillans.'

'We had better go and unpack,' said Debs.

'And I shall go and have a word with Mrs. Gilmour,' said Isobel, smiling at her.

'Come back, everyone, and tell me what is happening!' said Blair, also smiling. Murray's heart hurt.

'Why don't we take the gig, and you can come too?' he said, and Blair's smile transformed at once into something much more genuine. 'I'll go and send for it.'

Isobel, feeling suddenly very self-conscious, headed for the servants' quarters and Mrs. Gilmour's parlour. Should she have volunteered to do this? Was she being forward? She hoped that Murray had not thought, from her list of problems when he returned from Edinburgh, that she would not be capable of directing a household like Letho. Not that she might ever have the opportunity in her own right.

'Mrs. Gilmour?' she called, knocking at the door. Mrs. Gilmour opened the door at once, and curtseyed.

'How may I help you, Miss Blair?'

'Mr. Murray has asked me to let you know that the Wedderburns are staying a little longer. I hope that does not cause much inconvenience.'

'Indeed not, miss. I believe the beds have already been changed, so I shall make any other arrangements necessary.'

'Thank you. Is all else well?'

'I think so, miss.'

'Have you been much about the parish at all? Have you had the chance to make any acquaintances?'

Mrs. Gilmour smiled.

'Not yet, miss. There has been more than enough to do here!'

'Well, when you do, if we can help let me know. There is a housekeeper at Dures, the home of Mr. Francis George, but I'm afraid I cannot speak for the other big house, Collessie.'

'Collessie, yes, well, it was always badly run, miss.'

'Oh, you've heard that, have you?' Isobel laughed, though

perhaps she should not encourage a new servant to be quite so critical of the neighbours. Mrs. Gilmour seemed to think the same.

'I beg your pardon, miss: I spoke out of turn, repeated gossip I had heard.'

'Well, in this case … Anyway, no doubt you will see some of the neighbours at church tomorrow. Mr. Robbins will have told you of our usual arrangements.'

Mrs. Gilmour flushed.

'I'm sorry, miss, I have made my excuses to Mr. Robbins for church tomorrow. Women's troubles, miss.'

'Oh, of course. Don't let me keep you standing about, then, Mrs. Gilmour. No doubt you have plenty to do!'

Mrs. Gilmour curtseyed again as Isobel left the small, neat room. It was only as she returned along the stone corridor to the now empty entrance hall that it struck her: Mrs. Gilmour had seemed very certain of her gossip. How had she heard about Collessie?

Chapter Forty-Eight

The village was busy, with people finishing off work or cleaning or tidying in preparation for the Sabbath next day. The goats that grazed on the green had a harassed look as people cross back and forth around them, including a boy driving a pig. Dr. Feilden was just arriving at his own house in his gig. Mrs. Helliwell was coming out of a cottage with a covered basket, evidently taking food to the less able of Letho. Ninian Jack was striding purposefully up towards the church, no doubt to see to some technicality before the service in the morning – the central stove, or the door latch, perhaps. Blair was delighted at the opportunity to view all this activity, and Murray felt guilty that he had not taken his old friend out more often. The Blairs' visit had so far been eventful, but not particularly pleasurable, for Blair himself, at least.

'I shall head on north,' said Mr. George, riding beside them, 'though perhaps I should have another word with the innkeeper, first, since we're here.'

They had stopped beside the inn, which sat at the foot of the triangular green.

'And anyway,' said Blair, taking his attention away from the longer view and looking closer to hand, 'there is Mr. Macduff himself!' He jiggled, as if he would have sprung from the gig, and then remembered he could not. Murray hoped he would be able to help if Blair needed anything: it was rare indeed that Blair went out these days without Smith loyally by his side.

But there indeed was Macduff, talking to a woman in a grey gown. In a moment, Murray recognised her: it was Mrs. Warner, his erstwhile stand-in housekeeper, the one who had so urgently wanted to leave the house. He bore her no grudge, and was sorry that she had had to be detained in the village until Macduff would let her go. Isobel had said something about her considering a post at Collessie, which showed either determination or desperation.

Murray guided the gig as close as he could to where Macduff and Mrs. Warner were standing, without inconveniencing them, and jumped down to join them.

'… been at Collessie?' Macduff was asking.

'Since yesterday evening,' Mrs. Warner was explaining. 'If I must, I can remain a while longer, but it is not an ideal situation. For one thing, the mistress herself is in two minds about staying. For another – well, such an establishment!'

'Oh, good day, Mr. Murray,' said Macduff, noticing Murray. Mrs. Warner turned in alarm.

'Oh! Mr. Murray! I beg your pardon!'

'Not at all, Mrs. Warner – I had no wish to interrupt, but I need to talk with Mr. Macduff when you're finished.'

'Mrs. Warner was just telling me she has taken a position at Collessie, sir,' said Macduff, expressionless.

'I hope you will be very happy there, Mrs. Warner,' said Murray, equally bland.

'I'm sure I shall, sir,' said Mrs. Warner, 'for a while, at least. And now I must complete my errands, if you will excuse me, sir.' She curtseyed and departed, marching up one side of the green and mixing in swiftly with the comings and goings there. Murray drew Macduff over to the gig, so that Blair could be part of their conversation.

'See what we have found!' said Blair, who had been holding the pocketbook and watch, wrapped in a cloth. He revealed them like a magician. Macduff made a gratifying noise.

'Is those Mr. Pillans', then?'

'His name is in the pocketbook, and his initials are on the watch,' Murray assured him. 'And inside the pocketbook, we found this.' He removed the note with as much delicacy as he could, and spread it out on Blair's lap for Macduff to study.

'Well, now, there's a thing,' said Macduff, after a moment. 'Who's Sarah O'Rourke?'

'No idea,' Murray admitted.

'We think she might be Irish,' said Blair.

'Like your two engineers?'

Blair and Murray looked at each other.

'That had not even occurred to me,' said Murray. 'But there are many Irish people in Scotland, I should say.'

'Not so many in Letho, though, sir,' said Macduff. 'And, well, they'd have been awful handy there if they'd wanted to kill him, and be home for their supper.'

'An educated hand …' said Blair, staring down at the note.

'Mind,' said Macduff, 'I'd have said that was a woman's hand, myself, but it would be worth checking, do you not think, sir?'

'I do indeed,' said Murray, feeling stupid again.

'Well,' said Macduff, 'I suppose we should take these back to Mrs. Pillans – would you like me to do that, sir?'

It was one thing feeling stupid, but it was quite another sensing that Macduff agreed with him.

'I think we should like to accompany you, Macduff,' he said. 'Perhaps Mrs. Pillans knows who this person is. Then, if there is a possibility that she is in some way connected with my engineers, let us go at once and speak with them.'

'Aye, sir. That would be very helpful.'

Was he being sarcastic? It was difficult to tell with Macduff. Murray, annoyed with himself, was glad that Isobel had not been there to see him making a fool of himself.

'I'm afraid there's not much room in the gig. Do you have your mule nearby?'

'It'll be ready in no time at all, sir,' said Macduff. 'I dinna want to keep you back – just a wee minute.'

'I feel like a fool,' Murray said to Blair when Macduff was out of the way. 'Irish engineers just nearby – what if that's the answer? What if they did it?'

'Then I should be very disappointed,' said Blair sadly. 'They seem such competent engineers – and Mr. Sweeney produces such wonderful drawings. Perhaps, if they were to go to trial, you might ask the judge if they could finish the work first?'

It was not really what Murray had wanted to hear. He sighed, and watched the people on and around the green while they waited for Macduff. He wondered what errand Mrs. Warner was on, and whether or not they would overtake her on the way back to Collessie.

But they did not, and Murray assumed she had taken the shortcut from the village across his own land and through the woods, the way that Mr. Rieder must have done when he fled the body snatchers. Poor Mr. Rieder: he had had an unfortunate time in Letho. But then so had Mrs. Pillans and her mother: maybe the village was not the refuge he had hoped it would be this summer. No: he could not allow himself to think of his home this way: he had to present it to Isobel as her future home, as his home which he would invite her to share. But would she want to, after all of this? His servants had always been a little wayward, collectively – but she should know that. Would she be prepared to take them on? To take him on?

They were at Collessie before he had realised it, and by the look on Blair's face his silence since they had left the village had been noted. Murray steered the horse to the main door, and looked about for a stable lad, but none was in sight. He caught Macduff's eye and called across to him.

'Shall we tether the beasts to the railings? There is nothing else. The day is not too hot, fortunately. If I get the chance I'll ask for some water to be sent out.'

'Aye, sir, I suppose that's best. Here, you go first, sir – the mule doesna mind so much where she's put.'

Indeed the mule seemed to be looking forward to a cosy chat with the roan pulling Murray's gig, and was already nosing back along the railing to make her better acquaintance. Murray hoped they would behave. The only sound part of the railings, which were intended optimistically to prevent people falling into the basement area, was at the extreme right side of the house, where there was a little shade anyway. He and Macduff guided their animals over to what looked like the safest part. Murray climbed out, and turned to Blair. 'Now, how can I help you out?'

Blair's mouth turned down at the corners, thoughtfully.

'Do you know,' he said, 'I think I might stay here?'

'Are you sure?' Murray was taken aback. He was sure Blair had wanted to see Mrs. Pillans re-united with her husband's belongings. 'If you tell me what to do, I'm sure I can manage.'

'No, dear Charles – that is, I'm sure you could manage, but I think I would prefer to stay here just now.'

Murray glanced about, wondering what it was that had

attracted Blair's attention, but there was nothing obvious. The windows at this side of the house were all shuttered, probably not currently used. To the other side were trees, slowly encroaching on the building. Murray expected that in only a few years the house would be a crumbled ruin in a wild forest.

'Well .. we shouldn't be long, if you're sure you will be comfortable ...'

'Go along, Charles, please! I shall be quite content here.'

Reluctantly, Murray left him, and led Macduff to the front door of the ramshackle house.

'His watch!' cried Mrs. Pillans, as soon as the cloth was folded back. 'And his pocketbook! Oh, thank you!' She bit back tears as she picked up both objects, holding them close. 'Oh, where did you find them?'

'Someone had, ah, removed them, unaware of their importance to you,' said Murray carefully. She shot him a look, but said nothing.

'Oh, it's still ticking away!' said Mrs. Skead fondly. 'You'll need to remember to wind it.'

'It's a good watch, he always said,' added Mrs. Pillans.

'We had to look inside the pocketbook, of course, ma'am,' said Macduff, 'and we found a note. It referred to a Sarah O'Rourke. Do you know the name?'

'Sarah O'Rourke? But she used to work in the Oriental Warehouse.'

'Used to? What happened? Why did she leave?'

'Oh ...' Mrs. Pillans frowned, trying to remember. 'I'm not sure. It was after – after I left.'

Her gaze flickered up to Murray and back down again.

'Did you know her well?'

'Not really. She was a little older than me. Ambitious, I thought. And very pretty. We all assumed she had found some job she thought was better, I think.'

They all thought they had somewhere better to go. Was that not what Susan Knox had said?

'When you say it mentioned her, how do you mean?' asked Mrs. Skead.

'It was an anonymous note. It seems to have been what drew

Mr. Pillans to the icehouse – suggesting that he might find out what the writer knew about Sarah O'Rourke.'

'Why should he care?' asked Mrs. Skead.

'I was hoping you might have an answer to that, ma'am, or Mrs. Pillans might,' said Macduff.

'I don't believe he said much about it,' said Mrs. Skead. 'Did he, dear?'

'He mentioned that she had gone without giving notice,' said Mrs. Pillans, 'and he was a little cross because it meant that Mrs. Miller had to find a replacement. Now that I come to think of it, it did cause him some distress – I think he was not completely happy after that. He always liked a very high standard in his shop girls,' she added, lifting her head a little. She was, indeed, a very pretty woman.

'Do you remember hearing anything more about her after she left? What date she left, perhaps?'

'It would have been some time in … let me think … the end of February or the beginning of March, I believe. I don't think I could tell you more closely than that. It was not much remarked upon, and in any case, I did not often go into the warehouse after I – after I left. My dear Gordon could fetch me anything I desired.' She held the watch close, and sadly stroked its white metal case with her thumb. 'Anything I desired.'

Chapter Forty-Nine

They questioned Mrs. Pillans gently for another few minutes, but it was clear she remembered very little about Sarah O'Rourke, and had no idea why anything mentioning her name should be in her husband's pocketbook. Murray met Macduff's eye, and they gave up, wishing the ladies good day.

But just as they were about to leave, they heard the distant clanging of a bell. Knowing that by the time the servant answered the door they could be away, Murray and Macduff headed off nevertheless, and were surprised to meet Mr. George in the hallway.

'I'm glad I caught you before you left here,' he said, a little breathless. 'You remember I intended to take a look at my brother-in-law's papers, to see if there might be a clue to his whereabouts?'

'What have you found?' asked Murray.

'This.' Mr. George drew a doubled sheet of writing paper from his pocket, and unfolded it carefully. Inside was a cutting from a newspaper, the width of a column, and two or three inches long. The hallway was dark, and the three men moved over to the window. The servant who had answered the door had already disappeared.

'"Lammermuir Cottar Hanged",' read Murray, as the cutting was too small for both him and Macduff to read at the same time. '"On Wednesday last a most melancholy sight presented itself when the murderer of an innocent farmer was taken to the gallows to meet his end. William Skead" – Skead?' Murray dropped his voice, with a glance towards the staircase they had just come down. '"William Skead had confessed to killing Robert Almond and then stealing his purse and watch on the Haddington road last October. A crowd had gathered before dawn outside the tolbooth to witness the miserable creature brought forth. Before the final act was carried out, Skead, with the encouragement of the crowd, claimed that murder was never his intention, and that Almond's death had been accidental, but he was widely known to be a violent man of ill-controlled temper." It just goes on to describe the execution.'

'So you see,' said Mr. George, 'Rocheid knew something that linked him to Pillans!'

'Well, yes,' said Murray, still scanning the cutting, 'but would that not incite Pillans to kill Rocheid, rather than the other way around?'

'Rocheid could have been blackmailing him ... no,' Mr. George admitted, 'again, why would he kill Pillans?'

Macduff cleared his throat.

'There's one person we've maybe not thought much of in all of this, and I canna think why, now,' he said. 'And that's the very person – or even people – who might be most affected by this. If the ladies up the stair are really – what, now, the wife and the daughter? – of this fellow Skead who's been hanged, are they no the ones most interested in keeping that quiet? With Mr. Pillans' nice wee business popular with the gentry, and his coothy house in Newington, and all that? Who's to say that Mr. Pillans kenned at all about this?'

'We need to talk to Mrs. Pillans and Mrs. Skead,' said Murray.

Outside, Blair was anxiously awaiting news.

He had seen Mr. George canter up the drive, and a rough individual come and take his horse away, but Mr. George had not noticed him stuck in the gig at the corner of the house, nor heard his greeting as he rushed up the steps and tugged on the bell rope. It was a wonder the rope had taken the assault, Blair had thought, curiosity burning through him to his fingertips. Why was Francis George in such a hurry? Had he found Lord Rocheid? Was he here for Macduff as the sheriff's man, or for Murray, or to talk to Mrs. Pillans? He waited for a long moment, but no one came rushing out of the house again – George had not been here to summon Macduff or Murray to a scene of awful carnage somewhere, or to some emergency, at least. Anyway, the ruffian who had taken George's horse had removed it, and it might take some time to retrieve it. Blair hoped the horse was being looked after properly. Unable to do anything more, he had been chirruping kindly words to Murray's horse and to Macduff's mule, but the two beasts had ignored him so far.

The advantage of the gig over, say, his own carriage, was that he could look all about him. He was situated in the shade of the trees, near where the path that led from the village over Letho land reached Collessie. Low growth undoubtedly concealed the place where Herr Rieder had hidden, and from which he had seen Mr. Pillans' body being removed from the house. Blair watched wrens darting about there for a while, interested in their ability to vanish so completely into nothing. A treecreeper worked its way meticulously up the ash next to him. He thought about Rieder, his nocturnal wanderings, his nervousness, his reasons for being here. Was he just a symptom of Mrs. Pillans' social ambitions?

A movement amongst the trees caught his eye. A figure was making its way along the village path, heading his way – a woman. It was Mrs. Warner, the housekeeper.

'Oh! Mr. ... Blair, is it not? Has no one attended to you, sir?'

'Oh, no, I sort of chose to be here! But some water for the beasts would be most welcome.'

'I shall see that it is brought at once,' she said. 'And some refreshment for you, too, sir.' She looked tired, and Blair felt sorry for her.

'How are you finding your new place?' he asked.

Something about Blair always encouraged servants to talk.

'To be honest, sir, it is a struggle. I thought I could perhaps improve the place, but I fear I have overrated myself. I don't think I shall stay long: as soon as the sheriff's man says I may leave I shall return to Edinburgh and seek a position there again.'

Blair pursed his lips.

'When a house has a history of bad service, somehow it perpetuates itself, does it not? Have you family in Edinburgh?'

'No, sir, but I have friends. It is a pleasant town to work in, though the weather can be harsh. Please allow me to go and see that your horse is attended to, sir, and to send something out for you.'

He let her go, seeing how weary she looked, and settled down to wait again, this time with some prospect of – what would it be? Tea? Wine? Brandy? It was enough to keep him mildly occupied for another few minutes.

Mrs. Skead stared down at the newspaper cutting, then passed it in silence to her daughter. Her daughter gave a little gasp, jerking back as though the cutting were something sharp.

'A relative?' asked Mr. George, not unkindly.

'Where did you get this?' asked Mrs. Skead, just as Mrs. Pillans spat,

'My father.'

'I found it amongst the belongings of Lord Rocheid,' said Mr. George.

'Of Lord Rocheid?' Her look of surprise did not quite convince Murray. Had she known something of this?

'Your father was hanged for murder,' said Macduff. 'Did Mr. Pillans know about this?'

Mrs. Pillans met her mother's eye.

'He did,' she said. 'We thought it would be best to tell him – before anything formal was arranged between us. I loved him, and I dearly wanted to be his wife, but the thought of him finding out later, when there was no going back ... that would have been terrible. So I told him.'

'And what did he say?'

'He vowed to protect her – to protect us both,' said Mrs. Skead, her voice cold. 'We told him how William had treated me – treated both of us, over the years. Violent, aye, he was that. It was only a matter of time before he was hanged.' Tears came then, and she scrabbled for a handkerchief. Mrs. Pillans laid a hand on her mother's arm.

'He said he would make sure that no one in Edinburgh would ever find out.'

'Did you know that Lord Rocheid knew?' asked Murray.

'Why should I?'

'Do you know the manner of the link between Lord Rocheid and Mr. Pillans?' he tried.

'I didn't know there was one. I suppose,' she said, frowning, 'I mean, Lord Rocheid, he's one of the high heidyins down that way. He was not our landlord, but we knew his name. Maybe that was why he had the cutting, do you think? Because he knows the place? Maybe heard about – about what happened?'

'Had you met him before the other day?'

'No, never. Not until my husband's funeral.' She said the words bravely. Murray was almost convinced.

'Did your husband ever mention him?' asked Macduff. Murray was aware that the three of them could perhaps look a little intimidating, standing in the drawing room firing questions at Mrs. Pillans, but she did not seem concerned about that. Again she was frowning, trying, apparently, to remember.

'I think Lord Rocheid might have been a customer, but I'm not sure. My husband had several titled customers who admired his warehouse very much.'

'But you never met him as a customer?'

'Oh, no! No, I was not there for very long, really, at all. Just when we first came to Edinburgh. Is that not right, Mamma?'

'Not that long, really,' said Mrs. Skead, nodding.

'Tell me,' said Murray after a pause, 'how well did you know the girls who have gone missing? Mary Johnston, Jean Soutar, and Maggie Daniels. Did you work alongside them? Did Mr. Pillans say anything about them at home – before or after they disappeared?'

'No, no, he did not,' said Mrs. Pillans, showing the first signs of agitation. 'No, he barely talked about the warehouse at home. I had only just met – I don't know, maybe two, maybe all three of the girls? I was barely at the warehouse before I married. It was not the kind of life I was used to, you see. And then I married my dear husband, and that was all I had to do with the place. Absolutely all.'

'I don't believe her,' said Mr. George as they descended the stairs and crossed the hall to let themselves out – no servant had appeared to answer the bell. 'I should say she had been at the warehouse longer than she claims, and was well used to that level of life, wouldn't you?'

'She's trying hard to better herself even yet,' said Macduff, with a hint of admiration in his voice. 'I'd be interested to see where her next marriage takes her.'

'You're not saying she's only doing this for money, are you?' asked Mr. George. 'I had her down as more innocent than that.'

'Did she know Rocheid before? They came from the same area,' said Murray, more interested for now in the past than in the future. 'Did she know that he and her husband were connected?'

'We dinna know they definitely were,' muttered Macduff.

'Or was she herself the connexion?' Mr. George suggested. 'As you say, from the same area. Perhaps they had an alliance that pre-dates her wedding?'

They emerged from the house, and Murray looked round for Blair. He was still in the gig, and waved at them excitedly.

'Look down there,' he said, pointing into the basement area.

The low-level path around the basement was rank with rotting leaves and stagnant pools of water, except in one place. Along the path was a door, which must, by the sweep of cleared leaves, open outwards. On its latch was a new, cheap-looking padlock – Murray could almost hear Ninian Jack telling him how poor it was.

'What do you think is in there?' asked Blair.

'I don't know,' said Murray. 'Coals?'

'No servant at Collessie would be organised enough to order coals in May,' said Francis George.

'That is true,' said Blair, kindly. 'But that padlock is new: it is the kind that will rust in the least damp. And that path is very recently cleared by the sweep of the door. Do you think – could we maybe ask if we might see inside? Humour the curiosity of an old man,' he added, making a pathetic face. Murray laughed.

'All right, then, let's see who has the key, and we'll ask them.'

'I'll ask, sir,' said Macduff, and limped around the house in the direction of the servants' door. Mr. George, Murray and Blair watched him go. Murray was not sure if the sheriff's man was genuinely curious, or was just indulging them.

A few minutes later he hirpled back, accompanied by a shilpit manservant who wiped greasy fingers on the tail of his neckcloth before tucking it into the front of his waistcoat. The manservant bowed sketchily at the gentlemen.

'Never seen the lock before in my life, sirs,' he announced without preamble. 'I'd just kick it in, if I were you. Lock's probably stronger than the door.' Having given his opinion, he stood back and began picking his teeth, mildly interested in what they might do next.

Blair looked at Murray, who shrugged. Neither Blair nor Macduff was as strong as he was, in a door-kicking context, and Mr.

George, too, was older. Murray went to the broken stone steps, and made his way down to the area.

The door did not look up to much, it was true. He took a look at the lock, and then at the hinges. Then he braced himself, took a deep breath, and kicked.

The door broke so easily it almost fell on him. He staggered to one side, steadied it and laid it down, then looked inside the opening. He paused, then called up to the others.

'We've found Lord Rocheid.'

Chapter Fifty

Murray had not liked Jacob Rocheid – in fact, the man seemed to have gone out of his way to be difficult to like – but he would not have wished this on him.

Rocheid lay on his side on the filthy floor of the chamber – not part of the house but a kind of cellar extension on the other side of the area path. One arm stretched out before him and the other lay awkwardly bent to his waist, the close-fitting coat no longer so flattering. He had been struck on the back of the head, evidently. The dim daylight, just reaching him, showed a face pushed out of shape by the blow. Had he realised that his death was imminent? Murray was not sure, but by the look on that face it was possible. His expression was terrified.

'Oh, aye, that's the fellow,' said Macduff, joining Murray at the doorway. Francis George was right behind them, keen to make sure of the identification.

'Is it he?' called Blair with grammatical precision, unable to descend to their level.

'It is,' said Murray, backing out to allow room to Mr. George and Macduff. 'Struck on the head, as Pillans was.'

'Is he – how long is he – oh, dammit!' muttered Blair. There was a rattle, then a cry and a loud thump. Murray stepped back to try to see what had happened, but Blair was on the ground and already struggling to rise.

'Wait!' cried Murray. 'I'll help you!' He darted back up the rough steps and round to the gig, where Blair was trying to work out how to pull himself up with only one half-working knee. Murray bent and hauled, and supported him until he was steady, then gave him an arm to help him round to the steps.

By the time they had descended to area level, Mr. George was propped regardless against the damp stone wall opposite the broken door, and Macduff was re-emerging from the chamber, swiping his hands across each other.

'They've no cleaned yon place in a while,' he said, in mild disgust.

'Is he definitely dead?' asked Blair, stooping to brush grit off his own breeches and boot.

'Oh, aye, he's that,' said Macduff. 'Since last night, I'd say. He's cold.'

'Like Pillans, too,' said Murray, letting Blair go ahead of him now to see what could be seen. 'Killed at night in a damp, underground chamber. Struck on the head.'

'I suppose there's no chance he killed Pillans, then,' said Mr. George. 'Someone else killed both of them. But he's dead – do I really need him discredited as well?' He reflected for a moment. 'Can you imagine what state my sister will be in when she finds out?'

Murray gave him a sympathetic look, not sure what to say to comfort him. He turned to Macduff.

'Did you look to see if he had anything in his pockets?'

'Oh, aye,' said Macduff, and fished in his own pocket. 'A gold watch, ken, a cut above poor Mr. Pillans. I didna take off his gold ring, mind. Three sovereigns and some odd bits in a wee pooch. A handkerchief. Should I give them to yourself, Mr. George, sir?'

'I suppose,' said Mr. George. 'And then, I suppose, I shall have to take him home.'

Blair was tired, and stiff from his fall. It took the other three to get him back into the gig and settled, and some persuasion on Murray's part to make him acknowledge that they did not have to wait at Collessie to watch Macduff speak with everyone there: Macduff agreed to report to them at Letho when he had finished, with Blair warmed and bathed and comfortable. Blair eventually consented, but he was uncharacteristically grumpy on the drive back to Letho.

'I'm thinking,' he said, when challenged. 'At least I can still do that.'

Mr. George rode next to them the length of the drive, then begged leave to hurry on to Dures.

'I want to tell my sister before she might happen to hear in any other way,' he said. 'And I daresay Macduff will want to come and speak with her later, and see Rocheid's things – I'll need to prepare her for all that. I'm not sorry he's dead – I should be a hypocrite to say I was – but I do fear the effect this will have on her.'

Blair took dinner in his room, while Isobel and the Wedderburns heard Murray's news of Lord Rocheid's death.

'He seemed like the kind of young man who would meet an unfortunate end,' said Debs, superior.

'He seemed to me more like the kind of young man who is very adept at avoiding trouble for himself,' said Isobel. 'But I daresay the fact that he is dead proves me wrong.'

Debs smiled.

'We'll hear what the sheriff's man has to say, no doubt, after dinner,' said Murray.

But it was almost supper time when Robbins appeared to announce the return of Macduff.

'Have you eaten?' asked Murray at once, seeing how tired the man looked.

'I have not, sir,' he admitted. 'The housekeeper at Collessie was at least kind enough to offer me something, but I thought it best to decline.'

'Will you take something now? We can wait until you are more comfortable,' said Murray.

Macduff looked for a second as if he might refuse, then sagged.

'Aye, sir, that would be most welcome.'

Robbins took him away again to the servants' quarters, and in twenty minutes brought him back to his audience.

'There's hang all to tell you, ladies and gentlemen,' he began, when they had persuaded him to sit. 'There's not a soul there will say that they saw his lordship except at the funeral. And that's from Mrs. Pillans down to – well, it's difficult to say which of them is at the bottom there. And it's not like they've all agreed on a story, either – they're all saying different things and argifying with each other, but no one saw him – or saw anybody put yon new lock on that door. To be honest,' he said, looking to Blair, 'the way you just picked it out, there, it was like they wanted him found.'

'And there was no attempt to hide Mr. Pillans, either, was there?' said Blair, pleased with himself. 'It was as if they wanted a little privacy for the actual murder, but after that they just wanted a moment to breathe before the body was found.'

'I think it's time,' said Murray, 'to take a good look at what we know, and see if there's something we're not seeing.'

Blair, his mood recovered, bounced in his chair.

'Yes, yes, dear boy! Do you have notes? Or paper and a pen? Let us do it at once!'

'I don't know if you want to stay,' Murray said to Debs and her husband. 'You might find this very dull.'

'Our maid,' said Wedderburn simply, 'and my wife's jewellery. We have an interest in this, Murray.'

'Indeed. Then feel free to contribute at any point.'

Murray stepped across to the library and fetched pen and paper.

'Shall I write things down?' asked Isobel. 'I have a sketchbook I can lean on.'

'Of course.' He smiled and passed the paper and pen to her. He lost track for a moment when she smiled back, then sat down again. 'Where do we start?'

'Finding Mr. Pillans' body,' said Debs at once.

'Further back than that,' said Isobel. Debs raised her eyebrows, but Murray nodded.

'A murder never seems to be the beginning of anything,' he explained. 'It's the result of other events. We need to think about Gordon Pillans' journey here, for instance. We need to think about his possible association with Lord Rocheid.'

'Surely they must be connected!' said Isobel, looking up from the paper – not that she had written anything so far.

'But we don't really know how, or why. Let's see, though: Lord Rocheid's estate is somewhere near the Lammermoors, and Mrs. Pillans and her mother come from there.'

'Amongst Mr. Pillans' belongings was a copy of *The Bride of Lammermoor*,' said Isobel, 'with a warning inside.'

'Yes!' said Blair. 'That was strange!'

'Well, Mr. George seemed to provide the clue to that,' said Murray, glancing at Macduff.

'Aye, sir,' said Macduff, and told them about the newscutting and William Skead's unfortunate end.

'Oh, poor Mrs. Pillans!' said Debs, though she was clearly intrigued. 'She would not want people to know that!'

'No, indeed – yet someone seems to have warned Mr. Pillans that they did know.'

'Could that have been Lord Rocheid?' asked Mr. Wedderburn.

'Well, it could,' said Murray, 'though that does not explain why they are both dead.'

There was a moment of silence while they considered this.

'What about the missing girls?' asked Debs. 'They must be connected.'

'I believe so,' said Murray.

'And we have dates for those,' said Blair, 'which is just the kind of thing we can write down, is it not?'

Isobel waved her pen. Murray applied himself to remembering.

'Mary Johnston disappeared on the thirtieth of March. Three days later, in Gordon Pillans' account book for his gambling club, there is an entry where someone called "J.R." pays "G.P" several guineas. A fortnight later, on the thirteenth of April, Maggie Daniels disappeared. Similarly, three days later the same thing appears in the accounts.'

'Ah, but the next one was different, wasn't it, Charles?'

'Yes. On the fourth of May, Jean Soutar vanished, but there is no payment made. Instead, a payment was made on the twenty-third of April, with no disappearance attached.'

'Payment in advance?' suggested Mr. Wedderburn, and Debs nodded.

'Maybe. Maybe something went wrong on the twentieth of April, but the payment went through anyway?'

'And then is there another one?' asked Debs. Isobel was writing down the dates neatly in columns.

'There is – on the fourteenth of May.'

Debs nodded gravely.

'Our maid,' she confirmed. 'She absconded on the eleventh. With my jewellery, which has reappeared in the belongings of Gordon Pillans and Lord Rocheid. Hm.' She nodded again, as if to confirm that both men had got what they deserved.

'I suppose it's possible that, if they were prepared to take your maid, they also took women from elsewhere,' said Isobel, 'which would explain that extra payment.'

'That's true,' said Murray. 'But what about the payment for Jean Soutar?'

'She was the soldier's widow, was she not?' asked Blair. 'Is it possible that she was more capable of defending herself than the younger girls?'

'Oh, do you mean she might have escaped?' Isobel sat up, cheered at the thought.

'But then why did she not go back to the warehouse?' asked Mr. Wedderburn. 'Or tell the police office what had happened?'

'Too frightened?' suggested Isobel. Debs nodded.

'That could be it.'

'Or,' said Isobel, 'or, maybe, could she have decided to take revenge?'

'A woman?' said Mr. Wedderburn incredulously, then glanced at his wife and shut his mouth abruptly. Clearly he could picture Debs taking revenge. Murray noted Isobel suppressing a smile.

'It could have been a woman,' he said. 'I suspect both men were lured or tricked to where they were found, and then taken by surprise – would you agree, Mr. Macduff?'

'Oh, aye, sir. As long as she could reach, in the dark and all a woman could do that. Particularly if she was angry enough. And Mr. Pillans could have been drugged – remember the flask you found?'

'It's in the library,' said Murray. He stepped over to the door, but the flask was nowhere to be seen.

'I'm sure I left it on the desk,' he said. 'I didn't give it back to you, did I, Macduff?'

'No, sir.'

'Odd. One of the servants must have moved it.'

Isobel nodded. Murray had the feeling there was more she wanted to say, but was holding back for now. He watched her for a moment, then caught himself and tried to remember where they were.

'"G.P." seems, more than likely, to be Gordon Pillans, of course – unless the gambling club used a less obvious code. Lord Rocheid's Christian name was Jacob, so he could be "J.R.". Lord Rocheid admitted to bringing Mr. Pillans to Letho but said he had only met him along the road. Lord Rocheid also says they quarrelled along the way, and because of that, Rocheid spent Friday night at Collessie, waiting to see what Pillans would do. He left there, by all accounts, on Saturday night, drove to the village, found out that Pillans was dead, and drove on to Newport, only returning to Dures on Sunday evening. The Newport bit has not been confirmed, but he claimed to be with a woman there.'

'Good heavens,' muttered Mr. Wedderburn, though whether he was appalled at the woman or the location it was hard to say.

'Do we know who the woman was?' Isobel asked.

'We might never know now,' said Murray. 'I don't know if Mr. George asked him.'

'It strikes me that, without her, we have two strange women arriving in Letho at around the right time,' said Isobel, with a quick glance at the servants' door. 'If we entertain the idea of a woman, perhaps Jean Soutar, taking revenge for what had happened to her and perhaps to the others, too, then there are two women who might fit the bill.'

'Of course,' said her father.

'The housekeepers,' said Murray. 'Mrs. Warner and Mrs. Gilmour.'

Chapter Fifty-One

'The musician, Rieder, he said he saw a woman,' said Murray, suddenly remembering.

But before they could even begin to think about the possibilities, the doorbell rang. All of them froze, as if they had somehow summoned the murderer. Who else could it be, calling at this time of the night?

Daniel the manservant appeared, attempted to straighten his coat, ignored the company and headed for the front door. Whoever was out there, he did not immediately usher them inside.

'Should you no be round the back?' they heard him ask, dubiously.

'I'm here to see Mr. Murray. This is Letho House, is it not?' The voice was light and female, but confident. 'I have to speak to him in person.'

'But –' said Daniel, but Murray sprang to his feet.

'Miss Knox!' he cried. 'Let her in at once, Daniel, and bring more tea for everyone. Miss Knox! What has brought you here?'

Susan Knox had lost none of her assurance through being away from Edinburgh and the Oriental Warehouse.

'What has brought me here, Mr. Murray, is the last of your money and a man in a gig – who seemed to think I owed him more than the coins we had agreed! I had to walk up from the road. Oh!' She suddenly realised that the entrance hall was full of people, and curtseyed. 'I hadn't realised – I thought in a place this size you'd be in some kind of drawing room or salon, or the like.'

'Ladies and gentlemen,' said Murray, 'this is Miss Susan

Knox, of the Oriental Warehouse.'

'Late of the Oriental Warehouse,' she corrected him. 'I'm not going back there – even if they'd have me.'

'But why are you here?' asked Isobel, a little shortly. 'I mean, Mr. Murray was expecting a letter from you. I had no idea you were going to arrive in person.'

Susan Knox looked Isobel up and down, then saw Blair, and blinked.

'Mr. Blair! Good evening to you!' She curtseyed once again, this time with genuine friendliness. 'We heard you had an accident, sir, and we were all so upset! Forgive me,' she added to the company generally, 'I know we are not supposed to notice customers if we see them outside the warehouse, but sir, I'm so glad to see you looking well! I shall send word to the others as soon as I may.'

'Goodness,' said Debs, but quietly. Daniel brought in the tea, and Murray found a chair for Susan to sit down. She seemed tired, buoyed up less by energy than by excitement at having reached them. She took her cup and saucer with enthusiasm, and disposed of the contents at speed.

'Now,' said Murray, 'have you eaten?'

'I had a pie in Cupar,' said Susan. 'I could have managed two, but I had no time to spare. I came here as quick as I could.'

'What news have you? We'll get more food organised later.'

She shot him a grateful look, and Isobel refilled her cup.

'Thank you, miss. Well, I went to Newington, as you bade me.'

'To Mr. Pillans' house?'

'That's right. It was easy enough to get in and talk with that silly maid: she was glad of the company. Dear love the girl, she has not had much of a life to teach her not to be silly.'

'What did she tell you?'

'She told me she was worried, because the master had not come back and a strange man had visited. She had tried to contact the cook – she seems to like the cook – but she had not been able to. I'm not sure she can write, mind you.' Susan took a deep breath, as if reminding herself to keep on track. 'Anyway, she said a man collected Mr. Pillans in a gig the day he left – a man who looked a bit like him, but very fashionably dressed. I think she was impressed. Off they went and she never saw either of them again. So I asked her what life was like at the house. She didn't mind talking to me because I was from the warehouse, you see – she thought she might get a place there herself, one day.' Susan sighed. 'She said she quite liked working there, except when the mistress and her mother were away. She didn't like the men coming. And she didn't like it when they brought the girls.'

Susan Knox met Murray's eye, then looked around at the rest of her audience, making sure they were paying attention. Reassured by what she saw, she continued.

'She said the girls came, one at a time, when the mistress was away and when the men weren't there. They came in a closed chair, on their own.'

'When the men weren't there?' Debs could not resist making sure.

'That's right, ma'am – I asked the same thing. The girls came, and stayed the one night. The maid had to see them to a room that was prepared for them – nothing special, just a plain spare room – and wait on them.'

'And what happened next?' asked Blair anxiously.

'Nothing. The girls left the next day. A carriage would call for them, and off they would go – quite excited, she said.'

'Could she describe any of them? Did she have any memory of the dates they had been there?'

'Could she describe the carriage?' Wedderburn added.

Susan shrugged.

'I shouldn't think so. I mean, maybe, sir, if you went back and asked her what the weather was like, or something like that – but not exact dates. She thought there were maybe half a dozen girls altogether, but she didn't say she'd even seen any of them clearly – nor the carriage, either. Dark, was all she said, a big dark carriage. A big, dark carriage,' she repeated, and Murray thought he caught a shiver.

'Never mind: if we can find the cook or the maid they might be more helpful. Well done!'

'There's more, sir,' said Susan. She set down her cup and saucer, and her hands wound together on her lap. 'This was on the Friday morning, when your letter arrived. I sent word to the warehouse I wasn't coming in, said I wasn't well, and went straight to the bank to take the money you offered me, sir. I thought it best to have it straight, and I would return anything I didn't spend later.'

'You lied to them?' asked Macduff. She glanced at him and took in his position in the household – or outside it – in an instant.

'I did. I wasn't going to tell them I was off finding out about missing girls, and I wasn't going to leave them with nothing – that would mean they would tell the police and they would be after me as another missing girl. What else was I to say? I could have sent in my notice, but that would be nearly as bad – and anyway, at that point I thought I'd be back.'

'You thought you'd be back?' Isobel queried. 'You mean you don't intend to return now?'

'I do not,' said Susan, definitely. 'Not after that evening in Newington.'

She had a fine sense of drama, thought Murray, as Susan paused again. He would have thought it all for effect if he had not seen how the muscles in the corners of her eyes were twitching. He let the silence lie, hoping she would go on in her own time.

'I thought I had everything I could find out from her,' she said, 'but I hadn't realised how long it had taken. It was dark outside when I left. But Newington's a respectable place, I thought. I tugged my shawl around me and tied my bonnet tight, and headed off to go back to the Old Town.'

'Go on,' said Debs, breathless.

'Of course there are lights, but there aren't as many as there should be.'

'Oh, I agree!' said Debs. 'The Council should do something –'

'Debs,' said her husband, and she subsided.

'I'd reached a dark bit – I think I was in Gray Street, maybe? And I heard wheels behind me, on the squaresets. Gritty, and heavy. More than one horse, two, maybe. Like a carriage, not a light thing. I looked back, and there were two lamps, high up. And darkness behind them. Well, I thought, none of my business. Just someone coming home, or heading out. So I hurried on, and then the carriage catches up with me, and gets that wee bit ahead of me, and then it stops.'

She had been staring down at the floor in front of her. Now she looked up, at Isobel, then at Debs.

'I daresay ladies don't find themselves out on their own after dark. Let me tell you, miss, ma'am: there's times ... well. Well, I hope you never need to know.

'The carriage stopped, and I tried to cross the road behind it and go on past. But the driver called out to me.

'"Hi," he says, "Did you just come out of yon house there?" I thought I'd just ignore him, but quick as a flash he was down and in front of me. "I asked if you came out of that house there?"

'"Which one?" says I, hoping he'd pick some other house and I could say no and be on my way. "That one there," he says "belongs to a man named Pillans."

'I should still have said no, but it didn't matter. He went on, before I could answer.

'"Are you the new one?" he asked, and his hand was on my arm, and I knew he was stronger than I could ever fight off. "Are you? The new girl?"

'"I don't know what you're talking about," I said, trying to sound as high and mighty as I could. "I work in Mr. Pillans' warehouse. I'm no new girl."

'"Oh, one of the shop girls?" says he. "We've no had one of them for a while. Hop in, dearie, and let's be going. It's a fair distance we have to go tonight." And his hand tightened on my arm.

'I was shaking. Was this what had happened to Maggie, and Jean, and Mary? And to my friend Sarah, and all? I tried to think what to do – I felt so stupid, letting myself get caught, when I knew what had happened before. What had I thought I was doing, staying so late?

'Then from somewhere, I had an idea.

'"Listen, you," I said, shaking my arm to show him his hand was not welcome. "If you touch me, you'll be in trouble. I'm in charge of this operation – I'm not some shop girl to be taken away and disposed of! You ask Mr. Pillans!"

'"Ask Mr. Pillans?" he repeated, not sounding so sure of himself.

'"That's right," I said, taking a chance, "Mrs. Miller and I are working on this together. Now, off you go – no new girl tonight. Try next week."

He turned, and looked back at the carriage, as if some answer might present itself. And I ran. I ran until I was well out on South Clerk Street, but then I feared he could easily come after me, and I ducked down the lanes and stopped and hid until I was sure he wasn't following me. Then when I was sure he wasn't around, I went straight down to the coach office, and hid myself for the night – oh, but the North Bridge is a long, straight road to walk when you're trying to hide! – and took the first coach in the morning. I have all your money accounted for, sir,' she added, taking a piece of paper from her reticule and handing it to Murray. 'If there's anything you think I should not have spent, I shall pay it back. I have a little money put aside.' She frowned suddenly, and Murray wondered if she had just realised that she might need that to live on, until she found another position.

'Thank you, Miss Knox,' said Murray. 'I am extremely grateful to you for all you have done, and the risks you have taken in this matter – if I had realised the danger I should never have asked you to go.'

'I went for Sarah's sake, sir. You just showed me where to go.'

'Sarah,' repeated Isobel. 'Not Sarah O'Rourke?'

'That's right,' said Susan. 'Did you see her at the warehouse?'

Isobel looked at Murray.

'The account book,' he said at once, and went back into the library. He was already flicking through the pages as he returned to the entrance hall. 'What date was it that she left, did you say?'

'The second of March. A Friday.'

Murray reached the beginning of March.

'The fifth of March – a payment from J.R. to G.P of three shillings. The first missing girl.'

'Is that proof that she was one of them?' asked Susan Knox. Her voice shook a little.

'I think so,' said Murray. 'I think so.'

Isobel looked at Miss Knox, and took her arm gently. Murray realised that the shop girl had turned quite pale.

'Well,' he said, 'the least we can do is make sure you are fed and have a safe bed for the night.'

'Shall I take her to Mrs. Gilmour?' asked Isobel.

'Would you, please?' He watched them leave the entrance hall. Was Isobel easing into the position of mistress of the house? Or was she just aware that he was short of maids?

Isobel smiled at Susan Knox and led her down the stone passage to the servants' quarters.

'You'll be safe here,' she said, 'and you'll have time to decide what you want to do next.'

'Thank you, miss. And maybe find out if Mr. Murray discovers what happened to my friend.'

'I'm sure if he does he will tell you.' They reached Mrs. Gilmour's parlour, and Isobel rapped at the door.

'Oh! Miss Blair!' Mrs. Gilmour spun and curtseyed, and smiled brightly, though none of that could hide the fact that she had been crying. 'I've decided – that is, I feel much better, and I've decided,' she drew breath, as though her announcement was to be startling. Isobel prayed she was not about to resign. 'I've decided I shall go to church in the morning.'

Chapter Fifty-Two

'I want to know how Lady Rocheid is,' said Isobel at breakfast. 'Has Mr. George sent word?'

'No,' said Murray, 'there has been nothing. Perhaps I should go over before church and see if everything is all right. Macduff said they were taking the body there late last night.'

They were on their own in the dining room with Blair: the Wedderburns were not early risers, and last evening had been tiring for everyone.

'I feel so much that we are almost there,' said Blair. 'One of the housekeepers could be Jean Soutar. But which?'

'You're sure that neither Susan Knox nor Mrs. Gilmour showed any sign of recognising each other last night?' Murray asked Isobel.

'Mrs. Gilmour was much more intent on telling me that she was going to go to church this morning. It seemed to be important to her. I wasn't looking at Susan Knox, but she certainly didn't cry out "Oh, Jean!" and shake her hand.'

'She told us lots of useful things,' said Blair, wistfully. 'Could she have been working with Jean Soutar, perhaps? She wants to find out about her friend.'

Murray set down his coffee cup, propped his elbows on the table and sank his head into his hands.

'I feel as if we are going round in circles. If we cannot trust Susan Knox, then we don't know if anything she said last night is true and we don't know whether or not Mrs. Gilmour is Jean Soutar.'

'Where was the carriage taking them?' asked Isobel.

'Out of Edinburgh, presumably, if it existed,' said Murray. 'To Lord Rocheid's estate?'

'That could be discovered,' said Isobel. 'You could ask Macduff to write there.'

'He never let Lady Rocheid go there,' said Murray, thoughtfully. 'A dark carriage. He favours dark blue, I believe. It could have been his.'

'If it existed,' said Isobel again, and smiled at him. He looked quickly down at the table. When was he ever going to find courage and opportunity at the same moment? It had to be soon.

'Well,' said Blair, 'if they are working together, we shall soon find out, I should imagine. Because now they are here, together. What could they want to do next?'

'If it's revenge … the murderer has killed both the men we know were involved,' said Murray, pulling himself up. 'Unless Mrs. Pillans had a hand in it somehow. Could she be the next victim? Oh, could there be some connexion here – is that why Mrs. Gilmour now wants to go to church, to find Mrs. Pillans?'

'She wouldn't kill her at church,' said Isobel firmly. 'Not by the previous pattern.'

'No, but she might lay her trap.'

Isobel sighed.

'I think we're heading off on the wrong track. I don't believe that Susan Knox and Mrs. Gilmour had ever seen each other before in their lives until last night.'

'Oh,' said Blair, sadly. 'Then at least, dear Charles, your housekeeper is probably not a murderer.'

'Every cloud has a silver lining,' said Murray, making a face.

'I like Mrs. Gilmour,' said Isobel. 'I don't want her to be a murderer.'

'Then let us hope she is not. But I should go to Dures before church, and ask how Lady Rocheid is.'

'May I come too?' asked Isobel. 'Perhaps, as a woman, she might speak to me.'

'I'll see you on the village green,' said Blair, nodding approval. 'It's a fine morning: no doubt people will gather there before the service. Who knows what I might hear in the course of conversation? Who knows, indeed?'

At Dures, they could sense the tension before the butler even opened the door. He had a harassed look not typical of Dures servants.

'Ah,' he said, 'Mr. George is from home, sir.'

'At this hour?' asked Murray in surprise.

'He had to go to Cupar last night, on business, sir.'

Cupar again! Mr. George's business must be very compelling. In the distance, he heard the sound of breaking crockery – no doubt a nervous servant at work.

'Is Lady Rocheid receiving visitors? We have really come to enquire after her,' said Isobel.

'Lady Rocheid ...' said the butler, uneasily. It was about then that Murray noticed a reddening about the man's left eye, the first hints of a terrific black eye. Surely ...

'Lady Rocheid ...' the man began again, paused as they all heard glass shatter somewhere nearby, and managed to carry on. 'She received the news last night - the sad news of Lord Rocheid's death. The housekeeper made her comfortable.' He nodded to himself. Murray realised that the housekeeper had probably given Lady Rocheid some kind of sedative. 'And she slept very well. But now she is awake, and ... and very upset.'

'Perhaps if I went to speak with her?' Isobel suggested.

'I wouldn't advise it, miss,' said the butler quickly. 'She really is very upset.'

'Is Lord Rocheid's body here?' asked Murray.

'Oh yes, sir. She has spent some time sitting with him, of course. But now she has called for his gig to be harnessed, and is intent on ... on going out.'

'Going out? With her husband's body here?' Isobel was taken aback.

'Aye, well, miss,' the butler sighed. 'There's no stopping her. Here comes the gig now.'

He nodded to where the dark blue vehicle was being drawn up beside Murray's own gig, the groom calming an excited horse.

'When do you expect Mr. George back?'

'Not soon enough,' muttered the butler darkly, as Lady Rocheid, clad head to toe in black, rushed into the hallway and pushed past the servant. She barely seemed to see Murray and Isobel, and flung herself down the step and across to the gigs. It seemed more by good luck than anything that she climbed into the right one.

'We'd better follow her,' said Isobel. 'Lady Rocheid, where are you going?'

'I'm going to kill her,' said Lady Rocheid, breathily. She whipped up the horse, and it plunged off down the drive. Murray was already halfway to his own gig.

'Stay here,' he said to Isobel.

'My weight will help,' was all she said in response, as she climbed in beside him.

'Oh, heavens,' said Murray, and urged his own horse to follow.

Gigs were not stable vehicles. Lady Rocheid was already tipping to the side as she spun through the gate and on to the main road.

'I pray there's nothing coming!' murmured Isobel, clinging to the side with both hands. Murray agreed. Lady Rocheid had turned towards Letho village. Who was she intent on killing?

They reached the end of the drive and paused only to check for other traffic before hurtling right in pursuit. The road was not straight: they caught glimpses of the other gig now and then, tilting dangerously. Was she drawing ahead?

'Hold on!' he urged Isobel, wondering if he could make his horse go any faster – wondering if he should. The corners were tight – the last one into the village was the worst of the lot. Would either of them make it?

'Oddly, I am holding on,' said Isobel. He risked a glance at her. She was intent on the road, on the pursuit, willing the horse on.

'Will you marry me?' he shouted above the noise of hooves and wheels.

'Yes, of course,' she shouted back. She must have misunderstood. He turned quickly to look at her again. She was grinning at him. 'If we survive! Pay attention!'

They were almost at the turn into the village. Lady Rocheid had slowed, showing some reason at last. Even so, the gig tipped perilously as she went, and Murray reined in his own horse as gently as he could behind her. Lady Rocheid made it, the gig straightened, and she drove straight on to the green, then stopped. There were too many people about. Murray drew up beside the grass, and he and

Isobel hopped out. He realised he was grinning like a mad man, and made himself sober up before hurrying to catch the grieving widow.

'Lady Rocheid,' he said, reaching out to her.

'Where is she? Where is that woman Pillans?'

Murray looked about him. Mrs. Pillans and her mother were indeed on the green, with a small contingent from Collessie – heaven knew what power Mrs. Skead had over servants, but the Collessie pews would be more packed today than they had been for years. The Letho people had also arrived, with Blair propelled by Smith in his wheeled chair. Seeing them arrive, Blair gestured to Smith to push him over to Murray.

'I don't think it's Mrs. Gilmour,' he whispered, as soon as he could do so.

'Why not?'

'I don't have a why not. But I think Mrs. Warner is more probable. She was at Letho and then she was at Collessie, wasn't she?'

Murray looked around again. Both women were there. Mrs Warner appeared to be keeping the Collessie servants in line. Mrs. Gilmour, standing talking with Robbins and his wife, looked about her nervously. Of the two, Mrs. Gilmour looked much more likely. But Lady Rocheid had spotted Mrs. Pillans, and now Murray was having to hold her back.

'You!' cried Lady Rocheid. 'You are the cause of all of this!'

'Me?' Mrs. Pillans looked confused. 'What have I done now, your ladyship?'

'Nothing better than a murderer's daughter! You killed your own husband, and then you killed mine! I know. I know who you are! My husband told me!'

'Oh …' Mrs. Pillans had turned pale, and propped herself on her mother. Mrs. Skead, by contrast, was angry.

'You've no call to go shouting things like that at my daughter, Lady Rocheid. A child canna choose her father. And Lord Rocheid was no better than he ought to be – aye, his reputation round the Lammermuirs is well kent!'

'Oh!' cried Lady Rocheid, her face scarlet. 'I shall – I shall – '

'Lady Rocheid,' said Blair mildly, 'would you like to take a seat? I hate to see a lady standing about.' He had manoeuvred himself, with Smith's help, out of his wheeled chair, and offered it to Lady Rocheid. Breathless, she hurled herself into it. She looked exhausted.

Murray removed his hat and ran a hand through his hair, wondering what to do next. But Isobel had an idea.

'Miss Knox,' she called, seeing the shop girl with the Letho staff. 'Will you be good enough to step over here, please?'

Susan Knox, looking surprised, did as she was asked. Isobel gestured to the crowd, now gathered more closely to see what was going on.

'Miss Knox, do you see anyone here you know? From the warehouse, perhaps. For example,' she said, indicating Mrs. Gilmour, 'is that by any chance Jean Soutar?'

'No, it's not,' said Susan Knox. 'Do you think Jean is here?' She scanned the crowd. 'I can't see her.'

'Susan? Susan, is that you?' Mrs. Pillans, with a wary look at Lady Rocheid, came up to them.

'Annie!' The two women embraced.

'What are you doing here?'

Susan opened her mouth to reply, then stopped, clearly not quite sure what to say. But before Isobel could interrupt or Mrs. Pillans question further, the sound of carriage wheels grew louder. Susan jerked back, spinning to see where the sound was coming from. As far as Isobel was concerned, it was enough to show that her story of what had happened in Newington was absolutely true.

The open carriage came slowly towards the green. Lady Rocheid stood. Susan Knox stared.

'Now that's odd,' she said. Isobel looked at her, then back at the carriage. It drew to a halt, and Mr. George, beaming, allowed the coachman to lower the steps before he stepped down. He turned to reach a hand to the woman beside him.

She was not in the first flush of youth, but was nevertheless a very handsome woman. The smile on her face was very much like that on Mr. George's.

'Ah, Murray, Blair,' said Mr. George. 'Miss Blair, forgive me, good day to you. May I present my wife?'

'What?' demanded Lady Rocheid, sinking back into the wheeled chair.

Isobel curtseyed as the men bowed. And Susan Knox pushed

forward, mouth open.

'Now,' she said, 'that is Jean Soutar.'

And the new Mrs. George looked at her, and laughed in delight.

Chapter Fifty-Three

'Well, that rather destroys our theories,' said Isobel quietly, as Mrs. Pillans, Susan Knox and the new Mrs. George greeted each other eagerly.

'That's what he was doing in Cupar,' said Murray. 'He must have had her stay there until they were married. An honest man at last!'

'But it does mean that neither of the housekeepers is Jean Soutar,' said Blair sadly.

'But she is alive,' said Murray. 'Which explains why there was no payment after her disappearance. She was never intended to be abducted. Now what?'

'Now we have a word with Mrs. Warner,' said Isobel suddenly.

'Why with her?' asked Blair.

'Because she is trying to leave quietly. Just over there.'

Murray turned. Mrs. Warner was edging down the green, away from the Collessie crowd, and watching the erstwhile employees of the Oriental Warehouse with an intense wariness. Then she saw Murray and Isobel watching her in turn, took to her heels, and fled.

Murray had barely had the chance to start after her when she cannoned into an unsuspecting Ninian Jack, sending him barrelling to the ground. A cry came from somewhere behind Murray, but Mrs. Warner recovered fast and carried on, the slight hill giving her momentum. She rounded the inn at the foot of the hill, making for the main road, but just at that moment Macduff the sheriff's man emerged in his Sunday best, just placing his hat on his head. Mrs. Warner crashed straight into him, sending him staggering back against the wall of the inn – but his instinct was clearly to grab whatever had hit him, and to hold on tight. Murray came up behind her. Mrs. Warner was trapped.

'Is this the one we wanted, then?' asked Macduff. 'Is this Jean Soutar?'

'No,' Murray began, 'but –'

'Mrs. O'Rourke!' came a voice. 'What are you doing here?'

Susan Knox, still grinning from her happy reunion with Jean Soutar and Mrs. Pillans, had skipped down the hill after Murray.

'Mrs. O'Rourke?' asked Macduff. 'I thought her name was Warner.'

'It is,' said the housekeeper, then gave a resigned sigh. 'Warner's my own name. O'Rourke was my husband.'

'And the first missing girl – your friend,' added Murray to Susan Knox, 'was your daughter?'

'She still is my daughter, whatever they've done to her,' said Mrs. Warner – O'Rourke.

'Is she alive?' asked Susan Knox, on a gasp.

'I believe so. But some would say she would be better off dead.'

The conversation could not be left until after the kirk service. Murray, Blair (with Smith), Isobel and Susan Knox followed Macduff and Mrs. Warner into the inn's parlour, just as the innkeeper himself was setting off for church.

'Aye, go on,' he said. 'I daresay there'll be no violence.'

Murray hoped not.

'You went on looking for Sarah,' said Susan Knox, before they could even sit down. 'I didn't know. I mean, I would have helped you.'

'You had your position to think of,' said Mrs. Warner. 'I just prayed you would be safe, that they wouldn't take more girls. But they did. From the warehouse and from other places, too – one of them was someone's maid, and another was from the shop next door to the warehouse.'

'The payment we hadn't identified,' said Murray, half to himself. Isobel smiled.

'To Lord Rocheid's estate in the Lammermoors?' asked Blair, unable to keep quiet.

'Aye, that's right, sir,' said Mrs. Warner. She was shivering now, though the parlour was warm. Isobel found a blanket on a chair, and placed it across the woman's shoulders. Mrs. Warner clutched it close. 'With so many of the girls going from the shop, I thought Mr. Pillans must have had something to do with it. I went to Newington, to his house, and I watched – just on Friday nights, for I knew that was when the girls went, and the evenings were dark, so no one saw me, I think. Mr. Pillans was not about, but then I saw a girl arrive, and leave.'

'And you let them be taken away?' demanded Susan Knox. Murray nodded to himself. Miss Knox would not watch quietly, he suspected. Mrs. Warner shrugged under her blanket, a thin movement.

'I needed to know what was happening. I saw a dark carriage collect the girls, one by one – they went quietly, the poor fools! They made no trouble. When I had seen one or two, I began to follow the carriage, believing it was not going far, but I lost it when it sped up at the edge of the town. So I got a cart, and followed it bit by bit, asking at each place I passed. I lost them once again, and went back to where I knew they had been, and waited for the next time, and followed them again. They must have realised I was following, surely, but I don't think they even cared. Lord Rocheid seemed to be that kind of man.'

'You went all the way to his estate?'

'I did. That was how I knew who he was. The girls are kept there for – for entertaining his gentleman friends. Some kind of gambling club he runs there, according to the people in the village. The girls are a recent addition, for his Lordship was the kind to think everything should be under his command, and at his fingertips. I managed to talk to one of the girls through a window, but my daughter would not speak to me. She was too ashamed.'

'What did the girl say?'

'She said they were locked in – there was only a barred window, and the bars were thick and strong. She told me they had all been offered good places, with more money, in Edinburgh, by the man who had driven the coach. One of Lord Rocheid's men. Mr. Pillans must have given information about them, because he caught each of them on their way home from work, just far enough from the warehouse – or wherever. There was one, though, the coachman had taken a liking to, a lady's maid, and he persuaded her to steal some of her mistress' jewellery before she left. But Lord Rocheid had found out, and taken the jewellery as well as the girl.'

'Did you tell the police office?'

Mrs. Warner shrugged.

'What was the point? My word against Lord Rocheid? The local people would not speak out against their laird. I had to do the job myself. I found out Pillans had taken a house in Fife for the summer. I got in with some of Lord Rocheid's servants in Edinburgh and found he went to the same place, too. So I tried to find a way of getting here, and then I heard that you were looking for a housekeeper, sir. So I applied.'

'And thereby discovered the old icehouse,' said Murray, not best pleased at how his property had been used.

'Those lads running round, and the engineers working – I knew it would not be long before he was found,' said Mrs. Warner, 'but I thought, too, that they would muddle things nicely. I needed time to get to the other one, too.'

'You sent Mr. Pillans a note to meet you.'

'I did,' she said. 'And he came. Very gratifying. I mean, everything else had been such a struggle. But he wanted to talk to me. He wanted to tell me that he was ashamed, and he wanted to stop. Such a talker he was, there, in the dark. Lord Rocheid had found out something about his wife, but he had decided that enough was enough. He was going to talk to his wife, and put an end to it.'

'Did you not believe him?'

'Oh, I believed him, all right,' said Mrs. Warner, ice in her voice. 'But he had done enough damage. He had to go.'

'A hard thing to do,' said Isobel softly. 'How did you manage it?' She was holding Mrs. Warner's hand now, encouraging her.

'I used some of the medicine from the stillroom, from the old housekeeper's stores. Just to slow him down. I'm quite strong, but no match for a youngish man, I think. He sat down slowly, then lay down, as if he was going to sleep. And then I hit him, hard. And then I hit him again, and – and I'm not quite sure when I stopped.'

The room was silent for a little, only the heavy beat of the massive clock ticking over, for those who had seen it, the memory of that awful face.

'So,' said Murray at last, 'the same thing worked for Lord Rocheid, when you found a similar place in the basement of Collessie.'

'Och,' said Mrs. Warner, 'you could murder twenty people at Collessie and find hiding places for all of them, and nobody would ever notice. It's a terrible place.'

'But you weren't planning to stay long,' said Macduff. 'You were going to head off, were you no?'

'I was. Back to … well, to be honest,' she said, 'I'm not sure what I was going to do next. I had made up my mind that I would never get Sarah back, and that this was all that could be done. If by killing them I could somehow … I don't know, break the spell? But honestly, I'd lost all hope. And now, well, I suppose there really is no hope.'

'So now, I suppose we really must go home,' said Debs Wedderburn. Before her on the table lay the rest of her stolen jewellery, discovered amongst Lord Rocheid's things at Dures.

'We have heard almost all the answers,' agreed her husband. 'Poor Mrs. Warner.'

'Macduff has sent word to the Rocheid estate and to the local sheriff's man. The girls will be freed,' said Murray. 'Of course, the irony is that even if they bring Sarah O'Rourke back, it will be to see her mother hang for the deeds that rescued them all.'

'Poor Mrs. Pillans, too,' said Debs. 'What will she do?'

'It's clear that Lord Rocheid's knowledge of her father's character gave him a hold over Pillans,' said Murray. 'Pillans was very protective of his wife, trying to help her – help them both – to rise in society, too. I should think that Lord Rocheid insisted that the transactions, if I may call them that, were recorded in the account books of the gambling club, so that he had extra security if he were ever challenged.'

'So she can at least assure herself that his motives were sound,' said Isobel, ironically. 'But as to what will now happen to the warehouse – she may not have the money to sustain an Edinburgh house and the lease on Collessie, nor her new music tutor, Mr. Rieder. Never mind all the staff required for two establishments.'

'Ah, well, Mr. Rieder is to stay in the parish, nevertheless,' said Blair, his eyebrows reaching for his wig.

'Really?'

'Oh, yes. He is to go as music tutor to the new Mrs. George. Lady Rocheid's marriage gift to her new sister-in-law.'

'In that case, if Mrs. Pillans stays, she may well yet benefit from his skills. That is excellent,' said Murray, always happy to see music promoted in the parish.

'As to staff,' said Debs, 'what is amiss with your housekeeper?'

Isobel, Blair and Murray grinned.

'Nothing at all, now!' said Isobel. 'Mrs. Gilmour turns out to be Ninian Jack's missing daughter, Kate!'

'What?' asked Debs. 'After all these years?'

'Yes, indeed,' said Blair happily. 'It appears she has led a very interesting life. I don't think we have heard the whole story yet.'

'I'm not sure she will ever tell her father the whole story!' said Murray. 'Ninian Jack is a very respectable man – and he will want to set a good example to his new apprentice.'

'He's taken on Janny?' asked Isobel.

'He has – for now, anyway,' said Murray. He was almost more pleased with that than with anything else that had happened in the last few days. 'So we are rid of Janny, in part. But the establishment has grown – Mrs. Gilmour is keen to stay and I am keen to keep her. And Susan Knox, for want of anything better, has asked if she can take up a position as maid here. She has done it before, apparently. And after all, a larger establishment seems more appropriate for a married man.'

'A what?' asked Debs, though by her expression she knew what was coming. Blair was beaming from ear to ear.

'A marriage is intended,' said Murray. 'Miss Blair has consented to become my wife.'

'Now all we need,' said Blair, 'is those engineers to fix the water problem in a thoroughly ingenious way, and my happiness will be complete!'

About the Author

Lexie Conyngham is a historian living in the shadow of the Highlands. Her historical crime novels are born of a life amidst Scotland's old cities, ancient universities and hidden-away aristocratic estates, but she has written since the day she found out that people were allowed to do such a thing. Beyond teaching and research, her days are spent with wool, wild allotments and a wee bit of whisky.

We hope you've enjoyed this instalment. Reviews are important to authors, so it would be lovely if you could post a review where you bought it! Here are a few handy links ...

Visit our website at www.lexieconyngham.co.uk. There are several free Murray of Letho short stories, Murray's World Tour of Edinburgh, and the chance to follow Lexie Conyngham's meandering thoughts on writing, gardening and knitting, at www.murrayofletho.blogspot.co.uk. You can also follow Lexie, should such a thing appeal, on Facebook, Pinterest or Instagram.

Finally! If you'd like to be kept up to date with Lexie and her writing, please join our mailing list at: contact@kellascatpress.co.uk. There's a quarterly newsletter, often with a short story attached, and fair warning of any new books coming out.

Murray of Letho

We first meet Charles Murray when he's a student at St. Andrews University in Fife in 1802, resisting his father's attempts to force him home to the family estate to learn how it's run. Pushed into involvement in the investigation of a professor's death, he solves his first murder before taking up a post as tutor to Lord Scoggie. This series takes us around Georgian Scotland as well as India, Italy and Norway (so far!), in the company of Murray, his manservant Robbins, his father's old friend Blair, the enigmatic Mary, and other members of his occasionally shambolic household.

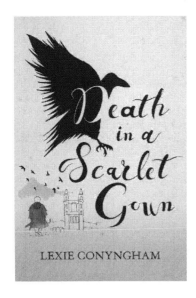

An Abandoned Woman

Fellowship with Demons

The Tender Herb: A Murder in Mughal India

Death of an Officer's Lady

Out of a Dark Reflection

A Dark Night at Midsummer (a novella)

Death in a Scarlet Gown

The Status of Murder (a novella)

Knowledge of Sins Past

Service of the Heir: An Edinburgh Murder

Slow Death by Quicksilver

Thicker than Water

A Deficit of Bones

The Dead Chase

Shroud for a Sinner

Hippolyta Napier

Hippolyta Napier is only nineteen when she arrives in Ballater, on Deeside, in 1829, the new wife of the local doctor. Blessed with a love of animals, a talent for painting, a helpless instinct for hospitality, and insatiable curiosity, Hippolyta finds her feet in her new home and role in society, making friends and enemies as she goes. Ballater may be small but it attracts great numbers of visitors, so the issues of the time, politics, slavery, medical advances, all affect the locals. Hippolyta, despite her loving husband and their friend Durris, the sheriff's officer, manages to involve herself in all kinds of dangerous adventures in her efforts to solve every mystery that presents itself.

A Knife in Darkness

Death of a False Physician

A Murderous Game

The Thankless Child

A Lochgorm Lament

The Corrupted Blood

Orkneyinga Murders

Orkney, c.1050 A.D.: Thorfinn Sigurdarson, Earl of Orkney, rules from the Brough of Birsay on the western edges of these islands. Ketal Gunnarson is his man, representing his interests in any part of his extended realm. When Sigri, a childhood friend of Ketil's, finds a dead man on her land, Ketil, despite his distrust of islands, is commissioned to investigate. Sigrid, though she has quite enough to do, decides he cannot manage on his own, and insists on helping – which Ketil might or might not appreciate.

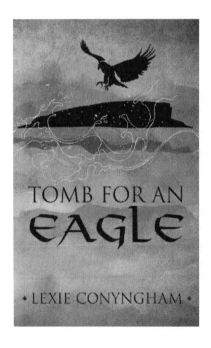

Tomb for an Eagle

A Wolf at the Gate

Dragon in the Snow

The Bear at Midnight

Other books by Lexie Conyngham:

Windhorse Burning

'I'm not mad, for a start, and I'm about as far from violent as you can get.'
When Toby's mother, Tibet activist Susan Hepplewhite, dies, he is determined to honour her memory. He finds her diaries and decides to have them translated into English. But his mother had a secret, and she was not the only one: Toby's decision will lead to obsession and murder.

The War, The Bones, and Dr. Cowie

Far from the London Blitz, Marian Cowie is reluctantly resting in rural Aberdeenshire when a German 'plane crashes nearby. An airman goes missing, and old bones are revealed. Marian is sure she could solve the mystery if only the villagers would stop telling her useless stories – but then the crisis comes, and Marian finds the stories may have a use after all.

Jail Fever

It's the year 2000, and millennium paranoia is everywhere.
Eliot is a bad-tempered merchant with a shady past, feeling under the weather.
Catriona is an archaeologist at a student dig, when she finds something unexpected.
Tom is a microbiologist, investigating a new and terrible disease with a stigma.
Together, their knowledge could save thousands of lives – but someone does not want them to …

The Slaughter of Leith Hall

'See, Charlie, it might be near twenty years since Culloden, but there's plenty hard feelings still amongst the Jacobites, and no so far under the skin, ken?'
Charlie Rob has never thought of politics, nor strayed far from his

Aberdeenshire birthplace. But when John Leith of Leith Hall takes him under his wing, his life changes completely. Soon he is far from home, dealing with conspiracy and murder, and lost in a desperate hunt for justice.

Thrawn Thoughts and Blithe Bits and *Quite Useful in Minor Emergencies*

Two collections of short stories, some featuring characters from the series, some not; some seen before, some not; some long, some very short. Find a whole new dimension to car theft, the life history of an unfortunate Victorian rebel, a problem with dragons and a problem with draugens, and what happens when you advertise that you've found somebody's leg.

Printed in Great Britain
by Amazon

16910666R00203